THE HOUSE
·OF WOMEN·

Alison G. Taylor

BANTAM BOOKS
New York   Toronto   London   Sydney   Auckland

THE HOUSE OF WOMEN

A Bantam Book

PUBLISHING HISTORY
William Heinemann hardcover edition published 1998
Bantam paperback edition / May 1999

ISBN: 0-553-58145-7
Published simultaneously in the United States and Canada

Bantam Books are published by Bantam Books, a division of Random
House, Inc. Its trademark, consisting of the words "Bantam Books" and
the portrayal of a rooster, is Registered in U.S. Patent and Trademark Office and in other countries. Marca Registrada. Bantam Books, 1540 Broad-
way, New York, New York 10036.

PRINTED IN THE UNITED STATES OF AMERICA

OPM   10   9   8   7   6   5   4   3   2   1

For Aaron

'—fortune is round like an orb, and, I need hardly add, does not therefore always fall on the noblest or the best.'

Ludwig van Beethoven (1770-1827)
in a letter dated Vienna, 29 June 1801 to
Franz Wegeler in Bonn

1

Her irritation increasing by the mile, Janet Evans drove back and forth three times between the roundabout by Safeway's in Upper Bangor and the Antelope Inn by Menai Bridge before she found the name plate, all but hidden beneath a riotous growth of privet tumbling over a high brick wall beside the main road.

Glamorgan Place was a short, hilly cul-de-sac, well-tended and suburban, quiet in the torpor of an August afternoon. She parked by the kerb half-way up the right-hand side, feeling heat sear her face and bare arms as soon as she stepped from the car, and looked up at the large, attic-windowed Victorian villa which was home to a Mrs Edith Harris. Overhanging beech and horse chestnut trees secluded the house from its neighbours, dropped leafy shadows on shrubs and wilting perennials and parched lawns, and darkened the short gravelled drive to the front door, where an overweight girl of uncertain years suddenly appeared, beads of sweat hanging like dewdrops from her hairline and a fat tabby cat clinging to her shoulder.

'I'm Detective Constable Evans,' Janet said, holding out her warrant card. 'From Bangor police. The doctor called us.'

The girl retreated into the hallway, treading in pools of coloured light which poured down the staircase from a stained glass window on the landing.

Stepping in the same pools, Janet asked: 'Are your parents in?'

'Mama's upstairs with the doctor.' The girl's eyes clouded and she hefted the cat to her other shoulder. 'He came to see Uncle Ned, but he was too late. He's dead,' she added mournfully.

Bathed in streams of the wonderful light on the elaborately carved staircase, Janet turned. 'How d'you know?'

'I saw him.' The girl trudged off down the hall, the cat's bright eyes looking over her shoulder.

A faded, once pretty woman in a shapely dress hovered at the turn of the stairs, her skin and clothing vibrant with the same rich colours. 'Did Phoebe tell you?' she whispered, wringing her hands. 'You can always tell, can't you? Phoebe's never seen a dead person before, but she knew, didn't she?' Her whole body shivered gently and Janet thought she must be of the same age as her own mother, marooned in that sterile time between biological redundancy and death. 'I called the doctor right away, but he said the police would have to be told, and I can't think why! Ned's been ill for *years*, but the doctor won't sign the death certificate.' Her fingers snapped around Janet's arm, cold and claw-like. 'Can't *you* tell him?' she whispered urgently. 'Can't you *make* him sign it?'

Pulling herself away, Janet went up the remaining stairs and along a wide landing towards the room at the end, where a thin, grey man, clad despite the heat of the day in a high, stiff collar, a faded silk tie and a suit, slouched in a dark plush chair ornate with curlicues and carvings. A pair of wire spectacles hung awry from the end of his nose, his mouth was clamped shut and his wide-open eyes stared blankly into hers.

The doctor was ready to leave. 'I can't stay, and there's nothing I can do, anyway, and although Mrs Harris would like nothing better, I can't certify cause of death because I don't know anything about the deceased.' He shrugged on a pale linen jacket. 'Edward Jones was one of Dr Ansoni's patients and he's on holiday until Monday.'

The air was sweet with flower scents, and dusty with the odour of old books and papers stacked in piles everywhere about the room. Beneath the open window stood a huge desk, littered with more books and documents, an ancient typewriter, and a scattering of pens and pencils and paper-clips. Stepping around teetering columns of books, Janet placed her fingers on the dead man's neck, eyes averted from his watery stare, and wondered fleetingly if the image of God were imprinted on his retina, as her father would claim. Striated with weals and marks, the cooling flesh was still beneath her own, undisturbed by any pulse of blood or twitch of life. He smelt of fresh air and ivory soap and death, and she felt suddenly nauseous.

'You don't need to check,' the doctor said gently. 'He's definitely dead, even if I can't say why, although it's more than likely to be natural causes of some kind. Anyway, the autopsy will tell us.'

'When did he die?' Janet asked.

The doctor glanced at his watch. 'A couple of hours ago at most, say between two and two thirty. Now I really must be off, so I'll leave you to it.'

She heard his feet pound down the staircase, crunch over the gravel and away, then close behind her, felt Edith's short panting breaths lift the hairs on her neck.

'Did he sign it?' Edith demanded. 'Shall I call the undertaker?'

Edging her out of the room, the cloying smells sickening, Janet said: 'I'm sorry, Mrs Harris, but we'll have to inform the coroner. The doctor can't determine the cause of death.' Closing the door on the dead man's eyes, she added: 'Is he your brother? Only your daughter called him "Uncle Ned".'

'Of course he isn't! And why do you have to involve the coroner?'

'It's standard procedure in cases of unexplained death,' Janet said, wearily. 'And the forensic team will have to examine the room. Nothing's been disturbed, has it? They'll need to know.'

'Disturbed?' Edith's voice rose. 'Of course it hasn't!' She paced the landing, then back, and stood close beside Janet, breath rasping, eyes hectic. 'And don't take any notice of Phoebe! She'll make a mountain out of a grain of dirt!'

'She hasn't said anything, except that he's dead.'

'She will!' Edith insisted. 'Believe me, she will!' She laughed, a sound like a horse in pain. 'She's already said somebody must have killed him. Isn't that completely *ridiculous*?'

2

'The ground's sweating,' Dewi Prys observed, elbows on the window sill of the CID office. 'It smells like that tramp we had in the cells a few years back.'

'So?' Janet asked.

Watching a clutch of women fighting to board a bus, laden with plastic carrier bags from the new German supermarket, he added: 'So, arguably, the earth's a big body crawling with people the way we're crawling with microbes.'

'That's hardly an original thought.'

'It is for me.' He swiped at a dead wasp, curled elliptically on the white paint, then unfastened another shirt button. 'There's not a breath of wind, everything's covered in dust, and if the weather doesn't break soon, we'll run out of water.'

'Oh, don't be ridiculous!' Janet snapped. 'God, I wish you'd stop moaning. You get on my nerves! You'll be complaining about the cold in a couple of months.'

'Probably,' Dewi agreed. 'Christmas isn't far away, is it? Has your pa written his Yuletide sermon yet?'

'I wouldn't know. I haven't seen him since I came back from holiday.'

'Why not?'

'Because I haven't.'

'Seen your mother?'

'She gets on my nerves almost as much as you. Nothing but questions, one after another! "Been anywhere nice, dear?", "Met any nice people, dear?", "Got anything planned, dear?" '

'Your pa probably puts her up to it.' Dewi smiled. 'You should give her something worth reporting.'

'Such as?'

He grinned. 'A red-hot intrigue with Mr McKenna?'

'That's not funny!' She flushed.

'You fancy him, though. Don't you?'

'You're unbelievably adolescent!'

'Methinks the lady doth protest too much,' Dewi taunted. 'Or whatever the saying is.' Drifting away from the window to straddle a chair, he gazed at her thoughtfully. 'Mind you, that bitch Denise probably put him off women for life. Why doesn't he get a divorce and get shut of her properly?'

'You're needlessly nasty about her. She could be well rid of *him*, for all we know.' She pushed aside her report on the demise of the old man in Glamorgan Place, and stretched. 'Is he expected in today?'

'Don't think so. He's just back for Griffiths's retirement do.'

'I hope he gets the promotion.'

'It's supposed to be a foregone conclusion.' He admired the arch of her body as she stretched again. 'And as soon as he moves up the ladder from Chief Inspector to Superintendent, there's room for an enterprising detective constable like me who's passed his sergeant's exam.'

'The questions must have been particularly easy that day.'

'You're bitchier than usual at the moment,' Dewi said, rising from his seat, 'so I presume it's that time of the month. Anyway, I'm off to see a man about a car. Ring me if you want anything.'

'You're buying a new car?' she asked, trying to ignore the jibe. 'What sort?'

'One that doesn't blow its guts apart every time I try to start the engine.' Lingering by her desk, he scanned the half-written report, then asked: 'How was Edward Jones related to Edith Harris?'

'Third cousin twice removed, or somesuch. He was a sort of lodger.' She brushed away a tiny withered leaf which had drifted through the window and settled on the desk. 'It's a shame his own GP's on holiday, because the locum obviously couldn't certify cause of death. Mrs Harris was really upset when I said we'd have to notify the coroner, and I thought she was going to throw a fit when uniform arrived with forensics.'

'Can't be helped,' Dewi said. 'D'you think they'll find anything?'

'It's probably natural causes. Heart attack, or something. He wasn't young.'

'No signs of violence? Nothing suspicious?'

'According to Mrs Harris, he didn't have an enemy in the world.'

'People say things like that when they're trying to pull the wool over your eyes.'

'That's almost exactly what her daughter said.' Retrieving her pen, Janet added: 'She's called Phoebe.'

'And why should Phoebe say that?'

'Because she likes drama, apparently, and a natural death

is far too prosaic.' She shuddered gently. 'She gave me the shivers. She's fat and sort of lumpy, and she dresses like a bag lady, and she's got these really strange eyes which look right through you, so if the old man *was* murdered, she probably did it.'

3

Draughts of hot air riddled with the smell of exhaust fumes billowed through the car's open windows as McKenna waited for a break in the traffic hurtling down the road outside the main gate of the police headquarters.

'I'll never see this place again unless I drive by specially,' Owen Griffiths commented, craning his neck to look back at the tall grey building roofed with a forest of antennae. He wiped a bead of sweat from the end of his nose. 'I don't know whether to laugh or cry.'

'Either's good medicine at the right time.' Beside him on the rear seat, Eifion Roberts unfastened his collar button, loosened his tie, and fanned himself with the ends. 'Mind you, you'll have a laugh taking that cheque to the bank. How much did you get?'

'More than enough for two holidays.'

'Then somebody's pleased to see the back of you, because at one time, you'd only have got the gold clock, whereas you got both.' Prodding McKenna's back, Roberts said: 'I've never understood why folks get clocks when they retire. Do you?'

'It's a subliminal message,' McKenna offered. ' "Watch this space, your end is nigh." '

'God, you're cynical!' Roberts commented. 'Still, it's as well, 'cos if your masters' smiles and sycophancies were anything to go by, you'll be filling Owen's boots come Monday.' Smirking, he went on: 'You'll look more fetching in uniform, so you might score once in a while. I'm told women find power a real turn-on.' He nudged Griffiths. 'Isn't that a fact, Owen?'

'I wouldn't know.' Griffiths's voice was plaintive. 'A purple past must be nice, though, mustn't it? Something secret and special and all yours to think back on.'

'See?' McKenna felt himself prodded again. 'Owen won't be the only one missing nearly every boat to set sail. Get yourself a life while you can. You must be so short of the necessary your guts turn somersaults every time a bit of skirt passes by.'

'Oh, be quiet!' McKenna snapped, 'and stop bouncing on the seat. I don't have reinforced suspension!'

'I'm on a diet, I'll have you know.'

'About time, too!'

'As I've said before, I'll find vinegar in your veins when I come to cut you up,' Roberts said. 'And fag smoke invading every cell in your body.'

'And what makes you so sure you'll have the pleasure of me on your mortuary table?'

'Because I've calculated the amount of fag smoke gungeing up your innards already, so don't get cocky just because you're younger than us.'

'You two bicker like children,' Griffiths said irritably. 'And always about the same things. It's very boring!'

'Excuse us!' Roberts winked at McKenna in the rearview mirror. 'We'll try to confine our puerility to the beach. We should be there soon.'

'And why are three grown men going to the beach?' Griffiths wondered. 'What'll we do there?'

'Well, I'm going to buy myself a bucket and spade, and play in the sand,' Roberts said.

'And I could paddle, couldn't I?' Griffiths added.

'You could even take off your shoes and socks first,' McKenna suggested.

'And what will you do, Michael?' Roberts asked.

'I'll watch,' McKenna replied, turning off the express-way towards Llandudno.

Bedazzled by the glitter of water against a sky of almost tropical blue, McKenna sat cross-legged on a tartan rug from the car, Griffiths beside him with sand encasing his wet feet and clinging to the fuzz of grey hair on his shins, and a white handkerchief, knotted at each corner, covering his pate. Near the water's edge, Roberts dug vigorously with a yellow spade, gouging a channel to carry the tide into the moat around his lop-sided edifice. Every so often, he smiled winningly at the two near-naked young women stretched out nearby.

'He's quite brazen, isn't he?' Griffiths said. 'Still, I suppose seeing so much raw flesh on the move is bound to get him over-excited.'

McKenna grinned. 'He's in his element.'

'Second childhood, more like,' Griffiths commented. He looked down at his own disarray and smiled ruefully. 'You might say we're both in our dotage.' He sighed. 'But I've had my day, I suppose. A short one, but sweet in its own way. It's just a pity it seems so distant and hazy, like childhood.'

'I can imagine you both as kids,' McKenna said. 'Dressed in sailor suits and sun-hats, playing on some beach half a century ago.'

'Eifion, perhaps, but not me.' Griffiths smiled gently. 'My parents couldn't afford holidays, so I was sixteen before I saw the ocean. I saved every penny from my job shifting cinders at the railway yard and took a cycling trip to Devon and Cornwall.'

'You must have had days out. Your place was quite near the coast.'

'Summers went by bringing in the harvest, then battening

down the hatches and praying for a kind winter. We didn't travel the way people do these days, and anyway,' he added, grinning, 'we only had a tractor, and I don't think my mother would've taken to arriving at the beach in the trailer my dad used for his muck-spreading.' Watching the pathologist's castle collapse into its moat, he asked: 'Your ancestors worked the land too, didn't they?'

'They worked it to the bone. Some of the Irish peat lands are as bleak as moonscapes now.'

'You'll feel at home in Wales, then.' Griffiths smiled.

After a long silence, McKenna said: 'I've never felt at home anywhere. I'm Welsh to the Irish, Irish to the Welsh, and trouble either way to the English.'

'Come on! Your dad was Anglesey born and bred, like you.'

'Maybe so.' He picked up a marbled pebble, and rubbed it clean of sand. 'But the past always catches up with you.'

'What past? I imagine your grandparents left Ireland to escape from something, like every other emigrant. Poverty, oppression, whatever.' Griffiths paused, then added: 'Or to look for something better, like Dick Whittington, although nobody's ever found the streets of Holyhead paved with gold, except our latterday drug peddlers.'

'One of our kinfolk was executed by the British after the Easter Rebellion in 1916, and there's no escape from something like that, or what it means.' He frowned, massaging the pebble. 'And when my parents took me visiting our relatives across the water, I used to wave my toy gun around with the rest of the local kids, but we'd be playing "Irish and English" instead of "Cowboys and Indians". So what does that make me?'

'The sum of your history, like the rest of us, so quit bellyaching about it!' A huge dark shape eclipsed the sun as Roberts loomed over them, and dropped the bucket and spade by McKenna's feet. Filthy, sweat-stained, face ruddy with exertion, he went on: 'I haven't played on the sand for donkey's years, and I'd forgotten how bloody tired you get, so I'm going for ice creams. Who wants what?'

'You're on a diet,' Griffiths said.

'It starts tomorrow with my hols, and you can't have an afternoon at the beach without ices.' He smiled down at McKenna. 'Why don't you take off your shoes and socks, like Owen here, and go for a paddle. Loosen up, man! Get your feet wet, for once in your life. It'll do you no end of good.'

4

The white van belonging to the forensic team was still parked outside the house in Glamorgan Place when Dewi arrived. He walked to the front door, almost compelled to step over the long shadows thrown by the trees, and pushed the bell, looking at the manicured lawns and weedless borders, a drift of night-scented stock beguiling his senses. Behind the leaded lights of the half-glazed door, he saw a dark shape flitting towards him.

She pulled the door wide, smiling brilliantly. 'Hello! And who are *you*?'

Another perfume drifted towards him, a musky, heady scent which sent a frisson through his innards. 'I'm a police officer.'

'Are you, really? Come in.'

He followed, drawn by invisible threads into a cool hallway scented with polish, where the fading colours from the landing window lapped against the walls as the sun sank to the west. Watching her, he marvelled at the corn-coloured hair swinging to her waist, the golden silk of her shapely arms, and the beautiful moulding of hip and buttocks. She opened another door, and stood aside, then flitted away, leaving the perfume in her wake.

Still wringing her hands, Edith Harris perched on a dusky brocade sofa set at right angles to the grand fireplace inlaid with blue Delft tiles, tall vases of creamy pampas grass framing the unlit grate. Opposite, her youngest daughter occupied a matching sofa, the tabby cat on her knees.

'Yes?' Edith looked up, her eyes glittering.

'I'm Detective Constable Prys, ma'am,' Dewi said.

'What do you want? And why are those other people still here?'

'It's just standard procedure, ma'am.'

'That's what that girl said earlier!' Edith snapped.

'They took Uncle Ned away ages ago,' Phoebe offered. 'To the mortuary.'

Dewi nodded. 'I'm sorry about all the upset, but we don't have a choice.'

'It's ridiculous!' Edith insisted. 'All this fuss, when not a day went by without Ned having *something* wrong with him! One thing after another, day after day, week after week, year after year!' She fell silent, then announced: 'It must have been his heart! He's complained of pains in his chest for years.'

'What treatment was he having?' Dewi asked.

As Edith opened her mouth to reply, Phoebe intervened. 'He wasn't having any, because everybody thought it was all in his mind, so it's a waste of time cutting up his body, isn't it?'

'Phoebe!'' Edith exclaimed. 'Don't be so horrid!'

The girl's eyes, Dewi thought, were the colour of slate on a rainy day. He wondered how old she was, and if there was still time for the swan to vanquish a very ugly duckling.

'Somebody's bound to say Uncle Ned was mad,' she countered. 'You've said it often enough.'

'He had problems.' Edith's admission was reluctant.

'What sort?'

'The usual sort crazy people have,' Phoebe said acidly.

'Had he ever tried to hurt himself?' Dewi asked.

Edith looked at him warily. 'I don't know.' She pulled a handkerchief from her dress pocket, and dabbed her eyes. 'You'll have to talk to Dr Ansoni about that.'

'Well, I won't bother you any longer.' Dewi smiled. 'Can I have a word with my colleagues before I go?'

Edith wafted the little square of clean linen. 'Phoebe will show you upstairs. I'm really quite worn out.' She slumped in the sofa, the back of her hand against her forehead.

Gathering up the cat, Phoebe struggled to her feet, and as she led him into the hall, he glanced into the shadows, searching for the other girl. 'Who's the young lady who let me in?'

'Minnie. She's one of my sisters, but she isn't a lady.' Clumping up the staircase, the cat over her shoulder, she added: 'Annie is, though. She doesn't live at home any longer.'

'Where does she live?'

'Llanberis. She's a teacher.'

'And what does Minnie do?'

'You'll have to ask *her* that.'

'Why don't you like her?'

'You'll have to ask her *that*, as well,' Phoebe said. 'Why are you so nosy?'

'Because I'm paid to be.' As she paused at the turn of the stairs, shifting the burden of the cat to her other shoulder, he asked: 'Has that animal lost the use of her legs?'

'Don't be stupid! And he's a him, not a her.' She frowned. 'Well, he *was* a him. He's an it now. Will he know there's something missing, d'you think?'

'I most certainly would.' Dewi grinned. 'And whatever he is, he needs more exercise. He's quite fat.'

At the head of the stairs, she stopped, staring gravely at him. 'I'm quite fat, and I get lots of exercise.' She hugged the cat. 'I like holding him. He's a comfort.'

'What's he called?'

'Tom.'

'Couldn't you think of something more original?'

'He was already christened when I had him. Uncle Ned brought him from the farm.'

'What farm?'

'The family farm near Bala. It's called Llys Ifor.'

'Who lives there?'

'Auntie Gladys and Auntie Gertrude.' The slaty eyes darkened to basalt. 'Mama didn't know what to say to them, so she rang Annie and asked *her* to tell them about Uncle Ned.'

'You'll miss him, won't you?'

She nodded, clutching the cat.

'And I expect it was a terrible shock when you saw him dead. Is that why you said someone must've killed him?'

Gesturing towards a closed door at the end of the landing, she said: 'That's his room.' Then she began to walk away in the opposite direction, stopping by another door. 'I said that because it's true, and you'll find out I'm right, if you're any good at what you get paid for.'

He heard the creak of hinges, and the door thudded shut.

5

Janet stared. 'I *am* honoured!' Head swathed in a bluey-green towel, body in a matching bathrobe, she smelled, Dewi thought, of mountain streams and sun-warmed heathers.

He hovered on the doorstep. 'I've been to Glamorgan Place.'

'Then you'd better come in.' She walked towards the kitchen. 'I've just made a pot of tea.'

He followed, peering through open doorways. 'You've made the place very nice.'

She filled two mugs, then sat at the kitchen table. 'Not a bit like the manse, is it? No velvet drapes, no velvet sofas, no litter of ornaments, no knick-knacks on every surface.'

'And no parents,' Dewi added, looking around the bright room.

'Quite.' She lit a cigarette, and watched him through the smoke. 'Did you want to tell me something about Edward Jones? I was on my way to bed.'

'A stroll down the pier would do you far more good. It's a gorgeous evening, there's sure to be a little breeze off the sea, and you're beginning to look like a plant that's been shut in a cupboard.'

'I'm tired.' She clasped the mug, and smiled gently. 'So say your piece, then I can get some sleep.'

'Phoebe Harris thinks it was foul play.'

'I told you that this afternoon.'

'But you didn't take her seriously, did you?'

'Because there was no reason why I should. Sick old man drops dead. It happens every day.'

'He was fifty-seven. That's not exactly old.' Dewi stirred his tea, then dropped the spoon on the table. 'And according to Phoebe, he was much sicker in the head than he was in the body.'

'Then maybe he committed suicide.'

'She says not.'

'She's not the fount of all wisdom,' Janet said irritably. 'She's overweight, overwrought and over-imaginative!'

'She could still be right.'

6

The street where McKenna had made his home since the collapse of his marriage, in a rented three-storey house, more resembled a slum, Dewi realized, each passing week. A nasty smell hung in the air, from torn plastic bags spilling rubbish in the gutters, smears of dog dirt on the pavement, and the patches of dark green mould daubed on the once white walls of the terrace opposite, where purple loosestrife and dusty weeds sprouted from fissures in the chimney stacks. At the end of the street, rusting tyreless wheels squashing the weeds which burgeoned between cracks in the pavement, two derelict cars had been dumped outside the empty house from where, last Christmas Eve, the police had evicted a group of squatters.

McKenna opened the front door, bright yellow rubber gloves on his hands. 'What a stroke of luck!'

'What is, sir?'

'You are. I could do with another pair of hands.'

'For what, sir?'

Shunted down the stairs and into the basement kitchen, Dewi found himself holding the gloves and a sponge, a bucket of steaming sudsy water at his feet.

'It's that stain by the cooker,' McKenna said. 'It won't come out, even though I cleaned underneath the carpet. It comes back like Rizzio's blood in Holyrood House.'

'Serves you right for putting a carpet in the kitchen, if you don't mind my saying, sir.' On hands and knees, Dewi began to scrub.

'It's kitchen carpet. It's supposed to repel stains.' McKenna watched. 'And I put it down because slate floors get ice-cold in winter.'

'So what did you spill?' Sweat began to glisten on the younger man's face.

'Bolognese sauce.'

Dewi sat back on his haunches and brushed hair from his eyes with the back of his hand. 'You're probably stuck with it, then. Tomato stains worse than blood.'

'Fancy a drink?' McKenna asked.

'I've just had a cup of tea at Janet's flat, but something cold would be nice.' Wringing out the sponge, he brushed away the froth of suds, and surveyed the damp patch. 'It's not as bad as it was, but that's not to say it's gone for good.' He stood up. 'Who's Rizzio?'

'Mary Queen of Scots' secretary, and allegedly her lover. Some of her nobles had him stabbed to death one supper-time.' He filled two tumblers from a large bottle of cider, and sat at the kitchen table.

Sitting in the other chair, Dewi said: 'This could be my last visit, sir, because you can't drink with the lower orders when you're promoted. You'll have to do your mixing else-where, like the golf club, or even the Lodge.'

'*If*. Not *when*.'

'It's a foregone conclusion, sir. Inspector Tuttle said so before he went on leave yesterday.'

'And he said the same to me when I went to relieve him of his cat-sitting duties, but we'll see what Monday brings, shall we?' He smiled. 'Mind you, Eifion Roberts said the chief constable was being extraordinarily nice to me today.'

Pushing an ashtray within McKenna's reach, Dewi said: 'Shouldn't you think about moving house, then? This street's really horrible.'

'If I wait a bit longer, it might get gentrified.'

'Who by? The locals haven't got that kind of money, and all the English want to be on Anglesey. What happened to the old folk across the road?'

'One's gone to see out her days in a rest home, and the other two were carried out feet first in early April.'

'A lot of people die in the spring, don't they?' Dewi asked. 'Maybe they have to see the world turning again before they can leave it behind.' He drank half the cider without stopping. 'Then again, people die all the time. Janet was called out to a sudden death this afternoon, at one of those big detached houses in Glamorgan Place, and I've been back this evening.'

'Why?'

'Just to check things are sorted until the autopsy result comes through. The doctor couldn't certify cause of death, but it looks like natural causes.' Draining his glass, he added: 'It's a weird household. The dead man lodged with this relative called Edith Harris, and she's got three daughters, but there's no sign of a husband or other visible means of support.'

'So perhaps her lodger was filling the voids, as it were. It wouldn't be the first time.'

'Oh, I don't think so, sir. He was fifty-seven.'

McKenna grinned. 'A year younger than Eifion Roberts, and you should have seen him leering at the girls on Llandudno beach. Still, you can't blame him, I suppose. They don't leave much to the imagination these days.'

Dewi flushed slightly. 'One of Mrs Harris's girls is quite fetching. The youngest is so ugly I felt sorry for her. How they came out of the same pod is beyond me.'

'What about the third?'

'I didn't see her. She lives in Llanberis.'

'And the mother?'

'Neurotic, irritating, and prone to asking questions you can't answer.'

'She was probably in shock. It takes people different ways.'

'She struck me as being near hysterical most of the time.' He uncapped the cider bottle and refilled his glass. 'And Phoebe, the ugly sister, said her Uncle Ned was supposed to be crazy, but she also reckons he was bumped off, so maybe they're all crazy.'

'Why should she think he was murdered?'

'I had a chat with Mrs Harris after forensics went and things had quietened down a bit, and she says Phoebe's probably in denial. Ned Jones moved to Glamorgan Place before she was born, and they were very close.'

'Ned Jones?' McKenna frowned. 'Where did he come from?'

'A village called Penglogfa, not far from Bala. The family had a farm and his sisters still live there.' Quaffing cider, Dewi went on. 'Ned came years ago to lecture at the university, but they retired him because he was forever ill. His room's stacked from floor to ceiling with old books and papers, but nobody seems to know if he was doing anything constructive with them. Mrs Harris kept saying: "It's such a shame when that sort of thing happens, isn't it? Such a terrible waste of his talent, wasn't it?", which is what I meant about the questions, because I hadn't a clue what she meant.' As McKenna rose to go to the parlour, he added: 'Phoebe says the farm's called Llys Ifor.'

'I know.' Rummaging through the books on the shelves in the chimney alcove, McKenna found what he wanted, then handed it to Dewi, open at a page of photographs. 'See anyone you know?'

Dewi stared with undisguised amazement. 'It's you, isn't it, sir?'

'Many moons ago.' Retrieving the book, McKenna pointed to another face, hollow-eyed and melancholy. 'And that's Ned Jones, when he won the essay prize at the National Eisteddfod.'

Dewi scanned the text. 'And you got second prize. Why did you never tell anyone, sir? You could've been quite famous.'

'Because I would have preferred to be *very* famous,' McKenna confessed. 'I felt like strangling him. He came from nowhere and snatched the glory right out of my hands.' Seated on his old chesterfield, he cradled the Eisteddfod yearbook on his lap. 'That year's essay theme was "Identity in Crisis", so I wrote about my family's ruptured identity and cultural dislocation, and how I'd renegotiated myself out of an Irish past to a Welsh present.' He smiled wryly. 'I suppose it was a bit precious, but everyone expected me to win.'

Dewi sat beside him. 'And what was Ned's contribution about?'

'Guilt and atonement and visitation by the sins of the fathers.' McKenna lit the cigarette. 'His family owned other properties besides Llys Ifor, and huge tracts of land and a slate quarry, and because all that wealth came from the proceeds of slave-trading, he said he owed his existence to the black people his ancestors exploited.' He'd paused, drawing on the cigarette. 'He'd trawled the family records for biographies of some of the slaves, and described what he called their atomized private identities, how and where they died, what happened to their children, and so on.'

'Heavy stuff,' Dewi observed. 'Did it deserve the prize?'

McKenna nodded. 'I wanted to weep with envy.'

'Well, it's all swings and roundabouts in the end, sir. You're going from strength to strength, while the one-time Bard of Bala's in a drawer in the morgue.'

'Having died a bare stick, as the Chinese say.'

'That's another way of saying he had no offspring, is it?'

'And no wife.'

'That we know about.'

McKenna closed the book and put it on the floor. 'I think I might to go his funeral, and pay my last respects.'

'Mrs Harris was wittering about that, as well. She asked if we'd let Ned's sisters know when the body can be released.'

'She can tell them herself. They're her relatives.'

'I got the impression they're not on good terms.'

'Then she can ask her solicitor, or bank manager, or

whatever. It's not our job.' Noting the disappointment on Dewi's face, McKenna said: 'And you're not doing favours on the quiet in your time off. You weren't by any chance planning to ask the comely daughter to guide you through the wilds of Meirionydd to Penglogfa, were you?'

Dewi blushed from his feet to the roots of his hair.

McKenna sighed. 'You should find yourself a steady girl. She'd neutralize some of that testosterone galloping through your veins.'

The blush deepened.

'There are times when it interferes with your judgement,' McKenna went on. 'You get side-tracked too easily, waylaid by a pretty smile or a buxom figure.'

'I'm not promiscuous, sir.'

'I know you're not.'

'But I can't find anyone who doesn't disappoint me, sooner or later.' He chewed his thumbnail, then added: 'And I've probably disappointed a few, as well.'

'It's a matter of trial and error, but at some point, you might have to settle for a compromise. Most of us do.'

Cheeks still pink, Dewi summoned a smile. 'Maybe I'll be another bare stick.'

'I hope not. That would be rather a waste.'

'There's plenty about. You've only got to look at the lonely hearts columns in the papers. There's even one in *The Times.*' He grinned. 'D'you think Janet reads it?'

'I don't know what she does. Why did you go to her flat? Is there something going on I don't know about?'

'I just called in because she didn't seem very well earlier. In fact, she's been pretty miserable since she came back from Italy.'

'So perhaps she's pining for the handsome Latin she dallied with for a while on the shores of the Mediterranean.'

'D'you think so?' Dewi pulled a face. 'I wouldn't've thought a holiday fling with some dago was quite her scene.'

1

McKenna's front doorbell rang shortly after eight o'clock on Monday morning and, thinking it must be the postman, he padded upstairs in slippers and pyjamas.

'Morning, Michael,' the deputy chief constable said. 'Can I come in?' Reaching the foot of the staircase, he added: 'Well, thank God the inside doesn't match the outside. All the same, shouldn't you be living somewhere a bit more salubrious?'

'I like this house,' McKenna said, his stomach churning with anxiety, 'and I like the view.'

Walking to the open back door, his visitor glanced over the garden fence, then to the wall on the right, where McKenna's two cats basked in the morning sunshine. 'These the strays I keep hearing about?' Then, he sat carefully on the chesterfield, rearranging his uniform.

'Can I offer you a drink?'

'Coffee, please. Black and no sugar.'

McKenna hurried to the kitchen, poured coffee into his best china mug, and returned to the parlour. 'I'll get dressed.'

'No rush, Michael. Let's talk first, shall we?'

'What about?' Sitting in the armchair, McKenna lit his first cigarette of the day. 'What's happened?'

'Nothing drastic. Nothing to worry about, really.'

'Oh, no?' McKenna felt his temper rise. 'And how often do I get an early-morning visit from someone of your rank all dressed up in his handing-out-the-bad-news gear?'

'Don't be like that.' The other man frowned. 'I thought coming here was the least I could do in the circumstances.'

'What circumstances?'

The other man coughed. 'We've been instructed to hold back your promotion for a while.'

Drawing hard on the cigarette, McKenna stared at the floor.

'It's a political decision, and it was taken without any reference to us.'

'Why?'

'Why d'you think? Good God, man, you've just come back from the Irish Republic!'

'And what does that have to do with me, or my promotion?'

'Because as superintendent, you'd be involved with Special Branch supervision at times, for royal visits and other sensitive security matters, and the civil servants who tell us what to do don't think, apparently, that someone with your background and connections is quite the best person to have in that office at this present moment in time, because they reckon the Irish Republic's a bloody tinder-box, and always will be, and all the peace initiatives and cease-fires in the world won't make the slightest bit of difference.' Pausing to draw breath, he added: 'I'm sorry, but that's how it is. I think it's a very bad show, and so does the chief.'

McKenna ground his cigarette to pulp in the ashtray, hands shaking. 'You knew I was going to Ireland before I went, so why didn't you say crossing the water for my great aunt's funeral would turn me into a security risk?'

'Because we've only just found out she was cousin once removed to the one who got topped in 1916.'

'And she wasn't born until 1920, because her father was

in the trenches with his English comrades up to the end of the Great War, so don't you think it's rather academic, as well as ancient history?'

'Nobody's got longer memories than the Irish.'

McKenna lit another cigarette, and stared at his visitor. 'Who checked up on me? Who took the trouble to uproot my family tree?'

'It wasn't us.' The deputy chief smiled tentatively. 'But you know we're sometimes forced to abide by other people's decisions.'

'When it's convenient!' McKenna snapped.

His visitor rose, again rearranging the uniform. 'D'you want to extend your leave for a few days?'

'No, I don't!'

'Suit yourself, but I just thought it might be easier if you gave Griffiths's replacement a chance to settle in.'

2

Finding McKenna's office still empty at nine thirty, Dewi strolled along the corridor to Griffiths's old room, rapped on the door, and walked in, but instead of McKenna, glorying in his new seat of power, he was shocked to see a woman behind the desk, a smartly uniformed and sharply coiffed creature, talking to a uniformed inspector who was another total stranger.

'Yes?' She raised one finely pencilled eyebrow. 'Who are you?'

'Detective Constable Prys, ma'am.'

'I'm Superintendent Bradshaw, and this is Inspector Rowlands. He's standing in for Inspector Tuttle.' She gave Dewi a rather feline smile. 'And just so you know, I'm replacing Superintendent Griffiths. Now, what can I do for you?'

'I was looking for DCI McKenna, ma'am.'

'How strange! I've been doing exactly the same. He seems to have gone AWOL.'

Janet had disappeared too by the time Dewi returned to the CID office, but her bag still hung from the back of her chair. He waited for five minutes, staring at the clock, then went downstairs to the canteen, to find her sitting alone at one of the tables, drinking black coffee and looking very miserable. 'Have you seen her?' she demanded, taking a cigarette from the pack on the table. 'And the other one? Mr McKenna's apparently absolutely livid. He came in quite early, then went straight out again. The gossip is that he's gone to HQ.' She blew smoke towards the ceiling. 'One of the sergeants said Bradshaw's got an awful reputation.'

'For what?'

'Mowing down anyone who gets in her way. She's one of the fast-track breed, and she's been with the fraud squad until now, so she won't have clue about real policing.' Sipping her coffee, she added: 'What on earth could've stopped Mr McKenna's promotion? I think it's awful!'

'I expect he does, as well.'

3

McKenna's meeting with the chief constable brought no comfort, and although assured that he remained the virtually autonomous head of divisional criminal investigation, he realized that what had sufficed for so long was no longer enough. Persuaded that Griffiths's post was his for the asking, he had let himself anticipate what it would bring, only to find the prize wrenched from his hands at the last moment by something emerging from the shadows, as Ned Jones had done so many years before.

Driving along the road travelled with such optimism only three days earlier, he thought of Friday's little adventure with the two people he regarded as his closest friends, and drew into a lay-by, to sit with his hands on the wheel and his head on his hands, and to think of what else he had lost, apart from a friend, when Griffiths decided to put himself out to grass.

4

Diana Bradshaw preened herself when the two young detectives leaped to attention. She perched on Dewi's desk, displaying elegant legs and well-shod feet, her perfume heavy in the still air. 'I thought you might like an opportunity to bring me up to date.'

'There's not much on at the moment, ma'am,' Dewi offered. 'August is usually fairly quiet.'

'Don't tempt fate!' She smiled. 'Especially with Inspector Tuttle and several others on leave.'

'The division's always got a good CID complement. We're just spread over a large area unless something big crops up.'

'With DCI McKenna in charge.' She rose. 'Yes, I do know, Constable Prys, and I know exactly how many officers I have at my disposal, uniformed and otherwise.' Gazing at him thoughtfully, she said: 'I'm told a car fraud of rather massive proportions has outwitted you for several months, so Inspector Rowlands is now in charge of that, and I expect some real progress very quickly.' Making for the door, she added: 'Please come to my office in ten minutes, Miss Evans.'

'Shit!' Dewi muttered. 'How to cross a new broom!'

'Why does she want to see *me*?' Janet's voice squeaked.

'Perhaps she fancies you. Play your cards right, and you'll be well in.'

'Oh, shut up!' Janet seethed. 'Don't you think of *anything* but sex?'

5

By the time McKenna could bring himself to face his foreseeable future, Rowlands had given himself a crash course in the current state of divisional activity, and was waiting to meet the chief inspector of whom he had heard so much. When McKenna eventually walked into the office, he rose to his feet and held out his hand. 'Ian Rowlands, sir. Inspector from central area on CID secondment.'

McKenna took the other man's hand, then gestured him to a seat. 'I'm told you're here while Inspector Tuttle's on holiday.'

'Yes, sir.'

Lighting a cigarette, McKenna said: 'Is this your first stint as a detective?'

'At this rank, yes.'

'Then we must make sure it's a worthwhile experience.'

'Yes, sir. I hope so, anyway.' Eyeing McKenna, he said: 'May I smoke? I've spent rather a long time in Superintendent Bradshaw's smoke-free zone.'

'Feel free.' McKenna pushed the pack across the desk. 'She tells me she's put you in charge of the vehicle fraud.'

'I've mugged up on it, but thought I'd ask you before I start anything.' Savouring the cigarette, he added: 'Janet and Dewi Prys told me about this Ned Jones who died last Friday. The autopsy report's just arrived, and things don't look very straightforward.'

'Do they not? Why's that?'

'Cause of death was asphyxiation by acute inflammation of the trachea, due to an allergic reaction, but the pathologist can't say to what.'

Fiddling with paperclips, McKenna suggested: 'A bee sting in the mouth, perhaps? Fatal reactions aren't uncommon.'

'There's no sign of a sting. It was probably a drug, even though he was known to have high sensitivities. His GP was prescribing nothing but nitrazepam for insomnia, and antihistamines for the allergies, so I wondered if it could be an assisted suicide. He was quite poorly and in a lot of pain, so he may have wanted out.'

'Then what's wrong with unassisted suicide? And Ned's illnesses were said to be all in the mind, so he was quite capable of killing himself. He wouldn't need help.'

'With respect, sir, Phoebe Harris said he must have been murdered.'

'While I can't discount unlawful killing,' McKenna said, 'provoking a fatal allergic reaction is a very uncertain way of doing it. It was more likely sheer carelessness or a simple accident.'

'Why? It's a very subtle way of poisoning someone. You can keep at it until it works, and it'll still look more like accident or suicide than murder.'

Dewi leaned against McKenna's door. 'If you're looking for Janet, sir, Ms Bradshaw had her in the office, then she came out, went to the bogs, and disappeared.'

'And is there a connection, other than the one in your head?'

'Dunno, sir. It's not my place to ask.' He paused. 'Will you be very offended if I ask why you weren't promoted? Everybody expected it, and they don't like what's happened. It doesn't seem honest.'

'I'm told it was a political decision taken outside the force, and to do with my ancestry, but not necessarily irreversible, even though my family tree can't be uprooted and regrown into a more conventional shape.'

'Really?' Dewi wandered over to the window, to look out over the bus shelters. 'I'd say that's a load of bollocks, and I'm sure Mr Griffiths and Mr Tuttle'll agree with me when they find out.'

'Unfortunately, other people's aspirations will have to go on hold for a while.'

'Only if they stay in this division, sir.' He drifted over to the desk, and sat down. 'And only if Ms Bradshaw doesn't decide to move on.' He smiled disarmingly. 'Shall I go in pursuit of the vehicle bandits with Mr Rowlands, find out what's ailing Janet, or go and see Mrs Harris?'

'Show Rowlands the lie of the land, but get me an appointment with Ned's GP first.'

6

'Ms Bradshaw tells me she gave you the rest of the day off,' McKenna said, as Janet stood at the door of her flat, red-eyed and pale-faced. 'Are you ill?'

'No, sir. I don't think so.'

'And Dewi tells me you legged it after you were called to her office. Did she upset you?'

'No, sir.' Janet hung against the door jamb, wilting and weary-looking, her shirt damp with sweat.

'This isn't an easy day for me,' McKenna said, 'and you're not helping.'

She raised her eyes, and her face crumpled like a child's as tears welled out and ran down her face, then she stumbled into the flat, sobbing raucously.

McKenna followed, to find her sprawled on the sofa, still weeping bitterly. 'For God's sake, girl! What's wrong with you?'

She gulped and wailed. 'I've been sick!'

'So? It's probably a tummy bug.'

'I was sick yesterday, and the day before.' Her voice rose. 'And the day before that, and I'm terribly late, and my father's going to *kill* me!' Face ashen, she began to gasp, staring at McKenna with huge, bloodshot eyes, before launching herself into his arms.

7

'Did you call on Janet?' Diana Bradshaw asked, sauntering unannounced into McKenna's office. 'Is she any better? I was quite worried about her.' Sitting on the edge of the desk, she went on: 'I had a chat with her this morning about her prospects, because she's a bright, well-educated girl, and she *could* go right to the top. She doesn't have a bad sickness record, does she? That would be such a shame.'

'No.' McKenna pulled a cigarette from the pack, and flicked his lighter. 'She's usually bursting with rude health.'

'Oh, well, I expect it's a hangover from holiday tummy.' As smoke began to curl towards the ceiling, she placed her hand to her lips, coughing delicately.

McKenna nodded. 'I expect so.' As she coughed again, he said: 'DC Prys is helping Rowlands with the car investigation, and I have an appointment to see Ned Jones's doctor after lunch.'

'Good.' She smiled. 'You don't need to report to me all the time, you know. You're in charge of criminal investigation.'

'Superintendent Griffiths liked to have his finger on every pulse,' McKenna said, smiling too. 'His input was often invaluable.'

8

Like McKenna, Gabriel Ansoni was of immigrant stock, the grandson of ice-cream makers from northern Italy, but unlike McKenna, he remained a good Catholic.

'How's the family?' McKenna asked.

'Sufficient to keep His Holiness quiet for the time being.' The dark eyes smiled at him. 'And more than enough to tempt me to leave them with the relatives in Cremona!' The smile faded, and he sighed. 'Poor Ned won't ever know that feeling, for all he was so close to Phoebe Harris.'

'I sort of knew him.' Relating the long ago Eisteddfot contest, in his mind's eye he saw Ned again, a thin figure stooping even in youth, mounting the stage to receive his accolade. 'So if I'd taken it into my head to dispatch him after all these years, I'd be famous at last, wouldn't I?' He smiled briefly. 'But his flame burned itself out without my help. What was wrong with him?'

'What wasn't?' The doctor spread his hands. 'He had one illness after another, and all I could do in the end was give him attention, because he'd exhausted the limited resources of medical knowledge. The consensus among the countless consultants he'd seen was of a neurotic hyochondria of epic proportions. In other words, he'd driven himself half crazy.'

'Is there a history of mental illness?'

Turning to the computer to search the medical record, Ansoni said: 'He was admitted several times to Denbigh Hospital with depression, and even sectioned once when he went completely crazy, and he spent a good part of his childhood and adolescence in one hospital or another. Tonsils, appendix, joint pains, chest pains, ear trouble, balance problems, headaches, gastro-intestinal problems, virulent mouth ulcers.' He took his finger from the keyboard. 'No physiological cause emerged, so a psychiatric conclusion was inevitably drawn, and indeed, such diffuse symptoms often indicate depressive illness.'

'Did you think he was a suicide risk?'

'Not really, although there were times when he seemed near the end of his tether.'

'Such as?'

'The last time we spoke.' The doctor ran his fingers through his hair. 'Osteo-arthritis and ankylosing spondylitis are common conditions at Ned's age, and he had both, together with low blood pressure, and he often experienced minor loss of sensation in the extremities, but he'd convinced himself that something perfectly normal was extremely sinister, and would necessitate amputation of his legs in the not too distant future. I said he was talking nonsense and he told me to stop patronizing him, because as he knew his bodily workings better than any doctor, he knew these new pains and strange changes heralded disaster.'

'You're on a hiding to nothing in that kind of situation,' McKenna commented.

'Which is probably why I subscribed too easily, if not wholly, to the psychiatric diagnosis and consequently never went out of my way to shape a therapy for him.'

'You can't treat what isn't there.'

'He had real pain, even if it was the product of inner turmoil.'

'But you didn't prescribe pain-killers?'

'Most strong pain-killers are highly addictive, and we have enough junkies courtesy of the NHS, without making more. Anyway, he never asked.' He smiled again, fleetingly. 'He was always on the edge of a psychological abyss, and he stopped himself from toppling over by sheer strength of will, so he dealt with his pain the same way. He once told me he even derived satisfaction from it, because it enhanced his awareness of the world.'

'People on the borderline of insanity often have heightened perceptions and instincts.'

'And which causes which?' asked Ansoni. 'He said he experienced pain in varying degrees day after day and night after night. He was helpless inside a body constantly threatening to kill him, from which, as he put it, he had to have prior permission for every breath he took, so I'm not surprised he became obsessed with its rhythms and workings and almost paranoid about his physical self.' He paused, gathering his memories. 'He used to clip articles from newspapers and magazines, and he'd come across one about aneurysms in the abdominal aorta, so he lay in the bath watching the throb of his own aorta, thinking an aneurysm would be like a bomb in his guts, but he wouldn't know when the timer was set for detonation.'

'Sickness is an existentially precarious condition,' McKenna said, 'whatever the reasons. He was intensely conscious of the dichotomy between mind and body, and perhaps his mind just caved in to the pressure from time to time. I suppose you could say his social body never separated itself from his natural body.'

'To me, he simply personified the unbridgeable gulf between the sick and the well, but now his natural body's dead, you can be sure his social body was somehow the cause of it.'

'Have you any idea what he could have taken?'

The doctor shook his head. 'You'll have to wait on the toxicology report, but I've seen people near death after eating a few strawberries. It could be an idiosyncratic response to any number of things, but he certainly had no suspect medication because there'd already been a rather worrying reaction to antibiotics I prescribed last year for a chest infection.'

'What kind of reaction?'

'A lower level of the one that killed him, which made me wonder if there was some malfunction of the adrenal cortex. The tests I arranged were negative, so Ned got himself a bracelet, and I filled in the details for him.'

McKenna frowned. 'A bracelet?'

'An SOS bracelet. A waterproof capsule on a chain, with a long strip of paper inside to write down important data about medical conditions, drug sensitivity and so forth. He said his life might depend on it, so he wore it all the time, and I'm just beginning to realize how much I'll miss him, for all he exposed our limitations and upset the balance of power. He was a good man, and he didn't deserve the suffering he had.'

9

Rowlands felt slightly sick after being bounced for mile upon mile along the pot-holed lanes twisting between one run-down village garage and another. 'Are these people we've seen paid informants?' he asked, sucking a mint.

'No, sir,' Dewi said. 'I just know most of them, as you do.'

'And have they told you anything interesting yet?'

'You heard as much as me, sir.'

'I heard a gabble of Welsh, so I didn't understand a word.'

'Really? You should've said. We're not into language fascism, which is lucky for Inspector Tuttle, 'cos all he knows in Welsh are a few swear words.' Taking a blind bend without reducing speed, he added: 'Does Ms Bradshaw speak Welsh?'

Rowlands felt the seat belt lock tight across his chest. 'I doubt it. She's from Manchester.'

'How long's she been with our force?'

'Two or three years, I think.'

'Is she married?'

'I believe so.'

'Any children?'

Rowlands tried to ease some slack into the seat belt. 'D'you always ask so many questions? Doesn't McKenna mind?'

'He lets me know if I overstep the mark. He's straight.'

'And you're so confident you could almost be called brash.'

'I like to be straight, too, sir. And having my own opinions isn't disrespectful. Mr McKenna encourages us to use our initiative, under the right supervision. So did Superintendent Griffiths.'

'If that's a coded message for me to take back to Ms Bradshaw, you're wasting your time. I never met her before today.'

The car showroom, straddling a bleak hill above the Rhiwlas road, was an ugly ramshackle structure tacked on to the side of an old stone dwelling which now served as offices. Parking on a patch of gravel by the roadside, Dewi went first to peer through the glazed showroom doors, then to the other building. Opening the office door, he walked in, Rowlands in his wake. 'This is Geraint, sir,' he announced, nodding to the young man behind the desk, whose face blossomed with acne. 'Geraint and his dad got done by Trading Standards for dishonestly flogging a vehicle, but they coughed up their fines without so much as a squeal of protest.'

'Was that the Tigra clocked from 33,000 miles to 14,000?' asked Rowlands.

'It was.' Dewi sat on Geraint's desk. 'I don't think Geraint and his dad did the deed, but they won't tell us who did.'

His glance flicking from one to the other of his visitors, Geraint said: 'Can't you leave it be? It's over and done with.'

'Only till the next time,' Dewi said. 'I want to buy that car I looked at on Friday, but how can I trust what you tell me? For all I know it could be two halves out of fatal accidents, welded together in the middle, like the red coupé that poor woman bought from your pal Dervyn.'

'You've had an HPI check on the car you were drooling over,' Geraint said. 'You even checked the engine number.'

'I know I did, because somebody's stealing engines, regrinding the block, and stamping on a fake number.' He turned to Rowlands. 'It makes you wonder if there's an honest dealer in the whole of Wales, and when you look at the records of the likes of Dervyn, you begin to think criminals must be fatally attracted to dealing cars.'

'Who's Dervyn?'

'Geraint's old school chum, except neither of them spent much time in class. They used to go twocking, and now they've taken to clocking.'

'Stop showing off your language, Dewi Prys!' Geraint snapped. 'I don't have any truck with that Dervyn.'

'There's a remarkable incidence of small-scale criminal enterprise in the area,' Rowlands observed. 'In my experience operations like this are usually part of a ring.'

'That's what I've been trying to get through Geraint's thick skull. To give him his due, this is his first clocking offense and he says he was conned when he bought the car, but I don't quite believe him.' Noting Geraint's scowl, Dewi added: 'Which isn't surprising considering some of the other tricks he's turned, like sticking a loose nut behind a hub cap, then saying the clanking noise was a knackered drive shaft.'

'I only did it once!' Geraint whined, spots livid against

his pasty skin. 'And if you don't leave me be, I'm going to report you! This is police harassment.'

'No, it isn't.' Rowlands showed his teeth. 'Not yet.'

10

As McKenna went in through the back door of the police station, the duty sergeant reported on Diana Bradshaw's half-hourly attempts to locate him. Irritated, he walked slowly up the staircase, the heat within the building stealing his breath. Hearing his footfall in the corridor, she opened the door. 'There you are!' Her smile was brilliant. 'I expected you back ages ago! Did you really need to spend half the day with the old man's doctor?'

He leaned against the wall, sweat running down inside his shirt, feeling transient and insecure, like a bystander in an alleyway. 'I think that's a slight exaggeration, ma'am.'

Looking rather hurt, she invited him into the office, and sat behind her desk, her arms folded. 'I hoped we'd be friends, you know, and there's really no need for all this formality, except in front of the rank and file. I'm sure you didn't always address Superintendent Griffiths as sir.'

'We'd known each other a long time,' he said. 'People here take a while to feel at ease with newcomers, and in any case, a measure of formality often avoids the embarrassment of getting in too deep too quickly.'

'Really? Well, thank you for the advice, chief inspector. Now, the pathologist wants to see you. Quite urgently, I understand.'

11

A blue haze softened the distant mountain peaks behind the hospital, and, locking his car, McKenna felt the vicious afternoon heat almost as an entity. A young man sat on the kerb outside the psychiatric unit, the sun beating down on his head, a cigarette clutched in his shaking hands, and as McKenna approached, he lurched to his feet, and staggered blindly towards the casualty department.

The grass around the pathology laboratories was bleached and patchy, the shrubs tinder dry, and McKenna wondered if this weather, freakish even by local standards, was really the fall-out of nuclear tests in the South Pacific, as people were wont to suggest. When he pulled open the door, cooler air slapped him in the face, and the smell of the death-house wormed into his nose and settled at the back of his throat.

'I think Edward Jones is trying to tell us something,' the pathologist said. 'It's what you might call an unfinished dialogue between us and his corpse.'

Supine under the bright lights, Ned seemed smaller than McKenna remembered, almost as frail as a child on the huge steel table. Tracing his gloved finger along the autopsy incision, he said: 'Tidy work.'

'I was particularly careful. I didn't want to damage the torso any more than necessary.' Leaning over the body, plastic apron crackling, the green-gowned pathologist pointed to a riddle of welts and marks. 'See the scratches all around his neck? There was a lot of skin under his nails, which is probably his, so I assume he clawed at his neck when he couldn't breathe, as people do when they're panicking for air. Now, I thought at first those thin red lines of congestion on his chest were random, but there seems to be a pattern, and it became much clearer when the weals and swellings from the allergic reaction began to decay.' He lifted Ned's hands, and showed them to McKenna, first the finger ends, nails trimmed neatly and spotlessly clean, then the palms, slightly roughened and patchy with old calluses. 'Hands often tell a life history, but he's still holding back on me. I hear he spent his time shuffling paper and reading books, but these hands have done a lot of hard labour in their time.'

'He was brought up on a farm.' McKenna was suddenly touched by a sense of loss. 'Are you absolutely sure an allergic reaction killed him?'

He nodded. 'I've never seen such elevated levels of histamine and bradykinin, and most of this discoloration is *urticaria factitia*. Wholly consistent with, as it were.'

'Could he have been saved?'

'Only by performing a tracheotomy within minutes. Now then, if you look carefully at the thin red lines on his chest, what can you see?'

McKenna leaned over the body, the scent of death strong in his nostrils, staring at the mottled flesh around the neatly closed incision which would never heal. 'Letters, I think.' He narrowed his eyes. 'An "F" and an "E", and both back to front.'

'They're more distinct in the pre-autopsy photographs.'

'Nothing was mentioned when he was examined at the scene on Friday.'

Going back to the office, leaving Ned exposed on the table, the pathologist said: 'I wouldn't bother tearing a strip off the attending physician, because but for those marks, this would look like straightforward natural causes.' He sat behind the desk and opened a drawer, extracting a bagged shirt and a sheaf of photographs. 'Where the skin's been sensitized by allergic reaction, it can be marked with something sharp and thin, like a fingernail, producing what's called *dermatographia*, or, in plain language, skin-writing. The condition's also called *tache cerebrale*, but that's more specific to meningitis.' Spreading out the large coloured prints, he said: 'The letters are quite clear, but as they're the wrong way round, they could be mirror writing after da Vinci, or, as he was *in extremis* at the time, they could mean nothing.'

'Which hand did he use?'

The pathologist shrugged. 'Natural right-handers can sometimes do mirror writing with the left hand, so presumably, southpaws can do the same with the right. The pressure variations suggest he wrote from left to right, but don't take it as gospel.' He dropped another photograph on the pile, of Ned dead in his chair, dressed in his old fashioned clothes. 'But you can be sure somebody tampered with the body. That's taken at the scene, and he was still all neatly buttoned up in collar and tie when we got him.' Showing McKenna the white shirt, frayed around collar and cuffs, he added: 'You can see where he almost tore off the buttons, and there were shredded fibres from the tie under his nails, which according to the label, is made of Macclesfield silk, so it must be quite old.'

'When will you know what caused the reaction?'

'As soon as the toxicology results come back, which should be within days, but I expect he ingested an antibiotic, despite the known allergy. The reaction was very typical.' Stacking the photographs, he added: 'I know he hadn't been prescribed antibiotics since last year, but he could easily have swallowed a couple of left over tablets thinking they were something else. People get very careless with drugs.'

'He was careful to the point of neurosis, according to Gabriel Ansoni.' McKenna lit a cigarette, trying to chase away the taste in his mouth. 'And he wasn't senile. How was his general physical condition?'

'There's little to substantiate all the ills he complained about, apart from an interesting inflammation in the colon, so he could've looked forward to his three score years and ten, given the usual creaky joints and chronic backache. He badly needed a new set of false teeth, because the ones I took out of his mouth must be nearly as old as his tie, which is probably why he had a mouth full of ulcers.' The pathologist put the photographs in a large plastic wallet. 'You can take these, but I haven't finished with the clothing yet.'

'Did you find his SOS bracelet?' McKenna asked.

The pathologist shook his head. 'Not even in the lining of his jacket. Perhaps you need to search his room again.'

12

Diana Bradshaw glanced at McKenna, then at the photographs he had placed on her desk. 'Isn't it rather fanciful to suggest the old man scratched a message on his chest?'

'Not necessarily, and it's obvious he tore at his shirt and tie, and even more obvious that someone tidied him up before the doctor and Janet arrived at the house.'

'Well, yes, but perhaps the person wasn't thinking straight.'

'Or perhaps the person was trying to obscure those telltale marks.'

'But what tale do they tell?' She smiled again, a gesture McKenna had decided was an obfuscation in itself, and said: ' "F-E" and "E-F" don't make any sense, whichever way around they are.'

'Clearly, Ned died before he could finish, but there are issues here which need investigating.'

'Oh, I couldn't agree more! But until we know the cause of death, it wouldn't be wise to decide what those issues actually are. For the time being, just soft-pedal, and keep the questions discreet. Mrs Harris is well-respected, and not without connections, so it wouldn't do to upset her.'

'And if he ingested antibiotics, as the pathologist suggested?'

'Obviously, you'll have to find out where they came from.'

'And who might have given them to him?'

She frowned. 'I'm far more inclined to see this as a suicide. Everything points that way.'

'If Ned killed himself, I think he would have sat in his chair, or lain on his bed, and died quietly, but I think someone poisoned him, and when he realized, he made a frantic effort to tell us who.'

'We'll see, shall we?' She smiled again, pushing the photographs towards McKenna without looking at them. 'And I'm sure you won't be influenced by what that silly girl said to Janet. By the way, can you double up with Rowlands for a few days? The decorators are coming in on Wednesday, and I thought it would be a nice gesture if they did your office first.'

'So I get a lick of paint in lieu of promotion, do I?'

'Oh, dear!' She winced. 'I really hoped we'd get through this little difficulty without any bitterness.'

He rose, picking up the photographs. 'I wasn't aware you had a difficulty, ma'am, little or otherwise.'

'Then please make sure you don't create any.' Her eyes were flinty.

13

'Where are we going now?' Rowlands asked, peering through the windscreen.

'Mr McKenna wants me to show you the lie of the land,' Dewi offered.

'I've seen it. Mountains, more mountains, and the worst bloody roads on the British mainland.' He shifted his cramped legs. 'No wonder your suspension's knackered.'

'I was going to show you where Geraint's mate Dervyn works, sir, and then drive by the other outfits where dodgy cars've turned up in the past few months.' Reducing speed as the road entered Bethel village, Dewi added: 'We haven't been shirking on this investigation. We did a history on each car, looked for patterns in distribution and sales, trawled the auctions, checked out known car-ringing outfits, and came up with a blank at every turn. One minute everything's above board and legal, the next it isn't. And before we took over when the stolen engines started turning up, Trading Standards had spent months on it.'

'D'you really think Geraint's involved?'

Dewi shrugged. 'I doubt if he's got the nous to clock a car, and his dad's even dopier. I think somebody palmed off the car on him, like Dervyn got landed with the two-piece coupé, and they're both too scared to say anything.'

'I'm sure they got a backhander,' Rowlands commented. 'That garage can't turn much profit.'

'Selling cars is only a sideline, sir. Most of the work comes from repairs and maintenance and MOTs. The locals and the farmers depend on small garages like Geraint's to keep their vehicles on the road.'

'Would threatening to suspend MOT licenses loosen any tongues?'

'They'd tell us to bugger off and get on with it.' Dewi grinned. 'Why d'you think these parts are called the "Wild West"?'

'Because you're competing with the lawless mobs in Manchester and Liverpool, and from what I've seen, doing very well. Your crime statistics *per capita* are much higher than central division's.'

'How long have you been there, sir?'

'Four years last March.'

'And where d'you live?'

'In a civilized patch outside Ruthin, where the roads are flat, and there's not a mountain in sight.'

14

Phoebe Harris answered McKenna's summons at the front door, the cat draped as usual over her shoulder, and an ugly bruise darkening her cheek.

'I'm Chief Inspector McKenna,' he said. 'You must be Phoebe. Is your mother in?'

Before she could answer, he heard a high-pitched voice calling from inside the house, and she turned away, leading him into the sitting room, where Edith stood before the fireplace, fronds of pampas grass brushing the hem of her skirt. She smiled brightly at her visitor. 'Make a pot of tea, Phoebe, there's a good girl. And put that animal down, dear, please! I can't get the fur off your clothes, and his claws make little holes in everything you wear.'

Phoebe trudged from the room, still carrying the cat, and inviting McKenna to sit down, Edith began an endless stream of inconsequential chatter until her daughter returned with a tea-tray, the cat at her heels. 'I call him "Phoebe's little shadow"!' she said brightly. 'He's with her day and night.'

'He's the only friend I've got now that Uncle Ned's gone.' Phoebe sat down, opposite McKenna, and the cat jumped up beside her.

Edith tutted. 'Don't be silly, dear. You've got your friends in school, and two lovely sisters.' She sighed. 'I do wish you'd stop him sitting on the furniture. He moults everywhere.' She turned to McKenna. 'He moults all year round, you know. I've never known a cat like him. It's not normal, is it? Should I ask the vet to do something, d'you think?'

'He's got a very thick coat.' McKenna took the tea Phoebe offered. 'He's bound to shed, especially this weather.'

'Is he?' Edith frowned. 'I suppose so. It *is* hot, isn't it? D'you think we'll have a break in the weather soon?'

'He's a policeman, Mama, not a weather forecaster.'

'Isn't she forward?' Edith laughed, a sound like a spoon against glass. 'She's only thirteen, you know, but she's very bright.'

'He's not a child psychologist, either,' Phoebe added.

'Don't be so cheeky!'

'I'm going upstairs!' Nudging the cat to the floor, Phoebe picked up her tea, and made for the door. McKenna saw the glint of tears in her eyes, then heard her plod up the stairs, the cat mewling.

'Oh, dear!' Edith sighed again. 'Aren't they a trial at that age?'

'How did she come by the bruise on her face?' he asked.

'The bruise?' Eyebrows raised, she paused. 'Oh, that! She was fighting with Mina. Sisters do have their little scraps, don't they?'

'And what was the fight about?'

She sipped her tea, hands trembling. 'Phoebe needles her. She will insist on calling her Minnie, which Mina hates, of course, but that's why Phoebe does it, isn't it? I expect she's a bit jealous. Mina's very pretty, you know.'

'And what's her proper name?'

She smiled. 'Minerva. She's named for a Roman goddess. Isn't it lovely?'

'Unusual,' McKenna observed. 'And your other daughter?'

'We call her Annie, but she's actually called Anastasia, after the Russian princess.' The cup rattled in its saucer. 'She thinks it's terribly outlandish, so she doesn't in the least mind being called Annie, but then, she's not as pretty as Mina.'

'And does your husband live with you?'

'I don't have a husband any longer,' Edith said, her face unreadable.

'I see.' He fell silent, drinking his tea.

'What did you want? Is it something about Ned?'

'It is indeed, Mrs Harris.' He put his own cup in its saucer. 'I have a number of questions.'

'What about?'

'The actual sequence of events last Friday.'

She stood up, and began to pace the room. 'But I told the other police officers everything! I heard a noise, as if he'd fallen, then I didn't hear anything else, and when I realized, I went upstairs and found him like that, so I called the doctor!' She stopped by the fireplace, wringing her hands. 'I knew he was dead as soon as I saw him.'

'Where was he when you found him?'

'In his chair.' Collapsing on the sofa, she shuddered, wrapping her arms around her body. 'I'll have to put out the chair for the bin men, won't I? It's all stained, and it was his favourite.'

'And how was he dressed?' McKenna persisted.

'Dressed?' Edith's voice rose. 'In his suit.'

'It was very hot on Friday, so wasn't it rather odd for him to be wearing a suit?'

'He dressed the same, summer and winter, and if it turned really cold, he'd wear an old knitted waistcoat under his jacket.' She balled her hands into fists and stared at McKenna. 'He was brought up thinking it's indecent to show a shirt, let alone any flesh. They're all a bit mental on that side of the family, you know.'

'Did he always wear a tie, too?'

'Yes.'

'But his tie was undone when you found him, wasn't it? And his shirt?'

'Yes.' She nodded, then gasped. Leaping to her feet, she ran to the window, then to the door, then stood rigid, tearing at her hands. 'I wasn't thinking!' Her voice rose to a wail. 'He wouldn't want people to see him like that! I tidied him up, that's all!' Staring at him, the whites of her eyes showing, she asked: 'How did you know? How did you find out?'

'He tore at his tie and shirt, trying to breathe, and scratched his chest and neck in the process, so it was obvious someone tampered with his clothing.'

Stumbling to the sofa, Edith collapsed again. 'I'm so sorry! I never meant to cause any trouble.' Tears began to run down her face. 'I just didn't think!'

'I'll need a statement from you in due course, Mrs Harris.'

'Will I get into trouble?'

'Probably not, if that's all you did,' McKenna said. 'By the way, have you told his family we can't release the body yet?'

'Annie rang them on Friday to say he'd died. She went there on Saturday to see them, but it won't have made any difference, will it?' She pulled a handkerchief from her pocket, dried her face, then jumped up again, to rummage in a bureau. 'Would you let them know about the body?' She ripped a page from a leather-bound address book, and gave it to him. 'Tell Gladys. She's still got some of her wits.'

Folding the page in his wallet, McKenna asked: 'Who else was here on Friday?'

'Who else?' Edith's eyes goggled. 'When? What time of the day?'

'Late morning onwards.'

'Nobody! The cleaner only comes on Wednesdays.'

'Where were the girls?'

'Mina's got a holiday job. She's at the tech, you know, doing a fashion course.'

'And Phoebe?'

'Out. She goes for walks on her own, and it's such a nuisance, because the cat grizzles and frets like a baby until she comes back.' She tried a little smile. 'I've told her to try him on a leash, then he can go with her.'

'Where does she go?'

Edith frowned. 'I don't know. I do so worry about her sometimes, wondering if she'll end up like Ned's side of the family. She was a little stranger from the moment she was born. Some children are like that, aren't they?'

McKenna rose. 'Thank you for your time, Mrs Harris. I'll send someone to take a statement, and we'll need to look at Ned's room again.'

'Why?' The eyes goggled once more. 'And what about his things? Will you ask Gladys about them? I can't think *what* to do with all those books and papers.' Wringing her hands again, she said: 'Maybe George would know.'

'George?'

'He's at the university. Ned was helping him with some work, and he used to come quite often, even though Ned knew I didn't like having him in the house.'

'Why was that?'

'Why was what?' Edith asked. 'Oh, I see! Oh, George makes eyes at Mina!'

'There's nothing strange about that, surely.'

'It's not nice. She's got a steady boyfriend, and she doesn't need a black man trying to turn her head.

•   •   •

Leaving his car outside the Harris house, McKenna walked to the main road, crossed over to Safeway, filled a trolley with groceries and cat food, then sat in the supermarket coffee house, trying to catch up on his day's quota of cigarettes.

'I heard you asking Mama where I was on Friday,' Phoebe said, placing a glass of orange juice on the table. 'Can I sit down?'

'Of course.' McKenna nodded. 'Did you follow me?'

'Sort of.'

'Where's the cat?'

'Well, he's not under my skirt, despite what Minnie says about my skirts being big enough to cover an elephant's backside.' Slurping the juice, she added: 'Actually, he's in the back garden. I don't let him in the front in case he runs under a car.'

'Cats are generally quite sensible with traffic.'

'How d'you know? Have you got one?'

'I've got two, both strays. They decided to squat in my house.'

'Oh, that's really sweet! Are they male or female? What d'you call them?'

'One of each, as was.' McKenna smiled. 'Fluff arrived first. She's black and white, and quite plump, and I think Blackie must have some Siamese in him, because he's very elegant.'

'Do they fight?'

'Not often, but they chase around the house like lunatics at times, especially when it's windy.'

She giggled. 'Tom does, too. He frightens the wits out of Mama.'

'Did Uncle Ned like your cat?'

Phoebe nodded. 'He brought him from the farm for my eighth birthday.'

'You'll miss him, won't you?'

'Yes.' Slurping more of the juice, she said: 'I've known him all my life. He came to live with us when Minnie was a baby.'

'And how old is she now?'

'Nineteen. I hate her.'

'Why? Because she's your sister?'

'Because she's mean and nasty. I don't hate Annie. I think I might even really love her, because I sometimes get that lovely warm feeling for her, like when I cuddle the cat.' She paused, her eyes dark. 'I loved Uncle Ned, you know. He was like a father.'

Pointing to the bruise on Phoebe's face, McKenna said: 'Mina must have thumped you pretty hard.'

'She did. As I said, she's mean and nasty, and her boyfriend's even more horrible. He turns up with a bigger, flashier car every other week, and they drive around like they're starring in some American road movie. That's why I call them Bonnie and Clyde. They hate it!'

'You could be deliberately provoking some of her anger.'

'It doesn't need provoking! Uncle Ned said she's out of control, because Mama lets her do as she likes, and never, ever punishes her. I think she's scared of her.' She picked up McKenna's lighter, turned it over to read the inscription, then put it on the table. 'This is quite old, isn't it? How long have you had it?'

'My parents gave it to me on my twenty-first birthday.'

'And what does MJM stand for?'

'Michael James McKenna.'

'That's not a very Welsh name, is it?'

'My ancestors came from Ireland.'

'Half of mine come from Meirionydd.' She rolled her eyes. 'Mama says they're all batty, and she's dead scared I'm like them.'

'She mentioned you go for walks on your own.'

'I like to think, and you can't do that in company, can you? And I like watching the sky when it's cloudy and windy. Sometimes, I just walk half-way over Menai Bridge and look down at the water. It's dead scary.'

'Why?'

'Uncle Ned said water represents death, and a bridge represents what he called the ascendancy of faith.' She paused, gathering her thoughts. 'Menai Bridge seems like a tug of war between Anglesey and the mainland, something just balanced there, and not real or solid.' She drained the glass, and smiled briefly. 'Actually, he was quite right, because if you're on the bridge, you're alive, and if you fall off, you're dead.'

'Did he ever go out with you?'

'He took me out every day when I was little, and we'd still go for walks when he was well enough, but he was often too poorly to get out of bed, and that bitch of a sister of mine used to make as much noise as she could when she knew he was trying to sleep.'

'I expect she'll get married and leave home soon.'

'Some hope!' Phoebe muttered. 'They're saving up to buy a house first, and have a posh honeymoon, and an even bigger car. That's if she doesn't ditch Clyde for somebody with more cash to chuck about.'

'Your mother mentioned a student called George.'

'She hates him.'

'Why?'

'He's black, and Minnie's really got the hots for him, only he can't stand her. She gives him the creeps.'

'Why?'

'He knows what a cow she is, that's why.'

'Your mother said George fancies Mina.'

'Well, she would, wouldn't she? Mama's not going to admit little Minnie isn't everybody's flavour of the month. God! If only she knew!'

'Knew what?' McKenna tried to staunch his questions, mindful of the pitfalls of talking to lone children, but found himself bewitched by her gossip.

'The way Minnie carries on with boys. George knows, 'cos I heard him tell her one day he wouldn't touch her with a barge pole if she was the last female on earth. She'd been flaunting in front of him for weeks, asking him if he stuffed socks down his jeans or if he was just pleased to see her. He was quite disgusted.'

McKenna choked on his coffee.

'I'll bet Mama told you Minnie was out at work on Friday, didn't she?' Phoebe prattled on. 'That's where she was supposed to be, but I expect she was up a mountain somewhere in Clyde's car, doing whatever people do in the back seat.' She paused. 'Not that I don't actually know, to be truthful, but Mama wouldn't like to know I know, if you see what I mean, because she likes to pretend we don't know about tacky things like sex, even though Annie managed to have a baby without finding a husband to go with it. Mama actually said to me: "Annie's got herself pregnant", then burst into tears. Wasn't that stupid? You haven't met Annie, have you?'

'No. I haven't met Mina, either.'

'You'll like Annie, and little Bethan's really sweet, even though Minnie calls her a bastard.' Seeing his frown, she said: 'I told you she's nasty. You can see it in her eyes, and she always covers her ears with her hair, because they're small and tight and ugly.'

Putting cigarettes and lighter in his pocket, McKenna smiled. 'I must go, Phoebe, I've a lot to do. I enjoyed talking to you.'

'You left your car outside the house, so I'll walk back with you.' She peered inside one of the plastic carrier bags. 'Your cats have exactly the same food as Tom. Isn't that odd?'

'What if your mother asks where you've been?'

'I'll tell her I just happened to meet you on the road. She's not really interested in me, you know. She says she's given up trying to fathom my strange behaviour.'

She plodded beside him, carrying the bag of cat food, shapeless clothes hung about her podgy young body. He wondered why she dressed like a derelict old woman, and thought it was probably another expression of her individuality, a rebellion against the expectations of peers and parent. As they neared the house, she halted in her tracks, and moaned. 'Oh, no! Not again!'

'Not again what?'

Pointing to a late model silver Jaguar, parked half on the pavement, she said: 'He was here all yesterday, fawning over Mama and being all serious and pseudo-grief-stricken.'

'Who was?'

'Professor Williams from the university.' She waited while he opened the boot, and stowed the shopping. 'And he's probably brought his ghastly wife with him again. If Uncle Ned was neurotic, like everybody says, I don't know what you'd call those two.'

'Why's that?'

'You'll see when you meet them. She's a lot younger than him, and French. D'you think that's why she's so weird?'

15

McKenna found Rowlands and Dewi humping furniture and boxes and piles of documents, and dripping with sweat. 'What are you doing?'

'I'm moving into the general office while the decorators are in, sir,' Rowlands said, breathing heavily.

'I understood we would be sharing.'

'That seemed a bit unreasonable.' He dropped a heap of

papers on one of the desks. 'Anyway, it's easier for me to move for the duration than muck about changing again when the other office gets decorated.'

'And Mr Rowlands is here for at least a month, so Mr Tuttle'll be back from France before then,' Dewi offered.

'And does Superintendent Bradshaw know about the new arrangements?'

'Dunno, sir.' Dewi shrugged. 'She'd left for the day by the time we got back.' He wiped his forehead with the back of his hand. 'If you tell us what you want moved into the other office, we'll get on with it when we've finished here.'

'Desk, chair and filing cabinets, please,' McKenna replied, finding a vacant chair, and lighting a cigarette. 'Any joy with the cars?'

'Nope. Same story as last time and the time before.' Inching a filing cabinet into the gap between two desks, Dewi asked: 'What about Ned Jones, sir? Suicide, murder, or Mother Nature?'

'Take your pick,' McKenna said. 'Mrs Harris admitted to tidying up his shirt and tie, so that discrepancy's explained.'

'What discrepancy?' Rowlands asked.

'I asked Ms Bradshaw to bring you up to date. Has she not done so?'

'Like I said, sir, she'd left when we got back,' Dewi said. 'Nobody's told us anything.'

16

Slouching in a chair in the little garden at the rear of his house, McKenna watched the sun go down behind the old university building, gilding its tower, and pouring gold light and long shadows down the hillside. The cats lay by his feet, soaking up the heat trapped in the earth, then the black and white cat rolled on to her back, stretched her legs in the air, and subsided in a heap. The black cat looked up and yawned.

'I could always take early retirement,' he told them. 'My pension would take care of us, even if I couldn't get another job.' He stubbed out his cigarette, and lit another, the smoke fragrant in the warm air. 'And I really think Denise should fend for herself. She's not a moron or a cripple, so why should I beggar myself for her benefit, just because I married her?' The black cat rose and stretched, then curled around his ankles, nuzzling his legs. 'And who'll look after us if I can't? She'll argue that I left *her*, but I wonder if she'll ever say why?' He smiled bleakly. 'D'you know, she wouldn't have given you two house room. She thinks all animals are dirty, and cats especially.' He bent down to stroke the animal's ears. 'Perhaps you are. Who knows?' The cat purred. 'And who cares? You're much nicer company than most of the people I've ever met.'

The front doorbell interrupted the one-sided conversation, and the noise made his stomach lurch with memories of the morning. He waited, thinking of all the people he had no wish to see, but as the bell rang again, insistently, he went slowly up the staircase and along the hall.

Janet smiled tentatively. 'I wanted to apologize for the way I carried on earlier. I was a bit upset.'

He shut the door and followed her downstairs. Her dark hair was pulled back loosely and tied with a silk scarf, showing pretty ears and the curve of her neck, and, smartly dressed in pale linen trousers and a silk shirt, she bore no resemblance to the wreck of a girl who had wept in his arms.

He took another chair outside, and poured her a glass of wine.

'Things have improved since this morning, have they?'

'Being hysterical doesn't solve problems, sir.'

'So you've still got a problem?'

She took a gulp of wine, and nodded.

'Are you sure?' McKenna asked. 'My wife had a couple of false alarms, you know. Have you done a pregnancy test yet?'

'I'm too scared.' She sighed. 'Anyway, I know. Women usually do.'

'Not necessarily. Worry can upset your system. So can air travel, and changes in routine.'

'I'm quite sure, sir.' She rubbed her eyes. 'I knew almost as soon as it happened.'

'And when did it happen?' He lit another cigarette. 'On holiday?'

She flushed. 'Yes.' Her voice was low.

'Someone you met in Italy?'

'Yes. He was on holiday, as well.'

'Does he know?'

'No.'

'Can you get in touch with him?'

'Of course I can!' The flush deepened.

'I only asked, Janet,' McKenna said gently. 'I wasn't suggesting you went in for a one night stand with a total stranger.'

'Oh, I'm sorry!' She rubbed her eyes again. 'I feel so strange, like I don't belong to myself any longer.'

'Pregnancy out of wedlock is something of a crisis, Janet, and you can't avoid making a decision about it, so what choice will you make? Abortion, adoption, or being a single parent?'

'Those aren't really choices, are they? They're more like lesser evils.'

'You could tell the baby's father, and see what he's got to say. He has every right to know.'

'I've got to make my own decision. It's my life, and my body.'

'And his baby.' Watching her, he said: 'He might want to get married.'

'Oh, my parents would love that, wouldn't they? A shot-gun wedding, of all things!'

'They might well prefer that to the alternatives. In any case, weddings don't make a marriage. Why not talk to them, at least? Contrary to what you said earlier, I'm sure it wouldn't enter your father's head to kill you.'

'No, he'll simply disown me, and expect my mother to do the same.'

1

Early on Tuesday morning, McKenna was disturbed by the postman, pounding on the glass panels of the front door to hand over a recorded delivery letter. Trying to decipher the postmark as he crunched his toast, he could think of no-one he knew in Manchester who might need to be sure he received their letter. It had a bad feeling, he thought: more bad news brought by another early-morning herald.

He washed the dishes, and went out to a garden already sweltering in the brilliant sunshine. The cats were indoors, in the deepest, coolest shade they could find. As he lit his first cigarette and carefully opened the long buff envelope, he learned that Denise was suing for divorce, and intending to prove such unreasonable conduct on his part that he would be well-advised, her solicitor explained, to allow the petition and her application for maintenance to proceed uncontested.

He felt chilled to the marrow, unreasonably and inexplicably, for she was doing what he predicted. Heart fluttering, he ripped open the other envelope the postman had handed over, and read the chief constable's confirmation of the decision to delay promotion, a blow not lessened by the assurance that the delay was temporary and no reflection on McKenna's professional integrity or competence.

He put the letters and envelopes on the flagstones beside

his chair, and tried to distract himself with other thoughts, but the dazzle of paper intruded, and he glanced down, wondering if the stuff on which the letters were written might darken to the dreary colour of the failures they represented.

2

From his listening post by the door of the general office, Dewi could decipher nothing of what passed between Diana Bradshaw and Ian Rowlands behind the closed door of her office. He heard the shrill inflections in her voice, the rumble of anger in his, but the words eluded him. Rowlands emerged at last, slammed the door, and stood in the corridor, breathing heavily. Dewi slunk back to his desk, and was pushing papers around when the inspector finally gathered himself together.

'Morning, sir,' Dewi said. 'Lovely day again, isn't it?'

'No, it bloody isn't! It's a sodding bloody awful day, and don't pretend you don't know why!'

'I didn't hear a word, sir. I just heard the argument.'

'Bradshaw's very annoyed that we took it upon ourselves to move furniture.' Rowlands sat down, and lit a cigarette. 'And even though she'd never set foot in the place before yesterday, she's already decided general discipline leaves a lot to be desired!'

'She'd have been well primed beforehand,' Dewi commented. 'HQ are bound to have put about a load of crap to justify the situation.'

'She said the special constables are being used inappropriately, and getting out of their depth. They're only supposed to assist the regulars, not replace them. And that,' Rowlands added, looking round for an ashtray, 'is another sign of very poor management.'

'It's a sign of cutbacks and penny-pinching, sir, because we've lost a quarter of our manpower in the last ten years, so who else can we send out pounding the streets?' Watching Rowlands blow smoke towards the ceiling, Dewi thought how ordinary he looked, his height and build average, his hair mousy, his features regular and unremarkable. Out of uniform, he was almost nondescript. 'She can take her gripes to the next policy authority get-together,' he went on, 'and while she's there, she can ask for some horsepower.'

'Bangor's too small for mounted police.'

'We had two enormous horses at one time, and they were a bloody sight more frightening than plods on foot, especially at football matches.'

'And would you like to carry arms, as well?'

'We already do when necessary, only Joe Public doesn't know.'

'Joe Public doesn't know a lot of things,' Rowlands commented. 'Is McKenna here yet?'

Dewi shook his head. 'Janet's back, though. She's gone to the canteen.'

'Is she better?'

'Seems to be.'

'Then she can take Mrs Harris's statement, and get those girls to give their version of events.' Stubbing out his cigarette, he added: 'Haven't you any paid informants in this nick who could help with these cars?'

'They've been asked.'

'So what about coincidences in the history of the bent cars? Were they sold on by the same dealer, serviced at the same garage, ever owned by the same person?'

'No, sir, and we don't know the extent of the problem. Trading Standards or us only get to hear when something happens, the insurance companies and DVLA don't keep the sort of information we need, and even though we liaised with other forces and DVLA over the false MOT certificates, we didn't learn anything new.'

'I think we'll target six of the vehicles,' Rowlands decided, 're-interview the previous owners, and see if we can turn up Mr X. And although we'll have to go into other force areas to do it, I'm sure Bradshaw won't object to the extra costs. She's very anxious to chalk this up as her first successful detection.'

'With respect, ma'am, this is your first time in charge of a station.'

'I know chaos when I see it!' Diana Bradshaw snapped. 'And bad discipline! Why didn't you stop Rowlands moving out of his office?'

'He'd already moved, and now, instead of all of us playing musical offices, I need only move once.' McKenna paused, then said: 'I asked you to bring him up to date on the Jones case, but he tells me you left while he was out.'

'I'm not here to nursemaid CID! I went to a planning meeting at divisional HQ.'

'In future, ma'am, I'd appreciate knowing your plans, as I'm responsible for the station in your absence.' Rising to his feet, he added: 'And as good forward planning is crucial to crime management, you'll need my quarterly report for the next planning meeting. While reported rapes and burglaries were below expectations, our projections on homicide and crimes against children were quite unrealistic.'

Placing a mug of fresh tea on McKenna's desk, Dewi said: 'Inspector Rowlands wants permission to re-interview some of the former owners of the duff cars, only it means travelling.'

'How far?'

'Chester. The Wirral. Maybe Liverpool.'

'Then tell Cheshire and Merseyside you'll be on their patch.'

'Why?' Diana Bradshaw stood imperiously at the door.

'Re-interviewing former car owners, ma'am.' McKenna

rose to his feet. 'It could be more cost-effective than chasing aimlessly around North Wales.'

'I'm surprised you know the meaning of the term!' She moved aside to let Dewi pass, then faced McKenna. 'I've just seen the overnight incident reports.'

'None of which concerns CID, ma'am. I checked, even though divisional HQ classify all incoming reports.'

'They may not concern you, but they certainly bother me! I've never come across such waste of police time and public money!' She stared at him, eyes hard. 'I may not be able to shut the stable door on this particular horse, but in future, I intend to make sure the horse stays put, along with the smallest item of police property!'

'Ah, I see.' McKenna smiled. 'The donated toilet roll.'

'It is *not* funny when some stupid woman calls us on her mobile phone at midnight because there's no toilet paper in the public lavatory.'

'Well, it was arguably an emergency for her, and the loos are only across the road.' He sat down, bored with her carping. 'And we shouldn't let concerns about forward planning and cost-efficiency obscure our primary function of public service.'

'Our primary function is keeping the Queen's Peace,' she said, 'and I don't think you're making a very good job of it at the moment.'

As one woman left his office, another waited in the doorway, her face miserable, her mouth drawn in a sharp line, and he felt wearied by the sight of her, drained of energy and interest. 'Yes, Janet?'

'Inspector Rowlands told me to take Mrs Harris's statement, sir. Shall I confine it to her tidying up the body?'

'Use your initiative,' McKenna said.

'He said to interview the daughters as well.'

'Until there's more information from pathology, we'll shelve the formal interviews.'

She made slowly for the door, feet dragging, then said: 'Shall I look for the old man's bracelet?'

'Not yet. I want the room left as it is.'

'Right, sir.' Pulling a wad of tissues from her pocket, she wiped her forehead.

'Have you reached a decision yet, Janet?'

'No, sir.' She leaned against the door, staring at him. 'I can't find the right one.'

'As the situation isn't of your choosing, the best you can hope for is the least painful way of extricating yourself.'

'I can't imagine myself married, especially not like this.'

'If you book a few days' leave and arrange an abortion, no-one need be any the wiser.'

'Don't you think abortion's wrong, sir?'

'Unless it's a medical necessity, I think it's an abomination, but I'm not the one who's pregnant.'

She smiled wanly. 'If I don't make a decision soon, it'll be too late, so I won't need to, and in a few months, people'll know without being told. Even my father.'

'You'd be entitled to maternity leave.'

'My mother thinks I can't even look after myself. God knows what she'd say about my looking after a baby.'

'I imagine she'd help you.' He watched the doubt in her eyes brighten with hope, and said: 'If having the baby's become an option, you'd better see your doctor very soon.'

'I will.' She smiled again, and opened the door.

3

Professor Iorwerth Williams, the owner of the silver Jaguar, and Edith Harris's visitor, was the first incumbent of the Chair of Celtic Studies at the university. Parking his own car under the spreading branches of the beech trees which shaded the gardens and granite walls of the professor's house, McKenna wondered how the ordinary Mrs Harris could capture the interest of such an extraordinary scholar. Like the leaves which rustled overhead, Williams's reputation had flourished upon the chance discovery of some ancient Welsh manuscript texts, long thought to be lost forever. He published papers and books, lectured abroad, and won acclaim wherever he set foot. Stepping from the car into the sunshine, suddenly and unreasonably, McKenna saw Edith Harris as the harbinger of an autumn which might wither that reputation as the beech tree leaves would perish on the turn of the year.

The woman who came to the front door was a breastless, two-dimensional shape clad in black from head to foot, her face a pale mask beneath a cap of jet black hair. Body bejewelled even so early in the day, her slightly wattled neck sported a glitter of gemstones beneath the hard line of her jaw. Her voice was husky and heavily accented. 'My husband is not at home. He is busy.'

'Is he not in?' McKenna asked.

'He is busy.'

'I won't keep him long, but I'd like to speak to him.'

She shrugged, pulled the door wide, then clicked along the scuffed tiles of the hall floor, high heels elongating her body. Standing behind her as she knocked at a wide panelled door, McKenna detected the perfume Janet favoured, sickly in the heat, and mingled with a pervading smell of tobacco.

As the door swung open, Williams snapped: 'I told you not to disturb me, *chérie*!'

'There is a policeman to see you.' She walked away, and left the two men facing each other. Slightly hunched, thin and pot-bellied, clad in socks and sandals and unpressed clothing, Williams scowled at his visitor, eyes narrowed behind half-moon spectacles slipping down a nose greasy with sweat. His hair was sparse and greying, the hairline yellowed with nicotine stains.

'I'm sorry to bother you, professor,' McKenna said. 'I understand you're friendly with Mrs Harris.'

'What of it?'

'I'm investigating Edward Jones's death.'

'Why?' His eyes, McKenna thought, looked slightly bloodshot, the irises muddied. 'Edith said it was a heart attack.'

'Did she?' McKenna smiled. 'At the moment, we're not sure. It could be suicide.'

'Oh, I see. Then you'd better come in.' He stamped across the room to a swivel chair beside the desk, motioning McKenna to an armchair.

The study reminded McKenna of the derelict house at the end of his street, and smelled worse, the deep casement windows tightly closed, the burgundy velvet curtains discoloured with dust. Ashtrays overflowed on desk and windowledge, unwashed plates and cups decorated other surfaces, their contents rotting and curdling.

Williams followed his gaze. 'The cleaner's on holiday, and the cook won't do any cleaning. Bloody woman! I should sack her.' Swinging from side to side in the chair, he said: 'So Ned wasn't crying wolf this time? He finally got round to killing himself. He'd been threatening long enough.'

'Had he?'

'About twice a month, according to Edith. He made life very difficult for her. She's a bag of nerves.' He pulled a cigarette from an open pack on the desk, and rooted around for matches.

As McKenna held up his lighter, he noticed the professor's quivering fingers. 'How well d'you know the family?'

Williams puffed smoke towards the dirty window. 'We

knew her husband, so we kept an eye on her after he went. That's all.'

McKenna tried to place the alien intonation in the man's voice. 'What happened to her husband?'

'I thought you wanted to talk about Ned. If you want to know about Edith's affairs, ask her.'

Lighting his own cigarette, McKenna asked: 'Why did Mr Jones threaten suicide so often?'

'Because he was mentally ill, I imagine. He was in and out of Denbigh Hospital like a yo-yo.'

'He was also in considerable physical pain, I understand.'

'So he said.' Contemplating the tip of his cigarette, Williams added: 'But the doctors never found anything really wrong with him. He probably invented his aches and pains for sympathy. He was very manipulative, you know, very sorry for himself.'

'He had a gift for writing at one time. Perhaps his problems arose because he couldn't realize his potential.'

'One swallow doesn't make a summer,' the other man observed. 'And one Eisteddfod trophy doesn't make a bard. He never amounted to much because he frittered away his time on his own crazy ideas. The whole family's peculiar.'

'What ideas?'

'I don't know. I never cared to get involved.'

'Mrs Harris mentioned a student. Was Mr Jones supervising a thesis?'

'You must be joking!'

'D'you know the student? He's called George.'

'Yes, I know he's called George.' Mashing the cigarette in one of the ashtrays, scattering more dirt on the desk, Williams said: 'George Polgreen is reading philosophy, and if you want my inexpert opinion, he's no more *compos mentis* than Ned was, which would explain why they hit it off.' He smiled, exposing stained and yellowed teeth, and the vestige of a boyish charm which would once have made him attractive. 'Still, lunacy's probably a prerequisite in his discipline.'

'I'll get his address from the academic registrar,' McKenna said. 'Unless you know where he lives.'

'In term-time, probably in one of those student rat-holes in Upper Bangor, but his family home is a township in South Africa.' The teeth appeared again, but without the charm. 'He's the blackest person I've ever seen, and I've seen plenty. A real jungle bunny!'

McKenna rose. 'Thank you for your time, professor.'

As he walked towards the door, Williams turned in his chair, its joints squealing gently. 'Will there be an inquest?'

'When it can be arranged.'

'And will the funeral be delayed?'

'I don't know yet.'

With the light behind him, Williams was a dark, slack shape. 'Ned's family will want him buried on home ground, I imagine.' He turned the chair again, his back to McKenna, and reached for another cigarette. 'Edith can let us know, when the time comes. Goodbye.'

4

Janet's car was outside the Harris house when McKenna turned into Glamorgan Place. He parked behind, and walked to the wide-open front door. Phoebe materialized in the hall, the cat by her feet. 'Mama's talking to your detective. I'm not supposed to disturb them.'

She led him towards a door at the rear of the hall, the cat padding behind, and when they reached the kitchen, it leaped on to a chair between a green, unlit Aga, and a gleaming enamel gas cooker, staring at McKenna. As he reached out to stroke its ears, Phoebe snatched his hand away. Her flesh was cool, and felt immensely clean. 'He might scratch! He'll come to you when he's ready.'

'It's a pity they can't be trained like guard dogs, isn't it?'

She grinned, the bruise on her face rosy and shiny. 'Clyde's got a guard dog, or so he says.'

'Is he really called Clyde?'

'He's called Jason Lloyd. She might end up as Minnie Lloyd.' Opening the refrigerator, she said: 'There's some fresh lemonade, half a bottle of wine left over from last night, or you can have tea. Or coffee.'

'Tea's nice on a hot day.'

She filled the kettle, took mugs from a cupboard, dropped four tea-bags into a pot, and leaned against the worktop while the kettle boiled, arms folded across her chest. She was dressed today in a long white man's shirt and khaki cotton trousers, her feet in laced sandals. Her hair curled damply around her face. 'D'you know why Uncle Ned died yet?'

'No.'

'So you don't know about his funeral?'

'No.'

'Auntie Gladys phoned last night, but she won't come here.'

'Why not?'

The kettle boiled, and Phoebe made the tea. 'She can't drive. Uncle Ned couldn't, either.'

'She could get a bus.'

'She's old, and, more to the point, she doesn't get on with Mama.' Stirring the brew, she added: 'Anyway, Annie's going again later in the week. She's always kept an eye on them, so Uncle Ned wouldn't worry too much.'

'I take it she *does* drive?'

'She learned as soon as she was old enough,' Phoebe said admiringly. 'She had a new car not long ago. Jason got it off a mate at trade price.'

'What does he do for a living? Is he at college?'

'Don't be funny! He's thicker than Minnie. He does security work. Any moron can do that, can't they?'

He took the tea she poured for him. 'How old is Annie?'

'Old enough to be my mother! Nearly thirty-one.'

'And is she dark, like you? Mina's blonde, isn't she?'

'Darkish.' Phoebe picked up her mug. 'Minnie's dark, too. Her blonde comes out of a bottle, as I expect Jason's found out.'

'How could he?'

'You know what I mean.' She grinned at his confusion. 'Mama says I'm in danger of being obsessed with you-know-what, and she went ballistic when I asked her if old people get grey pubic hair, or if it just falls out.'

'It's a sign of your age.'

'Mama says it's sheer nosiness, but Uncle Ned said I should always find things out for myself instead of relying on second hand stuff.' She sighed. 'I miss him an awful lot. It hurts more every day.' She looked at the cat, now asleep on its chair. 'I couldn't bear it if Tom died, too.'

'There's no reason why he should.' McKenna put his cigarettes and lighter on the table. 'And I know you can't help grieving for Ned, but don't let his death make you forget all the happiness you had with him.'

'I won't, but it's awfully hard.' She stood up to take an ashtray from the cupboard. 'I loved talking to him, you know. We talked about almost everything, and he even told me about being in Denbigh Hospital. Me and George are the only ones who know what he went though in that place. He called it a human warehouse.' She rubbed her eyes. 'I keep wanting to rush upstairs to tell him something, and I can't, and I won't ever be able to again, and it's so unfair, because there was so much he loved in the world!'

McKenna pulled a cigarette from the pack, then flicked his lighter, wondering about her mercurial changes of mood and the depths they obscured. 'People have said he often spoke of suicide.'

'Which people? Mama? The professor?' Her voice was derisive. 'He might've *talked* about it, but he'd never *do* it!'

'Then what would he actually say?'

Phoebe picked up her tea, and drank slowly, a frown creasing her forehead. 'He had a lot of pain, and he used to say killing yourself is the only way to get away from pain like that, especially when you know there's more to come.' She paused. 'And he said being depressed was like having a war of attrition with yourself, only I never quite understood what he meant.'

'He probably meant that it wore him down.'

'I suppose.' She nodded, and buried her face again in the mug of tea.

'So perhaps,' McKenna said gently, 'it's not unreasonable to suggest he killed himself.'

'He was trying to explain how it *could* make you suicidal, not how it *would*.' She paused again, then said: 'There's a whole world between them, and I knew exactly what he meant, 'cos I've thought about what might make me kill myself, and I'd never do it, not even if Tom died.'

The door suddenly flew open, and Edith twittered: 'What a surprise! I could smell cigarettes, so I thought Phoebe's Uncle Iolo had arrived!'

Phoebe stood up and went to the sink to rinse her mug. 'He's not my "Uncle Iolo". He's not *anybody's* "Uncle Iolo".' Slamming the mug on the draining board, she snapped: 'And I won't *call* him "Uncle Iolo", even if Minnie does. Simpering cow!'

'Will you behave yourself?' Edith shrieked. 'Heaven knows what our visitors are thinking!'

'Why don't you ask them?' Phoebe countered, her face mutinous.

'You're a rude, naughty child! Go to your room! This instant!'

McKenna intervened. 'Phoebe's distressed about Mr Jones's death, Mrs Harris. They were very close.'

'It's his fault she's like this!' Edith insisted. 'All this talking! All these questions! It's not right at her age.'

'Mama wants to shut the door on an empty stable,' Phoebe said, 'but she can't.'

McKenna looked at her. 'I don't understand.'

'She was too wrapped up with my snotty sister to give me attention, and now she feels guilty because Uncle Ned looked after me when she should've done it.'

'How dare you!' Edith shrieked again. 'Go to your room!'

Grabbing the cat, Phoebe rushed through the door and thundered up the staircase, then the windows rattled as she slammed a door.

Sinking into a chair, Edith rested the back of her hand on her forehead, and began to gulp air.

'Who's "Uncle Iolo"?' McKenna asked.

Showing the whites of her eyes, she gasped, and subsided over the kitchen table, her body wracked with sobs.

'Shall I make her a cup of tea, sir?' Janet sidled into the room. 'I could stay for a while.'

McKenna rose. 'What's happened?'

'Nothing in particular. It's delayed shock, I expect.'

'I'd better have a word with Phoebe.'

As McKenna fidgeted by the door, Edith looked up once more, her face ravaged, and said, between choked sobs: 'I can't cope!'

'You and Phoebe are just overwrought,' Janet comforted.

'I can't cope with her!' There was an edge of hysteria to Edith's voice.

'Couldn't Annie come over for the evening?' McKenna asked. 'Or better still, couldn't Phoebe go to Llanberis for a few days?'

'Oh, no! Mina wouldn't like that.'

'Why ever not?' Janet asked.

'She'd have to stay in to look after me, and that's not fair when she's been working all day. Anyway, she's arranged to go to a nightclub with Jason.'

'It won't hurt Mina to put her family first this once,' McKenna said. 'She can go clubbing another time. DC Evans will ring Annie, and see what can be arranged.'

He went upstairs, passed the glowing stained glass window on the landing, and turned right, to find himself facing the sealed door to Ned's room. Retracing his steps, walking again through the puddles of colour below the window, he passed a bathroom, carpeted in pink, and went towards the door at the far end, behind which Phoebe spilled out her heart to the only friend she had left. He knocked, and waited, listening to Edith's fretful tones in the kitchen, and Janet's soothing voice, then knocked again.

'Go away!' Phoebe wailed. 'Leave me alone!'

'Your mother's downstairs, Phoebe.'

He heard rustling and shuffling, another protest from the cat, then she opened the door, standing wearily in a shadow that was like a pool of her own misery, her face blotched and swollen with tears.

'Janet's asking Annie to come over,' he said. 'I suggested you go and stay with her for a while.'

Phoebe sighed. 'Mama won't let me. She doesn't like being alone with Minnie.'

'Aren't you rather over-egging the pudding? You're all very tense, and could do with a break from each other.'

'I've *told* you! Mama's scared of her.' Seeing the impatience on his face, she said: 'I thought you were brighter than most people.' She pointed to her bruise. 'I'm not the only one who gets thumped.'

'She's hit your mother?'

'Yes, only Mama won't admit it.' Retreating into the

room, she sat on the bed, and began to stroke the cat. 'Minnie played a horrible trick on her, and when Mama didn't find it funny like she was supposed to, Minnie got hysterical, and Mama had nasty scratches on her face afterwards.'

'What did Mina do?'

'You haven't seen Uncle Ned's room yet, have you? It's three rooms, really. He had his meals downstairs, but he had his own bedroom, and a little bathroom, so he never used our toilet.'

'And?' McKenna prompted.

'Our toilet seat doesn't get put up very often.' The cat rolled over and stretched out, front claws kneading her pillow, and she pulled him away. 'You know we go in there, sit down, and use it.'

'Yes, Phoebe, I get the picture.'

'So that bitch thought it'd be funny to put cling film under the seat and over the pan, because that's the sort of nasty thing she finds amusing.' She paused, her hand was on the cat's back. 'She probably hoped I'd go in there first, but it was Mama, and she was absolutely mortified. She had to have a bath, and wash her clothes, and she kept scrubbing the floor because she thought it still smelled, even after she'd bought a new carpet.'

'I see.'

'So you understand why I can't go to Annie's, don't you?'

'Couldn't someone else stay here if Annie can't? Uncle Iolo perhaps? Whoever he is.'

'That's the professor,' Phoebe said. 'Professor Williams. Mama always calls him Iolo. It's short for Iorwerth.'

'I know.'

She smiled, a grotesque gesture on that tragic face. 'His wife can't get her tongue round Iolo, so she calls him "Ee-oo-low". It's hilarious. She can't say Iorwerth very well, either. Uncle Ned said French people can't manage some of the sounds in Welsh.'

'I met her briefly today, but I wasn't introduced. What's her name?'

'Solange. Uncle Ned called her a "trophy wife", probably because the professor picked her up on his foreign travels, along with all the honorary doctorates and whatnot for being so clever.' Phoebe grinned. 'In my opinion, she's more of a booby prize.'

'You don't like him very much, do you?'

'I don't like being *made* to like him. He's Mama's friend, not mine.' She picked up the cat and draped him over her lap. 'Anyway, he treated his first wife very badly, Uncle Ned said. She left him in the end. He chases other women, or at least, he did then.'

'Professor Williams told me he knew your father.'

'So did Uncle Ned. I don't really remember him, and Mama never talks about him.' She rolled her eyes. 'According to her, it was one of those tragedies only grownups can understand.'

'I should go, Phoebe. Will you be OK if Janet stays until Annie arrives?'

'I'll manage.' She smiled again. 'Getting a row is nothing new. Mama says we go round and round in the same circles. Will you be seeing George? He wants to talk to you.'

'I thought he was in South Africa with his family.'

'Who told you that? They live in Notting Hill. He came back from London yesterday, and he was here first thing this morning 'cos he read about Uncle Ned in the *Daily Post*. He's terribly upset.' She put the cat on the bed, and stood up. 'His flat's only round the corner on Baptist Street, so if you wait while I wash my face and comb my hair, I can take you to see him.'

Edith howled as McKenna walked into the kitchen, Phoebe and her cat at his side.

'I told you to stay in your room!'

'Phoebe offered to show me where George lives,' McKenna said.

'You don't bring him back here, d'you understand? I don't want him in the house.'

'I had no intention, Mrs Harris.'

She muttered, as if to herself. 'Mina will be back soon.'

'I managed to get hold of the eldest girl, sir.' Janet's face was putty-coloured. 'She's on her way over.'

'I'll see you later, then.' He frowned. 'Are you OK?'

'A bit of a stomach ache. I'm seeing the doctor this evening.'

'Good idea.' He turned to Phoebe, who was watching Janet with undisguised curiosity, and herded her towards the back door, the cat at their heels.

Most of the garden was lawned, overhung with old trees almost sodden with rich summer foliage, which shielded both sides from the neighbours' view. Another gravelled path meandered through the lawns, in and out of a cool, dark shrubbery, past a wrought iron bench in the shade of a horse-chestnut tree, and towards the green wooden gate set into an arch in the boundary wall.

'I used to sit there with Uncle Ned,' Phoebe said, as they passed the bench. She sighed. 'D'you know, I *knew* something awful was going to happen to him!'

'How?'

She gestured to the cat. 'He suddenly started sitting in Uncle Ned's favourite chair. Cat's do that when someone's going to die.'

The gate creaked as she pulled it open, its bottom edge gouging an arc in the gravel. She trotted across a cinder path, and through an opening in a broken down fence, which gave on to a patch of garden, overgrown with wilting docks and sun-bleached couch grass, which brushed against his trousers.

Phoebe wrinkled her nose. 'Stinks, doesn't it? All the local cats use it for a bog, mine included, and it's dense enough for adders to nest in. Did you know the professor was brought up in South Africa? That's why he stamps his feet when he walks, to scare off the snakes.' She surveyed the rank grass and fronding weeds. 'The landlord says he's going to fire the grass now it's dry enough to take.'

'I hope he doesn't. He'll burn down half the houses as well.'

Opening the door of a ramshackle glazed porch, she said: 'That wouldn't upset many people. Mama says these places devalue nice houses like ours.' She led him through a dark passageway, up three staircases carpeted with cheap brown cord, and to the top floor of the house. 'The students really get ripped off, you know. George pays an awful lot of rent, and he's only got one room and a gas ring. He has to share the bathroom. I'd hate that, wouldn't you?' She knocked at a door where a painted hardboard panel obscured the original mouldings. 'Five other students live here. Just imagine how much money the landlord's making.'

'Supply and demand.' McKenna leaned against the wall, listening for sounds from within, while the cat crouched by his ankles.

Phoebe knocked again, and called: 'George? It's Phoebe. Are you in?'

'I think he'd have heard us by now.'

'Oh, well.' She turned away reluctantly. 'At least you know where he hangs out.' Following him down the stairs, she added: 'What will you do now? Are you going to see Auntie Gladys?'

'Your mother asked me to phone her.'

'That was yesterday. Haven't you done it yet?'

'There's nothing to tell her at the moment.'

'You're just supposed to talk to her.'

Stopping at the foot of the last staircase, McKenna looked

at the girl who hovered on the bottom tread, and wondered why he found nothing objectionable in her directness.

'I wasn't being rude,' she said.

'I know.' He smiled. 'I'll call her later, if I have time.'

'What will we do with Uncle Ned's things?'

'Nothing for now.'

As he walked from the gloom of the passage into the searing heat, she touched his arm gently. 'How did he die? Did it hurt him? D'you think he was very frightened?'

'He died very quickly, Phoebe.'

She followed him to the gate in the wall. 'But he must've known.'

He waited until she and her shadow were through the gate, then pushed it shut, deepening the arc in the gravel. 'I suspect we all know when the time comes.'

She walked beside him, scuffing her feet, while the cat disappeared into the shrubbery. 'Dying must be the strangest thing. You can't imagine it, can you? I can sort of imagine being born, and even being inside Mama, though I can't imagine where I was before then.'

'Maybe the same place you'll be when you're dead.'

'Uncle Ned said there's another plane, where souls wait around for a new body, like everything's made up of layers, but you can only see one at a time.' She frowned. 'He'll know now, won't he?'

'He will.'

'I wouldn't be scared if he came back and haunted us, you know.' She smiled again. 'If he does, I'll ask him what happened.'

Edith and Janet had vacated the kitchen, and he found them back in the sitting room, each side of the ornate fireplace. Phoebe remained outside, trying to cajole the cat to play with a length of string.

'Did you find him, sir?' Janet asked.

'He wasn't in.' Turning to Edith, he said: 'If he calls, would you ask him to get in touch with me?'

'I told him not to bother us.' Edith wrung her hands. 'I can't stand much more of this!'

Tempted to ask 'much more of what?', McKenna bit his tongue. Standing by the door, he wondered if she had shared more than a house with her distant relative, and how much she had ingested of the churned up silt from the common gene pool, then realized she was just in fear, of what was probably her first excursion into mischief when she tampered with the body, and of her middle daughter. Perhaps she and Phoebe were hostages, he thought, in a conflict Mina had created for sport or for spite, or to make some small point which had become, like most flashpoints, the more remote and obscure as more blood was spilled.

5

Anchored by a sellotape dispenser amid the litter of files and pieces of paper on his desk in the temporary office was a message slip recording a call from the mortuary.

'The lab faxed some preliminary findings,' the pathologist announced, when McKenna telephoned him. 'Edward Jones ingested tetracycline, but there were no capsules or tablets at any stage of breakdown, so we must assume he took the drug in its powder form, probably from a split capsule.'

'No possibility of complete digestion?'

'He was blitzed as soon as it touched his system.'

'I'd better talk to Gabriel Ansoni.'

'I've already done that. The allergic reaction which raised the alarm last year was caused either by tetracycline or ibuprofen, or one potentiating the other, so both were listed on this missing SOS bracelet as potentially lethal. More to the point, Gabriel's the Harrises's family doctor, and he hasn't prescribed antibiotics of any kind in the last two and a half years.' The pathologist paused, and McKenna could hear the tap-tap of a computer keyboard. 'Mrs Harris is near as dammit to being a tranquillizer addict, and the one called Minerva — did you ever hear such a ridiculous name? — she's on the pill.' The keys tapped again. 'The girl's also had scripts for new generation anti-depressants. Misery runs a bit in that family, doesn't it?'

'It usually does.' McKenna lit a cigarette. 'Run in families. What else was in Ned's stomach?'

'Tea, milk, lamb, bread and butter, tomato, and a minute trace of honey, and as he died around mid-afternoon, that was doubtless his lunch. In theory, the tetracycline could have been put in the milk, but unless there was a huge amount, adding hot tea would substantially reduce its potency. There was also enough nitrazepam to suggest he took a sleeping tablet the night before he died, but no trace of antihistamine, and that's about it for now,' the pathologist said, 'so in my considered opinion, which I won't voice at the inquest, whenever that is, and bearing in mind the marks on his chest, I'd say you can rule out suicide and accidental death.'

McKenna sighed. 'What about the tissue under his nails? All his own, or not?'

'Don't know yet. Have you found out who tidied him up *post mortem*?'

'Edith Harris.'

'So apart from her, how many suspects have you got?'

'She's insisting Ned didn't have an enemy in the world.'

'Yes, but she's a tranxhead, so you'd be a fool to believe a word she says.'

Diana Bradshaw's office was empty. McKenna fidgeted by the open door, intensely irritated, both by her absence, and by her failure to advise him of it, and was returning to his own billet when he heard footsteps behind him.

'Were you looking for me?'

He turned. 'Yes, ma'am. New information from pathology about Edward Jones makes suicide or accident extremely remote.'

She stood with her hands behind her back, head tilted. 'So?'

'So I want Rowlands and Dewi Prys to assist a murder investigation.'

'I'll think about it.' Walking into her office, she closed the door firmly.

Phoebe answered the telephone. 'Annie's here, so your policewoman's gone. Mama's lying down and we're baking a cake for tea.' Before he could respond, she said: 'Will you be coming again?'

'Yes. I'll need to come again.'

'You can meet Annie, then. She and Bethan are staying until things get back to some sort of normal.'

As he put the telephone in its cradle, thinking Annie Harris and her child could well have a long and unpleasant sojourn, Diana Bradshaw swept into the room, and sat down. Watching her, he recalled Sigmund Freud's description of women as a dark continent, and, not for the first time, feared it was his lot to wander blindly through, bereft of navigational aids.

'Why have you suddenly decided Edward Jones was murdered?' she asked.

'The facts rule out the alternatives.'

He related the pathologist's information, and she pursed her mouth, frowning. 'Those facts are equally consistent with suicide.'

'So how did he come by the tetracycline?'

'He could have asked someone for it, of course!'

'Perhaps so,' McKenna conceded. 'Nonetheless, we must act on the presumption of unlawful killing.'

'I suppose so, but for the time being, you must make do with Janet, because I don't want to pull the others off the vehicle investigation.' She rose. 'Let me know in a couple of days how you're getting on.

'We'll need a plan of campaign, then,' Janet said, answering McKenna's summons to his office. Smiling, she added: 'Dewi won't be pleased. He's hoping for another chance to see the lovely Minerva.'

'Whose habits, according to Phoebe, are much less attractive than her appearance, and I don't think it's entirely sour grapes on her part.'

Janet looked through his notes on the discussion with the pathologist. 'I'm not surprised Edith needs tranquillizers. She's probably driven herself up the wall.'

'Long term use of psychotropic drugs creates unstable moods and behaviour,' McKenna said. 'I wonder why Mina's had them. A girl of her age shouldn't need happy pills.'

'She's her mother's daughter,' Janet commented, 'so there's an inherited disposition towards popping pills at every opportunity, especially if they're the latest fashion.' She rubbed her forehead. 'Maybe I should get some, then I wouldn't care about being pregnant.'

'You can't be sure you are. Were you sick this morning?'

'I waited for ages, but nothing happened. I've got a griping stomach ache instead, so tomorrow, I expect there'll be another new experience. It's like an alien invasion.' She made a neat pile of the papers. 'Do we start formal interviews right away?'

'When we've established who was where on Friday, but I

want to examine Ned's room first. I'll get forensics to meet us there.'

'It's a mess, sir. Not dirty, but just full of things, as if he's kept everything he ever had, including every piece of paper.'

6

Rowlands's irritability grew mile for mile along the A55 towards Bangor. 'I'm not blaming you, Prys, but we should have telephoned these people first!'

'Well, sir, we didn't.' Overtaking a fast-moving truck, Dewi added: 'We can go again, when they're back off holiday.'

'Bradshaw will not be quite so laid back about the virtual waste of a day and God knows how many gallons of petrol.'

'We can always tell her it was raking over old ground, and we're therefore approaching the problem from another angle.' Dewi braked to take the Talybont turn-off. 'Trading Standards dumped the whole lot on us when a couple of stolen engines surfaced, but strictly speaking, there's nothing to connect those to the clocked Tigra and the welded coupé.'

'The Republic of Gwynedd can't support too many bent vehicle outfits.'

' "Republic of Gwynedd", sir?'

'As in the locals making up their own rules as they go along, without reference to the law of the land, but you wouldn't necessarily notice,' Rowlands said, gazing through the window. 'You're part of the same culture.' As the car flashed past an old granite house and the entrance to a lane, he turned in his seat. 'What's that? Surely to God you don't bury people at the roadside!'

'The gypsies live down that lane.'

'There's a grave by the road, with fresh flowers and a cross.'

'It's a shrine for a little gypsy girl who was run over a few years ago, on her way home from school.' Seeing the expression on Rowlands's face, he added: 'And it's not morbid, sir. We think it's rather touching.'

7

The silver Jaguar glittered hugely in the sunshine of Glamorgan Place, rays of light bouncing from its roof and bonnet and wings. McKenna drove to the top of the cul-de-sac and parked in the shade of a hawthorn tree. Its dying flowers tainted the air with a sour odour.

Eyes invisible behind dark glasses, Janet said: 'Where does Mrs Harris get her money?'

'I've no idea.' He walked down the short hill, stepping in her truncated shadow. She was wearing different perfume, a light, lemony scent. 'And it's unlikely to be relevant to Ned's death.'

'I'd still like to know. Maybe she'll tell me, if I ask her nicely.'

'Ask about her husband, too, if you have the opportunity.' He paused by the gate. 'I tried to prise some information out of Iolo Williams, but he wouldn't take the bait.'

'He seems very faithful, doesn't he? He must be one of those caring souls, so I expect my father knows him.'

McKenna walked up the path and rapped on the open front door, knocking again, more forcefully, when the hall remained empty.

The sitting room door was wrenched open, and Williams stamped towards them, screwing up his eyes as the sun struck his face. 'It's barely a couple of hours since you left. What do you want now?' As he moved restlessly, the odour of stale nicotine drifted from his clothing. 'You can't see Edith. She's lying down.'

'She needn't be disturbed,' McKenna said. 'We've come to examine Mr Jones's room.'

'Why? Have you got a warrant?'

'We don't need one, professor. This is standard procedure.'

'It's not convenient!'

'I'm sorry, but it's got to be done.'

'It can be done some other time!'

Another vehicle pulled into the road, and double parked beside the Jaguar. Williams pushed past McKenna and Janet, and flapped down the path in his sandals. 'Get away! Move that van now!'

McKenna followed him. 'The forensic team can park up the hill beside my car, but they're coming in.'

'I shall complain!' Williams stormed back to the house. 'You can't invade Edith's home and her privacy like this. You're treating her like a criminal!'

Phoebe appeared on the doorstep, her face sodden with tears. 'What's happening?' The cat crouched by her feet, tense and wary, then shot into the hall as two forensic officers came up the path, their overalls crackling.

'We want to examine Ned's room,' McKenna told her.

'Why are they here again?' She pointed to the overalled men. 'They frightened Tom!'

'Come inside,' Janet coaxed. 'There's nothing to worry about.' She put her arm around Phoebe's shoulder, and tried to persuade her from the doorstep, but the girl refused to move.

'Oh, get inside, child!' Williams snapped.

'I won't! You've no right to tell me what to do!'

He raised his hand, palm out, and Phoebe cowered away.

'Professor Williams!' McKenna caught hold of his arm. 'Leave her alone. Can't you see she's upset?'

Shaking himself free, Williams again pushed past Janet,

and returned to the sitting room, slamming the door. Phoebe leaned against the door, and began to sob, while the overalled men stood on the path, baggage at their feet.

'Go with DC Evans,' McKenna told them. 'I'll be with you soon.'

Sobbing as if her heart would break, Phoebe shook her head, tears running from her chin and making huge splotchy patches on her shirt. He took her hand, and led her to the kitchen. 'Where's Annie?'

She slumped into a chair, and leaned over the table, a parody of Edith earlier that day.

'She's gone to the shops.' The words were punctuated with sobs.

'Is Mrs Williams here?'

'I don't want to see her!' Phoebe's voice rose ominously. 'I hate her!'

'Then I'll stay with you until Annie gets back.' He took out cigarettes and lighter, and looked around for the ashtray. 'What's happened since we spoke on the phone? You were crying before we arrived, weren't you?'

The cat sidled around the door, and jumped on the table, bulldozing her shoulder with its head. She reached out to stroke him, catching her breath in a huge sigh. 'You'll have to use a saucer, 'cos they've got the ashtrays. Solange smokes like a chimney as well. Their house stinks, and they stink, and she stinks most because she doesn't have a bath very often. French people don't, you know. I expect that's why they invented perfume.' She tickled the cat's ears. 'His fur smells of cigarettes when they've been here, like a council house cat, but you can smoke if you want, because you're not like them. I expect you open your windows, and wash your clothes and hair, because you smell quite nice.' She smiled wanly. 'Like Uncle Ned, in a way. Maybe you use the same soap.'

'Maybe,' McKenna agreed, taking a saucer from the dresser. 'What's upset you?'

She wrapped her arms around the cat, and hugged him. 'It's silly, really. I said Annie and me were baking, didn't I? The cake looked so nice we decided to have some as soon as it cooled, only when I bit my piece, it tasted horrible, like sawdust, but there's nothing wrong with the cake. It's me.' She caught her breath again. 'Then I realized nothing's tasted the same since Friday, and when I went into the garden, the flowers smelled almost rancid, and it's all cold and damp under the tree where I used to sit with Uncle Ned, not cool and fresh like it was last week. Everything's gone flat and sad, like it's all over.'

'You're grieving, Phoebe. You've lost someone you loved very much, who's always been part of your life.'

'It hurts,' she whispered. 'It hurts so much!'

He stroked her hair. 'Does Annie understand?'

'She hurts, too. And little Bethan keeps asking where Uncle Ned's gone, and we don't know what to tell her.'

'The truth is best.'

'But could she understand? Annie wants her to go to the funeral, but Mama said it'd be cruel, because she's far too young.'

'Even if Bethan can't understand now, she'll remember when she's older, and be able to put the whole picture together.' He rapped ash into the saucer. 'She won't be afraid of some terrible mystery, or think people simply disappear off the face of the earth.'

'I suppose.' Phoebe sniffed, scouring her face with her hands.

'Does your mother miss him, too? Is that why she's so distraught?' He heard a rustle, felt a gentle draught.

'My mother barely tolerated him.' Annie Harris walked into the kitchen, plastic carrier bags in one hand, a small child with wispy fair curls clinging to the other. She dumped the bags on a worktop, and turned to face McKenna, the child leaning against her legs. 'And my mother isn't distraught. She's retreated into drug-assisted hysteria, which is her usual response to stress.'

McKenna rose, and held out his hand.

'Michael James McKenna,' Phoebe intoned. 'Detective chief inspector. My sister Anastasia and my niece Bethan.' Annie shook his hand briefly, then ruffled her sister's hair. The child gazed up at him, blue eyes wide. 'You'll notice,' Phoebe went on, 'that Bethan's got blonde hair, only hers is genuine.'

Annie smiled. 'You also have noticed it's impossible to get Phoebe to shut up.' Turning to her, she said: 'I thought you'd gone for a lie-down.'

'I had, then Mr McKenna came, and the professor had a tantrum. He's sulking in the sitting room with Solange.'

'Well, I hope they don't plan to stay for dinner.' Annie began to empty the carrier bags, and said to McKenna: 'Janet Evans is still waiting on the stairs, you know, with the men in what Bethan calls spacesuits.'

'They're forensic officers,' Phoebe said. 'They were here on Friday, and now they're back to turn Uncle Ned's room inside out for fingerprints and that sort of thing.'

'Why?' Annie stopped emptying the bags.

'Yes, why?' Phoebe demanded.

Still on his feet, McKenna fidgeted with his lighter.

'Please don't prevaricate,' Annie added. 'I need to know what to tell my mother.'

'Ned was killed by an allergic reaction to one of the drugs listed as potentially lethal on his SOS bracelet, which is still missing, so at the moment, we're treating his death as suspicious.'

'I told you!' Phoebe announced, shock draining the colour from her face. 'Didn't I tell you?'

Annie sighed. 'Yes, child, you told me. Now get the cat off the table.'

• • •

The seal around the door of Ned's room was intact. McKenna watched as it was opened, then went in, Janet at his heels. Unaired for over four days, its leaded windows catching the full force of afternoon sunshine, the room was stifling, the smell of old books and musty paper overpowering.

Janet wrinkled her nose. 'Can we open the windows?' Noticing the chair in which Ned died, its plush seat stained and crinkled where his bodily excretions had dried out, she added: 'And can we move this? Phoebe's quite likely to come nosing.'

'When it's been re-examined,' McKenna said.

'Apart from the SOS bracelet and any tablets, what else are we looking for?' She surveyed the desk and shelves, the stacks of papers and books, and wandered through a shaft of sunlight drifting with dust motes to look at two old wood caskets, roughly bound in brass, which stood on one of the shelves built into each chimney alcove.

'Don't touch those! Please!' Phoebe stood in the doorway.

'Don't come in,' McKenna told her.

'You mustn't open them!' Her face began to crumple, more tears imminent. 'They were Uncle Ned's. He called them his Box of Dreams and his Box of Clouds.'

'And what's in them?' McKenna asked.

'Dreams and clouds,' Phoebe said, 'and if anyone opens the boxes, they'll blow away.'

Making his way back to the door, careful not to touch any surfaces, McKenna said to Janet: 'Take care of the boxes. I'll be downstairs.'

Phoebe clumped down ahead of him, to the waiting cat. 'Are you going to take our fingerprints? Mine'll be all over Uncle Ned's things.'

'We'll take everyone's,' McKenna said, herding her back to the kitchen.

'Even the professor's?' Her eyes gleamed. 'He won't like that.'

'I'm sure he'll appreciate the need.' Hand on the kitchen doorknob, McKenna asked: 'Has he ever hit you?'

She shook her head. 'He just shouts. He's always raising his hand like he did earlier. He does it to Solange when he's annoyed.'

'And what does she do?'

'Smack him down, and mutter rude things in French.'

Bethan sat on a stool by the table, sucking orange juice through a straw. Pink rubber gloves on her hands and a butcher's apron around her shapely waist, Annie chopped onions, tears streaming down her face. 'Wipe my eyes, Phoebe. I can't see a thing.'

Tearing paper towel from a roll, Phoebe obeyed.

'And make a pot of tea while I finish the vegetables.' She glanced at the kitchen clock. 'Shouldn't Mina be home by now?'

'She wasn't back 'til midnight last night.'

'Well, it's her loss if she misses dinner,' Annie said. 'Do those two in the sitting room get tea?'

'They've got a bottle of wine. I expect they'll go when it's empty.'

'Good.' Laying out a tray with mugs and biscuits, Phoebe waited for the kettle to boil, surveying McKenna. 'I'll take Bethan to play in the garden when the tea's ready, so you can grill Annie while we're out of the way.'

'My baby sister's taken quite a fancy to you.' Annie topped up McKenna's tea, and poured her own. Iolo Williams and his wife had left, Solange dumping two wine glasses, both smeared with fingerprints and one with lipstick, and an empty bottle, on the kitchen counter, and then, with ill grace, the ashtrays, collected from the sitting room at Annie's request.

'She's got something about her,' McKenna said.

'She has, hasn't she? And whatever it is, Uncle Ned saw it, too.'

'I need a lot of information.' He stubbed out his cigarette in the saucer. 'It's difficult to ask your mother, and Phoebe's too young.'

'So you're left with the option of grilling me.' Annie smiled briefly. Her eyes were the same colour as Phoebe's, darkening or gleaming as the light touched them. 'Mama isn't usually like this,' she went on. 'She's a perfectly competent mother, but like many people, she can't cope with severe emotional stress.'

'I understand she uses tranquillizers.'

Annie leaned back in her chair, hands thrust into the apron pocket. 'She's an NHS addict.'

'She's not alone in that, either.'

'It's too easy, isn't it? You take the tablets to blank out some pain, and before you know it, you can't get through a day without them. Like you and cigarettes, I imagine. Mina's had drugs as well, but she was probably trying to blank out herself.'

Childish yelps and shrieks came from the garden, and through the window, he saw Bethan and the cat chasing Phoebe. 'I've not met her yet.' He lit another cigarette. 'Phoebe talks about her a lot.'

'She's pathologically jealous of Phoebe. That's why there's so much hostility. Don't assume looks are everything, Mr McKenna. Phoebe's very bright, and she has the gift of making contact with people. Uncle Ned was the same. They shared a type of warmth you don't come across very often.' Rising to stir the pot of meat and vegetables simmering on the gas cooker, Annie added: 'Mina resented Phoebe from the moment she was born. She'd ruled the roost until then, and had no real competition, because I was so much older.'

'What happened to your father?'

'Nothing remarkable.'

She wedged the lid on the pot, and sat down, hands in apron pocket again. She had a quality of stillness he found restful, an unusual economy of movement and effort far from her mother's incessant agitation, yet she was unmistakably Edith's daughter. Watching the play of light on her face, he wondered if Edith had once shared this full-blooded womanliness, before life sucked it from her.

'Did Phoebe tell you Father's a civil engineer?' Annie asked. 'He's in North Africa at the moment, building roads in inhospitable places. He's worked abroad for years, and earns much more than he would here, which is how he managed to keep Mama out of his hair and the rest of us in relative comfort.' She smiled fleetingly, mischievously. 'So now you can stop fretting about where the money comes from!'

Nonplussed, he cast around for something to say.

'I was about eight when he first went overseas,' she went on, 'and I realized afterwards they'd actually separated. Then he came back, and they "tried again", as the saying is, but it didn't work, so he left, not long after Mina arrived.' Her eyes darkened. 'I was glad when it was over. My childhood was marked out by their tears and misery and screaming rows, but I never knew what it was all for, and it seemed such a waste. I used to wish Uncle Ned was my father, because he certainly loved us far more than my real father ever did.'

'But your father must have come back yet again,' McKenna said.

She nodded. 'And Phoebe was born. It was quite peaceful for a while, but I suppose there was too much history, and it got the better of them. We haven't seen him for almost seven years. He sends cards and presents at the right times, but that's all.'

'When did your mother start taking drugs?'

'When Mina was a baby. I think she had post-natal depression, then she almost went to pieces when my father left.' Rising again to stir the pot, she said: 'That's why Uncle Ned came, and that's why Mama could never relax with him. He reminded her of the bad times, just by being here.' She leaned against the counter. 'And her own weaknesses, too, I imagine. That can't be comfortable for anyone.'

'Wasn't he rather an odd choice of surrogate guardian? He had his own problems.'

'He was family, and he was always a lot more together, as Phoebe would say, than people ever gave him credit for.'

'I accept that, but there's a long history of mental illness.'

'The whole family's weird. Ned's depressions were nothing.' She lifted the lid off the pot, then turned down the heat. 'And anyway, they didn't drop from the sky, even though troubles can be like rain.' Sitting again, she added: 'He never took the kind of drugs Mama gorges like Bethan would wolf sweets, because he'd suffered too much from the treatments forced on him in hospital. He wanted to get her off tranquillizers, but she wouldn't even try to help herself.'

'What treatments did he have?'

She shrugged. 'Dr. Ansoni could probably give you the details, but Ned called them "chemical restraints", as opposed to the straitjacket, presumably. They left him with the shakes, you know. Jumping legs, chattering teeth; that sort of thing.' Her eyes darkened again. 'Mina was a bitch to him at times! His teeth had fallen out years ago, probably because of the drugs, and his false teeth clicked when he spoke, which annoyed her, so she sneaked them from his room one night, and he was frantic. He didn't eat for two whole days, then I found them in her schoolbag. She'd hide those two boxes Phoebe was worrying about, too.'

'The Dream Box and the Cloud Box. Did he make up the names for her, like a story?'

'Possibly. He was very imaginative. He made you see things differently.'

'I know. He beat me to the Eisteddfod essay trophy.'

'Phoebe said.' Annie smiled. 'She'd remembered your name from the yearbook, and because she couldn't get at Ned's copy, she went to the public library.'

'She never mentioned it.'

'She wouldn't. She likes to know more than you think she does. She's probably got a huge Box of Secrets under her bed.'

'I'll need to take a formal statement from her. And from your mother and Mina.'

'And from me?'

'Were you here on Friday?'

'I hadn't been since Wednesday. I usually call once a week, and go to the farm the day after. Have you spoken to Gladys yet?'

'Your mother asked me to, but there's nothing to say at the moment.'

'I'll be going again, anyway. Mama just wants Ned's things out of the way.'

'Have you any idea if he made a will?'

'He didn't need to,' Annie said. 'His entire estate reverts to the surviving family members, through his father's will. A tontine, I think it's called.'

'Complicated,' McKenna commented. 'So who benefits when Ned's side of the family dies out?'

'No, you misunderstand: the *whole* family, Mama and us included. We'll each receive a portion of Ned's estate. Effectively, it can go on for ever.'

'And what's the estate worth?'

'Not much, and a lot less than it used to be.' She sighed. 'D'you remember what I said about his depressions? His father left Ned and his sisters some stocks and shares, quite separate from the contents of this will, and Ned sold most of his to buy rare books and manuscripts. At the time, he was in lodgings in Hirael, and the house went up in flames one day because someone overloaded an electrical socket. Most of his collection was destroyed, and he was ill for quite a long time afterwards.'

'Was he not insured?'

'Only partially, but he was devastated because the books and documents were irreplaceable. I think he'd hoped to save them for posterity.' She rose to give the pot another stir, the smell of simmering beef and herbs and vegetables filling the kitchen. 'Not to be rude, but it's getting near dinnertime, and I want to get Bethan to bed soon.'

McKenna stood up. 'Thank you for your time.'

'Will your people be much longer in Ned's room? I don't want to wake Mama until they've gone.'

'I'll see. The room will be sealed again, and we'll arrange to take statements as soon as possible. And we also need everyone's fingerprints for elimination, including Bethan's.' He took a card from his wallet, and left it on the table. 'Get in touch if you want anything.'

Annie read the details of work, home and mobile telephone numbers, and slipped the card into her apron pocket as Janet appeared at the door.

'We've finished for now, sir. I don't think we should start rummaging through the papers until we know what Ned was working on.'

'George knows exactly what Ned was doing,' Annie offered. As Janet went back upstairs, she said: 'Is she pregnant? I had that same look on my face when I knew Bethan was on the way. It's as if you turn in on yourself, and shut down all the non-essential systems.'

8

When McKenna returned to the station, after leaving Janet and the forensic officers to remove papers and personal effects from Ned's room, he found Rowlands and Dewi eating sandwiches and drinking coffee.

'Ms Bradshaw's left for the day, sir,' Dewi said.

'Any joy with the cars?'

'The people we wanted to see had gone on holiday.'

'Are you actually telling me you didn't contact them beforehand?'

'Sorry, no,' Rowlands said. 'My fault.'

'Yes, it bloody is!'

'It's mine as well, sir,' admitted Dewi.

'You're like bloody children dodging school!' McKenna seethed. 'Have you wasted the whole day?'

'More or less.'

'Then you can start making up for it when you've finished at the trough!'

'Bradshaw told us about Ned Jones,' Rowlands said.

'That was kind of her!' McKenna snapped.

'And she said we're to leave off the cars and concentrate on finding out who laced his food with poison,' Dewi added.

Janet knocked on the office door as McKenna finished the last mouthful of a Cornish pastie.

'Aren't you supposed to be seeing your doctor?' he asked.

She sank into a chair. 'It's too late now, and I'd rather wait to see the woman GP. She's on leave this week.'

'Is that such a good idea?'

'Pregnancy isn't an illness, sir.'

He tried to discern the differences in her face so clear to Annie, but saw only an unseasonal pallor and smudges under her eyes. 'If you feel up to taking statements this evening, you and Rowlands can interview Professor Williams and his wife.' He drained his tea. 'I want to find George Polgreen.'

'When shall we interview Edith and the girls? Edith may well have done more than tidy Ned's shirt and tie. The SOS bracelet isn't in the room, and the only drugs we found were an almost full bottle of nitrazepam and a few antihistamines in his bathroom cabinet. There was an uncashed script for more antihistamine on his desk.'

'Everyone knew about the bracelet, so what's the point of hiding it?' McKenna said, lighting a cigarette. 'Have you brought back all the financial records?'

'We removed all the papers apart from the books and manuscripts. They really need an expert opinion.'

'George Polgreen should be able to help there.' He stubbed out the newly lit cigarette. 'I'm sorry, Janet. I'll try not to smoke in front of you.'

She smiled wryly. 'I went through a whole pack last night. I'm finding it hard to sleep.'

'Can't you see a woman doctor at the family planning clinic? You shouldn't keep putting it off.'

'I won't.' She rose, gathering up handbag and pocketbook. 'You didn't say when we're to interview Edith.'

'We'll wait until she's retreated from the edge a little bit, otherwise we'll push her right over.'

Before leaving the office, he called Annie, to say the four Harris women must be available for interview the following day.

'Phoebe's a minor, so she must have someone with her,' Annie pointed out. 'Apart from Mama or me. We must be suspects.'

'You said you hadn't been at the house since the Wednesday.'

'But you've only got my word for that, haven't you? I'll call our solicitor.'

Dewi protested when McKenna dumped on his desk the large boxes overflowing with Ned's papers and personal effects. 'What am I supposed to look for?'

'Motive.' McKenna explained the provisions of the tontine. 'Money, to or from the deceased. Things which don't add up, literally or metaphorically. Love letters. Hate letters. The names of friends, acquaintances, enemies.'

Blowing at the silvery residue of fingerprinting powder which lay on the documents, Dewi said: 'Why are we sure Ned was murdered, sir? It seems like a bloody great leap in the dark to me.'

'We aren't sure,' McKenna said. 'We're proceeding on the assumption, based on the pathology, without entirely discounting suicide or accident until we have more information.'

'As long as we're not just dancing to Phoebe's tune.' Dewi placed an untidy pile of paper on the floor beside his desk. 'Are you getting a search warrant for the house?'

'Only if Edith won't co-operate.'

'She probably will, because if she's clever enough to dream up a killing like this, she won't leave the evidence around after.'

9

The young man who opened the door to the attic flat of the house on Baptist Street was also the blackest person McKenna had ever seen, but hardly the 'jungle bunny' of Iolo Williams's bigoted view. George Polgreen was tall, his face and body beautifully proportioned, his skin like polished ebony, and McKenna could understand why Mina found him so entrancing.

'Phoebe said you called earlier,' George said, inviting him in. 'I was down at the police station, strangely enough, because I thought someone had been in here while I was away, but nothing seems to be missing, so nothing's being done about it.'

'Does your landlord have keys?'

'Only for the latch lock.' George pointed to the door. 'I put the deadbolt on myself. I'm afraid our rooms get done over quite often.' He hovered over McKenna, the light through the dormer window casting a long dark shadow. 'Would you like a drink? It's still so bloody hot, isn't it?' Graceful and elegant as a big cat, he went to the kitchenette and stooped to pull out two stone crocks from under the sink. 'Cider or lemonade. Take your pick.'

'Cider shandy, please,' McKenna said.

He took two tankards from the cupboard, and carried crocks and tankard across the room. 'Ned gave me these,' he said, showing McKenna the ancient crocks and their stone stoppers. 'They came from the farm.' He sat down opposite, in an armchair draped with a brightly woven throw, the tankard in his hands.

Like the chair and its cover, the room was spotlessly clean and immaculately tidy, books, and papers in racks and rigid plastic files, a computer neatly aligned on the desk below the window. A small digital cat chased smaller digital mice across the blanked out screen of the monitor, each mouse turning paws up as it was napped.

'You don't have curtains,' McKenna said, into a lengthening silence.

'I don't need them. They're untidy things, anyway.'

'Why did you think someone had been in?'

'Just a sense of disturbance, I guess. Things not being exactly where they should be.'

'Yes, you'd notice.' Sipping the frothy brew, McKenna said: 'As you can imagine, we're having problems sorting through Ned's effects.'

An expression of near anguish passed over the fine face. 'What happened to him? Phoebe said he was poisoned with a drug.'

'Can I smoke?' McKenna asked. George nodded, and he went on: 'We can't completely rule out suicide or accident, but both are remote.' As he lit the cigarette, the smoke was snatched by a gentle draught from the open window. 'Although we were told Ned didn't have an enemy in the world, he wasn't exactly loved by some people.'

'Edith and that ghastly Mina.' George stood up, to pass McKenna a small earthenware bowl for his ash. 'Edith's a headcase. Civil and even smarmy one minute, screaming at you to get out the next. God knows how Phoebe stayed sane! If Ned hadn't been there, she probably wouldn't have.'

'And Mina?'

'Potentially more of a headcase than Edith, in my opinion. I don't like her, and she knows it.'

'Edith said you make eyes at Mina.'

George smiled briefly, showing perfect, white teeth. 'She'd be so lucky! I'll admit to looking at her, but that's all.'

'Why would you do that?'

'You haven't met her yet, have you? When you do, you'll see for yourself what a puzzle she is. She looks drop-dead gorgeous at first sight, but she's got a funny atmosphere.' He frowned, searching for the right words. 'She makes *you* feel odd; uncomfortable, even, but you can't tell why, and it's not to do with sex.'

'D'you know her boyfriend?'

'Clyde? I had a run-in with him once. He told me to leave her alone, and I said I wouldn't touch her with a barge-pole.'

'He's not called Clyde,' McKenna said.

'I know, but Phoebe's views stick, don't they? They have unconscious validity, so they're powerful.' He took a long drink. 'Phoebe's powerful, actually. Annie is too, but not so much. I think having Bethan tempered her.'

'And Ned?'

'I'm a better person for knowing him.' He fell silent, then said: 'He got right under your skin, and I'm going to miss him. So will Phoebe. She's changing already, from the child I knew to a person learning to be alone.'

'Ned could have engendered hate in an equal measure,' McKenna pointed out. 'Phoebe seems to have adopted his persona, and I can see how she must rile some people.'

'Like him, she's direct, uncompromising, naive, and incapable of dissembling, which truly creative people usually are. The force of their inner life stops the ego-self developing.' He fell silent again, thinking. 'People thought Ned was mad because his mind was open to any possibility, any idea, any influence, and sensitive to everything. He seemed balance and unbalanced at the same time, which is very threatening to people whose mental processes generally revolve around themselves and the fears induced by conditioning and experiences of probability.'

'You're losing me.'

'I don't think so. Phoebe told me about your excursion into the world of *eisteddfoddau*.'

'Are you Welsh speaking?'

George nodded. 'I took my first and master's degrees in Celtic languages and cultures.'

'I thought you were reading philosophy?'

'I'm doing a doctorate.'

'Perhaps I misunderstood Professor Williams.'

'I doubt it.'

'Then why isn't he supervising your thesis?'

'Because his qualifications aren't up to it, so he sees me as personifying his inadequacy, which wouldn't even be tolerable if I were white. He's the most arrogant bigot I've ever met, hence the picture he painted for you.' He leaned down to uncap the crocks, and refilled the tankards. 'The head of the Welsh Department's my supervisor. He was the one who put me in touch with Ned.'

'I'm surprised to hear about Williams.'

'Academic fraud isn't confined to students, you know. He's no scholar, in the real sense of the word. All he can lay claim to is unearthing a few early texts, and he's ridden on that. He entered the Eisteddfod year after year, and never even got a mention.' Wiping a smear of froth from his lips, George added: 'And he's so gratuitously nasty I'm hard pushed at times not to shove his remarks back down his throat.' He balled his fists, the knuckles gleaming. 'When he interviewed me for the doctorate, he said in his experience, which was considerable, black people are the dark side of man's psyche, and being black is a congenital disease, which in a way it is, but not quite on a par with syphilis, as he believes.'

'That rubbish was put about by an American psychiatrist called Benjamin Rush, and a very long time ago,' McKenna said. 'How come you were accepted in the face of such hostility?'

'I complained to the Principal, so he sent me to the Welsh Department.'

'Wasn't that a bit risky?'

'What? Complaining? Oh, you learn by experience.' George held out his hands, palms up to show the ugly scars defacing his wrists. 'London coppers use handcuffs held together with a rigid bar, which can break your bones with the slightest pressure, and after they'd banged me up for the fifth time and smashed several bones in my wrists, I sued for false arrest and personal injury, and got enough compensation to pay off my parents' mortgage and finance my doctorate.'

'And why were you arrested?'

'Because I'm black and I was there. To a lot of London coppers, we're all jungle bunnies, which could be why so many of us act like savages.'

'What will you do with your Ph D?' McKenna asked.

George smiled, eyes gleaming, and McKenna sensed in him the same swift, disconcerting changes of mood so characteristic of Phoebe. 'Become an upwardly mobile nigger!'

'What do your parents do?'

'My dad works the railways, like a lot of black people, and my mother's a house-slave, like a lot of women.'

'You're becoming a bit tedious.' McKenna lit a cigarette, watching the other man through a drift of smoke. As the sky beyond the window faded into summer twilight, and the room grew darker, he became like a shadow.

'You'll still be able to see my teeth and the whites of my eyes,' George said.

'I have some idea of the way immigrants feel.' McKenna's voice was tetchy. 'It's a hangover of the empire mentality.'

'And nothing to do with skin colour. The English blame us for losing it all. You're as white as the whitest white trash, and you probably have more problems than I do, because you don't expect them.'

'I came to talk about Ned, not myself,' McKenna said. 'Who were his friends? Who loved him?'

'Phoebe. Annie. Me.' George paused. 'And perhaps that tramp they call after the Prophet of Bangor. He's known Ned's family since the year dot.'

'You mean Robin Ddu? Black Robin?'

'That's him, but he's not black. He's an unwashed white man.'

'The last time I saw him was when he tried to smash Burton's window for some new gear, so we locked him up for the night.'

'Did you delouse the police station afterwards?'

McKenna smiled. 'And itched for days, wholly unreasonably.'

'It's measure of prejudice, isn't it?' George commented. 'Edith wouldn't have him in the house, so he and Ned used to get together in a pub.'

'Did Ned ever go away?'

'Occasionally, but only to the farm. He found travelling stressful and uncomfortable and frightening because it reminded him of the enforced journeys to Denbigh Hospital, which is what I meant about conditioning and experiences of probability. When outer life intrudes on inner life, it can change your mental climate from fair weather to foul, and, as Ned couldn't trust that a journey intended to end somewhere else wouldn't terminate in Denbigh, he did most of his wandering within touching distance of base.'

'What's the subject of your thesis?'

'How, when and why the Welsh diaspora came about, and its effects.'

'As when Madog ap Benfraes allegedly discovered America long before anyone else knew the place existed?'

'And left a tribe of Indians speaking Welsh to prove it.' Emptying his tankard, George added: 'Ned was helping me with the cultural impact of Welsh emigration for people on the receiving end, and the inward movement which arose as a consequence.'

'The family slaves,' McKenna said.

'The men worked the slate quarry, and the women tended the house and farm. Quite a lot of them are buried in the village churchyard, but one had a granite headstone in that sea of slate because he was a free man by the time he died. He wouldn't be cowed in death by the slate which enslaved him in life.' Rising to go to the kitchenette, he said, 'I'll make coffee.'

Standing with his back to McKenna, waiting for the kettle to boil, he put sugar and cream on a tray and spooned instant coffee into mugs. 'You know, Ned understood concepts most of us don't even know exist, and not only because he was at odds with normal society. Until he went to university, he'd never set foot outside his home territory, never seen the sea or a city, never moved beyond that huge massif between here and where he came from. Those mountains were an impenetrable barrier, both physically and psychologically, defining the psychological distances of Wales and the nature of the psychological landscape, and once he went beyond them, he became a refugee.' He poured boiling water on the granules of coffee, and returned to his chair, setting the tray on the floor. 'He taught me to look at the solid world in its metaphysical sense and see the endlessness of possibilities and connections, and in the broadest sense, the infinite impacts of human interaction.'

'So, that's one legacy we know of.' McKenna picked up his mug. 'Even if it's intangible. We're having problems with his physical leavings. Could you help us sort his books and documents? They haven't been touched so far.'

George nodded. 'I don't think he owned anything of real value. He lost most of the good stuff in a fire, and what's left of his share in the farm reverts to the rest of the family.' He paused. 'The farm's well named, isn't it? Ned said it was poetic justice.'

'You've lost me again.'

'In a famous mediaeval poem, there's a house called Llys Ifor which falls into ruin. Ned reckoned the memory of all that's happened in a place survives, so as the Jones's Llys Ifor housed the family's greed alongside the slaves' misery, he thought it only right the house should eventually collapse under the weight of negative emotion.' He paused, coffee mug half-way to his lips. 'His ideas took on a life of their own, you know. My head must be as full of his thoughts as Phoebe's.'

'She was desperately anxious we shouldn't try to open the Box of Dreams and the Box of Clouds. D'you know what's in them?'

'Dreams and clouds, I guess. I don't think they can be unfastened, anyway. They're sealed right around with brass straps.' George smiled. 'Did you find the Box of Lies, too? I know that opens, because I often saw Ned sticking bits of paper in there.'

'What does it look like?'

'It's an old shoe-box, made from that thick, brown, old-fashioned cardboard.' George smiled again, teeth gleaming. 'He had another one like it, which he said was for pieces of paper with dark intentions, but I don't know if that had a name, as well. He was obsessed with paper.'

'I gathered that from the state of his room.'

'Edith called it a germ's paradise, and said it was no wonder he was never well. She'd stand at the door sometimes, clucking and fidgeting, almost begging Ned to agree to a good clear out, but he wouldn't, of course. He once told her everyone's history is written down somewhere, including all her deepest fears and secrets, and psyched her up so much I thought she'd collapse.'

'That wasn't very kind, and it could be construed as blackmail.'

'Oh, come on!' George taunted. 'Ask Iolo Williams how crucial paper is: his whole career's built on a few scraps of it.'

10

Hazy streaks of pink and purple, the lingering remnants of the day, lit the sky to the west as McKenna locked his car and went through the back entrance of the police station, the harsh white interior lights dazzling his dark-adapted eyes.

Behind a desk completely overwhelmed with paper, Dewi laboured, reading and puzzling and sorting, neat piles growing at his elbow, and on the floor by his feet. 'Before you ask, sir, I've nothing to report,' he said. 'This is only phase one. Phase two starts when I finish putting this lot into some kind of coherent order, which will probably be,' he added, indicating the stack of boxes as yet untouched, 'some time next month.'

'Have you come across a Box of Lies yet?' McKenna asked. 'An old brown cardboard shoe-box?'

'If you look in that carton by your feet, sir, you'll see it's full of old brown cardboard shoe-boxes.' He leaned back and stretched, rolled-up shirt sleeves grimy with dust. 'And unless there's a label to tell me, how will I know which one's got lies in it?'

'I've no idea.' McKenna yawned. 'Anyway, either to-morrow or Thursday, depending on Edith's state of equilibrium, you're to help George Polgreen sort the books and papers we left in Ned's room.'

'Is there an actual point to this paper-chasing, sir? The drugs and bracelet are more important.'

'You're looking for motive.' McKenna glanced at his watch. 'And you can pack up for tonight, as I've no wish to be rumoured a slave-driver by the canteen gossip.'

'I'll finish this batch first. By the way, Inspector Rowlands is waiting in your office. He had trouble with the statements.'

Rowlands was dozing in McKenna's chair, head nod-ding, mouse-brown hair ruffled by a breeze through the open window. He jumped like a frightened cat when McKenna coughed.

'You should've been away long ago,' McKenna said, tak-ing another chair. 'It's a long drive to your home territory.'

'I might look for digs for the time being. My wife said it's less disruptive if she knows I'm away for good, rather than not knowing what time I'll get in of an evening.' He reached for a cigarette, pushing the packet towards McKenna. 'I'm a bit concerned about Janet. I had to send her home.'

'Why?'

'She interviewed that sulky French piece while I talked to the professor, and twice I heard her rush upstairs to the bathroom. She said the woman's perfume was making her feel sick.'

'She was supposed to see her doctor this evening, but she missed the appointment because I kept her late.'

Rowlands smoked in silence, then said: 'She's pregnant, isn't she? My wife was just the same both times.'

'Have you said anything to Dewi?'

'Good heavens, no! It's Janet's business. I just told her to see the doctor first thing in the morning.'

'Let's hope she takes more notice of you than she does of me, then,' McKenna said. 'She can be very wilful.' He tapped ash into an overfull tray. 'How did you get on with the Williamses? Did you take sample fingerprints?'

'I got on extremely badly, and so did Janet. They were hostile, rude, arrogant, and completely uncooperative, and if we want their prints, even for elimination purposes, we'll have to get a court order.'

'Didn't you say we could arrest them for obstruction?'

Rowlands nodded. 'He stood there quivering with rage, a huge glass of neat gin in his hand, and she stood beside him, sneering as only the French can, calling us "*les flics*", which is French for the lowest form of police life. Maybe you should have gone, and thrown your rank around a bit.'

'Oh, I wouldn't rank high enough to make the difference.' McKenna smiled wearily. 'Perhaps Ms Bradshaw will oblige us.'

11

When McKenna arrived home, his two cats were draped along the parlour window-ledge, while in the garden, two of their friends performed an open-air concert. When his joined in a chorus, he thought their music sounded rather like Schoenberg. As soon as he opened the back door, the two songsters scarpered over the wall, his own in pursuit, and he lingered for a while, waiting for them to return, night scents drifting past and occasional traffic on the distant main road disturbing the edge of the silence around him.

He made supper, put out fresh food and water for the animals, and tried to call Janet, to find she had switched on her answering machine. Wondering if Edith had surfaced from her drugged stupor, he fell asleep on the chesterfield, not to stir even when the feline pursuit began to chase its own tail as the two songsters rushed through the open back door and took flight up the staircase, his own animals close behind.

1

The postman delivered only a few circulars to McKenna on Wednesday morning. Relieved, he read the invitations and exhortations on every garish piece of paper in each envelope, before tossing them in the bin.

A strange car occupied the space next to his parking bay in the station yard, a big angular vehicle the colour of shiny coal, with alloy wheels, smoked glass windows, and a soft top folded neatly down to expose a chic functional interior.

'Nice car, isn't it, sir?' Dewi lounged against the back door. 'It's also got fuel injection, power steering, and it'll easily top 130.'

'Very impressive.' He stood back, surveying the lines, imagining himself behind the wheel on the open road. 'Whose is it?'

Dewi grinned enormously. 'Mine.' He left his vantage post, and walked over. 'I bought if off Geraint, and it's definitely totally legit. There's even a Stealth tracking system, in case some bugger tries to nick it.' Reaching into his pocket for a handkerchief, he rubbed at a minute smudge on the wing. 'I got a decent trade-in, so it hasn't quite put me in hock for the next twenty years.'

•   •   •

Shrouded in grubby dust-sheets, the corridor outside Diana Bradshaw's office was a jumble of ladders, rags, cans of paint, cartons of white spirit, and brushes in many sizes. As McKenna sat down beside her desk, she yawned, and he thought that with her face devoid of make-up, she looked more human and approachable. 'Hard to sleep when it's so hot at night, isn't it?' he ventured.

She stared at him, eyebrows drawn together, her eyes a little bloodshot. 'Are you trying to be funny?'

'Of course not. No-one sleeps well this weather.'

'Especially not when they're disturbed every half-hour or so?'

'I don't understand.'

'Don't you know what happened overnight?' She tapped the single sheet of paper on the desk, and he noticed her chipped nail varnish. 'Because the officers in this station don't seem to be able to deal with the most trivial matters a rookie straight from training college would take in his stride, I had barely two hours sleep!'

'May I?' Taking the paper, McKenna read of a summer's night riven with human and animal endeavour. An elderly woman, putting a milk bottle on her doorstep, had watched a polecat wriggling along Mount Street, its tail brushing dust off the road, then 'Trumpton', as the fire brigade was known, were called just before midnight to quench a late-night barbecue which tipped over and set fire to a hedge, while a young mother in Maesgeirchen, retrieving her washing from the line, found someone had forestalled her and filched her new lace brassiere and matching knickers. Pushing their state of the art vehicle to its limits, the traffic police chased a boy-racer from the wealthier shores of Anglesey, joy-riding in his mother's turbo-charged sports car, hurtling over Menai Bridge as some poor young men from Bangor's council estate crossed from the mainland to the island by walking the bridge suspension chains rather than the footway. 'All we need follow up is the washing line theft. There was a spate of those last summer, too.'

'Was Superintendent Griffiths consulted over every little incident?' she asked coldly.

'No, ma'am, because he didn't insist on prior consultation before manpower or money was deployed, as you did. So, unless you allow people to use their initiative, you can look forward to many more disturbed nights.' As she opened her mouth to speak, he went on, irritated beyond deference. 'We have experienced officers at all ranks in this sub-division, and twenty-four hour back-up at divisional HQ. If you need to know of something, you'll be told, and on the odd occasion when communication or judgement fails, we pick up the pieces later.' He rose. 'By the way, are you particularly busy this morning?'

'Why?'

'Professor Williams and his wife were singularly uncooperative to wholly reasonable requests, and they might be less inclined to argue with you than they were with Rowlands.'

2

Iolo Williams's silver car again flaunted itself in the sunshine of Glamorgan Place, and edging his own unremarkable motor into the space behind, McKenna decided the vehicle was as vulgar as its owner.

Rowlands examined the Jaguar's leather interior and in-car toys. 'Being a professor is more lucrative than I thought.'

'He writes books, as well, and goes on lecture tours.'

'He'd need to sell thousands of books to cover the insurance,' Rowlands commented. 'And what about the big Edwardian house on Menai Strait? And the hired help?'

'Maybe someone left him the house. There was money in

Wales at one time, you know. Ned's family had plenty, and Edith isn't exactly shooing wolves from the door.'

'We know where their loot comes from. I think I'll check out the professor.'

'Why? Maybe his wife's rich. Maybe his first wife won the pools and paid him to leave her.'

'And maybe not.' Rowlands walked up the path. 'Has he got any kids? And where *is* wifey number one, anyway?'

'I don't know! And I don't think kids or first wife are relevant.'

'According to Prys, without knowing the facts, you can't know what's relevant and what isn't.'

'You're beginning to sound like him,' McKenna said, waiting for someone to answer the door. 'As for facts, it's a relevant fact that the professor is here, rather than sitting in his big Edwardian house, where Ms Bradshaw and Janet expect him to be.'

The other man raised his eyebrows. 'Surely Bradshaw will have telephoned first, to make sure they're in?'

Solange answered the summons, dressed again in black, but embellished today with a necklace of heavy gold box links. Matching ear-rings stretched her lobes with their weight. Squinting in the sunlight, she looked them over from head to foot, then tossed her head and clicked off along the hall, calling: '*Les flics! Encore!*' before disappearing into the sitting room.

Iolo erupted from the kitchen. 'What the hell d'you want now?'

'A little civility wouldn't come amiss,' McKenna said. 'My superintendent is on her way to see you, as you were so unhelpful last night.'

'What?' The professor's face, pasty and sour-looking, paled to the hue of dirty flour.

'Superintendent Bradshaw is on her way to see you and

Mrs Williams about the unfinished business of statements and fingerprints.'

Edith sidled around the sitting room door, wispy and pallid. 'What's happening? Why is everybody shouting? I've got *such* a headache.'

Iolo turned to her. 'We're not shouting, dear. Everyone's a little tense. We've got to go.' For the first time, McKenna heard soemthing other than harshness in his voice.

'Why?' She tilted her head, like a child.

'Professor Williams wasn't able to finish his statement last night,' McKenna said. 'Two officers are waiting at his house at the moment.'

'Statements about what?' Edith peered at the men on her doorstep. 'He hasn't done anything.' She bowed her head, and McKenna watched tears squeeze from her eyes. 'I can't stand this! I really can't!'

McKenna took her arm, persuading her to the kitchen and into a chair. 'Where are the girls?'

'I don't know.'

'Are they out?'

'I don't know!' She looked around the room, then jumped to her feet, snatched a bottle of tablets from the counter, and clutched it to her chest.

'You must have some idea where they are?'

'Why can't you leave me alone? I told you about Ned's shirt, and you said it'd be all right, and now you won't leave me alone!' More tears trickled down the side of her nose. Her eyes were bloodshot and her whole body trembled.

McKenna sat down and lit a cigarette. 'You already know what we must do, and why.'

She began to struggle with the bottle top.

'Are tablets the answer?' he asked. 'They could make you feel worse.'

'They make me feel better!'

'Aren't they more like a crutch which keeps collapsing when you least expect it?'

'I need them!'

He reached for the ashtray on the counter, and found it full of lipstick-stained butts. 'Why was Mina prescribed drugs?'

'*She* needed them.'

'Why?'

'She wasn't happy.'

'Is she happier now?'

'I don't know! She won't talk to me!' She slumped like a rag doll. 'I'm her mother, and she won't talk to me, and Phoebe speaks to me as if I'm stupid.' She fell silent, turning the bottle round and round in her hands.

'You were left to bring up the girls on your own, and that's hard for anyone. I haven't met Mina, but you should be proud of the other two.' He dropped ash on top of the stained butts. 'I know Phoebe can be challenging, but that's her, and her age.'

'She's very clever, you know. Ned said she could do anything she wanted.'

'She's grieving for him.' He paused. 'And you're probably doing the same. He lived here a long time, and died very suddenly in very distressing circumstances.'

'I'm afraid,' Edith whispered. 'It's all so threatening. *You're* threatening.'

'Yes, I know.' He stubbed out the cigarette, spilling ash on the table, the stench from the ashtray nauseating.

'I'm not always like this,' she added.

'I don't expect you are.' He smiled. 'And I don't think you need to be afraid.'

'But I am, because if somebody *did* kill Ned, they might come back for the girls, or even me.'

•　•　•

The bruise on Phoebe's face had changed colour. 'Annie *told* Mama we were going shopping. We've only been out half an hour. The solicitor's coming at half ten.'

The kitchen was crowded with women and shopping bags and the child, who leaned against her grandmother, staring at McKenna.

'Where's Mina?' he asked.

'In her room,' Annie said.

'Having a sulkfest,' Phoebe added. 'And she didn't eat any breakfast, so she's probably getting anorexic. She's prone to hysterical responses.'

'Cassandra would be a better name for you,' Annie told her. 'Make yourself useful, and put away the shopping.'

Methodically piling foodstuffs in cupboards and refrigerator, Phoebe said: 'George calls me a *venticello*. It's Italian for a little wind, or in other words, a gossip.' Seeing the bottle of tablets still clutched in her mother's fist, she groaned. 'Have you taken some more?'

Sighing, Edith relinquished the bottle, dropping them on the table with a little clatter, and rose to her feet, stiff and bent like an old woman. Bethan caught hold of her skirt, and, as she ruffled the child's hair, McKenna felt a twist of sympathy for her.

'No, dear. They don't really help, do they?'

'We've been telling you that for years.' Exasperation sharpened Phoebe's voice.

'Take Bethan out to play while your mother sorts herself out,' McKenna told her. 'The house is a bit like a three ring circus.'

'Have you seen George yet?' she demanded. 'And did you telephone Auntie Gladys?'

'Yes, no, and I don't want a lecture.'

She stared mutely, then took her niece by the arm and trudged outside. He saw the cat crouched on the doorstep,

waiting for her, and watched the little trio go up the path
and disappear through the gate in the wall.

'You've hurt her feelings,' Annie commented.

'She'll get over it,' Edith said. 'She's far too pushy at
times.' She poured water into the coffee percolator, and
flicked the switch. 'My solicitor's coming to look after
Phoebe's interests,' she told McKenna, 'but I'm not sure
Mina doesn't need him more.'

'Why?' Annie asked.

'Because.' Filling a tray with cups and saucers, Edith
again turned to her visitor. 'Will you take her statement? I
think I can trust you not to hurt her.'

By lunchtime, McKenna had learned only that Edith, faced
with a situation beyond her control, harboured a reservoir
of fortitude beneath the surface instability, and his estima-
tion of her grew.

Barricaded behind her cat, its front paws spread over her
knees like tiny portcullises, Phoebe punished his rebuke
with monosyllabic, almost truculent, responses, and gave
no further definition to the hazy picture of a family going
about its usual business on a sweltering August afternoon,
in complete ignorance of impending tragedy.

Then Mina came to sit beside the family solicitor in the
cool airy sitting room, and, although inclined to be preju-
diced by all he had heard to her detriment, McKenna still
found himself half-enchanted by her. She was dressed simply, in pale blue jeans and a white T shirt, the corn-coloured
hair held back from her face by two thin braids, obscuring
the ears of which Phoebe was so critical.

'I was at work all day Friday,' she said, her voice tenta-
tive. 'I've got a holiday job with Merlin Security. They'll tell
you if you ask.'

'When did you last see Ned? Or speak to him?'

'I can't remember. I went out with my boyfriend on Thursday night, straight from work. He works for Merlin, too.'

'Did you see much of Ned?'

'Not really. He only had meals with us.'

'Did you go to his room at all?'

'When?'

'Any time.'

'Mama made me take him a drink, sometimes. Or messages.'

'How did you get on with him?'

She glanced at the solicitor, then twisted her hands together. 'I don't know.' She leaned forward, hair swinging around her face.

'Did you like him?'

'I don't know. He could be a bit frightening.'

'Why?'

'Because he was old. His false teeth clicked when he talked, and sometimes, they made a sort of hissing noise, and you could see flying spittle in the sunshine.' She shivered, wrapping her arms around her body. 'And he seemed to be lots of different people inside one body, and you never knew which one you'd meet. Annie said his pain and illness made him like that. She didn't mind. Phoebe didn't, either, but I couldn't know which person I was supposed to be with him. I couldn't trust him.' She looked up at McKenna. 'Do you know what I mean?'

'Does it matter?' the solicitor asked. 'I can't see the relevance.'

'Did you ever go into his room when he wasn't there?' McKenna persisted.

She flushed, then nodded, her whole body stiff.

'What did you do?'

Twisting her hands until the knuckles whitened, she said: 'It was like Annie and Phoebe were his own daughters, and

I was someone who'd been left on the doorstep. He loved little Bethan, too.'

'What did you do?' McKenna repeated.

'Mama said I was just trying to get him to notice me.'

'Mr McKenna,' the solicitor intervened, 'just what is your point?'

'I've been told Mina played tricks on Mr Jones.'

'What kind of tricks?'

'Interfering with his things, hiding his false teeth.'

'That's a far cry from giving him drugs she knew would probably kill him, which is what I think you're implying.'

'I'm trying to establish the nature of his relationships with everyone in this house, and elsewhere, and it seems his and Mina's wasn't very satisfactory.'

'He didn't like me!' Mina's voice rose. 'He never liked me!'

'Why not?'

'I don't know! He used to upset me when I was little.'

'How?'

She dragged her hands through the sumptuous hair. 'I can't explain!' She was close to tears. 'He was cold with me, but he was sweet with Annie. He talked to her, and took her for walks, and he did the same with Phoebe, right from when she was born, but he just ignored me, and I don't know why.'

Edith had no answer to the puzzle when McKenna again questioned her. 'Some people simply don't like each other. You can't do anything about it. Anyway, Mina made her own friends. She's always had lots of friends.'

'But she must have resented the situation.'

'I suppose so.'

'And perhaps you resented Ned's attitude, on her behalf? That would be only natural.'

'You know I didn't get on with him very well. We had nothing in common, and even though he came because I had needs, I was useful to him and his needs, as well.' Reserves of strength well in hand, she added: 'You can't make it into something it isn't. Families always have their little feuds.' She frowned. 'And I don't like you digging up these things. They might be trivial to you, but they're private to me, and you haven't got the right to pry like this.'

'We'll go on digging until we unearth the motive for his death.'

'Well, you won't find it in this house!'

'So would you know where else I can look?'

'Of course not!' For a moment, she looked like Phoebe. 'Why should I?'

Lighting another cigarette, McKenna said: 'You probably knew him better than anyone.'

'Why? Because we were of an age? That means nothing. Phoebe was closest to him, then Annie, I suppose, and that George. He wasn't easy to know, and he didn't like revealing himself. I expect he'd had too many psychiatrists poking and prying over the years.'

'Forgive my asking, but have you ever had psychiatric treatment?'

'When Mina was a baby, I started having upsets, so my doctor put me on tranquillizers. He didn't warn me about the addiciton.' She paused, toying with a half-consumed cup of coffee. 'Perhaps he didn't know. I didn't, until I tried to stop taking them. Sometimes, I hate the way they make me feel, then I'm terrified of how I might feel without them. In the end, you don't know who you are any longer.'

'And has Mina ever had psychiatric treatment?'

'No.' Edith's voice was sharp, defensive. 'And I don't want to talk about her like this. I know Phoebe's been gossiping, and I expect Annie's had her say. There's little or no privacy between them.' She fell silent, then added: 'Maybe Mina stopped talking to me because she's just trying to keep some of her life to herself.'

'Phoebe told me about the incident with the lavatory seat, and the way Mina reacted,' McKenna commented. 'Are you afraid of her?'

'I was afraid *for* her. Afraid she'd get like Ned, or even worse, like me, so I took her to the doctor. He tried her with this new anti-depressant, but she said it made her feel "out of herself" and very strange, so she stopped taking it.' She paused again, tapping her fingeranils on the table top. 'But of course, Phoebe's never let her forget it. She's very judgemental at the best of times, and quite cruel towards Mina, and this wretched curiosity of hers gets the better of any consideration for other people's feelings. Ned could be just the same.'

'I see.' McKenna too fell silent, watching her, irritated by her involuntary restlessness, the twitching fingers and eyelids. Now and then, she smoothed her dress over her belly, as if to remind herself of the place from which the girls of whom they spoke had struggled head first into life.

'I've always felt I have to protect Mina,' Edith went on. 'Be there for her more. The other two had Ned, but she had no-one.' She clasped her hands tightly together, and shivered. 'I know what you're thinking. You're making up a picture of her not being quite right in the head, and so jealous of Phoebe and Annie that she killed Ned out of spite.'

'And don't you fear the same?'

'I did!' She shuddered so violently the table rocked. 'On Friday, I did. But then you said he would've died as soon as he took the drugs, so I knew it couldn't be her.'

'We still don't know how they were ingested. Can you remember anything else about that day? Something Ned might've done out of the ordinary, or different from his usual routines?'

'I've told you!' she insisted, near exasperation. 'I made

sandwiches for lunch from the remains of Thursday's roast, he came down about two, and we ate in the kitchen, then he went back upstairs. And he died.' Tears glimmered in her eyes. 'He was all alone when he died.'

'Did he ever make his own snacks and drinks in his room?'

'Why won't you listen? He wouldn't have foodstuffs lying around. I know his room looks a mess, but it's not dirty. He was very clean, very particular, and he said food encourages insects and mice.'

'Did he ever use sugar?'

Edith sighed again. 'None of us does. You've taken what's left of the packet I bought months ago. Annie used some for cakes, and I'll rub sugar on roasting lamb if there's no honey, but I didn't on Thursday. I used honey, and a touch of rosemary.'

McKenna stubbed out his cigarette in an ashtray now overflowing with his own leavings. 'We'd like you all to give urine samples for testing. The antibiotics must have been in something everyone had.'

'Wouldn't we have noticed?'

'Not unless you had Ned's sensitivity.'

'But isn't it rather late? Any trace would be long gone.'

'Not necessarily. I'll get some sterile containers delivered.'

'I'll tell the girls,' Edith offered, then glanced at him warily. 'What will you do with these bits of us you're taking away? First you took our words and our fingerprints, and now you want stuff from our bodies.'

'Unless required for evidence, they'll be destroyed.'

3

The offices of Merlin Security, where Mina Harris filled the days of her long summer vacation, were housed in a converted chapel at the lower end of Bangor High Street, but the main depot occupied a small unit on the industrial estate, at the bottom of a hill close to the railway line. McKenna parked his car outside the high chain-link fence around the site, and nodded to the three young men, stripped to the waist, who lay on a patch of scrubby grass under a fierce afternoon sun.

'I'm looking for Jason Lloyd,' he said.

'Who wants me?' The youth raised himself on his elbows, chest muscles rippling.

McKenna showed his badge. 'Police.'

Jason scrambled to his feet, brushing dust and shards of grass from his torso and trousers. 'What took you so long?' Grinning at his mates, he strutted into the shed-like building.

Until his eyes adusted to the sudden gloom, McKenna was almost blind. Following the shadowy figure, he passed white vans with fluorescent stripes and logos, hoisting tackle and racks of tools, skirted puddles of stinking oil on the rough concrete floor, and edged down an alleyway between strong steel cages bolted to floor and wall, which were stacked higgledy-piggledy with packages and cartons.

Barging into a lighted cubicle at the back of the building, where a fat elderly man sweated his way through the day in a miasma of fumes, Jason said: 'Out! I gotta talk to the police.'

The man struggled upright, swearing under his breath, shirt button straining over his pink belly, then waddled out, leaving a vapour trail of sour sweat and tobacco. Jason took the newly vacant chair, and pointed McKenna to its rickety twin. 'I keep telling him about bathrooms being invented,' he said, waving his hand towards the departed figure, 'but he takes no notice. He smokes so much he sweats nicotine.'

'There are worse things.'

'Like what?' Jason asked, eyes gleaming. 'Putting a miserable old sod out of his misery?' As he leaned forward, the overhead light glinted on the tiny silver crosses and studs piercing both his ears. 'I've heard it would've been a kindness to put Ned Jones down like a sick old animal, and you can ask Phoebe Harris if you don't believe me.' He smirked at McKenna. 'I suppose you're here to see what you can pin on me, aren't you?'

'Why should I be?'

'Because I'm here, and you lot hate me. Why, I can't imagine!'

'Because you were a pain in the arse from the day you started walking, and it's only luck you never got caught! We haven't forgotten your juvenile pranks.'

'And that's all they were,' Jason countered. 'A bit of skylarking.'

McKenna looked around the windowless little office. 'When you're done with the civil rights bit, perhaps you'd tell me how long you've worked here?'

'Since I finished the YTS. I got lucky and got a job, so don't bugger it up by making nasty untruthful insinuations to my boss.'

'Does Mina Harris come here at all?'

'Only if the boss sends her. She works in the main office.' He gave McKenna a tight, wolfish smile. 'She was there all day Friday.'

'I know. I've already checked. Where were you on Friday?'

Jason tilted the chair, and reached behind him for a wad of worksheets clipped to a board. Thumbing through, he said: 'I was on a bloody split shift for starters, because we've got one off sick and two on holiday. I worked six in the morning 'til two in the afternoon, went home, had a kip, woke up, had tea, and came back on at ten. You can ask my mam.'

'What time did you finish?'

'Seven o'clock Saturday morning.'

'You do mobile patrols, don't you? Can you give me route details for both the shifts?'

'I can, yeah.' Jason nodded, grinning. 'But they won't be

much use, because there's only my word for what I did and where I did it. I often don't see a soul, except your lot poncing around in their flash cars.'

'You must call in every so often?'

'Yeah, and I could be calling from the top of Snowdon, and nobody any the wiser.'

'When did you last go to the Harris house?'

'Yesterday.'

'Before then.'

'Sunday.'

'How often are you there?'

Jason shrugged. 'Quite a lot. Edith likes me. Dear little Phoebe doesn't, as she's no doubt told you.'

'And had you ever been in Mr Jones's room?'

'I've been everywhere in the house.' He grinned again. 'Know what I mean?'

'Edith Harris would probably like you a lot less if she knew that,' McKenna commented.

'I shan't be telling her, and if you do, it'd be from spite.'

'Does Phoebe know?'

'I expect so.' Anger glittered in his eyes, and pulled at his mouth. 'She knows bloody everything else!'

McKenna rose. 'I'll want your fingerprints. Did you eat at the house at all between Thursday and now?'

'Can't remember.'

'We're taking urine samples as well as prints, so I think we'll include you in the sweep.'

'Please yourself.' Jason stood up, casting a distorted shadow across the desk. 'I've nothing to hide.'

4

Diana Bradshaw sat in McKenna's office, her chair under the open window, smells of paint and white spirit larding the air. 'Are we wasting our time?' she asked. 'Prys is almost invisible behind that mound of paper, Janet's making another mound from all the statements, and there isn't a shred of evidence pointing towards either motive or murder.'

'How did the professor and his wife conduct themselves with you?'

'Very well. I don't know what the fuss was about.' She uncrossed her legs and smoothed her skirt. 'Did you know Solange Williams was quite a famous model before she married? She's still very chic, isn't she?'

'She's certainly well-dressed,' McKenna agreed. 'She has a nice line in jewellery, too.'

'I said she must find life in Bangor very dull after such an exciting career, but she said not. She goes to France quite often, anyway.'

'Rowlands commented about their high standard of living. He hadn't realized professors do so well.'

'He's a writer, too.'

'I wouldn't imagine his books sell more than a few hundred copies.'

'Dear me! You men are so competitive, aren't you?' She smiled. 'Ned Jones probably never amounted to anything because he couldn't face the competition, so he gave up, and retired into ill health.'

'Iolo Williams said much the same,' McKenna said. 'By the way, did either of them go to the house on Friday?'

'They last called on Wednesday afternoon, went away on Thursday night to London, and didn't return until Saturday. He was at some do arranged by his publisher.'

'We're taking urine samples from everyone who might have eaten or drunk at the house last week.' McKenna smiled winningly. 'I'm sure the professor and his wife will take the news better from you.'

• • •

Dewi swore as McKenna caught the edge of the desk with his hip, knocking one of the piled-up boxes to the floor. Kneeling to retrieve the scattered pieces of paper, McKenna said: 'Why didn't you have the sense to fasten them up with rubber bands?'

'Because I can't find any! Because nothing's where it should be 'cos of the bloody decorators!'

McKenna sat back on his heels, looking through the sheaf of papers. 'These are all bits and bobs about Iolo Williams, going way back.' He scanned the pages. 'Press cuttings, book reviews, details of lectures, copies of the manuscripts he discovered . . .'

'Every one of those shoe-boxes is full of stuff about the professor,' Dewi said.

'So where's Ned's Box of Lies?'

Dewi shrugged. 'Take your pick, unless it was just a joke.'

McKenna arranged for the pathology department to deliver sterile containers for the urine samples, and to collect them the following day.

'The professor and his wife must've taken to Bradshaw,' Rowlands observed. 'They agreed immediately.'

'I think they've found some common ground,' McKenna said. 'At least, the ladies have. Ms Bradshaw found Solange very "chic".'

'Did she? I'd be more inclined to call her sluttish, spiteful, rude, and ill-bred, whatever fancy clothes she's wearing.'

'Different races have their own frames of reference,' McKenna pointed out. 'French men, for instance, feel almost obliged to have a mistress as well as a wife, and French law accommodates the *crime passionnel*, which to us is no more defensible than any other unlawful killing.'

'Dewi says Jack Tuttle's having a French girl on an exchange visit.'

'He's having two, one for each of his twin daughters. They went to France last month, so Jack's taken his wife touring for a couple of weeks before they collect the twins and the exchanges.'

'Well, I'll give him a week at most before he's desperate to invite Madame Guillotine over to join them.'

'D'you speak from experience, or simple francophobia?' McKenna asked.

'My sister did the exchange thing years ago, and we got landed with this absolutely awful girl from somewhere near Montpellier. She was the most spoiled, selfish brat I've ever come across, and so sullen and surly and sulky you could've throttled her! Solange has got exactly the same attitude, like you're the dog shit she's just scented under her nose.'

'That diatribe was riddled with alliterative "s" sounds.'

'You've got a weird thing about words, haven't you?'

'I read a lot. I even used to read the labels on bottles and jars, every word on hoardings in the street, and newspapers and magazines from cover to cover.'

'You must be afraid of missing something.' Rowlands smiled. 'Maybe you should take over from Dewi.' He rose and stretched. 'We could ask George Polgreen if he knows why Ned had five boxes crammed with stuff about Williams. I'm sure he'd say, seeing as the man's no friend of his.'

'D'you think Iolo's the killer?'

'Not really. I know he comes over to us as a nasty, arrogant sod, but we've seen his other side in the way he treats Edith. And when do we ever see the best in people? I think he's just shit-scared. Fear makes people very aggressive.'

'Then he must have a lot to fear.'

'People caught up in murder investigations get frightened. It's normal. Anyway, he hasn't got a discernible motive.'

'Nor has anyone else.'

'We'll find out who has, eventually.' Sitting down again and reaching for a cigarette, Rowlands added: 'It could even be someone we haven't come across yet.'

'This was a very intimate crime.'

'So who's in the frame? I expect Annie's got hidden depths, like most people, but I can't see her harbouring secrets worth killing for. She's got too much to lose.' Blowing smoke towards the ceiling, Rowlands talked on. 'I don't think the lovely Minerva's got enough between the ears for this scam, because it was quite a clever crime, and Edith would have been more likely to bash him over the head with a poker in a fit of hysterics.'

'So that leaves Solange.'

'And Phoebe, and I wondered if her almighty curiosity perhaps got out of hand. As Ned encouraged her to find things out for herself, she might have taken it into her head to feed him the drug as an experiment, to test his allergy.'

'You're describing a psychopath.'

'How do we know she isn't? D'you know, when she's older, I can see her in a lab grafting monkey heads on to human bodies, or *vice versa*, to see what happens. And,' he added, warming to the theme, 'Dewi said Ned could've been trying to write 'F-E-R-C-H" on his chest, which is Welsh for "daughter".'

'With the three of them under our noses, that obvious association of ideas is no brilliant piece of deduction,' McKenna commented. 'I'd say Phoebe's conscience controls her curiosity, but as asking questions is as natural to her as breathing, she picks up far more information than she knows, and it worries me that Ned's killer might realize that.'

5

Briefly released from drudgery, Dewi gunned the engine of his new car, sending plumes of smoke pulsing from the twin exhausts. Sunglasses on the bridge of his nose, bare arm resting on the door, he roared out from the yard behind the police station, turning heads as he cruised past the swimming baths and towards the pier. More heads swivelled when he parked, motor idling, to spend a few minutes watching yachts tacking down the Strait from Beaumaris to Menai Bridge, sails tautened by an off shore breeze. The sun, drifting towards the west, was searingly hot, the people who watched him in his gleaming car wilting in the heat. He reversed slowly out of the parking lot, then drove up the hill towards Siliwen Road, plunging into a green darkness of overhanging trees before emerging again into hot white light. At the end of the road, he made a sharp left turn into Holyhead Road, then into Glamorgan Place.

She was at the door before he reached the step, face shadowed by the wonderful hair.

'Are you really called Minerva?' he asked.

She nodded, gazing over his shoulder. 'Is that your car?'

'Why? Would you like a ride in it?'

She had no smile for him today. 'I just wondered.' Turning on her heel, she left him standing on the doorstep.

Nonplussed, he waited, then walked into the hall, and knocked tentatively at the sitting room door.

'There's nobody there.' Mina spoke from the rear of the hall. She was like a ghost, or a cat, appearing and disappearing without respect for the rules of solid matter. 'Annie's taken Mama and Phoebe and Bethan for a drive.'

'I'm supposed to meet my boss here,' Dewi said. 'And George Polgreen.'

'Oh, they're upstairs. You can go up.'

Long legs elegantly crossed, skin gleaming like the paint

on Dewi's car, George lounged in a battered leather arm-chair beside the desk, while the chair which had cradled Ned in death stood vacant in the far corner, already gathering dust.

McKenna sat on the dusty window-ledge, smoke from his cigarette drifting through the open window. 'It took me about four minutes to get here,' he commented, 'and I left after you. I suppose you went detouring in your tart-trap.' As Dewi reddened under his tan, McKenna added: 'Not that I blame you, but now you've arrived, you can pitch in with George, while I have another look over Ned's clothes and whatever.' He regarded the stacks of books and mounds of paper with dismay. 'Although we're probably wasting our time.'

'What was he doing with this lot?' Dewi hefted a pile of books on to the desk.

'Research,' George said, clearing a space. 'He'd spent the last twenty odd years analysing the influence of Welsh culture on European culture from the eighth century onwards. When we last discussed it, he'd got as far as 1750, and before you ask, a great many people all over the world would be very interested in what he was doing, so I was wondering,' he added, looking at McKenna, 'whether you could find out from the family if they'll let me finish his work.'

'Well, there's another motive.' Dewi opened the first book on the pile, its pages brittle and fragile, and began to read a copperplate inscription on the flyleaf. 'Mr McKenna killed him out of pique because he lost the Eisteddfod trophy, and you did it from greed because you wanted to steal his scholarship.'

'Are you serious?' George said. 'I should learn to keep my mouth shut in front of coppers, shouldn't I?'

'Why don't you both shut up?' McKenna asked equably, taking one of the brass-bound caskets from its shelf.

'They're not supposed to be opened, sir,' warned Dewi.

Shaking the box and hearing nothing, McKenna said: 'They must come undone somehow.'

'I don't think so.' George looked up. 'You can see where the brass straps were welded together, or whatever you do with brass.'

McKenna shook the other casket, again in vain, replaced both on the shelf, then took hold of the huge shell beside them and put it to his ear. Smiling, he crossed the room, held the shell to Dewi's ear, then to George's. 'It's true you can hear the sea, isn't it?' He touched the casket lids. 'I'd have thought dreams and clouds would have their music, too.' He went towards the door in the far wall, and up the remains of a servants' staircase to the bedroom.

Ned had slept in a high bed with carved head- and foot-boards, his head on plump feather pillows covered with white embroidered linen, his body under an old quilt sewn from patches of pretty silks and cottons. From his bed, he would have looked through the leaded casement window over tree-tops and the jumble of gables and roofs, towards a glimmer of sea in the distance.

A tall wardrobe to match the bed stood in shadow in the far corner, a companion chest under the window, its top filmed with dust. A tortoiseshell tray, leached of its rich colours by years of sunshine, held old silver cuff-links, a comb with a few strands of grey hair caught in the teeth, and a brush, backed with the same cloudy tortoiseshell, snarled with more strands of the same hair.

As McKenna opened the top drawer in the chest, scents of clean linen and old wood drifted up from a pile of neatly folded shirts, their cuffs and collars beginning to fray, the white cotton a little starchy and spotlessly clean. The next drawer housed three pairs of striped winceyette pyjamas with corded waists, and three pairs in paisley-patterned cotton for the warmer months, all meticulously clean and folded. In the bottom drawer were stacks of creamy inter-lock underpants, cut the old-fashioned way, a pile of dark grey woollen socks, all paired, two worn leather belts, and two pairs of elastic braces.

Ned's winter dressing gown hung on the back of the door, his few suits in the wardrobe, with his shoes, slippers, and one pair of walking boots in a tidy row under the window. In the wardrobe drawer, McKenna found the knitted waistcoats Edith had described, together with some well-worn jumpers, their elbows meticulously darned. Within reach of the bed was an ancient record player, housed in a walnut cabinet with its door slightly ajar, and, seating himself on a rush-seated oak chair, McKenna began to examine Ned's store of records.

Of Paul Robeson he knew, and John McCormack's plaintive tenor had never failed to bring tears to his mother's eyes, he recalled, reading the labels on the shiny black 78s, but Hubert Eisdell was unknown, as were some of the other artistes. The records were probably valuable, he thought, taking care not to rip the brown paper sleeves as he put them one by one on the floor, and even the newer vinyl LPs in plasticized wrappers would interest a collector. He tried to imagine the old man sitting in his bed, perhaps with one of his many books in his hands, perhaps just listening to his music, dreaming his dreams and remembering his memories, and was touched again by the sense of loss, of something gone from his own life before he realized its worth.

From the other room, he could hear the rustle of paper, the clump of book placed upon book, the low murmur of voices. He put the records back in the cabinet, closed the door and watched it move open again, then went through a low arched doorway into the bathroom, stooping to avoid the lintel.

He leaned against the half-tiled walls, looking at the white washbasin, the white lavatory with its wooden seat, the deep white cast-iron bath, and wondered why he had come here again, and what he hoped to find that the previous day's search had failed to unearth. Back in the bedroom, he knelt down to look under the bed, and dragged out a battered pigskin suitcase, almost holding his breath as he unfastened the worn straps, but apart from a lining of pale watered silk, faintly scented with old lavender, it was empty. He rose, brushing bits of fluff from his knees, and, glancing through the window to the back garden, saw a big marmalade cat sloping towards the gate in the wall, tail low to the ground.

6

Telephone receiver in one hand, McKenna pulled a cigarette from the packet with the other, and flicked his lighter. 'How long will the urine tests take?'

'Not long, as we know what we're looking for,' the pathologist said. 'You should find out who eats and drinks what in the Harris household, in case some of the tests are negative.'

'Why? He was poisoned by his lunch.'

'And whoever spiked his food probably refrained from eating the same.'

McKenna watched a smoke ring form itself above his head, then disperse. 'I'm going to Meirionydd to see his family later this week. Can I give them a time scale for release of the body?'

'Not until we have a date for the inquest.'

'Fine.' He tapped ash from the cigarette. 'Could you do me a favour?'

The other man sighed. 'Eifion said he never gets a minute's peace when you've got a mysteriously dead body. What d'you want?'

'Could you use your computer to take a short cut? I want to know if anyone with access to the house was prescribed tetracycline, say within the last three years.'

7

Shortly after four o'clock, Mina knocked on the door of Ned's room with a tray of tea and sandwiches. Silently, she cleared a space on the desk, put down the tray, and disappeared.

'I reckon you'd give a year's pay for a ride with her in your new car,' George said, biting into a sandwich.

'So?'

'So, be warned. She's a prick-tease, for one thing, and a headcase for another, and if Clyde sees you making eyes at her, he'll give you a hiding, because she belongs to him, and he's another headcase.'

'How d'you know?' Dewi asked.

'He threatened me not long ago because she said I'd been making eyes at her, then got very nasty when I said I wouldn't touch her with a barge-pole, and wanted to know what was wrong with her.'

'Have you got a girlfriend?'

George grinned. 'I'm thinking of advertising in the lonely hearts columns. What about you?'

'There's no-one at the moment,' Dewi admitted.

'There will be, before long, with that car.'

'Have you got a car?'

'Yes, but it's more often off the road than on. It needs a new engine.'

'Geraint'll fix you up, and he won't charge much if you say I sent you,' Dewi said. 'I'll give you his number.' He put his teacup in the saucer and opened a box file of loose papers. 'We haven't got very far, have we? Mr McKenna's hoping we'll somehow strike gold.'

'Ned was very secretive. I knew some things about him, Phoebe and Annie knew others, but nobody knew the whole man.'

'So are we wasting our time?'

George shrugged. 'McKenna asked me about the Box of Lies, but I'd never seen inside it. He said you've got five boxes all the same, all filled with stuff about Williams.'

'Press cuttings, book reviews, odds and sods like that.'

'Nothing personal or confidential, like letters?'

Refilling his teacup, Dewi said: 'I've not seen any letters apart from one from the Benefits Agency, threatening to suspend his incapacity benefit because of new eligibility rules, a couple from the Inland Revenue about taxing his pension, and a few old ones from his solicitor about family matters.'

'That's odd. He corresponded with a lot of people abroad about his research, and those letters aren't here. He wrote to the family, as well, and I know they wrote back quite often, because he'd read out bits of news and gossip.'

'Where else could they be? Could someone have them for safekeeping?'

'His solicitor in Bala, perhaps?'

'I spoke to him yesterday, and all he's got is a copy of the father's will. I'd better check with him again.' Retying the string around a stack of papers, Dewi put it aside, and reached for another. 'Who was Ned writing to abroad?'

'Celtic scholars, historians, linguists, musicologists; loads of people. Look in his address book: it's huge.'

'I haven't found an address book, huge or otherwise.'

8

Diana Bradshaw paced McKenna's office, executing neat turns, the soles of her elegant shoes sliding on the carpet.

During the course of the day, she had put make-up on her face. 'You only have this Polgreen's word for it. No-one else has mentioned letters, or an address book, so it's rather precipitate to question Edith Harris under caution.'

'She admitted tampering with the body,' McKenna pointed out. 'She conceded this morning that she feared her daughter had killed Ned, and she's extremely overwrought.'

'*Anyone* would be overwrought with what she's going through!' She sat down, rather suddenly, and stifled a yawn. 'And I don't want to be responsible for a complete breakdown because we put her under too much stress.'

'People have accused Ned of retreating into illness. Edith could be doing exactly the same.'

'Perhaps the letters and address book were removed after Janet attended the scene on Friday.'

'Uniform and forensics were there all the time, and Dewi stayed until the room was sealed. No-one went in, and nothing was taken. I checked.'

She leaned back in the chair, legs crossed, and swung one foot rather jerkily. 'Actually, I'm not happy about this Polgreen character being involved. Professor Williams doesn't have a good word to say for him.'

'George is the only one who knows anything about Ned's activities, and this isn't the first time Williams has badmouthed him.'

'I don't want him involved.' She rose. 'It's inappropriate.'

'I'll pass the word,' McKenna said. 'What about Edith?'

'I don't have much choice, do I? Call in a doctor, just in case , as well as her solicitor.'

Edith had exhausted her supply of fortitude. Face chalk-white, eyes red, hands trembling uncontrollably like dry twigs in the wind, she faced McKenna and Janet across the table in the interview room, her solicitor by her side. The pretty dress which had looked so fresh that morning hung around her body like grave-rags.

'You contacted the GP at around three forty-five on Friday afternoon,' McKenna said. 'Before he arrived, some fifteen minutes later, you straightened Ned's clothing. Is that correct?'

She nodded, her neck stiff. 'Yes.'

'And only you and Phoebe were in the house?'

'Yes.'

'Did Phoebe enter Ned's room?'

'I wouldn't let her. I didn't want her to see him.'

'You had lunch together, downstairs, at around two o'clock. Is that correct?'

'Yes.' Her voice was little more than a croak.

'What did you do afterwards?'

'I can't remember.'

'Please try, Mrs Harris. Did you wash the dishes?'

'Yes.' Her face brightened a little. 'Yes, I washed up and tidied the kitchen. Then I made myself some coffee.'

'Then what?'

'I took it to the sitting room.'

'What did you do there? Were you reading, watching television? Did you perhaps telephone someone?'

'I think I read the paper. I like to read the paper every day.'

'When did Ned return to his room?'

'As soon as we finished lunch.'

'What would he usually do in the afternoon?'

'I don't know. Write, or listen to his records, I suppose, if he wasn't going out.' Snatching a handkerchief from her pocket, Edith wiped her eyes, then began to tear at the fabric.

'You said you heard a noise, like a fall. What time was that?'

'I don't know.'

'Approximately.'

'I don't know!'

'Before three? After?' McKenna asked. 'How much time passed between your hearing a noise and going upstairs?'

'I don't know!' She balled the handkerchief, knuckles white. 'I thought he'd just dropped something. I started peeling vegetables for dinner.'

'Where were you when you heard the bump?'

'In the sitting room, I think.'

The solicitor intervened. 'Mr Harris made a number of alterations to the house. Originally, there were six ground floor rooms, but he knocked the breakfast room and sitting room into one, blocking off the back staircase, and partly extended the kitchen. As you know, Mr Jones's room faces the back, but the floor area is partly over the sitting room.'

'I could've heard it from the kitchen, as well,' Edith added. 'Sounds go up and down the staircase.'

'So when did you begin to worry?' McKenna asked.

'It sort of fretted at me, not being able to hear him. I even went into the hall once or twice to listen. You know, for shuffling noises, moving around noises.' She fell silent, tearing at the handkerchief again. 'It *felt* different, like I was alone in the house, and I knew I wasn't, so I went up again, and knocked very hard on the door.' Tears began to trickle down her cheeks. 'He didn't answer, so I went in, and found him like that.'

'Where exactly was Phoebe?'

'When?'

'What did she do after lunch?'

'I told you. She went for a walk, and the cat was wandering in and out of the kitchen, waiting for her. He kept getting under my feet.'

'When did she come back?'

'I can't remember. It's all a jumble in my head.'

'After you called the doctor? Before?'

'After.'

'Which way did she come into the house?'

'The back door. She uses the gate in the garden wall.'

'Did you see her come in?'

'I heard her.'

Shuffling through his notes, McKenna said: 'How many keys are there to Ned's room? We found his in the desk.'

'Two?' Edith said. 'I'm not really sure. I keep spare keys in the bureau in the study.'

'Who knows about the spare keys?'

'Everybody.'

'Jason?'

'Jason?'

'He's a frequent visitor,' McKenna said.

'Mina might have told him, but I wouldn't. There's no need for him to know, is there?'

'Do Phoebe and Mina have their own house keys?'

'Mina does. Phoebe's too young. Annie's got a key, too, and Lolo and Solange.'

'Why do the professor and his wife have keys?'

'In case I'm ill,' Edith said.

'Was Ned in the habit of locking his door?'

'Sometimes. He liked his privacy.'

'When would he lock the door? Day? Night? When he was out?'

'I don't know! I never checked!' She looked at the rag of linen in her hands. 'I remember opening his room now and then for the cleaner.'

'She comes every Wednesday, doesn't she? How long is she in the house?'

'All day.'

'Did she do Ned's room every week?'

'She did the bathroom and bedroom.' A brief, sad smile touched her lips. 'And the parts she could reach in his study. She was always complaining about only being able to do half a job in there.'

McKenna glanced through his notes. 'Did you hear any other odd noises on Friday afternoon?'

'Like what?'

'Anything unusual, out of place.'

'I don't think so.'

'Were the front and back doors open?'

'I can't remember about the front door. The back door was open because it was so hot.'

'Can you tell me how you buy your milk?' McKenna asked.

'Milk?' Edith's bloodshot eyes goggled.

'The antibiotics may have been dissolved in milk.'

'Oh.'

'Well?'

'The milkman leaves three pints a day.'

'What happens when you run short?'

'Phoebe goes to the shops.'

'Did you run short any day last week?'

She frowned. 'I'm not sure. I might've done.'

'Remembering that you're making this statement under caution, Mrs Harris,' McKenna said, 'is there anything you want to add, remove, or amend, in respect of the information you've already given?'

Edith looked to her solicitor. 'Is there?'

After Edith left, almost welded to her solicitor's arm as if that were another crutch, McKenna returned to his office. 'That was a total waste of time, and I've completely scuppered the chance of further co-operation from her.' Janet leaned on his desk, one hand massaging her abdomen.

'Have you seen the doctor yet?' he added.

'I'll live.' She smiled wanly.

'You look very pale, and people are beginning to notice your less than blooming health.'

'By "people", you mean Dewi Prys, I suppose.'

'No, not Dewi. Rowlands commented, and Diana Bradshaw asked if you had a dodgy health record.'

'Perhaps I should stick up a notice in the canteen: "Janet Evans is pregnant. Volunteers required to give the good news to her father, the Reverend Edwin Evans." '

'Have you seen him lately?'

'We spoke on the phone the other day. I can't face either him or my mother at the moment.' She sat down, and took cigarettes and lighter from her bag. 'And please don't lecture me about smoking, sir. I'm trying to cut down.'

'I wasn't going to. Have you been in touch with the baby's father yet?'

'I haven't done anything. I don't know what to do for the best, so I'm doing nothing. I decided yesterday I wanted the baby, and felt very proud, very confident and really happy.' She inhaled deeply, then coughed, rubbing her throat. 'And today I feel absolutely terrible, as if I've lost all control over my life, so God knows how I'll feel tomorrow.'

'D'you want to go home?'

'I'm OK. Having a moan can be very therapeutic.' She smiled again, more warmly. 'Something's puzzling me about what Edith said. If the noise she heard was Ned falling, why didn't she find him on the floor? D'you think she put him in the chair, as well?'

'Is she strong enough? She's quite lightly built.'

'He was probably only a little heavier than she is, and Phoebe could move mountains if need be.'

McKenna fidgeted with his own cigarettes. 'We must ask her about buying extra milk. You'd better do that, as I've blotted my copybook there, too.'

'You like her, don't you?'

'She has unusual qualities.'

'Inspector Rowlands thinks she's like a loaded gun minus the safety catch, and her curiosity's enough to kill most of the cats in North Wales.'

'I know.'

'Don't you find her rather odd, sir? She goes from one mood to something completely different in the blink of an eye, and for no apparent reason.'

'She's very young, Janet, and she has a somewhat abnormal existence with a near-addict mother and a potentially delinquent sister. Apart from that, she's had a terrible shock. She was very close to Ned.' Lighting the cigarette he had been rolling between his fingers, he asked: 'Have you come across any discrepancies in the statements?'

'Only odds and ends, mostly to do with timing, but people hardly ever remember things like that with any accuracy. Inspector Rowlands suggested doing a cross index of significant times, activities and people, to see what shows up. He's started something similar with the dodgy cars.'

'That's very enterprising,' McKenna commented acidly.

Janet watched him, the smoke from her cigarette drifting upwards and sideways, entwined with that rising from his. 'I know you're always telling us not to gossip, sir, but people talk, and when something unexpected happens, people talk even more.' She paused, waiting for a response, then went on: 'For instance, there's going to be an awful lot of talk about me, sooner or later.'

'It won't amount to more than a nine days' wonder.'

'I know. Women fall pregnant all the time, married or not.'

'So?'

She moved uneasily in the chair. 'Everyone expected you to be promoted.'

'And?'

'Inspector Rowlands said his wife heard some talk. Apparently, it's nothing to do with you. Your promotion was held back because Superintendent Bradshaw had to be moved, and this was the only station with a vacancy.'

Annie telephoned as McKenna was about to lock his office.

'How's your mother?' he asked.

'Like a cat on hot bricks,' she said, 'but less upset than I expected. Iolo's here again, so I imagine he's keeping her mind off things. I can't think why she doesn't charge him rent.'

'Don't you like him, either?'

'I'll take the Fifth Amendment,' she said, a smile in her voice. 'Actually, I wanted to know if you're coming to the house again tomorrow. During the holidays, I usually go to the farm on Thursdays, but I can put it off if necessary. Gladys will understand.'

'There's still a great deal of work for us to do on Ned's papers.'

'That's not the problem. Are you planning more interrogations?'

'I can't say what we're planning.'

'Silly question, wasn't it?' Annie said.

'I meant that I don't know. It depends on what information arises, among other things. Dewi might come up with something.'

'He didn't look very fulfilled,' she commented. 'You work them hard, don't you? He didn't leave until well after seven, then he and George swanned off together in that flash car.'

'Is your sister in?'

'Which one?'

'Mina.'

'For once, I thought she was resisting the siren call of the local night-life, but she disappeared with Jason a while ago, both of them giggling like idiots, which isn't surprising, as there probably isn't a complete brain between them.'

McKenna smiled to himself. 'And where's Phoebe?'

'Last seen in the dining room, writing in one of her many notebooks, with that blasted animal moulting all over the table. I told her to take herself and the cat into the study, but she wouldn't.' She paused, then added: 'She's been quite morose this afternoon. I think you upset her.'

'I owe her an apology,' McKenna said. 'Would you ask her to come to the phone?'

'I'll ask, but I can't guarantee she will.'

Sounds of footsteps and distant voices came down the line, the noise of door hinges, then he heard a little clatter as the telephone was retrieved.

'Yes?' Phoebe's voice was dull.

'I upset you today, Phoebe. I'm sorry.'

'I wasn't being cheeky.'

'I should be used to your questions by now, shouldn't I?'

'Are you going to arrest Mama?'

'I can't answer that. Not "won't", but "can't", as in "don't know".'

'I wish you'd arrest the professor! Can't you lock him up for harassing us? And her, too. I'm sick of seeing them. They had dinner here, and now they've got Mama hostage in the sitting room, wanting to know what you said to her.'

'It's only natural they should be curious.' Before she could intervene, he went on: 'I asked your mother if she'd bought any extra milk last week, but she couldn't remember.'

'D'you think Uncle Ned was poisoned with the milk? Which day?'

'Any day after Monday or Tuesday, I suppose.'

'I'm thinking.' The silence lengthened, disturbed again by noises from within the house, and the girl's faint breaths. 'I had to go to the shop on Monday, because we ran out of polish, and the cleaner gets uppity if everything isn't right for her.'

'Are you sure it wasn't Tuesday? She wouldn't need the polish before Wednesday.'

'Mama realized on Monday. She had to wash the dining table because Tom was lying on it where the sun shines very early in the morning. She polished it afterwards, and asked me to go before we forgot.' Phoebe fell silent again, then said: 'I know I didn't buy anything on Tuesday, because I spent the whole day with Uncle Ned.' Her voice tailed away, and he heard a deep sigh. 'I bought some milk from Safeway on Wednesday afternoon.'

'Are you sure?'

'I had to, 'cos Mama said Solange and the professor were coming round later, and she likes lots of cold milk in her coffee. Quite sick-making, in my opinion.'

'How much did you buy?'

'One of those big plastic bottles with a handle. Four pints, or whatever it is in litres. Mama was a bit annoyed, because she said we didn't need so much.'

'Did Ned drink milk? Did he have cereal?'

'He didn't drink it neat. I don't, either, because it's a bit sickly. He had cereal sometimes, but not very often. He liked toast and scrambled egg for breakfast.'

'And can you remember when the Safeway's milk was opened?'

'I don't know. I don't do the food. Minnie was using bottled milk for breakfast on Thursday, but the milkman'd been by then, and she prefers skimmed anyway.'

'And Friday?'

'I can't remember. I'm awfully sorry.'

'Ask your mother to come to the phone, please, Phoebe. Tell her it's important.'

The receiver clattered again, then he heard Iolo Williams's

voice, raised in angry protest, before Edith whispered down the line.

'Yes? What d'you want?'

'I'm sorry to bother you again, Mrs Harris. Phoebe bought a carton of milk on Wednesday. Can you recall when you opened it?'

'Oh!' She gasped. 'I threw it away!'

'Why? When?'

'It didn't taste right. Oh, my God!'

'Please, Mrs Harris. When did you open it?'

Her breath came to him like the breath of a frightened animal. 'It needed using up, so I put some in the jug on Friday morning, and we had it for lunch, and Ned had two mugs of tea, and I used it for the coffee I told you about, and that's why I threw it away, even though it was nowhere near the sell-by date, because it tasted so sour.'

'Why didn't you remember when we talked earlier?'

'I don't know.' She sighed deeply, then said: 'I can see it now, that's how I can remember. I can see the big carton in the 'fridge, and I remember being annoyed with Phoebe for buying so much, and I can see my hands pouring the milk into the jug, and thinking it would take for ever to use up.'

'Was the cap seal broken?'

'Mina used it. She had some for her breakfast, but she said it didn't taste very nice, so she opened a bottle.'

As he walked down the stairs from his office, McKenna met Diana Bradshaw on the way up, dragging herself along the banister rail, her face waxen, clothes and hair in disarray. When she saw him, she stopped, breathing heavily.

'What's happened?'

'I've been shot at.' Hauling her body to the top stair, she leaned against the wall. 'I was driving home along the expressway, and this car pulled out to overtake, and when it drew level, a girl leaned out of the passenger window and shot at me.'

'You're joking!'

'If only!' Diana said, a tremble in her voice. 'I was absolutely terrified, and God alone knows how I managed to stop without crashing.' She made for her office, creeping along the wall, McKenna beside her. 'Traffic rescued me.'

'Where's your car?'

'In the yard.' Slumped in the chair, she folded her arms. 'It must have been a water pistol, because there's just a smear of something on the driver's door, but my God, I was frightened!' Recovering a little equilibrium, her voice sharpened. 'Of all the stupid, dangerous tricks! She could have caused a dreadful accident.'

'I suppose you didn't get the make, or registration number?'

'No, but I'd recognize the girl if I saw her. She was tossing her hair, and she had this crazy expression on her face, like it was the funniest thing in the world.' She paused, her breathing still tense. 'I can't be sure, but I think they followed me from here, as if they'd been waiting outside the yard. I kept seeing the car in the mirror, slowing down when I did, accelerating after me, but never overtaking, and when they finally pulled out, it was a relief, because they were beginning to get on my nerves.' The telephone rang, and she jumped, then picked up the receiver. As she listened, her face reddened with anger.

'Bloody bitch!'

'I beg your pardon?'

'They've just hosed down the car, and the paint's come peeling off the door. She must have had brake fluid in the water pistol. Bloody bitch!'

9

As a pale moon drifted in the sky, casting eerie tree shadows down the flanks of Bangor Mountain, McKenna sat in his small parlour, his cats perched on the back doorstep like relics from a pharaoh's tomb. From a neighbouring back-yard, he heard the opening bars of another nocturnal concert, and saw their ears twitch in unison. Dreading a further recital of atonal modernism, he rose wearily to shoo them into the little garden, praying the animals could discover instead a minimalist work composed of prolonged intervals and non-existent notes.

The letter from Denise's solicitor lay on the table, half folded, unanswered. On his way back to his seat, he read again the curt words, and felt again the same chill, undiminished by the passage of time.

1

McKenna woke as the cathedral clock chimed twice, into that dead time when yesterday had gone while tomorrow still gathered strength to begin. Sticky, overheated, he pushed the thin quilt to the bottom of the bed, and lay on his back, staring through the uncurtained window at a clear night sky and millions of stars, trying to recall the noise which disturbed him.

Voices drifted in from the street in front of the house, breaking up the night silence like static on a radio, and, rolling from the bed, he padded barefoot across the small landing into the room opposite, looking down on an overhead view of a large, dark car and two dark heads, and hearing a cadence of voices.

'He'd want to know,' Dewi was saying.

'You can't wake people at this time of the morning,' George Polgreen replied. 'We've done all we can for now.'

Hauling up the bottom sash window, McKenna leaned out. 'What the hell are you two doing?'

Two startled faces turned upwards, one pale as the moon, the other dark as the night, white teeth flashing. Dewi vaulted over the car door, while George opened the passenger door, and stood in the road like a long shadow. 'Somebody's done over George's flat, sir. The bastards kicked the door in.'

McKenna closed the window, retrieved his dressing gown from behind the bedroom door, and staggered downstairs, almost sleep-intoxicated. 'You'd better come in.'

Dewi fussed over his car, setting the immobilizer switch and checking the alarm, before following George and McKenna to the kitchen, where he began, uninvited, to brew tea, while McKenna slumped at the table and George sat quietly in the other chair.

'Why are you both out so late?' McKenna demanded.

'We went for a drive,' Dewi said, 'after we'd finished at the house, then stopped off for a meal at a place George knows in Dolgellau. When we got back, he asked me up for coffee, and we found his flat'd been burgled, so we called the station. Uniform and forensics are there now.'

'When were you last in the flat?' McKenna asked George.

'Before I went to Edith's. Dewi and I went straight out from there.'

'What's missing?'

'I've no idea. We didn't touch anything.'

'Any damage?'

George shrugged, rather helplessly. 'I don't know. I hope no-one's touched the computer. All my thesis work is in there.' Taking the mug of tea Dewi offered, he added: 'I've got back up copies on disk, but someone could've put in a virus. It'll have to be checked and reconfigured.'

'George said he thought someone was in the flat while he was away,' Dewi said, leaning against the counter, 'and he also said we should've found a lot of photos with Ned's things.'

McKenna gave up trying to sleep as the cathedral clock struck seven, and staggered down to the kitchen once again.

Dewi and George had returned three hours earlier to George's invaded territory, to find stern-faced police officers in possession of a chromium chain-link bracelet attached to a water-resistant screw top capsule, found with George's small collection of cuff-links and tiepins in a carved wooden box. The letters 'SOS' were inscribed on one side of the capsule, a St Christopher medallion on the other, and in concertina folds inside, a long thin strip of paper bore the name and address of Edward Jones, and the list of substances likely to prove fatal to him.

Arrested and processed, George was now confined in the bridewell, waiting to explain what Dewi at least considered inexplicable. 'I can't believe it, sir,' he had said, back in McKenna's kitchen as a summer dawn cast new shadows over Bangor Mountain. Their wings tipped gold, gulls wheeled in the sky, mewling and chattering, irritating the cats in slumber by the back door.

'You're too quick to judge a book by its cover.'

'He was devoted to Ned. Why should he kill him?'

'Only yesterday, you yourself came up with a good motive.'

'That was a joke.'

'And, as the saying goes, many a true word is spoken in jest.'

2

Leaving for work before the postman made his way along the narrow street, McKenna saw the blue-garbed figure with his big heavy bag toiling up the steep hill towards his house as he drove down, and as the postman waved and smiled, wondered what more unsuspected horrors lurked in the depths of that bag.

Diana Bradshaw was also early to work. 'I hear you have Polgreen in custody,' she said amicably, then suddenly frowned. 'Is it true Prys was out with him last night?'

'He's already been counselled over the matter,' McKenna said. 'Is there any news about your car?'

'My husband bought it not long before we moved, you know, and it hadn't even had a scratch, and now it needs a total respray.' She looked unaccountably saddened, he thought, rather than angry, as her words suggested. 'Why do people do these things? Is it mindless vandalism, or sheer envy?' She tapped her fingers on the desk, and he noticed her nails were newly lacquered. 'At one time, if people wanted something, they earned it for themselves, but now, they just destroy what others have worked and saved for, because they think the world owes them a living. It makes me despair!'

'Did you give a description of the girl?'

'All I saw was a typical bottle blonde. You know the type: hard-faced and completely amoral. You see it in their eyes.'

'We could turn up thousands looking like that,' commented McKenna, making his way to the door.

The decorators were squatting on upturned paint cans outside his vacated office, smoking, and drinking from an array of thermos flasks by their feet. 'Bloody hot again, isn't it?' one of them commented. 'Too hot for the paint to dry hard. It's still tacky, so we might have to come back to finish off when the weather turns.'

Rowlands waited by the door of the temporary office. 'They've been sitting there for the past half hour.'

McKenna scowled. 'They can sit there all day as far as I'm concerned. Shut the door, and sit down.' Pulling cigarettes and lighter from his pocket, he said: 'Janet passed on a bit of gossip you'd passed on from your wife. I don't like people talking about me behind my back.'

'It's not like that.' Rowlands lit his own cigarette. 'My

wife's friendly with the wife of an inspector at headquarters, and it's the talk of the place. I've heard plenty of comment here, as well.'

'I've already discussed the matter with the chief constable.'

'With respect, sir, I don't imagine for one moment he gave you the real facts, because he'd lose too much face admitting to such shenanigans.' Reddening slightly, he took a deep breath. 'Bradshaw's fraud unit was investigating the director of that construction company which collapsed owing millions, and put hundreds out of work. He'd been skimming off profits for years, moving the cash way outside our jurisdiction into offshore accounts, under company covers which were nothing more than a name and a box in some remote place. The job was a nightmare.'

'So?'

'So, hard-faced bastard that he is, he set up a new business, buying society repossessions at real knock-down prices, then reselling at a huge profit.' Pausing to knock ash from his cigarette, Rowlands went on: 'One couple who'd lost their home were sued by the building society for an outstanding mortgage balance of nearly fifty grand. Their house had been sold for £23,000, when it was worth at least £100,000, even in a depressed market, so they alerted us.'

'Very interesting, and a fairly typical sign of the times, but I don't see the connection.'

'By trawling Companies House records, one of Bradshaw's team discovered the owner of the property business was the man they were investigating, but she told him to forget it. He carried on digging, anyway, found all the houses were valued for very much less than they were worth by one surveyor working for one estate agent, and went back to her. She threatened him with disciplinary action for disobeying her orders.' Smiling rather bitterly, Rowlands stubbed out his cigarette. 'He soon discovered she'd bought her nice new house through the same channels, but *after* she'd first been alerted, so he grassed her up to the hierarchy, and here she is. So, basically, sir, you've been stitched up.'

'Or turned into a fleeced lamb fighting a wind tempered to another, and it's history anyway, neither makes a difference,' McKenna commented. 'However, I'm not alone in weathering that kind of storm, so perhaps you could deploy your energies to absolve George Polgreen of responsibility for Ned's death, in the face of evidence to the contrary.'

The forensic evidence taken from Ned's rooms was processed and tagged, matched and cross-referenced with the fingerprints and other samples taken from Edith, her daughters, and her visitors. At some time or another, all of them had entered his room and left residues to tell the tale, but in his conflict with death, Ned tore flesh only from his own body, leaving its shreds under his nails. Except for Mina's, all the urine samples showed varying traces of tetracycline, while the chrome bracelet was bereft of even a smear of fingerprints.

'That's unusual,' Janet observed, leafing through the spill of paper from the fax machines. 'Jason Lloyd's fingerprints are almost non-existent.'

'Why?' McKenna stifled a yawn.

'There's a lot of abrasion.'

'Not uncommon with manual workers and people who handle chemicals. We wouldn't get decent impressions off the decorators, either.' Yawning again, he asked: 'Have the other tenants at George's house been interviewed yet? Did anyone hear the burglary?'

'He's the only one of the students not away for the summer vacation,' Janet said. 'And the neighbours heard nothing because there was a very rowdy party going on in someone's back garden.' She made a neat pile of the flimsy paper, and placed it on the desk. 'What shall I do now, sir?'

'Sit in while Rowlands interviews George, then check his whereabouts last week, because unless he was here in Bangor when he claims to have been at home in Notting Hill, he couldn't have tampered with Ned's food.'

'Unless he had an accomplice,' Janet suggested, 'but I think whoever poisoned Ned deliberately planted the bracelet.'

'Quite, which leaves us back where we started,' McKenna said testily. 'Dewi's at the house examining the rest of the books and documents, and looking for the letters, address book and photos George says have gone missing. If he doesn't find them, you and Rowlands can consider executing a search warrant later today. I'm going to see Ned's family.'

'Edith'll have a nervous breakdown if we arrive with a warrant.'

'I've already alerted Dr Ansoni, and Ms Bradshaw knows we'll need extra bodies for the search.'

'Her car's an awful mess. Have you seen it? I didn't know brake fluid could do that to paint.' She rose, pushing a loose strand of hair behind her ear. 'She must be having a courtesy car while hers is away, because I don't know how she'll get home tonight without one. I saw the breakdown truck when I was downstairs getting these faxes.'

As McKenna walked quietly along the corridor on his way out, Diana waylaid him, throwing open the door of her office, and smiling brightly. 'I need a favour,' she admitted. 'I want my car done today, if possible, so could you recommend a reliable repair shop?'

'But Janet saw the breakdown truck take it away not long ago.'

'What?' Her face blanched. 'She can't have done! Oh, my God! It's been stolen!'

•   •   •

Leaning against the wall outside the interview room, waiting for George to be brought from the cells, Rowlands said: 'I suppose this is what hell breaking loose might sound like.' Telephones bleeped, fax and teletype machines chattered, footsteps rattled, and voices shrilled, Diana Bradshaw's the most stridently. 'All this fuss over a bloody car!'

'It's a nice car,' McKenna commented.

'And a nice price, too,' added Rowlands. 'Maybe she's got shares in the property company.'

'Heed a word of advice, Ian, before it becomes necessary to give you a word of warning,' McKenna said. 'You're fast becoming very hostile towards her, and it's fast becoming very noticeable. Others will be only too eager to follow your example, and I don't want rumours about sexual or other kinds of harassment finding their way to headquarters. Nor do I want to be accused of promoting slander.'

'Point taken, sir.' Pushing himself away from the wall as George came into view, trudging in the wake of a uniformed constable, he added: 'I think she'll manage to dig her own grave, without my help, but I'll keep my fingers crossed.'

3

No silver car graced the sunlit quiet of Glamorgan Place, but Dewi's stood at the kerb, bodywork pristine, hood folded down. McKenna parked in the gap behind, and sat for a moment, admiring the other vehicle and savouring an unwholesome delight in Diana Bradshaw's loss, for although no compensation for his own, it might augur enough for retribution.

As he walked up the drive, Edith appeared at her front door and skittered down the steps, agitated and almost feverish. 'Is it true about George?' she panted, snatching at his arm. 'I can't believe it! I simply can't! He would *never* hurt Ned, not in a million years!'

'I can't discuss him,' McKenna said. 'I'm sure you understand why.'

'You've made a mistake.' Edith blocked his progress, jerking from one foot to the other like a bird. 'You've made a *terrible* mistake.'

'I can't talk about it,' McKenna insisted.

'Then tell me if the drugs were in my milk. I've a right to know.'

'Can we go indoors?' He moved on, Edith almost running at his side. 'You seem rather tense and upset.'

She stopped suddenly, and swore. He turned to face her, unreasonably shocked, to see tears in her eyes. 'What did you say?'

'Something very coarse!' she snapped, brushing away the tears impatiently. 'I'm sick to death of being treated like a child or a simpleton! I'm tired of being patronized, of having people tiptoe around me as if they're treading on egg shells, or even worse, as if they're in a minefield.' She stamped up the front steps, and into the hallway, forging a passage through the colours splashing down the staircase from the landing window. 'Yes, I am tense,' she announced, pushing open the sitting room door so violently it ricocheted off the wall, 'and yes, I'm upset! I've had a murder in my house, and now you've arrested the one person, the *only* person, who couldn't be responsible. George wasn't here last week. He hadn't set foot in this house for almost a month.'

'I see.' McKenna stayed by the door, watching her pace the room.

She wore another of her shapely, pretty dresses, the long skirt flowing in the draught her movements created. As she reached the fireplace at the end of her second circuit, she halted. 'And I expect I'll become even more tense and upset,' she added. 'I've stopped taking those bloody drugs. I flushed them all down the lavatory, so by this evening, I'll probably be climbing the walls, and by tomorrow, I'll no doubt want to slash my wrists. But whatever I do, *I'll* be doing it, not those cursed tablets!'

'You don't have to go cold turkey. There are medicines to assist withdrawal.'

'I know there are.' Edith nodded. 'Different bloody drugs to snare you like a gin trap. I'd rather suffer, thank you!'

'You will, too. Don't you think you should tell your doctor?'

'Why? What's he going to do? It's a doctor's fault I'm like this to start with.'

'The determination that's keeping you going at the moment won't last,' McKenna said. 'I know. I've tried to stop smoking.'

'Phoebe will help me.' A smile flickered in Edith's eyes. 'She helped me throw the things away. Annie will, too.'

'Isn't it a large burden to put on their shoulders?'

'They can bear it. They're strong.' She sighed. 'Mina isn't, poor child! She's too much like her father.'

'Where are the girls?'

'Mina's at work, Annie's gone to the farm with Bethan, and Phoebe's upstairs with your young man, making sure he doesn't damage Ned's things.'

'He's not a vandal, Mrs Harris.'

'I didn't mean that kind of damage! She's doing what George should be doing, only he can't, because you've locked him up.'

Phoebe had been crying. Tell-tale blotches disfigured her face, exaggerating the relics of her fight with Mina. 'You've got to let George go!' she told McKenna.

'I can't talk about George,' he said. 'And neither can Dewi.'

'Oh, him!' She favoured Dewi with a look of near disgust. 'He acts like he works for MI5 instead of the local cops. Still, I suppose with his fancy car and some pretend big secrets, he feels more of a man.'

'You're being rude,' McKenna said. 'And on the subject of secrets, someone mentioned you like a few of your own. Is there anything you should have told me that you haven't?'

'Who said that?' she demanded.

'Never mind who.'

'People have no right to talk about me when I'm not there!'

'Everybody gossips,' Dewi said. 'It's fun, and you do plenty.' He shifted a pile of books to the window-ledge. 'And it *wouldn't* be fun if the person you're talking about could hear, so stop acting silly, and answer Mr McKenna.'

She looked from one to the other, then said, rather sulkily: 'I'd tell you if there was.'

'Good.' McKenna smiled.

'And will you tell us about George as soon as you can?' McKenna nodded.

'He didn't do it, you know.' Phoebe was adamant. 'He wouldn't, and he couldn't, anyway, 'cos he wasn't here.'

'So your mother said.'

She picked up another stack of pamphlets and loose papers from the floor, and held them in her lap, one hand on top. 'We chucked Mama's tablets down the toilet. Did she tell you? I only hope Annie gets back before Mama needs her next fix.'

'I suggested she call Dr Ansoni,' McKenna said.

'She won't.' Phoebe was certain. 'She'll just suffer. I dare say we will, too.' She gazed through the window, a strange expression on her face. 'I wonder what sort of person she'll become when she's off the drugs.' Turning to McKenna, she asked: 'Will we have a different mother, d'you think?'

'I don't know, Phoebe. I don't know if tranquillizers change a personality, or just blunt the sharp ends of it.'

'Minnie's tablets didn't do much for her, except make her rattier than usual. I didn't see that happy feeling people talk about.'

'Not everyone reacts the same.'

'Obviously not!' the girl said tartly. 'Else we'd all be dead, like Uncle Ned, wouldn't we?' Her face suddenly threatened to crumple into misery again. 'That's why Mama threw away her pills. She said if she hadn't been drugged out of her skull, she might've noticed something wrong, or chucked the milk before Uncle Ned had any, and he'd still be alive.'

'It's not her fault, and we're not sure the milk was to blame.'

'Oh, you are patronizing!' Phoebe slammed the papers on the desk, and stood up. 'You really are!'

'I think it's one of those times when we can't say right for saying wrong, sir,' Dewi offered. 'Phoebe's pretty angry about George getting arrested.'

'Phoebe's *very* angry about George getting arrested!' She mimicked his voice, deliberately provocative.

'I'm not surprised you get the odd smack in the mouth off your sister,' Dewi told her. 'You're lucky I'm trained to keep my temper under control.'

'Is there any prospect of constructive input from either of you?' McKenna asked wearily. 'Or will you fight like cat and dog all day?'

'Tom!' Phoebe wailed, rushing to the door. 'Where is he?' She ran along the landing, calling, then they heard a huge sigh, a sudden laugh, as the cat came into view, stretched out across the top of the stairs in a bright beam of sunshine.

'Go easy on her,' McKenna said quietly.

Dewi smiled. 'She's a good kid. I like her sort of spirit.'

McKenna sat on the window-ledge, and lit a cigarette. 'You may be called back to the station. Ms Bradshaw's car was hijacked from the yard right under our noses.'

'You're kidding!'

'Janet saw the breakdown truck taking it away, and, like several others, thought nothing of what seemed a very obvious and logical thing to be happening to a damaged car.'

'That's very, very clever,' Dewi commented. 'And how do the villains know which car to nick unless it's been marked for them beforehand, in more ways than one?'

'Rowlands is way ahead of you.' McKenna smiled. '"Sprayed by brake fluid" has already been added to his rapidly growing cross index.' He rose, brushing dust from his trousers. 'I'm off to see Ned's family, and I don't expect to be back until late.'

'D'you want to borrow my car?' Dewi asked, taking the keys from his trouser pocket. 'It's a nice day for an open-top drive.' He grinned. 'And unlike us last night, you could get lucky, and find the woman of your dreams. *We* got tagged as a couple of queers, out posing.'

4

Until he was out of the city's convoluted one-way systems, McKenna treated the car with reserve, assessing its strengths and idiosyncrasies, but at the bottom of Port Dinorwic bypass, he let it go. Air currents snatching his hair, the whine of a slipstream in his ears, and the speedometer needle quivering on the hundred mark, he rocketed past other traffic on the wide, curving hill, grinning from ear to ear.

Here and there along the Porthmadog road, the sun raised shimmering heat mirages, and seared the top of his head and his arms while he waited behind a queue of trippers to pay the toll on the Cob, beyond which all that remained of Klondike explosives factory were a few deep wounds in a hillside strewn with slivers of corrugated iron. He stopped for lunch just east of Penrhyndeudraeth, eating in a garden shaded by banks of glorious hydrangeas, above a dusty road meandering through the river-cut valley floor. Bees hummed around him from flowercup to flowercup, while a lone wasp stalked the girl at a neighbouring table, as she flirted with her boyfriend, oblivious to danger. Ripe and summery and almost overblown, she reminded him of Mina, and he thought of the time when the heat would desert her relationship, leaving her to face winter alone.

On the road once more, the cubic concrete edifice of Trawsfynydd power station rose ahead, gleaming on the edge of a dark lake so contaminated, some said, that the fish from its depths were monstrous. Fields and sheep folds and dour granite buildings slipped by behind low stone walls and clipped hedgerows, a collage of land speckled with thousands of sheep. Denuded of fleece, they grazed pastures grown lush on spring rains and toxic caesium, the legacy of another power station thousands of miles to the east, which, like the last testament of Ned's father, might never be exhausted.

Turning for the Bala road, he drove through sparse forestry plantations and a tide-like wilderness of molten earth set into slopes and cones and bleak unstable escarpments, while above him, a red kite flirted with the sun, swooping and soaring and dazzling. The car cut a swath in the hot still air, while a little breeze, scented with the tang of pine, stirred off the peaks and ruffled the meagre waters of Llyn Celyn reservoir, rustling through the wind-tangled scrub around the shoreline. He slowed to take the hairpin bend which dragged the road around the flank of the moun-

tain, looking for the ruins of submerged hamlets and railway line, then accelerated once more, passing the dam
holed decades before by guerrilla soldiers of the Free Welsh
Army. The light hurt his eyes, the sun burned through his
shirt, and the hot draughts swirling inside the car parched
his skin and filled his nose with the lingering stench of the
charnel house. He saw the cattle incinerator from the corner of his eye, a blackened ramshackle building up a dirt
track behind a copse, greasy smoke befouling walls and
fences, and black soot stuck to the leaves.

Bala's streets were choked with tourists and cars, and
he fretted behind a stream of slow-moving traffic, overwhelmed by smells of frying food and exhaust fumes, before leaving the town behind for the gentler wooded hills to
the east, and the tall Celtic cross, wreathed for remem-
brance with brilliant red silk poppies, which marked the
junction for Penglogfa. The village was a tiny place of old
cob and stone cottages and tapering lanes, with a church at
its heart like the hub on the wheel of life. Lavish pink and
white and purple fuchsias dripped over garden walls, and
dropped their blossoms in the road beneath his tyres. He
and his car attracted attention, women who turned from
their gossip to look, children who gathered in small groups
and followed him at a run, and old men, who simply
watched, shaking their heads, and he thought they probably
knew who he was and why he had come, by that ancient
process which carried knowledge as the eagle rode the wind
from mountain to mountain.

Fortress-like behind a high stone wall, Llys Ifor strad-
dled the side of a hill at the end of a lane built for horse-
traffic, and barely wide enough for a car. Untrimmed bushes
and small trees slapped their branches against the windscreen, dragged over the fairings and brushed his head and
shoulders, leaving shards of leaf and blossom and another

perfume on his clothes. He drove through an arch in the wall and parked in the courtyard beside a smart blue hatch-back with a teddy bear strapped in the driving seat.

For all its size, the house was a simple structure of four walls and a roof in the tradition of Welsh vernacular archi-tecture, devoid of embellishment apart from a heavy string course at first floor level, and high chimneys at either end, corbelled out from the walls, where a drift of grey smoke hung over the one to his right. Angled architraves sur-mounted the door and window openings, set deep into walls built with boulders from the mountains.

Annie appeared in the courtyard, dressed in jeans and a pale silk shirt. 'Phoebe rang to tell us you were on your way.' She smiled. 'And that you'd borrowed Dewi's car. Which way did you come?'

'Through Porthmadog.'

'It's quicker through Corwen,' she said, escorting him into the kitchen, 'but not quite so scenic.'

The room was massive, and filled with ancient shadows, plastered walls dark with age and smoke, great slabs of blue-veined slate on the floor, the ceiling criss-crossed with beams of black oak. The wall to the right was almost filled with an enormous hearth, where a fire crackled and glowed, and he doubted if room or fittings had changed since the day the house was built.

'It's a listed building,' Annie told him, 'and it's falling into ruin because Gladys can't afford the upkeep. She lives in a few rooms and the rest are empty.'

'How old is it?'

'Mostly late fifteenth century, but some of the outbuild-ings are older, and the land deeds go back to 1257.' She took a stone crock from an alcove in the wall, and filled a glass jug with lemonade, setting out jug and tumblers on a tray. 'Henry III granted the title to Ifor Hael, no doubt for services rendered.'

'It would make a wonderful guest house,' McKenna said, watching her. 'Gladys could make a fortune.'

'I expect she could, but that wouldn't be practical.' She picked up the tray, and made for a low, wide door set in a wall feet thick.

'Where's Bethan?' he asked, holding open the door, and feeling the age of the wood beneath his fingers.

'As on every other visit, rain or shine, she's having a riding lesson with Meirion. He and his cronies help Gladys with the stock.'

He followed her along a slate-floored passage bisecting the house, and through another low door into a parlour brilliant with the sunshine of an August afternoon.

Perched on a long oak settle, feet crossed at the ankle, fire-tartan criss-crossing her lower legs, and a pinchbeck brooch at the neck of her dress, Gladys Jones looked like a wrinkled Phoebe, dressed in black. She smiled and gestured like Phoebe, her eyes were the same slaty-blue, and she had the same expression about her. As she shook McKenna's hand, she nodded towards the mess of a human being bundled up in shapeless dark garments, asleep in a tattered wing chair beside a hearth filled with apple logs. 'This is our sister, Gertrude,' she said. 'She's quite deaf.'

'And almost blind, and dumb of speech,' added Annie. 'But she still keens and moans, especially when the moon's full.'

'Hush, child!' Gladys chided, inviting McKenna to sit beside her.

Annie handed him a tumbler of lemonade, the glass beaded with dew, then like Gladys, watched him in silence, weighing him as a person, seeking changes wrought by a changed environment. A Jacobean brass clock ticked crankily on a mantel festooned with dusty black mourning, birds rustled and chirped in the trees beyond the open windows, and the deaf woman whuffled like a sleeping animal. He heard sheep bleating in the distance, then nearer, the bark of a dog and Bethan's laughter, and wondered if memory and sense might still flicker in the mind of the decayed woman in the fireside chair. 'What's wrong with your sister?' he asked Gladys.

'Old age,' the old woman began.

'Ignorance and stupidity,' Annie interrupted.

'Gertrude's seventy-eight, I'm seventy-one. Old age is bound to get us, but Annie won't have it.'

'She's been like this as long as I can remember.'

'Annie's convinced Gertrude's afflicted with mad cow disease, but I've told her she was never quite right in the head, even as a girl.' Gladys smiled gently. 'We're all a little strange, as I expect you've realized. Edith thinks the isolation turns our minds. Is it true she's thrown away her tablets? She'll be like a one-legged man without his crutch.'

Gertrude twitched violently, rocking her chair, them began to snore, dribble trickling from her half-open mouth. Annie wiped the crazed skin with a napkin, then tucked the cloth under Gertrude's chin.

'She's very foolish to stop taking her tablets so suddenly,' Gladys went on. 'But then, she's a foolish woman in many ways, and she's made some very stupid mistakes in the past, and suffered for them, but she wouldn't hurt Ned, even though they never liked each other very much.' She paused, watching him, then said: 'She wouldn't let anyone else hurt him, either.'

'She's said Ned didn't have an enemy in the world,' commented McKenna.

'That didn't stop you arresting George,' Annie commented.

'We had no choice,' McKenna said. 'Ned's SOS bracelet was found in his flat.'

'After someone made sure you searched it.'

'That may well be, but we still had no choice.'

'Ned wrote about George quite often,' Gladys said. 'I

hoped to meet him one day. He sounds a decent young man. Phoebe likes him too. She said I should tell you to let him go, but I told her she'd have to wait on the fullness of time.'

'Time often needs help,' Annie interjected.

'So Phoebe reminded me.' Gladys nodded. 'Mind you, she'd like to run the world, or at least, her small part of it. She wants me to go to Bangor, but there's not really much point, because we'll bring Ned back to be with the rest of the family in the chapel yard. Did you know our great grandfather laid the chapel foundation stone in 1854?' she asked McKenna. Then grief clouded her eyes and etched deep lines about her mouth. 'When can Ned come home? When can we bury him?'

'We're waiting for the inquest date.'

'Why?' Annie asked. 'There's no mystery about his dying.'

'There might be argument,' McKenna said.

Gladys rose. 'I'll make tea.' She patted her sister's withered hands, then trotted to the door, remarkably spry for her years. 'Show Mr McKenna the farm,' she added, 'and after tea, he can look at the photo albums.'

'Auntie Gladys virtually reared Ned, you know,' Annie said. 'She's taken it hard.'

She led him through another low door into a flagged hallway from which a wide stone staircase, treads worn hollow in the middle, led to the upper floor. A drying, cloying smell filled the air.

'I can smell dry rot,' he said.

'There'd be something wrong with your nose if you couldn't,' she retorted, dragging open the front door. Cut from black oak, studded, banded and hinged with iron, its bottom corner screeched along the stone, and a shower of coins dark with verdigris fell about their feet. 'Aunt Gladys puts coins over the front door every New Year's Eve,' she said, stooping to retrieve them, 'and she'll be long cold in her grave before they bring any good fortune to this house.'

'Why can't she sell up, or hand it to the National Trust?'

'Because the will says it must stay in the family, and she can't risk the legal costs of asking for a variation in the terms. A court wouldn't necessarily rule in her favour, however reasonable the request.' Leaving the door ajar, she went outside. 'And she can't afford her contribution to a restoration grant. She barely keeps body and soul together as it is.'

Unmown lawns of yellowed weedy grass fronted the building, bordered with unclipped hedges and shrubs. Looking back at the dark house, its windows ablaze with the light of the westering sun, he said: 'Ruination of a place like this would be tragic.'

'Ned thought it was poetic justice.'

'I know. George told me.'

'You can't really believe he killed Ned.'

'I can't discuss the matter.'

'Mama said you can be patronizing, and so did Phoebe. We have a vested interest, you know.'

'That's the problem.' McKenna's bare arm was almost brushing her. 'I think George was very crudely fitted up, which leaves the real killer still on the loose, and it could be any one of you.'

'I've already told you it wasn't me, but I can't prove it, and I've already told you that.'

A flight of crumbling steps led from the lawn to a cobbled yard flanked by shippons and haybarns. Against the perimeter wall, a rectangular space which was once the floor of another building had been covered in sand, and here Bethan sat astride a palomino pony trotting in circles, pursued by a brace of black and white sheep dogs.

A craggy man, aged by the elements, sat on a stump of mossy wall, watching child and pony. He smiled briefly at Annie and nodded stiffly to McKenna as they passed.

'That's a beautiful pony,' McKenna said.

'Gladys started breeding palomino cobs a long time ago, probably when she realized she'd never have children.' Annie waved to her daughter, who studiously took no notice. 'Megan's the latest in the line.' She made for another arched opening in the wall, pushing open a sun-bleached wooden gate on to a sweep of pasture, where three more golden horses sheltered from the sun beneath a stand of massive oaks which looked as old as the house. The neighbouring fields were speckled with sheep, like the fields he passed on his journey. 'That's Tara.' She pointed to a graceful animal rippling with shadows. 'She's Megan's dam, and I ride her quite often. The slightly darker one is Bella, her dam, and the big colt is Bryn, Megan's brother.' She smiled. 'You ride, don't you? Dewi Prys told Phoebe.'

'Did he also tell her I fall off?'

'He said you had a bump last year, but everyone comes off some time. Bella chucked Gladys over a wall in the spring. She broke her arm, but it hasn't bothered her. She says horseback is the only way to bring the sheep off the mountains, which is her excuse for enjoying a good gallop.'

'And she looks very good for it. Does she have help around the house?'

'Meirion's daughters do the heavy work, and the district nurse comes twice a week to bathe Gertrude.'

'Can she walk?'

'She can totter from her chair to the little room off the parlour where she sleeps, but she can't toilet herself, or dress herself, or even eat by herself. I'm sure she's an early victim of the new strain of Creuzfeldt-Jakob, but Ned and Gladys reckon she was cursed for bringing May blossom into the house when she was little. Then again, I wonder if the whole family isn't hexed.' Talking over her shoulder, she set off along a well-trodden path through the grass beside the boundary wall. 'Their great grandfather's brother went to America in 1860, bought a huge tract of land from the government for next to nothing, and built a farm. Two years later, he lost his scalp to the Sioux in the Minnesota Massacre.'

'These things happen,' McKenna said. Waist high fronds of grass dropped seeds on his clothes as he passed by. 'Senile dementia's very common, and Gladys did say Gertrude was always rather strange.'

'Senile dementia runs in families, and they're all very strange, but Gertrude's the only one to go completely gaga.' Annie stopped, surveying the hills and pastures, and her perfume drifted towards him, mingled with the scents of the land.

Standing at her side, he said: 'There's a tide of sheep out there, isn't there? As far as the eye can see.'

'And most of them belong to Gladys.' She moved on, brushing her hand through the plumes of grass. 'I expect you saw thousands more on the way here, but there isn't a cow or calf for miles around. They've all be slaughtered.' She fell quiet, walking slowly along the path, then added: 'I'm not the only one who thinks Gertrude caught mad cow disease, you know. Most of the village believe she did. They watch each other all the time, looking for what they saw in Gertrude so long ago, and hoping desperately not to find it.'

The sun drifted further to the west, dragging long shadows over the earth, and walking close behind her, McKenna thought of death in its many guises, creeping across this beautiful landscape. One of the horses whinnied, and he turned, to see the three of them streaming across the field, bucking and kicking. 'D'you think animals have any conception of death?' he asked. 'Or do they simply accept it as the natural end to life? It would save a lot of grief if we could do the same.'

'But we never can, can we?' She watched the horses, pensively, then walked on. 'We always find regrets, for what we've lost, or not done, or not said, or just for the way death comes, even though it's always a thief. It stole Ned, and

Phoebe, and George, and the rest of us, and we'll never know how big or small each theft was.' Opening a rotted wooden gate under another arch in the wall, she added: 'But then, we rely on sex and death to keep the world turning, don't we?'

Through the gate, an unbroken length of a barn wall reached into the courtyard, where Bethan now stood on an upturned crate at the side of the little mare, reaching high to unbuckle the girth straps. Here and there in the ancient masonry, McKenna saw signs of clumsy repairs, and, at intervals under the eaves, galvanized iron hooks held lichen-stained roof tiles in place.

'When she's groomed and fed Megan, she'll have tea in Meirion's mansion.' Annie smiled, and, instead of entering the courtyard, turned westwards along the path towards a tiny stone structure built into the wall. A little stone staircase ran up its gable end to a minute arched doorway, under a round window with wooden shutters. 'It's the oldest building on the land, and we've no idea what it was for.' Going around to its other gable end, she opened the door, stooping below the lintel. 'It was our playhouse when we were younger, and it's always been a den for the farmhands. In the winter, they sit in here with a roaring fire, playing cards and setting the world to rights.' She pointed out a row of old wooden pegs rammed higgledy-piggledy into the twisted beam above the iron grate. 'Their caps hang there in a row, every one with finger marks in the same place where they tweak them off.'

Four old upright chairs stood on a floor of dried earth, around a table askew on its legs, and through the one small window, he saw a new view of the woods above the village, so distorted by the old glass it wrenched the eyes. On the worn stone window-ledge, casting a blurry shadow, the *doppelganger* of Phoebe's cat surveyed him with glassy eyes.

Annie giggled. 'Tom's one of her kittens. Phoebe calls

her "*Ur*-cat", as in the "mother of all cats", and don't try to stroke her, because she's likely to have your arm off. She only lets Gladys, Phoebe and Bethan touch her.'

'Not you?'

She shook her head, smiling. 'Not since I conned her into a carrying box for a trip to the vet.'

'And not Mina?'

'Mina doesn't like animals, and they don't like her. I suppose they sense something they need to fear.' The smile died, like a cloud over the sun. 'She hated coming here when she was younger, and she got so bored we'd find her chasing the sheep, worrying them like a rogue dog.' She leaned against the wall, hands in pockets. 'She's so lacking in imagination I feel sorry for her, and with the best will in the world, I can't understand why she's so different from Phoebe and me.'

'Even as your sister,' McKenna said, 'she's entitled to her differences and individuality.'

'You're an only child, aren't you? It shows, somehow. You must feel isolated from the moment you're born.'

'And even more so when all the memories that created you die with your parents, so I can't imagine the sort of continuity which exists between you and Phoebe and Mina.' He smiled. 'All I can do is feel envious.'

'There's little but blood between us and Mina.' She moved away from the wall, stepping into a beam of light, dust motes drifting about her hair and clothes. 'Even at my age, I find this place enchanting, but where Phoebe and I see magic, Mina sees a dirty hovel.' She grinned again. 'Bethan thinks it was built for the fairies, although in this neck of the woods, it was more likely a hide out for witches and hobgoblins, or even of the Ingrams's estate.' Wiping dust from her hands, she laughed. 'Their fame won't have spread to Bangor, but they're supposed to be very wealthy. Martha'r Mynydd, who lives in a farm beyond Bala, says Mr

Ingram and his pretty young daughter often come to her evening gatherings.'

'And?'

'They don't exist, and as far as we know, they never did. Martha's another crazy woman.' She nodded to the cat, and made for the door. 'Gladys will have fed Gertrude by now, so we can go back. Unappealing sights like that are best kept private, aren't they?' She sighed. 'I can't help thinking Gertrude's death would make better sense than Ned's.'

'Death isn't meant to make sense,' McKenna said. He glanced at his watch. 'I told the solicitor in Bala I might call.'

'Why? Gladys can show you her father's will, if it matters, and she'll know if Ned lodged any papers there. She's had power of attorney for years, because with Ned and Gertrude both so prone to being *non compos mentis*, there was no option.'

The front door was still open, but instead of returning to the parlour, she took him up the stairs. The upper floor was divided by partitions of blackened, coarsely-grained oak, and at the head of the staircase, the reek of dry rot was overpowering. Hefting her shoulder against a door to the right, she pointed to webs of fungus garlanding the ceiling beams. 'That's what you can smell,' she said, then closed the door with a thud.

Ned's old room was on the other side of the stairwell, along a short corridor lit only by sunlight seeping through from the landing. That door, too, fitted ill in its frame, and jammed itself into the floor with a dreadful screech as Annie eased it open.

Tall cupboards and heavy chests, crudely carpentered from old dark wood, and dull with age and neglect, lined one wall, and against another stood a beautiful mahogany desk and a battered captain's chair. The brass bedstead, tarnished now, and lacking one of its finials, was covered with a handmade quilt, a history of the family's life stitched together, and now so worn in places that only a few fine threads of silk halted total disintegration. More black fabric was draped over the oil paintings which hung about the walls, dressing the house in mourning, and as McKenna moved around the room, trying to decipher the landscapes and faces behind years of dirt on the canvases, the floorboards creaked under him and he felt a disconcerting bounce in the joists below, as if they too were ravaged by the fungus. Treading gingerly, he skirted a washstand with a fine oval mirror on its chipped marble top, and stood by the window, looking into the heart of the village.

So close he could hear her breathe, and smell the scent of fresh air and sunshine about her, Annie said: 'When he was a boy, Uncle Ned used to stand where you are now, like a prisoner in a high tower. If you look to the right, you can see the chapel roof beyond the trees by the church, although there's only one cemetery, which Phoebe, of course, calls the "flesh-farm".' Elbows on the washstand, she added: 'Church folk are buried this side of the trees, chapel folk the other, and little Amos is there with the rest of the family. He died from polio when he was four, so I suppose he'll always be "little Amos", and we'll never know if his death was a bad thing or not.'

'Who was he?'

'The youngest child. Their mother went into a virtual collapse when he died, which is why Gladys reared Ned, and not long afterwards, Gertrude's little daughter died. She was four, as well.'

'And Gertrude's husband?'

'She never had one. Madness isn't all we inherit.' She turned away. 'When I had Bethan, everyone but Ned and Gladys treated me like an outcast. Mina said I'd ruined her reputation, and Mama was so bitterly hurt and disappointed she had a relapse. She's still convinced I've wrecked any chance of a decent marriage.'

'What about your father?'

'He pretends she doesn't exist. He hasn't been back since she was born in any case, but he never sends birthday or Christmas gifts, or even cards.'

Gertrude slept again in her chair, smelling of soap instead of bitter old age, a rug woven from the strange colours and ancient symbols of Welsh tapestry wrapped around her knees to ward off a chill seeping through the threadbare carpet. McKenna noticed an oval chamber pot poking out from under her chair, its inside stained, its outside scattered with posies.

While Annie washed dishes in the kitchen, Gladys sat beside him on the settle, an album of faded photographs in her hands, turning pages spotted with mildew, and pointing out the few quick and the many dead among the pensive, proud, troubled and self-conscious faces in this tribal record. Such Welsh faces, he thought, watching her spindly fingers, and in profile, some were almost concave, like the wicked witches in fairy stories. As she chattered on, he realized there was not a black face to be seen, and wondered if that collision of memory and history were more painful than the rest.

'Have you pictures of the slaves?' he asked. 'Or rather, their descendants? George said some of them stayed as free men and women.'

'Only because they had nowhere else to go at the time.' Annie quietly came back from the kitchen, and took up her seat beside Gertrude. 'They couldn't get away fast enough when the heavy industries developed in South Wales, even though it was only an exchange of one slavery for another.'

'You've always had socialist leanings,' Gladys said to her. 'But do they do you any good?' Then to McKenna, she added: 'We had quite a few photos at one time, and some other very old pictures. Ned had them for his essay, but I don't recall him sending them back.'

'They seem to have disappeared,' McKenna told her. 'Like most of his letters.'

'How strange! Why should anyone steal them? They're no use, are they?' Turning to the back of the album, she showed him a double page of small black and white snapshots. 'Apart from the baby photos you've already seen, I've no other pictures of Ned. He had the rest.'

Ned Jones in youth smiled warily at the camera, the shadows of melancholy already about his eyes, and even then, he was thin and frail. In most of the snapshots, he wore a high-collared shirt, a broad tie, waistcoat and breeches, thick wool knee-socks and hob-nail boots, and stood mostly alone, before the farmhouse door, in the courtyard, or beneath the wonderful ancient trees where the golden horses now grazed. Only in two photographs was he in company, beside another young man with a shock of thick unruly hair on his head who was much taller and very plump, and who wore shirt and trousers and shoes wholly lacking in style or distinction.

'Who's this?' McKenna asked.

'His friend from Aberystwyth University. He came visiting once or twice, but I haven't seen or heard of him for over thirty years. We called him Eddie, because he was another Edward.' She closed the album with a little snap. 'I think they lost touch. Ned never wrote about him.'

'May I see the letters Ned sent you? They might provide some insights.'

'I haven't kept them,' Gladys confessed. She gestured about the room, where lighter patches on the walls told of pictures once hung there, and indentations in the floor

planks and squares of deeper colour on the faded carpet betrayed the shapes of the furniture which had rested there.
'I've given up collecting things. People do when they get
old, you know. You tend to keep just what you need, and
find the rest a burden.'

'That's not quite true, is it?' Annie said. 'You've sold an
awful lot. I remember the dressers and settles and tables
and chairs, and that wonderful Elizabethan buffet which
ran the length of the kitchen wall, not to mention tin toys
and teddy bears and old china so fine the sun shone through
it. All you've got left is the junk and broken bits, like that
double-handled cup and deep saucer you use for Auntie
Gertrude.'

'I got a decent price from the sale-rooms in Bala,' Gladys
said. 'I might be old, but I'm not stupid.' She turned to
McKenna, touching his arm. 'Before the money ran out
from my father's stocks and shares, we lived well enough,
but sheep eat people round here, and the house gobbles up
whatever's left. There's no point feasting your eyes on pretty
pictures while hunger-rats gnaw your empty belly.'

'Or chopping up antique chairs to feed the fire,' Annie
added.

'You're a silly child at times, you know. Contrary for the
sake of it,' Gladys told her. 'Most of the money goes in wages
to Meirion and his family, because we'd be in a sorry state
without them.' She smiled at McKenna. 'You never really
escape poverty once it's come to your door, do you? I can't
tell you how often I've longed for one of those little cottages
in the village, with central heating and just enough space for
Gertrude and me, and not a single sheep to worry about.'

'You'd hate it,' Annie said. 'And where would you put
the horses?'

'I can still dream, even at my age.'

'Where did the slaves live?' McKenna asked.

'There's a gate at each compass point in the boundary

wall,' Gladys replied, 'and you'll have passed through three on your tour, but the east gate's so choked with bushes and brambles I doubt it's been breached since Ned was writing for the Eisteddfod. It leads to a track up the hillside, and the building where the quarry workers lived, which has gone to rack and ruin like the rest. Every so often, the English come, offering me a near fortune, but I can't sell.'

'Uncle Ned said he trudged back and forth in all weathers from the quarry,' Annie added, 'trying to imagine he was a black man. He said the quarrymen's lodgings were no better than a cattle shelter.'

'What about the slaves who worked in the house?' McKenna added. 'Where did they live?'

'In the barns,' Annie replied. 'With the other animals.'

'You've got a bitter little streak in you, child!' Gladys snapped. 'And if that's what socialism does for a body, you want to leave it alone, before it eats into your heart.'

5

The clatter of paint cans and the thump of the decorators' boots came from McKenna's office, along with the vapours of paint and white spirit. Diana Bradshaw coughed. Janet coughed too, as if in sympathy, then rose quickly and disappeared along the corridor.

'What *is* the matter with that girl?' Diana demanded.

'A stomach upset, I imagine,' said Rowlands.

'It's lasting rather a long time.'

'Can we discuss Polgreen instead, ma'am? We can't continue to hold him without charge, and as he was in London at the crucial time, I don't think we can set any store on finding the bracelet in his flat.'

'He *says* he was in London, and you'll hold him until the

Metropolitan Police show me incontrovertible proof that he didn't have the time or opportunity to come to Bangor and poison Edward Jones.'

'Edith says he hadn't been near the house for weeks, and we know the drugs were in food or drink Ned had on Friday.'

'We don't *know*. We're surmising, on circumstantial evidence, which could be sheer coincidence, or back-up plan if the other one went wrong.'

'What other one?'

'The other plan Polgreen devised, when he thought up the scheme to report a non-existent break-in at his flat, then wreck the flat and have some guillible policeman with him when it was discovered!' She paused for breath. 'I'm absolutely furious with Prys! Not content with spending most of the day with Polgreen, he goes out with him for the evening afterwards. Doesn't he realize people like that can't be trusted? Professor Williams has the measure of him, even if you don't.'

Fiddling with one of the many pieces of paper littering his desk, Rowlands said: 'Ned had boxes of clippings about the professor. We should ask him why.'

'You'll do no such thing!' Diana snapped. 'You will *not* pester someone of his standing on account of a half-senile old man. There's neither rhyme nor reason to Edward Jones's actions.'

Mindful of her reputation, he said: 'Aren't we in danger of letting the professor dictate the course of our investigations? And as for Polgreen, if he sues for wrongful arrest and detention, I'd say he has every right. We could be looking at compensation running into six figures.'

'Or we could be looking at an immensely devious person who ruthlessly plays the system. He might have got compensation from the Met, but I'm afraid he'll find out the hard way that I'm not a soft touch for ethnic minorities.'

'And I think we'll find out the hard way that we're all making the wrong moves for all the wrong reasons,' he said mildly.

'Don't you dare challenge my authority!' Her face whitened with rage. 'Get out of here, and find my car! And take that snivelling girl with you!'

'If I do that, ma'am, and neglect a murder inquiry in the process, people might say you're abusing your power.'

6

Rubbing an aching back, Dewi bent to retrieve the paper which had fallen from one of the hundreds of books, and, grimly fascinated, began to read a recent cutting from one of the broadsheets, which discussed in graphic detail the circumstances where guillotine amputation of a human limb might be necessary.

Peering over his shoulder, Phoebe asked: 'What's that?'

All afternoon, helping with the thankless task of sifting Ned's artefacts, she had haunted him with memories, relentlessly recreating the dead. The cat, spread along the window-ledge, was motionless for long periods, occasionally shifting with the fall of the sun.

She scanned the cutting. 'Uncle Ned said his legs would have to come off eventually, so he was collecting stuff about amputations and artificial limbs. Dr Ansoni said he was being morbid, as well as mad.'

'The pathologist didn't find anything life-threatening,' Dewi told her.

'That doesn't mean there never would have been.'

'You're a real prophet of doom.'

'I'm a realist.'

'Not all the time. I'll bet you and Ned often had your heads in his Box of Clouds. And talking of boxes, George mentioned a Box of Lies, only I can't find it. We've got five boxes all the same down at the station, and every single one's full of stuff about the professor.'

'Really?' Phoebe widened her eyes. 'How peculiar.'

'You can't help, then?'

'Maybe it was stolen, like the letters and photos and address book.'

'I'm beginning to wonder if any of it ever existed.'

'Of course it did! Don't be stupid! And if you've got five boxes like the Box of Lies, they must all be full of untruth, mustn't they?'

7

Frowning, Rowlands glanced at Janet's pasty face. 'You can go home if you want. Nobody need know.'

'Ms Bradshaw's got me under surveillance. Anyway, I'm OK.'

'She's got us all under surveillance.' He dumped a huge pile of Ned's papers on her desk. 'And you look far from OK to me.'

'You know, don't you?' Janet asked wearily.

'I've seen it all before. Twice, in fact, and we've got two kids to prove it.'

'Did your wife have awful stomach ache?'

'She had whatever you care to name, and it was hell on earth for both us in the first three months, then everything simply disappeared, and she felt wonderful.'

'I can't wait.'

Glancing at her again, he found her expression as ambiguous as her words. 'D'you mean you can't wait to feel better, or you can't afford to wait to find out if you will?'

He watched a tear trickle from the corner of her eye and come to rest on her cheek like a bead of dew. 'I don't know.'

'You're torturing yourself with indecision. Why don't you make up a balance sheet and see how it works out?'

'My father's reaction would obliterate any credits.'

'He's not the one having a baby, and you won't get through this by any rules except your own.' He put another pile of papers on his own desk. 'And if you're not making your own rules yet, this is the time to start.'

'You don't know my father!'

'Don't prejudge, Janet. He might be thrilled once the shock wears off.' Lighting a cigarette, he added: 'Bradshaw's prejudging, and it's going to cost.'

'Refusing to bail Polgreen isn't unreasonable.'

'Refusing to ask Iolo Williams why Ned collected reams of paper about him is, though.'

'Not necessarily. He might've been Ned's secret hero.'

'I'd credit Ned with better judgement. Williams is hardly the stuff heroes are cast from. He's a weasel sort and his wife's a harpy, and I still want to know where his money comes from.'

As soon as Diana Bradshaw went home, Janet followed suit, leaving Rowlands alone in the deserted offices. The smell of paint grew rancid about him and a mug of coffee cooled at his elbow as he fiddled with the computer controls, trying to reduce the glare of the bright green images flickering on the screen and searching for the secrets which riddled the machine's guts.

By his own account, George despised secrets, knowing they would sooner or later break through the weight of time and deception like weeds through concrete. Pausing with his finger on the scroll lock button, Rowlands thought of the huge and handsome black man, still incarcerated in the bridewell, and, inconsequentially, of Janet, who, during the morning's interview with George had shivered now and then, her sensitivities, heightened by pregnancy, perhaps re-acting of their own accord to the man's exotic atmosphere. In other words, he thought, releasing the scroll lock, she had the hots for him, like Mina Harris, and as data skipped from bottom to top of the screen, he wondered if Solange ever dreamed of those fine black hands and scarred wrists chart-ing her body, then shivered himself as the image of her in lust with her pot-bellied spouse sprang to mind.

Iolo Williams had no record of any delinquency attached to his own name, but accessing the file reference which flanked his address, Rowlands discovered that a Mrs Mar-garet Williams was twice convicted of theft many years be-fore, and escaped a custodial sentence because her mental equilibrium had fallen foul of her hormones. Her last known whereabouts were on one of the city's council estates.

8

McKenna felt unable to leave Llys Ifor without saying farewell to Gertrude. She was like the ghost at a banquet, an unresolved mystery who would remain a fixed point in the existence of all who knew her.

Gladys solved the dilemma for him. 'Mr McKenna's got to go now. He's a long drive ahead of him.' Her sister snuf-fled, head sunk in her chest. Then, holding out her hand, Gladys said: 'It was kind of you to come, and I hope you'll let George go soon. I know he wouldn't hurt Ned.' Her palms and fingers were calloused with toil, the skin on the back of her hands freckled with liver spots. 'Will you give him my regards? Tell him to come and see us when he can.'

Annie took him back through the kitchen. 'It'll be dark soon,' she commented, looking at the sky to the east, dusky with impending twilight. 'If Mama's still attached to the floor, I might stay here overnight.'

'We need to search your mother's house for Ned's missing things, but I'd be grateful if you don't alert her yet.'

'Not tonight, surely?'

'Tomorrow.'

'That's another day, and anything could happen. All your questions could be answered by a stroke of magic.'

'I doubt that.'

She fell silent, looking up at the sky, then at him. 'Could you do me a favour? I'm not taking advantage of knowing you, but I've got a problem and it won't go away. At the moment, it's a little one, but I'm afraid it's getting bigger.'

'I can't promise, but I'll try. What is it?'

'The car.' She nodded towards the vehicle, gleaming beside the other dark beast of a machine. 'I bought it last November, and in March, I received a fixed penalty notice about a parking offence in Shrewsbury. I haven't been to Shrewsbury in years, so I filled in the form which came with the notice, and sent it back. Then another one came, about the same offence, so I added a letter, and last week, I had a final notice. I rang Shrewsbury police, but they say I'm the last registered owner, and therefore liable.'

'I'll see what we can do.'

As he walked towards the car, Annie a few paces behind, Bethan came around the corner of the house, Meirion beside her, and began to run towards her mother, curls flopping. One of the dogs shot past his master in a flurry of black and white, and collided with the child, knocking her to the ground. She lay there, stunned, a little heap of flesh and bone in bright summer clothes, and McKenna ran towards her, gathering her in his arms. She sobbed briefly, rubbed her eyes with her fists, then smiled at him, and wrapped her arms around his neck. As he carried her to Annie, her hair like gossamer against his cheek, her sun-warmed flesh against his, he realized he had never before held a child, and felt such a pain pierce his heart he needed to cling to her, for the comfort she brought, as Phoebe clung to her fat tabby cat.

Hesperus, the evening star, hung between the mountains like a guiding light. Save for the odd farm vehicle, the road was almost deserted, and, where the old railway viaduct marched in silhouette over the horizon to one side, and the bulk of Arenig Fach cast a massive shadow to the left, McKenna glimpsed a tiny shape pacing ahead like a piece of landscape on the move. Drawing near, he saw the shape for an old man, clad in shirt and britches, tumbledown boots on his feet, his skin like tanned leather, an empty fertilizer sack tied around his middle, and a knapsack bouncing between his shoulder blades. He stopped the car, dust and stones spinning from the rear wheels, and reversed. 'Can I give you a lift? We're a long way from civilization.'

The man halted his trudging, a little smile tweaking at lips bedded in stubble. He leaned on the car door, the smell of tobacco and sackcloth strong about him, and laughed at the transformation of McKenna's face as recognition came.

'Robin Ddu!'

'Not quite so black as last time we met,' the old man said. 'I get a good scrub now and then at the mansion farm near Bronaber. I've been working there the past few weeks.'

'Where have you been today?' McKenna asked, pushing open the passenger door.

'The same place you just came from, most probably.' Robin dropped heavily on the seat. 'I stayed last night at Martha's, then went on this morning to pay my respects to Ned's folk.' He eased off one of the boots, exposing a wash-worn sock. 'You and your fancy car are welcome to me. I've got a blister on my heel from this terrible heat and my new socks.'

'And what have you been up to since I saw you last?'

'This and that. Here and there.'

'Where did you spend the winter?'

'The usual places.'

Resting almost on the horizon, the sun cast his face into sharp relief, reddening the weathered cheeks. He was a large man, bony and ill-proportioned, with raw-boned hands strong enough to wring the life from a sickly lamb or a dog gone bad. His scalp was fluffy with wispy grey hair, his eyebrows bleached by the sun, and his eyes that clear, far-seeing blue, peculiar to the true Celt.

'Martha's offered me a roof this year,' he added. 'If she's not dead by then.'

'The one they call Martha'r Mynydd?' McKenna asked.

'She's the only Martha in these parts. D'you know her?'

'I'd never heard of her until today. Annie Harris told me about the Ingrams.'

'She's a bonny young woman, isn't she? And the little one's as pretty as a picture.' Robin smiled, exposing raw pink gums. 'More than even God Himself could say for Martha. Poor soul! She's been so sick they took her to the hospital in Bangor for a couple of nights.'

'What was wrong with her?'

Rummaging in the knapsack between his feet, Robin pulled out a dog-eared book and waved it under McKenna's nose. 'Ned gave me this last time we met. It tells how the English found us in centuries past.' He turnéd the pages slowly, one expression after another beguiling his face, and, his words in counterpoint to the whining slipstream, said: 'They reckoned the country was the fag end of Creation, the animals were the rubbish from Noah's Ark, and what passed for houses nothing more than nasty hovels dripping with damp, where the farmer, his family, his servants, and his animals all lived together, and they were all such brutes you couldn't tell one from the other.'

'What's that got to do with Martha?'

'She still lives like that, only it's just her and the animals.

She caught something off one of them, and it made a huge cyst on her neck, and when it burst, she said the room was almost flooded, then this huge tapeworm crawled out and slithered down her body and away through the bloody stuff from her neck.'

'For God's sake!' The car swerved, rocking wildly for a moment.

'It's true,' Robin insisted. 'You ask the nurse who does for Gertrude Jones if you don't believe me.'

McKenna thought of the ignorance on which Annie blamed Gertrude's tragedy, and, glancing at the man beside him, whose age he could not even remember, of others brutalized by that ignorance.

'Martha's been very miserable since she came back from the hospital,' Robin went on. 'She had some turkeys in the barn, ready for Christmas, only a fox got in and killed all but three. Then the next night, there was a great wind, and the barn roof caved in and finished off the rest, like God smashing His fist on her. She wants me to go back before the weather turns to make the hole good.'

'Did she know Ned?'

'She knows the whole family, and she said the friend he brought back from college stuck out like a sore thumb.'

'That was over thirty years ago,' McKenna said.

'So? He was a foreigner, so he stuck in the mind. Folk like to remember some things, as when Ned won at the Eisteddfod. They were all very proud.' He smiled the toothless smile again. 'Robbed you of your glory, didn't he?'

'Is there anyone in Christendom who hasn't heard that story?'

'Probably not. It's a good story, and you'll be remembered for it.' He rubbed the blister on his heel. 'So let's hope it's not spoilt by folk saying you didn't have the brains to find out who killed him. Gladys tells me the young man you locked up isn't the right one.'

'No, I don't think he is, but we had no choice.'

'We've always got a choice.'

'You choose to live like this, do you? Never knowing where your next crust's coming from, never knowing if you'll have shelter of a night?'

'I had the choice to slave for another man's profit, or be where I am, beholden to nobody.' His right hand still holding the old book full of English spite, Robin waved his left airily about him. 'Look around you, man! It's a sight to break your heart! Is it any wonder I chose to walk the roads?' He grinned, gums raw in the cavernous mouth. 'I'd be a gyppo if I could afford the pony and caravan.'

'You're nuts,' McKenna said equably. 'You always were. So's Martha, by the sounds of it. You've probably been drinking water from Trawsfynydd Lake.' Reaching the bottom of the pass, he slowed the car. 'I'm going to Porthmadog. Where are you heading?'

'The farm at Bronaber.'

'I'll drop you off, then. It's not far.'

'No need. You've already saved me three hours or more.' Leaning down, seat-belt cutting across his chest, he put the boot back on his blistered foot, and methodically tied the laces, breath wheezing. 'Stop where the road forks, and we'll part company for the time being.' The boot laced, he sat up, and grinned again. 'I dare say I'll call on you one way or another when I'm next in Bangor.'

'We'll always give you a bed, if you're desperate. You don't need to smash up the town to get inside the police station.'

'That was the last time I saw Ned, you know,' Robin said. 'When you locked me up for the night.'

'Did you ever write to him?'

'I'm not one for having my thoughts on paper for others to know about. Gladys kept me up to date.'

'How long have you known them?'

He shrugged. 'Who keeps tally? I've helped out since their father passed on. I can strip a sheep of its fleece faster than anyone this side of the mountains.'

McKenna stopped the car, wheels cutting deep wounds in the grass verge. Reluctant to abandon his passenger, he asked: 'Have you any cash to tide you over?'

Robin patted the pockets in his britches, and McKenna heard the jingle of coins. 'I get a wage at the farm, and I've no outgoings like the rest of the world.' He clambered out of the car, and reached in for his knapsack. 'I'll be fine. This is my land, isn't it? I know it better than the backs of my hands.' He shut the car door, hefted the knapsack on his back, then leaned over, gazing at McKenna. 'Next time you see young Annie, tell her about the Ingrams, will you? I forgot earlier. We were too busy with Ned.'

'Tell her what?'

Robin looked towards the horizon, where the sea glimmered like molten metal between the fall of land. 'I slept in Martha's barn, under the stars I could see through the hole in the roof, because folk wouldn't think it seemly for us to share the house, even at our age.' He put up his hand, shielding his eyes from the setting sun. 'And nobody knows where the tapeworm went, do they? Anyway, very late last night, I heard noises from the house, so I went to look. There were shapes flitting back and forth behind her curtains, and a man talking in a deep voice, and a girl laughing, and Martha joining in with the fun. So there you are. You never know, do you?'

9

Still dressed in the clothes he wore the night before, George was stretched out on his bunk, staring at the ceiling with his hands laced behind his head. A book lay spine up in his lap, and an empty plastic mug had toppled over on the floor. When Dewi opened the cell door, he turned his head slowly. 'As I'll be here at least one more night, d'you think I could have a shower and change of gear?'

'The duty officer's on his way.' Dewi leaned against the wall, imagining the black man like a caged panther. 'You should've been released. It's as plain as a pikestaff somebody fitted you up.'

'Not according to the lady *bwana*. She's explained how she worked out my elaborate plot to kill Ned by remote control, so I can steal his work.'

'She doesn't really believe that, does she?'

George put the book on the floor, then sat up. 'She's managed to convince a magistrate.'

'But you were in London.'

'Who says? Me? My parents?' He smiled bitterly. 'Get real, Dewi! Nobody believes people like us, unless we're confessing to crimes.'

'Other people would've seen you.'

'Yes, and if I could remember where I went and when, your mates in London would know who to ask, but I can't.'

'Edith said you hadn't been to the house for weeks.'

'She goes out, doesn't she? She can't know for sure.'

'Jesus! You sound like you don't know yourself.'

'I'm telling you how others view it,' George said, 'so I don't expect to see daylight again in the foreseeable future.' He rose, his energies uncoiling like springs, and began to pad from one corner of the small cell to another, unshod feet almost silent. 'Is my room secure? Has anyone been back?'

'Forensics went to check on a few things, and I called in to make sure the door's been repaired and the lock fixed.'

George halted suddenly. 'Why did forensics go back?'

'Mr McKenna sent them, in case the excitement of finding the bracelet made them a bit slipshod looking for other things.'

'Such as?'

'Signs that it was a genuine break-in, and that someone got in while you were away, though I don't see how they could. No-one's got a key for the mortice, have they?'

'Ned had one.'

'Why in God's name didn't you say so before?'

'I didn't think last night because the door was kicked in, but I told whoever took my statement when I reported the suspected break-in. You can check.'

Rowlands sighed. 'You've already had one bollocking for consorting with suspects. Give her half a chance, and Bradshaw'll put you on a disciplinary charge, so it's a waste of time even thinking she'll listen to anything you've got to say about keys to George's room, faked break-ins, and planted evidence. As far as she's concerned, it's all over bar the shouting, and as from tomorrow, we're on other duties. She ripped up the search warrants on Edith's house.'

'Mr McKenna won't be told what to do,' Dewi said. 'Not when it's against his better judgement.'

'He might have no choice.' Looking at the younger man's eyes, bright with anger, he added: 'George saying he gave a key to Ned is the same as him saying he was in London last week. We can't prove it, and we can't disprove it, so we're left with balancing the odds.'

Dewi fidgeted with a ballpen. 'So why didn't we find Ned's letters and other stuff with the conveniently to hand bracelet?'

'Because he got rid of them. The bracelet's small enough to overlook.'

'We'll regret this.' Dewi's voice was ominous.

'Maybe, and maybe not, and quite frankly, I'm fast losing

interest. We've got cars to worry about, including hers, which is still somewhere in the wide blue yonder.' Rowlands smiled coldly. 'She's gone home in a little Fiesta. It was all she could get her hands on at short notice.'

'You want to be careful she doesn't pull her knife out of my back and stick it in yours, sir.'

'Haven't you figured out yet she'll have more than one knife? God! You haven't a clue how life works, have you? You've been part of McKenna's cosy little clique too long, and so has Janet.'

'You sound as if you resent the way we get on together, sir,' Dewi commented.

'I'm telling you how the situation looks to an outsider. It's no skin off my nose, because I'm just passing through, but you're stuck with Bradshaw.'

'I expect she'll learn to fit in, if she's staying.'

'First Phoebe Harris, then the unwholesome Iolo, now you!' Rowlands was exasperated. 'Is there something in the local water that goes to your head? You seem to think you can turn the world any way you want it.'

'That's the difference between the leaders and the followers,' Dewi said mildly. 'Not that I'd call the professor a leader. Would you?'

'And how d'you rate Bradshaw?'

'We'll see, won't we? When push comes to shove.'

'OK then.' Rowlands grinned suddenly. 'Let's give her a shove in the right direction. She flatly refused to let me interview Iolo about Ned's papers because she's besotted with the image he and the sulky Solange put over, whereas I think it's a long way from the reality.' He reached for his cigarettes. 'For instance, his income won't support mortgage, car finance, general living expenses, as well as her clothes and jewellery. His book sales are nothing to write home about, and his lecturing pulled in less than £500 last year.' He lit the cigarette, his smile lingering. 'I've been busy on the computer.'

'Solange probably gets her clothes cheap. She used to be a model.'

'She did indeed, but there are models and models. I'm not saying she advertised for punters in a Parisian telephone kiosk, although that could be how she met Iolo, because I imagine he's got a liking for the gutter. The French call it *nostalgie de la boue*.' He grinned again. 'I checked with immigration. She was a house model for a ready-to-wear clothing outfit in Paris, which is as unglamorous as it gets.'

'Her family could be well-off.'

'Her father managed a small ironmongery before he retired, her mother worked part-time in a wallpaper factory, they've got three other children, and live in one of Paris's poorer quarters. Solange just trolled around various shops and offices before she struck lucky at the clothing factory.'

'So what's that got to do with Ned?'

'I don't know, but there's some connection. Why else would Ned keep all those cuttings and whatnot?' Inhaling a lungful of smoke, Rowlands went on: 'Janet said he mig' hero-worshipped Iolo, but I can't see it, somehow.'

'We've got a potential source of information captive in the cells,' Dewi pointed out.

'Bradshaw would love that, wouldn't she? Anyway, George can't say which of the boxes is the Box of Lies.'

'Phoebe says *all* the boxes must be full of lies.'

'She doesn't know any more than George. She's making an assumption, and assumptions are dangerous,' Rowlands commented. 'None the less, Iolo was at Edith's on Wednesday, so he could have spiked the food.' He pulled a sheet of paper from a folder. 'Our problem would be proving he got his hands on some tetracycline. The pathologist checked on everyone with access to the house, and the Williamses have only had penicillin derivatives, although he gets a lot of sleeping pills. Mind you, I'd need sleeping pills if I had to lie next to her every night.' He handed over the paper, pointing out regular prescriptions for hypnotics in the name of E Iorwerth Williams. Nothing was listed for Jason Lloyd, nor for George Polgreen. 'I checked up on them,' he added. 'Apparently, they're both disgustingly healthy.'

'So?' Dewi stretched and yawned. 'They've both got family. What about them?'

10

Waiting for a while at the road junction, McKenna watched Robin trudging into the twilight, his hobbling figure shrinking and fading, and as he drifted out of sight around a bend, McKenna realized this landscape would be diminished with his passing. He gunned the motor and went after him, headlights catching the tramp full in the back and casting his shadow huge on the wayside boundary wall. 'Get in. Your foot looks bad.'

'I won't argue.'

'And ask the people at the farm for a dab of surgical spirit and a plaster. If that blister gets infected, you'll be laid up, then Martha won't get the hole in her roof mended.'

'I'm sure Mr Ingram could arrange for it to be done,' Robin said. 'Maybe he'll take his daughter to Ned's funeral, then the whole world can see them.'

'Will you go?'

The old man shrugged, staring into the distance. 'If I'm in these parts when he comes home, not that a funeral makes a difference. The world's already a colder place for knowing he's gone from it.'

• • •

Instead of turning in his tracks after leaving Robin by the
farm gate, McKenna drove south to Dolgellau, and lingered over dinner in a restaurant packed with tourists,
thinking of distances and savouring the horizons and perspectives he had viewed today, for they diminished his own
narrow perspectives and blurred the close horizons of his
failures. Acknowledging a great unwillingness to relin-
quish the day, he paid the bill and gunned the motor of
Dewi's car once more.

In his own, he would see only what surged into brief life
in the headlights, but now, he thought, he was face to face
with the night. As the road plunged into Coed y Brenin, the
air was awash with the scent of pine, and he heard rustlings
and the crackle of branches, then stamped on the brake
when a small deer erupted from the trees and shot in front
of him. Dense pockets of mist obliterated the road without
warning, throwing the glare from the headlights back in his
face and chilling his body, and he felt adrift, simultaneously
free and in peril, for there was not a soul in the world who
knew where he was, except perhaps the old tramp, who
could have but an inkling.

He passed the gate where he had parted company with
Robin, and saw Trawsfynydd power station in the distance,
blazing with energy of it's own making and casting its bril-
liance across the poisoned lake. About to take the Porthmadog turning, he changed his mind, and set out for the
Crimea Pass, slate tips as big as mountains on either side,
headlights bouncing off the broken walls and blind gables
of wayside cottages and lighting the eyes of wandering night
creatures. As he reached the high ground, a pair of Tornado
jets streaked overhead, red and green lights flashing on wing-
tips and tail, and glancing westwards, he saw them bank
steeply, flame shooting from the afterburners, then heard engines screaming above the whine of the slipstream. One
after the other, they pursued him the length of the Pass, a

pinpoint of heat from the laser sights hovering between his shoulder blades and boring into the back of his skull, until he slid from view beneath the densely wooded slopes overhanging Betws y Coed.

His own car, dull creature that it was, was neatly parked a few yards from his front door, with Dewi asleep in the driver's seat, a dreamy expression on his face. His back and shoulders aching, McKenna roused him. 'You should've gone home.'

Dewi glanced at his watch. 'I only left work half an hour ago. We've been paper-chasing again.' He checked his car for signs of injury, set the alarm, and followed McKenna into the house.

The cats shot into the kitchen as soon as McKenna opened the back door. He left it open, to dissipate the heat of the day trapped in the small room, and set about feeding and watering his animals, while Dewi sat by the kitchen table, yawning. When the kettle screeched, he rose to brew the tea. 'That stain's coming back on your carpet, sir. I told you it would.'

'So I must ask myself,' McKenna said, rinsing his hands, 'if you're ever wrong.'

'Not often.' He yawned again. 'And if I am, I keep quiet about it.' He splashed milk into two mugs. 'However, Ms Bradshaw'll find it harder to cover up *her* blunders, 'cos they're bigger. People are taking against her already, so she's getting a hard time. She'd been called back twice before I left.' He poured the tea. 'Some yobbos from Gwalchmai thought they'd have a free bus ride to Bangor, and the driver very bravely chucked them off at the next stop, so they started heaving bricks at his windscreen.'

'Nothing new,' McKenna said, searching for an ashtray. The cats looked up, irritated by his restlessness.

'And there was another fight outside Kentucky Fried

Chicken. A patrol car got its window kicked in 'cos the mob was trying to get at the prisoners in the back seat.'

Ashtray located, McKenna subsided into a chair. 'Pressure works both ways, and when she starts pushing back, you'll learn a lot about the human pecking order.' He lit a cigarette. 'The lower down you are, the nastier it gets.'

'As you say, sir, it works both ways, as I told Mr Rowlands earlier.' He smiled. 'How was the car?'

'Very exciting, but I gave Robin Ddu a lift, so it might need fumigating.' He laughed at the expression on Dewi's face. 'For once, he was quite clean, even if he is still full of strange ideas and tall stories.'

'So are you any the wiser for your trip to the back of beyond?'

'Annie Harris was there. She and Gladys fleshed Ned out a little, and filled a few gaps in the family history.' He fell silent, remembering. 'But there's clearly no property worth killing for. The house is a near ruin.'

After an hour of tossing and turning and thumping pillows in search of a cooler patch on which to lie, McKenna gave up the unequal struggle and went downstairs.

The cats were asleep on the hearthrug, twitching now and then in their dreaming, as Gertrude Jones twitched in her dim world. He opened the back door to the fragrant night, then sat at the parlour table playing solitaire, and, in the midst of the pointless turning of cards, was awestruck by the possibility that all human endeavour was an involuntary assault on life's naturally recurring tedium. Even this futile activity, he realized, flicking the stack again, held no satisfaction if it resolved itself without effort. Exposing the Queen of Hearts, he placed her neatly atop the King of Spades: red on black. The Queen of Clubs lay with the King

of Diamonds: black on red. In the next row, the Queen of
Spades sneered at him, defying resolution. Sneering back at
the cold, two-dimensional figure which so resembled Solange
Williams, he obliterated her contemptuous face with the
Knave of Diamonds, almost pitying the professor.

· FRIDAY, 24 AUGUST ·

1

'What's all this?' Diana Bradshaw demanded, jabbing a finger at the sheets of paper strewn across McKenna's desk. 'Have you nothing better to do?'

'We were trying to work out what Ned wrote on his chest, and how.' He picked up one of the sheets to show her. 'As you can see from the note on the top, this is how "FE" looks written with the left hand. And this is how it looks written with the right.' Shuffling the pile, he found another example. 'This is —'

She held up her hand to silence him. 'Who did these?'

'Dewi Prys, ma'am. We sat him in a chair and pinned the paper to his chest.'

'That's hardly replicating the circumstances in which Edward Jones scratched himself, is it? And whether he wrote "FE" or "EF" is irrelevant. Neither means anything.'

'It's possible he intended to write *ferch*.'

'But you'll never know, so you're wasting time.'

'Point taken, ma'am.'

A tiny breeze, risen off the sea during the night, swirled hot draughts and the stench of paint about the room, disturbing the sheets of paper. Diana moved a chair nearer to the window, and sat with her face in shadow.

'Was there something you wanted?' McKenna said, into a lengthening silence.

'Not particularly. I presume you heard about last night's hooliganism? Some of it was rather unpleasant.'

'Legal recreation's hard to come by for youngsters without cash in their pockets, so they resort to anything that might alleviate the tedium of hopeless poverty.'

'You sound like a book at times.' Humour flickered briefly in her eyes. 'In my opinion, the sociological view of criminals as victims is dangerously misguided. Not only do they make victims of others, but life is actually much simpler. The Welsh have a reputation for trouble-making, which they earned by drinking to excess, settling their differences with fist-fights, and pandering to notoriously over-sexed women, and *that's* why the cells are full this morning.'

'They'll empty before the day's out, one way or another.' He massaged his shoulder, his body haunted by the memory of being thrown from a horse. 'Local miscreants apart, we must make a decision today about George Polgreen. I can't support a charge against him, because there are too many others with an interest in Ned, and too much we don't know about his background.'

'Finding out about his background was supposedly the reason for going to wherever it was you spent all yesterday.'

'I had to eliminate certain possibilities,' he said. 'The terms of his father's will could provide motive for despatching any member of the family, only there's no property worth getting out of bed, let alone killing for.'

'Then I think the case should go on the back-burner, don't you?'

'And the search warrant on the Harris house?'

She shifted uneasily. 'Is it really justified?'

'The magistrate thought so when it was issued, and he isn't easily convinced.'

'I'll think about it.' She rose, smoothing her skirt. 'And I'll decide about Polgreen when I've reviewed the evidence.'

'Don't leave it too long,' McKenna warned. 'He has a good lawyer.'

'She ripped up the warrant,' Rowlands said. 'I thought you knew.'

'I can always get another,' McKenna pointed out. 'Have you asked the pathologist about scripts for the Lloyds and Polgreens?'

'I left a message.'

'Then while we're waiting, we'll have a proper look at those papers on the professor.'

'Why? They don't make any more sense than they did before Dewi finished sorting them.'

'We'll look. Where is he, anyway?'

'Getting ready to go with uniform to a demo at Welsh Water. Joe Public's voicing objections to a rumoured drought order.'

'And where's Janet?' McKenna asked.

'You tell me.'

Dewi had rationalized the welter of paper in the five old shoe-boxes into neat bundles, each indexed, and fastened with a coloured clip. Culled from newspapers and journals published in Britain, Germany, France, Austria and America, and beginning with the first announcement of Williams's discovery of the mediaeval manuscripts, the huge wad of press cuttings ran through to a very recent review of his latest academic paper. In a slimmer bundle, McKenna found copies of the originals in Middle Welsh, attached to articles about the age-old practice of copying and recopying, with translations into English, French and German, some in the rather spidery hand he recognized from Ned's workbooks.

'Ned was more of a linguist than I realized,' he said, comparing a German translation with the original.

'Can you read German?' Rowlands asked.

'Not well enough to know if Ned improved on the other. How about your French?'

'It's quite good, but as I can't read Welsh at all, I wouldn't know tit from tat.'

The third bundle, listed as 'Other Copy Manuscripts', was a collection of prose and poetic texts in Middle Welsh and Latin, in various hands and styles on various types of paper. His memory of Latin long gone, McKenna deciphered the Welsh, hearing the music of the poetry in his mind, his attention caught by a twenty line verse in the alliterative style of *cynghanedd*, where a child bemoaned his fate as the bitter harvest of his mother's seeds of love, which in their ripening broke her heart. 'Some of this is beautiful,' he said. 'I wonder where it comes from?'

'We could consult the expert, and give ourselves an opening for asking him why Ned collected this stuff.' Leafing through a bundle described as 'Miscellaneous', Rowlands added: 'I can read a couple of these. They're in English. "If you have a friend, then keep him. Let not that friend your secrets know, for if that friend becomes your foe, then all the world your secrets know." That's Ned.' He grinned. 'And I'll bet this is Phoebe: "Clyde and Bonnie sitting in a tree, K-I-S-S-I-N-G. First comes sex, then maybe marriage, or just daft Bonnie with a baby carriage." She's no budding Tennyson, is she?' He handed the sheet to McKenna, then began to read the next pages. 'And these are off a computerized fortune telling programme, saying what's in store for Ned, Phoebe, George, Annie, Edith, Bethan, Bonnie and Clyde, the professor and the lovely Solange, and Tom, AKA Phoebe's cat.'

'Is Ned's death predicted?'

'No.'

'George's arrest?'

Rowlands shook his head. 'Not a hint of looming disaster for anyone. At worst, Mina's warned to beware of deception.' He tossed aside the stapled sheets, and picked up the last bundle, scanning Dewi's index. 'These are "Historical Records". Some are in English, but the Welsh and German ones'll make more sense to you than me.'

Separating the bundle, he kept those he could read for himself, while McKenna discovered how, against all odds, thoughts and dreams committed to paper might survive history's chaos. Like other pages inscribed with trivia or world-changing moment, the mediaeval manuscripts Williams unearthed had criss-crossed Europe, in the custody of bards, scribes, foot-soldiers, pirates, monks, spies, merchants and refugees, then lain unread and overlooked for centuries, before chance brought them once more to light. 'Do you realize,' he said, 'everyone who ever touched those manuscripts left their mark on them?'

'It's a miracle they survived,' Rowlands commented. 'There's an article here about a tenth century book of Welsh laws which was found intact in 1945, in the bombed out ruins of a Berlin library.'

'A hair's breadth from destruction!' McKenna's imagination took flight. 'Suppose someone had used Iolo's manuscripts as a spill to light a fire or a candle, or wrapped them around a wedge of cheese or a paddle of butter?'

'Tough, especially on Iolo!' Rowlands lit a cigarette, gesturing to the computer predictions. 'Those won't do much for his twenty-fifth century counterpart, will they? Stuff from a machine isn't quite the same as what comes out of a person's head.'

'Computers will think for themselves long before then. Bangor's own boffins have already invented a teachable microchip.'

'Then let's hope they can keep it under control. I saw this

TV programme about software sort of giving birth all by it-self to new generations of something, and it was bloody frightening.'

'Computers are modern mythology,' McKenna said. 'Every culture makes its own to explain the inexplicable, which is why Ned said that what went into the making of Llys Ifor would bring it to ruin.'

'Red Indians believe things and places create their own spirit from what the parts absorb in the making,' Rowlands added. 'It's either good, or bad, depending.' He grinned. 'So Bradshaw's car is probably harbouring gremlins galore under its bonnet.'

'Like the other half million vehicles getting nicked every year,' McKenna said, making neat bundles of the scattered papers. 'Any luck with the cross index yet?'

'Not that you'd notice, but something might click, like the computer giving us Iolo's first wife. D'you intend to see her, or obey Bradshaw and put everything on hold?'

'We'll tie up some loose ends first, and see what pattern the knots make.'

'A nice tight noose round Polgreen's neck, I imagine,' Rowlands commented. 'I can think of quite few who went to the gallows on less circumstantial.'

'Rather than fret about history repeating itself, see Iolo about these papers Ned was hoarding, and take Janet with you, so she can throw in the odd reference to her father to raise the tone of the proceedings.'

Stubbing out his cigarette, Rowlands asked: 'Aren't you worried about her? She looks ghastly.'

'Short of frog-marching her to Ansoni's surgery, what can we do? She may look worse than she feels, anyway. Apart from throwing up every so often, she's functioning quite normally.'

'You don't think she's just soldiering on to the bitter end? Is she that kind of person?'

'I don't know. The life she's led so far wouldn't put her to the test.'

'Well, we'll see what she's made of soon enough. Women can change out of all recognition when they're pregnant. They're the oddest creatures, you know. Completely unpredictable.'

2

Mindful of female caprice, McKenna had left the house that morning before the postman made his way up the hill, but returning to check on the cats, aware of his long neglect the day before, he found another missive from Manchester on the front doormat, half hidden under an unsolicited catalogue for designer casual wear, and an invitation to apply for a credit card restricted to the over-fifties.

Standing in the hall, blood pounding in his head, he tore open the envelope, and found a polite prompt to reply substantively to the earlier letter within the next ten days.

He fed the cats, pulled down the top sash of the parlour window so they could come and go, and put the letter with its companion under a paperweight on the table, next to the ranked playing cards which refused to resolve themselves, the Queen of Spades sneering still over the shoulders of the Knave of Diamonds and obstructing all progress.

3

Phoebe was sitting on her front doorstep, dragging a toy mouse on a length of string back and forth, while the cat, which seemed larger each day, lashed out occasionally with his left front paw. 'He's tired,' she said, as McKenna walked up the drive.

'With what?'

'Eating and sleeping and eating, I guess, but I'm sure he thinks, too.' She rolled the string around the mouse's body, then rose in an ungainly fashion, a windblown leaf, perhaps the first fall of the year, clinging to the leg of her canvas trousers. She wore a smart cotton shirt with the trousers, but the clothes were already crumpled, pulled out of shape, he supposed, by the surplus flesh beneath.

'I'm sure my cats think, but I can't prove it,' he said, following her into the house.

On each visit he made to this house, the light from the wonderful window was different, its intensity and definitions changing with the passage of time. Now, the pooled colours were being angled towards the walls, rammed by the force of the sun, and he fancied they must flow out of sight under the skirtings as the sun set, to return with the dawn. As he lingered in the hall, the cat padded into the house behind him, and brushed against him, tail twined around his leg.

'See?' Phoebe said. 'He's decided he likes you, but he obviously had to think about it.' She made for the kitchen, and set about her tea ritual. 'I don't know if your cats watch telly, but Tom does, and for the last six weeks, there's been a series about big cats on Wednesday evenings. He's watched every minute, probably because they're snuff movies from his point of view. Anyway,' she added, dropping tea-bags into the pot, 'come half eight on Wednesday, he's in his favourite couch-potato position right in front of the telly, and he trashed the front room when the programme didn't come on, so that proves he can think, because telly programmes don't relate to taste or smell or food.' She poured boiling water into the pot and closed the lid with a little snap. 'Cats give you hell when there's a roast in the oven or fish on the table, but that's normal. Knowing what's on telly, and when it's coming on, is something else.'

'I met his mother yesterday,' McKenna said. 'I thought it was him at first, so he must recognize the big cats as relations, and for all we know, their activities might spark a common species memory.'

'It's still a sign of mental processing.' She sat at the table, arms folded. 'Uncle Ned said when you live with animals, you see the similarities, not the differences.' She looked at the cat, now supine on the floor, legs out as if crucified. 'Do you ever wonder how animals perceive themselves?'

'In a wholly subjective way totally inaccessible to others, like us, because there's no choice.' He stroked the animal's soft belly, feeling rather than hearing its purr. 'I rather envy them, because whether they think or not, they don't have to spend a lifetime constructing themselves, as we do.'

'Uncle Ned said you can't be true to yourself if you're always trying to please others, and being whatever different people want.'

'Being true to yourself is usually viewed as anarchy or lunacy, and neither is conducive to peaceful co-existence.' He wrenched his hand from the cat's reaching fangs. 'See what I mean?'

She grinned, then rose to pour the tea. 'In case you're wondering, Mama and Annie went to town for Bethan's school uniform.' Putting two mugs on the table, and an ashtray in front of him, she went on: 'She's starting at Annie's school next month, so there won't be any more worry about finding decent child-minders. Annie teaches the tens and elevens, but she could teach senior school if she wanted. She got a first class honours, and I keep telling her to do a post-grad, like George, then take up lecturing, 'cos she'd do a much better job than the professor.' She sipped her tea, looking at him over the rim of the mug. 'I suppose you've still got George locked up in your dungeons, haven't you?'

'I'm afraid so.'

'Mama's really furious about it, you know, which is a bit

odd as she doesn't like him. Then again, you don't have to like a person to resent an injustice, do you?'

'How is she?'

'Like the rest of us, I suppose, waiting for whatever happens when an addict stops taking drugs. I know she didn't sleep much last night. I heard her in the kitchen several times.'

'Then you can't have had much sleep, either.'

The relics of her fight with Mina were fading, but the skin beneath her eyes was blue-tinged. 'I haven't slept very well since Uncle Ned died,' she said, 'because I can't bear the waking up. It's almost a whole week since he went, but in my head it seems like only a few hours. Time's gone haywire.'

'Time's probably the most subjective thing of all,' he said. 'And completely fluid. Music time can squeeze a lifetime's experience into a few notes, or stretch virtually nothing almost to infinity, like psychological time.' He picked up his tea. 'And sometimes, a journey back takes a lot less time than the journey there, especially at night, as if other dimensions contract or expand according to invisible laws. When I was at the farm yesterday, I felt as if I'd travelled to a different time zone altogether.'

'That's because it's a different world, and so lovely I don't know how Uncle Ned could bear to leave.' She smiled. 'Annie said Auntie Gladys really took to you, and Meirion said you seem "passable, considering", which is quite a compliment coming from him, as I don't expect you even exchanged grunts. He doesn't talk to people on first acquaintance unless he has to.'

'I met Robin Ddu on my way back. He'd been to Llys Ifor.'

'He's never been here, 'cos Mama would go apeshit with a tramp in the house. Actually, I think Uncle Ned envied him. He said Robin's as near true to himself as a person can be.'

'He ekes out a brutal existence to prove it, and he'll

probably have an equally brutal death, with not a soul beside him to close his eyes.'

Phoebe ran her finger round and round the rim of her mug, frowning. 'I think that's what Uncle Ned meant. Robin's past bothering about what worries the rest of us, isn't he? He's part of the land he roams, so he'll happily rot away on a mountainside, like a sheep stifled by a blizzard, or the wild pony we once found above the farm. She'd died giving birth, beside this tiny, tiny foal which was just a bag of bones, and they were both so much part of the landscape we almost fell over them.' Light and shade coloured her eyes as she turned the knowledge Ned had bequeathed to her. 'Uncle Ned always felt like a refugee,' she added, 'because he couldn't see the land where his roots were laid down, like Robin can, day or night. He had pictures in his mind instead, and he said we all need a feeling of belonging to make sense of who we are. Otherwise, we spend our whole life groping like the blind, looking for something we can't recognize even if we find it.'

McKenna watched the smoke from his cigarette caught by a little draught through the open back door, and shredded to a wisp. 'On the other hand, perhaps being whole depends on a sense of exile, of knowing there's something missing.'

'Perhaps.' She felt the side of the teapot, as Gladys had done the day before, then topped up the mugs, and he felt for an instant as if caught in some warp of time, here and elsewhere simultaneously. 'I used to wonder,' she went on, 'if he had so much pain because he had a lot of love and nobody of his own to spend it on, so it just stayed inside, hurting him.'

'And did you ever tell him that?'

She nodded, memory again darkening the slaty eyes. 'He said that kind of love was a myth, and it caused a lot of misery, because people thought it was the be-all and end-all to life, when a bus was more likely to hit them than Cupid's arrow. He believed you could only be really happy in what he called the "company of the world", which is a fancy name for nature and whatever god you follow.'

'Do you think he was right?'

'I think it *became* right for him, when he realized there was nothing else on offer, and, for all I know, I might end up the same way.'

'I hope not. That would be a terrible waste.'

She smiled suddenly. 'We women can always have a baby to spend love on, can't we?' Then there was a deep, breath-catching sigh, almost a sob. 'But I know what he meant about loneliness.'

'You've got a very good brain,' McKenna said, trying to retrieve some comfort for her.

'I'm entitled to some compensation for a body like mine. I've often wondered if we got on so well because we're both such poor physical specimens, like with like against the prejudice of the rest of the world.' She frowned again. 'Minnie's a terrible body fascist, and so is Solange. My English teacher is, too, because when I wrote an essay about Llys Ifor, she said I was over reaching myself, and I know she wouldn't have been so bitchy if I were thinner, or prettier. Uncle Ned and George said the essay was good enough to enter in the Eisteddfod.'

'What did you write about?'

'Mostly ideas Uncle Ned put in my mind.' She ran her fingertip again around the rim of the mug. 'Mama let me stay at the farm for two whole weeks so I could really look at it, and think about what I was seeing, and what it meant, and how Llys Ifor and the land could go on without any of us, but how it couldn't, and –' She broke off, and stared at him. 'D'you really want to hear this?'

'Yes.'

'Why?'

'Because I'm interested, and because there's a lot of Ned in your thoughts. It helps me to know him.'

'Knowing him won't tell you who killed him.'

'It might.'

'It won't make the slightest difference. He died because he got in somebody's way, or knew something he wasn't supposed to know.' She rose, a little stiff, a little bent, a little more like Gladys, and he found himself hoping the resemblances would cease before Gertrude entered the picture.

'Reading the essay would be easier than listening to me rabbit on, wouldn't it?' She went into the hall, and he heard her footfalls on the staircase. The cat shot after her when the noise of a car engine disturbed the morning quiet of Glamorgan Place, and he stayed in the kitchen, listening to three generations of Harris women returning from their shopping expedition. Phoebe thundered down the stairs, adding a base note, then Edith came into the kitchen, a bright smile on her lips and the light of impending terror in her eyes.

McKenna rose, about to speak, and could think of nothing to say which was not patronizing or crass, then Annie appeared in the doorway, Bethan in her arms, she smiling as if he were the most welcome visitor, her child yawning.

'Bethan's always worn out after a day at the farm,' Annie explained.

'There was no need to drag her all the way back here last night,' Edith said mildly. 'I don't need a minder quite yet.'

'When we were having dinner, you said it wouldn't be long before you needed a straitjacket,' Phoebe reminded her, edging around her sister and niece, the cat beside her. She dropped an exercise book on the table by McKenna's cigarette packet, then filled the kettle. 'And you weren't joking, were you?'

'Cassandra rides again,' Annie said. Bethan stared at him over her mother's shoulder, just as the cat stared over Phoebe's shoulder. Taking a bottle of orange juice from the refrigerator, Annie added: 'Mama doesn't need things ramming down her throat every five minutes.'

'She does,' Phoebe countered. 'She needs the pills she flushed down the bog.' Swilling out the teapot, she talked on, as if to herself, while Annie leaned against the counter giving her child a drink, and Edith subsided into one of the chairs, right elbow on the table. There was electricity in the air between these women, he thought, little currents springing in arcs from one to the other, charging the atmosphere with tingling excitement rather than tension. Bethan coughed on her drink and Phoebe patted her between the shoulder blades, then tore off a length of paper towel to wipe away the tears springing to the child's eyes and the juice running down her chin.

'Is George still locked up?' Edith asked.

He nodded, aware of four pairs of eyes fixed on his face.

'But there's no more evidence against him, is there? And there won't be, because he had nothing to do with Ned's death,' Edith insisted. 'I do know who comes in and out of my house, and I've a good mind to go to police headquarters and make a formal complaint.'

'I doubt if that would make any difference, Mrs Harris.'

'You'd be surprised what can make a difference! It often depends on who's doing the talking, doesn't it? I'm sure Professor Williams would be only too happy to come with me. He's of the same mind as we are about George, even though they can't stand each other.'

'What?' McKenna realized he was gaping at her.

'Why must I repeat myself so often?' Edith demanded. She scrabbled in the pocket of her dress, extracted a pack of cigarettes and a gaily coloured disposable lighter, and lit a cigarette with a sigh of relief.

Phoebe sighed. 'Mama's a classic example of the addictive personality, hopping from one crutch to another.'

'Don't side with the killjoys until you know all the facts,'

Edith said. 'Nicotine's supposed to stop senile dementia, so it's a great pity Gertrude never took up the habit, isn't it?' Tapping ash from her cigarette, she added: 'And I must admit my mind feels clearer than it has for years, so apart from helping me get over the tablets, maybe your Uncle Iolo's right when he says smoking sharpens the wits.'

'Only if you've got wits to begin with!' Phoebe snapped. 'It hasn't done much for him or Solange, has it? And he is NOT my "Uncle Iolo"!' Her voice was hoarse with exasperation. 'And he's got an almighty cheek giving anyone advice! He's on a permanent drugfest! He smokes like a chimney, drinks like a fish, and pops enough pills to sink a ship.'

'He does not take drugs!'

'He does, Mama.' Phoebe was adamant. 'Uncle Ned told me.'

'How could he know what your Uncle Iolo does?'

'I've no idea.' Scalding the pot, Phoebe tipped the water down the sink, counted out six tea-bags, and poured in more boiling water. 'But Minnie's seen the bottles in the bathroom cabinet when she goes to the house for her fashion shows with Solange, though how she can bear to have that woman's clothes next to her skin is beyond me. They reek of stale sweat and perfume.'

Left arm resting along the back of her chair, Edith inhaled a mouthful of smoke, then let it dribble slowly from her nostrils, her pose unconsciously elegant. 'Did Mina tell you what was in the bottles?'

'She couldn't remember the names,' Phoebe said. 'She has trouble with long words.'

'Don't be so bitchy,' Annie chided.

'She's just being truthful.' Edith sighed. 'Poor Mina!'

'She's been "poor Mina" to you ever since she was a baby,' Annie said. 'Why?'

Edith shrugged, hiding behind her veil of yellowy grey

smoke. 'Take Bethan upstairs for a nap. The little mite can barely keep her eyes open, and you're going out again later.'

'Let me take her.' Phoebe picked up the child, tickling her tummy. 'I'll read a story if she wants.' As she passed, she said to McKenna: 'You can take my book home if you like, but you'll read it, won't you?'

When she was out of earshot, Edith asked: 'Is that her essay about Llys Ifor?' She turned pages until she came upon the long screed in Phoebe's rounded, immature hand. 'Look what that teacher wrote,' she said, showing him a vicious scrawl of red ballpoint in the margin. "This work is over-imaginative," he read. "You have over reached yourself, writing about ideas beyond your grasp. Stick to what you understand in future."

'I went to see her,' Edith told him, fidgeting with the lighter, 'and I said she should be ashamed to harbour such miserable, mediocre attitudes! Nobody should mock a child's imagination.' She rounded on her eldest daughter. 'And I hope you know better than to stifle that kind of joy in the world. I've often thought something like that must've happened to Solange.'

'Whenever I've called her a hard-faced, superficial harpy, you say she's done well for herself,' Annie said.

'She's done the best she can, in the circumstances, but she's not happy.'

'Greedy people never are,' Annie countered.

McKenna intervened. 'Does Phoebe know you spoke to her teacher?'

'If she doesn't know, she'll have guessed,' Annie commented. 'Not much gets past her.' She put a fresh mug of tea in front of him, her fresh scent mingling with the acrid smoke of Edith's cigarette.

'I wanted to ask her about a couple of things Ned may have discussed with her,' he said, lighting his own cigarette. 'Maybe you could help?'

Annie sat beside her mother, both waiting expectantly.

'Gladys mentioned a friend of Ned's from their university days,' he went on. 'And it seems Ned had a key to George's flat, but we haven't found it.'

'Oh, dear!' Edith's eyes, red-rimmed with lack of sleep, widened. Her mouth worked, thoughts trying to find voice. 'Oh, no! He wouldn't do that, unless they'd had a dreadful falling out nobody knew about.'

'What, Mama?' Annie asked.

'Ned could have killed himself after all, and arranged things to make George look guilty.' She stubbed out the cigarette and reached for another. 'He could have put his bracelet in the flat, thrown away the key, or hidden it, then killed himself, and nobody could say when he last had his bracelet, because it was always tucked up out of sight under his cuff.'

'Why would he do that to George?' Annie asked. 'They were like father and son.' She smiled gently. 'Your imagination's running away with you.'

'But it's possible, isn't it?' Edith demanded of McKenna.

'Unlikely, I think,' he said, then grasped the opportunity. 'Would you let us search the house? The whereabouts of the key is very important to George.'

Edith spread her hands wide. 'Whenever you want.'

Her fingers shuddered gently, convulsively, as he wondered if her suffering, as her body voided itself of the drug residues, was more or less than his, as his heart and mind neutralized the remains of his marriage. 'Does anything come to mind about this friend?' he asked. 'He was another Edward, known as "Eddie", and, from the snapshot Gladys has, he was taller than Ned, quite overweight, and had a lot of hair.'

Edith and Annie looked at each other, then shook their heads. 'I vaguely remember hearing about him,' Edith mused, 'but he doesn't sound like anyone we know now, and Ned had so few friends.' She inhaled another lungful of smoke. 'But couldn't you have a computer prediction made from the photo to show how he might have changed? I'm sure Professor Williams would know someone at the university who could help. How old would this Eddie be now?'

'Around Ned's age.'

'Apart from George, the only person Ned called a friend to my knowledge was that old tramp.' Edith grimaced delicately.

'I met him yesterday,' McKenna said. 'He'd been to the farm to pay his respects.'

'He was walking down the lane as we drove up,' Annie added. 'He frightened Bethan half to death, which was very odd, as he's no more of a gargoyle than Meirion.'

'She knows Meirion,' Edith pointed out. 'He's almost part of the family, and besides, she has to keep on his right side if she wants her riding lessons.' She turned to McKenna. 'And in case you think I'm being cynical, take it from me that girls know from a very early age which side their bread's buttered, even though some fool themselves into thinking they can have butter *and* jam on both sides.'

'That's probably a veiled reference to my lapse from the straight and narrow,' Annie told him. 'Mama's wilfully obscure at times, in the hope of acquiring an air of exotic mystery, which I suppose accounts for our outlandish names.' She turned to Edith. 'Didn't Father raise any objections?'

'He wanted to call you Joan, after your grandmother, but I wasn't having you stuck with another Edith sort of name.'

'And what's an "Edith sort of name", Mama?'

'One that's dull, miserable and designed to keep you out of mischief, and expects you to live down to its demands.' Inhaling deeply yet again, she added: 'Mind you, Anastasia is a bit over the top. I'm glad you don't use it.'

'Minerva's not exactly run of the mill.'

'That was another mistake, and the poor child won't ever

live up to it.' She sighed. 'I'm not surprised Phoebe calls her Minnie, you know. She recognizes her limitations.'

'Now who's being bitchy?' Annie said, close to laughter.

McKenna smiled too, and as something flickered to life in Edith's haunted eyes, and sounds of gaiety came faintly from the upper floor, where Phoebe must be playing with her niece, he thought he could spend a very long time in the warm company of these unusual women, and be happy. Then the spectre of the absent Mina drifted into his mind's eye, and he felt a chill crawl up his spine.

4

George padded around the cell like a caged jungle cat, Rowlands thought, half-expecting to be pounced upon and clawed to pieces. 'What's the lady *bwana* got planned for me?' George asked, his eyes muddy with fatigue. 'Your detention order's up soon.'

'Mr McKenna's refused to charge you.'

'Yeah, but he's not calling the shots, is he?' Leaning against the wall, George stared at his stockinged feet. 'Are you looking for the key I gave Ned?'

'We're looking.'

'But you don't expect to find it.'

'It's probably gone the same way as the letters and photos and address book.'

'And you don't expect to find those, either.'

'We don't know where to look.'

George bared his teeth in a smile. 'The lady *bwana* wouldn't be happy to hear you talking on equal terms to the likes of me.'

'You've a right to be kept informed.'

'Are you sure about that? I thought my rights were forfeit

to my colour. If I were a plain white honky, I wouldn't be here.'

'So who's showing prejudice now?' Rowlands demanded.

George resumed his stealthy padding. 'We've learned from bitter experience to be defensive about your prejudice, because whatever you say about equality, given the chance, you'll indulge in nigger-baiting until the blood runs.'

'Then there's nothing I can say, is there?'

'Not really. I've been here before, as one might say, and I expect I'll be here again. In fact, my whole life will probably be punctuated by intervals in some cell or another.' He stopped in his tracks and gazed at Rowlands. 'And each time you white honkies pander to your prejudice and lock me up because I'm a nigger, it'll be another black mark against me, not you.'

'Will you stop calling me a white honky?' Rowlands snapped. 'One run-in with flatheads from the Met doesn't give you the right to tar the rest of us with the same brush!'

'Why not?' George asked. He padded over to the bunk, and sat down languidly. 'You're a white honky until you prove otherwise.'

'Why should I prove anything? You're complaining because you're being asked to do exactly that.'

'So now you know how I feel.'

'It's a mistake to argue with people like you,' Rowlands decided. 'But because of your education, not your colour.'

'The lady *bwana* resents me on both counts.'

'Like us, she wants a result. Unsolved crimes are bad for public confidence.' As George opened his mouth to speak, Rowlands held up his hand. 'Don't say it! Wrongful arrests are even worse.'

'Actually, I was going to ask for a cup of tea, and if I've got to stay here another night, I'd like another change of clothes and something else to read.'

• • •

Rowlands found Diana Bradshaw in her office, her desk stacked high with the large bound books which held the photographs and personal statistics of known criminals. As he walked in, she looked up from a spread of faces, and frowned. 'Yes?'

'Polgreen's detention order lapses at five o'clock, ma'am.'

'So?'

'His solicitor must be told if you intend to apply for another extension.'

'I have the matter in hand.' She marked one of the photographs with her finger, her nail cutting a tiny crescent in the clear plastic which shielded the face of a young woman with dark roots in her dyed blonde hair. 'What have you and Prys done about the cars? And where's Janet Evans? I haven't seen her for hours.'

'Prys is updating paperwork,' Rowlands said. 'He has to be available for the demo at Welsh Water.'

'And Janet Evans?'

'She came with me to see Professor Williams.'

'What?' Her face paled with anger and the nail dug deeper into the plastic. 'You were specifically instructed not to bother him!'

'We needed advice about Ned Jones's papers, and no-one but Professor Williams has the necessary expertise.'

'You should have asked for my permission!'

'With respect, ma'am, we can't function efficiently without at least some autonomy.'

'But you don't function efficiently, do you? Polgreen has been in custody since the early hours of yesterday morning and you still haven't found enough evidence to charge him. Are you sure you're looking?'

He flushed. 'It's unlikely the evidence is there.'

'You people amaze me!' She smiled coldly. 'You're bending

over backwards to make sure you can't be accused of discrimination, without the least understanding of the way people use racial prejudice for their own ends. If you'd ever worked in an inner-city force, as I have, you might appreciate how ethnic minorities can get away with murder just because of who they are.'

'I don't think that's true, ma'am.'

'You can *think* what you like!'

'In that case, ma'am, I'll suggest you're keeping Polgreen in custody to prove something to yourself, knowing full well he had nothing to do with Ned Jones's death.' Quivering with rage, he added: 'And please don't bother to threaten me with disciplinary action. I know you won't tolerate criticism, even if you're well out of order. After all, you wouldn't be here otherwise, would you?'

Janet heard the thud as Diana Bradshaw's office door closed, then the footsteps she knew were Rowlands's pounding along the corridor and through the fire door at the head of the stairs. Gently rubbing the left side of her belly, where the nagging pain which had plagued her for days threatened to turn fiery, she realized she would miss Rowlands when he moved on, which might be sooner than planned if the blistering row which preceded the thudding door indicated the prevailing wind.

Unsettling and disconcerting, the winds of change were blustering all about her, defining new features wherever she cast her eyes, and whichever mirror she consulted showed a face changed almost beyond recognition, its features sharpened with worry and twisted with confusion. Pain curled inside her like the flame of passion from which it sprang, and she dug her fist into her distended belly, trying to staunch a flood of agony.

Returning from the canteen with a tray of tea and sandwiches, Dewi found her doubled-up over the mess of papers on her desk, fighting for breath as if she had run a hundred miles. 'Jesus! What's wrong?'

Gasping, she shook her head wildly, digging both fists into her sides. Her chest heaved, and sweat poured down her face and neck, making dark blotches on her shirt, then the pain went, like flame beneath a deluge of water, with barely a flicker left to tell of its passing, and her blood ran cold, draining from scalp to toes. Slowly and fearfully, she sat upright, laughing weakly at the expression on his face.

'You've got to see a doctor. Now!' he said urgently.

'I can't get an appointment at short notice.'

'Pain like that doesn't need an appointment. There's something really bad going on.'

'How d'you know?' She moved gingerly, expecting an onslaught, and was almost blithe when nothing happened. She wondered fancifully if the dragon in her belly had run out of fire. 'Ned was in pain all his life, for no real reason.'

'But you're not usually.' He leaned over her, appalled by the waxen face and bruised eyes. 'You look terrible! Far worse than any corpse I've ever seen.'

'Don't be ridiculous!' She shivered. 'I've probably been poisoned by the paint fumes. They absolutely stink!' She held a mug of tea to her lips, and he heard the porcelain rattle against her teeth.

'You could have appendicitis,' Dewi suggested. He bit into a sandwich, and released the stench of cheese and pickle.

She clenched her teeth. 'It was taken out when I was five.'

'Then you could have some obscure foreign illness.'

'I'd be ill all the time.'

He sighed. 'Then you must be pregnant, and whatever anybody's told you, this isn't normal.'

She felt no anger, no humiliation, no resentment that he

should know, and marvelled at the changes which made her care only about the absence of her pain.

'Silence generally means yes,' he added.

Finishing one sandwich, he reached for another, putting a new layer on what she imagined as a stack of smells piling up towards the office ceiling, and she thought about their colours, were they visible. Paint like slurry, she decided, undulating heavily about the floor and washing against the walls, spumed like an oily sea with wisps of dirty smoke from the cigarettes McKenna and Rowlands consumed with such relish. The sandwiches and steaming tea swilled like vomit, running down street gutters in slicks of rainwater. She put her hand over her mouth, waiting, but nothing happened. Perhaps, she thought, the dragon had consumed her innards and everything there.

'We'll tell Bradshaw you're ill,' Dewi said, 'but first, we'll get the doctor.'

'I don't want a doctor.' Her words were indistinct.

'What you want isn't relevant. It's what you need that matters.' He picked up the telephone, and saw her body suddenly riven with tremors as a deep red tide surged between her clenched thighs.

Summoned urgently from Glamorgan Place, McKenna found an atmosphere of taut anxiety at the police station. Diana Bradshaw had gone in the ambulance with Janet, and Rowlands was waiting for him, chain-smoking. 'I blame myself!' he said, as soon as McKenna arrived. 'I should never have said my wife had stomach pains. I misled her.'

'Any blame belongs with the wretched hagiarchy which makes the Welsh fear and despise what should be natural and joyous. Janet didn't go to the doctor because she can't forgive herself for sinning, and when she gets better, she'll accept this torment as her due.'

'Suppose she doesn't get better?' Rowlands asked, his eyes bleak. 'She was bleeding like a stuck pig. The paramedics couldn't get her to the hospital fast enough, and those bloody decorators just stood there, gawping and whispering. The news'll be all over bloody Bangor by tea-time.'

'Has anyone told her parents?'

'Dewi rang. They've gone to the hospital.'

'And where's he?'

'At the Welsh Water demo. The mob's getting bigger by the minute, and the mood's getting uglier.'

'Perhaps I should go to the hospital, as well.'

'Bradshaw's there.' Pulling hard on his cigarette, Rowlands said: 'She'll want to see you. We had a row over George, then it got out of hand, and I let rip about her trying to cover her blunders.'

'Oh, bloody brilliant!' McKenna snarled. 'I warned you to keep your mouth shut!'

'You're not exactly famous for your tact and reticence!' Rowlands snapped. 'Oh, hell! I'm sorry,' he muttered, then said: 'No, I'm not sorry! She bloody asked for it! Anyway, what I said wouldn't warrant dismissal, so the worst I can expect is a transfer to Holyhead.' The glimmer of a smile touched his lips. 'I hear it's worse than Chicago in Al Capone's heyday.'

'It's the same as it always was,' McKenna said testily.

'Look, I *am* sorry. I didn't mean to cause trouble.'

'People rarely *intend* to create chaos, but they manage, all the same.' His face grim, McKenna added: 'What's happening with George?'

Rowlands shrugged. 'Bradshaw said she was dealing with it, but she hasn't completed the application for an extension.'

'Then we'll leave it until she comes back.'

'We saw Williams, by the way, but he wasn't much help. He'd no idea why Ned collected all that stuff, and insisted the other poems and whatnot were just copies of what's been around for ages.'

'I haven't come across them before.'

'But you're not a Welsh scholar, are you?'

'Then ask George if they're familiar, because he's far more of a scholar than Williams will ever be.'

Shortly after Rowlands went downstairs with a sheaf of documents under his arm, Gabriel Ansoni called from the hospital. 'I was here with a patient when Janet arrived,' he told McKenna, his voice grave. 'She's still being transfused, because the haemorrhaging won't stop.'

'Was it a miscarriage?'

'It was an inevitability. She had an ectopic pregnancy, and the Fallopian tube's ruptured. She must have been in agony for days. Why in God's name didn't she come to see me?'

'I've left the papers with George,' Rowlands announced. 'They'll be quite safe because he's not going anywhere. Did you ring the hospital?'

'Dr. Ansoni called,' McKenna said. 'She had an ectopic pregnancy, and now she's in a critical condition.'

'Are you going over?'

'Diana's staying. She'll be a lot more use than we would.' Seeing the other man's mutinous expression, he scowled. 'Just stop making like Punch to her Judy, will you?' Rummaging in his briefcase, he went on: 'And as computers co-operate with you, find out why Annie Harris keeps getting these fixed penalty notices when she hasn't been to Shrewsbury for years.'

'Because her car came courtesy of Jason Lloyd, I imagine,' Rowlands commented, leafing through the documents.

'Anything connected with that arrogant little sod must be suspect. I can't think why Edith likes him.'

'Maybe she only pretends to, to keep Mina happy,' McKenna said, locating Phoebe's exercise book at the bottom of his briefcase. 'Stranger things have happened.'

'Like your opinion of Edith changing from negative to positive in the blink of an eye?'

'She's surprised me more than once this week,' McKenna admitted.

'I expect she's surprised herself even more, but with her sort, you can't tell which state of mind's calling the shots, so they're not exactly reliable. Phoebe's pretty much her mother's daughter, as well.'

'And I think they both have a core of honesty and strength. By the way, Edith said we can search the house, so we'll do it when Dewi's back.'

In her essay, Phoebe struggled at times to give full voice to her ideas, McKenna thought, but amid the unruly wrangling with words, they were none the less forceful and uniquely experienced, burned in the crucible of her own imagination before being set down on paper. She built Llys Ifor stone by stone, from its past as the raw, carpentered environment of its infancy, to its future as the few tumbled stones of a decayed ruin, and each era was a new manipulation of the earth on which it stood, a new rearrangement of mossy stone, weather-bleached wood and lichen-stained slate, each the record of its own history, and an indivisible partnership between man and nature.

Lingering over words and phrases, caught again between here and another place and time, he decided beauty could be defined only by the hunger it evoked, and thought of the gift she fought to bring to maturity. The taste of envy could still sour his throat when he remembered Ned's gift, and perhaps in that he was not alone, he realized, wondering who might have found the same gall too bitter to swallow.

The little breeze still drifted in from the sea, stirring dusty leaves on the trees outside and pulling cigarette smoke about the room. Sorting papers, he began to understand how his resentment and disappointment, and an unremitting sense of failure, impeded his own capacity to function, for the execution of police duties without malice or favour had implications beyond even-handedness. When Diana Bradshaw favoured her own comfort, she had set in motion the chain of events now leading him to fritter away his time escaping humiliation. Irritated beyond measure by his own stupidity, he telephoned Gladys to ask for a snapshot of Ned's erstwhile friend, and was then unreasonably pleased when she again invited him to visit Llys Ifor whenever he wished.

Through the half-open door, he saw Rowlands hunched over the computer console, chain-smoking in defiance of all instructions, pushing keys and frowning. 'Are you sure that car belongs to Annie Harris?'

'Of course it does.' McKenna went to the door. 'How else would she be getting fixed penalty notices?'

'Did she check the number with her own? People can get so upset by these notices they don't think.'

'I checked. It's her car.'

'Then as the computer's telling me that car belongs to a man from Rhyl, I think we've got a classic double-up on our hands. Who's got the *bona fide* vehicle, I wonder, and who's driving round in a stolen car and total ignorance?'

'Probably both of them. Why stop at two, with new registration documents there for the asking? Get Rhyl to find out where the car was bought, and check the engine and vehicle ID numbers, then ask DVLA to do a thorough trawl.'

'I'll put Iolo's toy through while I'm at it, and I'd better do Dewi's convertible, as he bought it off that villain Geraint.' He glanced at McKenna. 'Will you tell Annie, or shall I?'

Instead of quartering the cell, George was crawling around amid a litter of papers, studying one after the other and moving a sheet now and then to another heap. When McKenna appeared at the door, he sat back on his heels, brushing sweat from his forehead. 'If truth is misrepresented often enough, and with enough guile, the misrepresentation becomes a truth.'

'That's a very philosophical assertion,' McKenna commented. 'How is it relevant in the real world?'

'As something to bear in mind, and not just when you want to fit a crime to a suspect. You may well have the suspect under your nose, but not know the crime's taken place.' He gestured to the papers. 'Have you read this lot?'

'We read most of them. Dewi sorted them into loose categories.'

'Up to a point, his diligence obscured the issue.' George searched for a particular document, then read out the poem which had caught McKenna's attention, his execution of its ancient language quite beautiful.

'And?' McKenna enquired, sitting on the bunk and lighting the last cigarette from his packet.

'Williams said these texts have been around for centuries, but they're new to me, and I've seen virtually all the extant texts of the period.' He pointed to the heap of press cuttings telling of the professor's career. 'Did you read those?' As McKenna nodded, he said: 'What's missing, then?'

'How on earth should I know?'

'You're a detective.'

'But not a document specialist.'

'You don't need to be. It's staring you in the face, which is what I meant about misrepresentation of the truth.'

'So why not put me out of my misery?' McKenna asked, dropping ash in the empty packet.

'What's in it for me? The key to the cell door?'

'As far as I'm concerned, you can stay here until you turn white.'

'You put Rowlands to shame!' George laughed, teeth gleaming. 'He's scared shitless of being accused of prejudice, whatever he says to the contrary, and you don't give a toss.'

'I heard about the "white honky" jibe,' McKenna said, 'but I'm "white trash", so from that point of view, you and I are on a par. Now, what's missing?'

'Provenance of the texts Williams discovered. You'd expect to find analyses of paper, watermarks, inks, quills, writing style, words and phrases current to the place and period, and anything else that might verify their history. As Ned kept everything else, I can't imagine he'd overlook that.'

'Nor can I.' McKenna smiled slightly. 'Phoebe might well have been right about all the boxes being full of lies.'

'Which means Williams's whole career is built on a fraud, and Ned probably found out.'

'What about the other texts, like that beautiful verse?'

'They need the attention of document specialists and Welsh scholars, but I suspect some were written by the same person trying out different hands,' George said, then he grinned. 'You'll have to retrieve the originals of the professor's alleged discovery from the National Library, won't you? And as I've no doubt the manuscripts were accepted at face value, expect to see a cat the size of Phoebe's routing the academic pigeon coop.'

• • •

'It's amazing how you find things when you know what you're looking for,' Rowlands commented, happily punching computer keys. 'The man in Rhyl's spitting feathers, because the vehicle ID details on the car he bought relate to an identical model reported stolen by Manchester Police. And,' he added, pausing to light a cigarette, 'DVLA unearthed two others with the same registration, one local, the other in Shropshire, which is probably the parking offender. If they had a decent computer in the first place, these things would show up at the time, and the double-up racket would be a lot harder to run.'

'All over the station,' commented McKenna, 'there are notices in big red letters warning us not to smoke near computers.'

'Are there? I always smoke when I'm working on my own. Seems to help it to think, or whatever computers do with themselves.'

Tearing the wrapping from a new cigarette pack, McKenna related the conversation with George. 'We've been disgracefully negligent over these documents, but then, if George is right, so have some of the best brains in the field.'

'Do we haul in the professor, then, and hope he admits his deception?' Rowlands asked. 'Fat chance!' He put his cigarette in the lip of the ashtray, and returned to the computer. 'I've alerted the vehicle examiner about the suspect cars, and Shrewsbury Police will do their end.' He paused. 'And I called the hospital, but there's no change.'

'But she's been there nearly two hours. There must be *some* change.'

• • •

When she telephoned a little later, Diana Bradshaw could report only that Janet was still in the operating theatre, still losing blood, and still being transfused, while the distraught Pastor Evans roamed the hospital corridors, muttering to himself. Janet's mother simply waited, in stunned silence.

'Why didn't she tell me?' Her voice was subdued. 'Why didn't she ask me for help? You knew, didn't you? Just before she passed out in the ambulance, she said she wanted you to tell her parents.' She drew a deep breath, then said: 'And Prys knew. Everyone knew, except me!'

'Dewi probably guessed, which wouldn't be difficult in the circumstances,' McKenna said. 'Janet told me because she's known me a long time, and I know her family. She wasn't trying to hide anything from you, and nor was anyone else.'

'I didn't think you were!' The waspish tone was never far away. 'But at the very least, I might have persuaded her to see a doctor.'

'She wouldn't go. She missed an appointment the other evening.'

After a long silence, she said: 'Even if she pulls through, she might never be able to have children.'

'That isn't always a tragedy. Some women don't want children.'

'Only until they find they're barren, and then there's nothing on earth they want more.' Then, before he could respond, she rushed on. 'You'll have to release Polgreen.'

'Without charge, or on bail?'

'Without charge.'

'And are you returning soon? There are several things to discuss, Rowlands among them.'

'He lost his temper.'

'He tells me he was very much out of order.'

'And what d'you suggest I do about it? Set the disciplinary machine in motion? I don't think that would be warranted.'

'As I wasn't there, I can't give an opinion.'

'Quite, so we'll chalk it up to experience. What else did you want to discuss?'

'Some developments with regard to Ned, and Rowlands has struck lucky with the cars.'

'Tell him to find mine, then, and I'll forget what he said.' There was a glint of humour in her voice.

The aged scholar whom McKenna eventually located through the document curator at the National Library struggled to entertain the possibility of fraud more than Phoebe ever fought with words. While admitting that technical verification of Wiliams's discovery had not taken place, the need for such investigation, or the wisdom, was dismissed out of hand. 'D'you realize the best Celtic scholars in Europe scrutinized those texts?' he demanded. 'Are you trying to gainsay their judgement?'

'The documents appear to constitute evidence,' McKenna countered, 'so they must be properly examined.'

'You can't do that! Don't you know how fragile they are?'

'No harm will come to them, I assure you.'

'Why are you doing this?' The old voice was plaintive. 'People have known of those texts since they were first written, and if you look through the literature, you'll find hundreds of references and even quotations.' He paused, in obvious distress. 'By chance, every once in a blue moon, when the world thinks they're lost for good and we're all the poorer for it, there's a hint they might still exist, or a clue to their whereabouts, and that's how these were unearthed. The clues were there, but no-one saw them for what they were, until Eddie realized there might be a trail to follow.' He paused again. 'He got a job in Vienna during one of the long vacs, helping to sort some of the messes still left over from the war, and found the manuscripts among a pile of papers belonging to the Frenchman called de Tremont, who went to Vienna in 1809 as part of the French occupation, then returned to France in a hurry when there was so much trouble after the 1814 Congress. He left most of his stuff behind, expecting to collect it later, I imagine, but he never did.'

'Who is "Eddie"?' McKenna asked, almost holding his breath.

'Professor Wiliams.'

'His name is Iorwerth.'

'That's his second name. We knew him as Eddie.'

' "We"?'

McKenna could almost see the other man shrug. 'Me. Us. We were at university together.'

'I didn't know,' McKenna said, reaching for another cigarette. 'Did you by any chance know Edward Jones, too?'

' "Ned-soft-in-the-head", Eddie called him.' He laughed. 'He disappeared off to hospital nearly every full moon, but it never seemed to make a difference. He was such a melancholy person. Eddie visited his home a few times, somewhere in the back of beyond, and he reckoned the whole family was doolally.'

'He none the less won a major prize at the Eisteddfod.'

'And if he hadn't been so unstable, who knows what else he might have done? But it's water under the bridge, isn't it? And what you intend doing with these manuscripts is not only a waste of time and public money, but it could well be seen as an attack on Eddie's reputation, and on ours.'

'I trust you'll regard the matter simply as a necessary part of our investigations,' McKenna said. 'And at least, you'll have the provenance for your own benefit.'

'We don't need it.'

'Who first saw the manuscripts?'

'I did. Eddie came back from Vienna with a whole load of stuff he was pretty excited about, but when I saw those, I was ecstatic, and I asked my uncle to look at them. He was the top Celtic scholar of his day, and he'd be as proud as punch to see how Eddie's taken over his mantle.'

'I'm sure he would,' McKenna said, a grim smile on his lips.

'Women enjoy being inconsistent,' Rowlands commented. 'They think it keeps us in our place.'

'Diana had to agree to our interviewing Iolo,' McKenna said.

'Eddie,' Rowlands corrected him. 'You didn't need to ask for the photo after all, and if we'd had our wits in gear, the "E" before his name on the path lab printout would've alerted us.'

'Well, it didn't!' McKenna snapped. 'We had to rely on a suspect and a gullible old mate to point us in the right direction.'

'It's like a mountain fog anyway. Ned's papers are in such a mess they could mean anything or nothing, and the manuscript scam was up and running over thirty years ago.'

'We don't know the manuscripts are fakes,' McKenna reminded him.

'So why the cover-up, if not to hide the truth? Or, as George says, to create a new truth? Why didn't Iolo own to being Ned's old pal? He's had plenty of opportunities.'

'We'll ask him, when I've asked the first Mrs Williams if she can fill in a few blanks.'

'D'you think Edith's been economical with the truth, as well? Surely her woman's intuition would have detected their relationship?'

'Not if it was sabotaged by the drugs,' McKenna said, tidying his desk. 'D'you know something? You badger me the way Dewi does. You must share his dog-with-a-bone mentality.' He locked his briefcase and pulled on his jacket.

'By the way, Diana's staying at the hospital until there's some news about Janet. Let me know as soon as she calls.'

5

Driving slowly through the council estate in search of Margaret Williams, McKenna realized for the first time that the inadequates who passed through police hands with such depressing regularity were identifiable by the filth and neglect which marked out their addresses. Wondering briefly if the world might be a better place should some of them perish in the womb, he pulled up outside the spick and span dwelling where Iolo's first wife now lived.

Pristine double-glazed windows caught the afternoon sunlight, the front door and garden gate gleamed with fresh paint, and, bright with more paint, little stone animals foraged her garden; rabbits in herbaceous borders, a squirrel transfixed at the foot of an ornamental tree, a frog teetering on the edge of a tiny pond, and a cat crouched on the doorstep. Smiling despite himself at her whimsies, he walked up the path and rang the bell. Inside the house, a little tune chimed out.

An old man opened the door, smiling. 'Lovely day again, isn't it? What can we do you for?'

Showing his identification, McKenna said: 'I'd like to see Mrs Williams.'

'You took your time about it, didn't you?' Beckoning him to follow, the man trudged along the hallway, carpet slippers almost soundless on a thick pile carpet. 'We've been expecting you ever since word got out about Ned Jones.'

Shunted into the back parlour, McKenna found himself face to face with the wife who preceded the sombre Solange in the Williams's marital bed, and thought the professor might have come to rue the substitution, for even in age, this Mrs Williams had colour and vibrancy. She smiled, extending a plump pink hand. 'Iolo asked the other day if you'd been to see me,' she said, her voice soft with the residues of a Valleys' accent.

'Did he?' Taking the offered seat, he added: 'I didn't know you were still in touch.'

'They aren't, in the way you mean,' the old man told him. He padded to the door. 'I'll make the tea, then leave you to it. Maggie doesn't need me to hold her hand.'

'I met him in Tesco's,' she said. 'Trundling around with a trolley full of liquor. Solange said they were stocking up early for Christmas, which was just an excuse, of course.' Regarding him brightly, she asked: 'Did he give you my address?'

'No,' McKenna admitted. 'He's never mentioned you.'

'He's ashamed of me because I got into trouble, and ashamed of himself because I divorced him. So did you get my address off your files?' When McKenna nodded, she went on: 'Should I still be there? I mean, aren't convictions wiped off the records after a while?'

'They are, yes.'

'So why am I still here? It was a long time ago.'

'You're quite right. I'll look into it.'

'Not that it matters. I never made a secret of it. It was the only lapse I'd had, up to then.' She giggled. 'And since then, I haven't stopped!'

'Take no notice of her,' the man said, standing in the doorway. 'She likes to think she's a bit of a hell raiser.' He grinned at McKenna, his face a web of wrinkles. 'We never married, you see, and she still gets a kick out of living tally, even after all these years.'

'Don't the neighbours suspect?' McKenna asked.

'No reason why they should. I'm another Williams, and Maggie wears a ring. Mind you, we'd have wed if we'd been blessed with children, because it's not right to raise them the other way.'

As the kettle screeched in the kitchen, and her companion disappeared, she said: 'Harry would've made a lovely dad.'

'I'm sorry to get personal,' McKenna said, 'but our files mentioned a hormonal disorder at the time of the offences, and I assumed it was the menopause. Wasn't that before you met Harry?'

She nodded. 'The doctors thought the same, but they were wrong. It was Iolo. I'd stopped eating because I couldn't stomach food, so I lost a lot of weight, and got very run down, and my periods just stopped. I looked like an old hag, and felt worse.' She sighed. 'And as soon as I left him, everything changed.'

'Was he violent?' McKenna remembered the raised hand and vicious temper Phoebe provoked.

'He never hit me, but I was still afraid of his moods, and what he *might* do. And he was forever running me down, sneering about my voice and my clothes, and my lack of proper education. Iolo's not a nice man, you see. He's weak and selfish and spiteful, but I can't help feeling a tiny bit sorry for him now, because I'm so happy, and he's stuck with that Solange. She won't leave him while he can keep her in fancy clothes and trips abroad.'

Harry reappeared, with afternoon tea for two on a shiny silver tray.

'Stay,' Maggie told him. 'Mr McKenna won't mind. Get yourself a cup and saucer.'

'You won't be telling him anything I haven't heard, and more than once, and I want to finish weeding that border in the back garden.' Turning to McKenna he said: 'This heat's doing no good for my roses, but the weeds don't seem to care they've had no rain for nearly six weeks. They keep coming, bigger than ever.'

'There was an item on the news about a water shortage,' Maggie said, 'and a big demo at the Welsh Water place.'

'There'll be trouble to be sorted, then,' Harry commented. 'Folk like an excuse for mayhem.' He shuffled from the room, and, as Maggie stirred the tea and poured milk in the cups, McKenna heard the sounds of garden tools being dragged along paving.

'He loves gardening. He used to keep the parks for the council.' Lifting the teapot, she added: 'That was before the drunks and addicts took them over. There's nowhere now for a rest and a chat.' She passed him a cup. 'Help yourself to sugar, and have a scone. I baked them fresh this morning.'

He was spending another afternoon in the company of age, he thought, raking over the embers of the past, some cold, others which flared into new life as the oxygen reached them. As he bit into a crumbly scone topped with rich Welsh butter and strawberry jam, he tried to imagine the woman opposite in her earlier guise. 'Where did you meet Professor Williams?'

'I worked in one of the university libraries.' She smiled again, licking butter and jam from her fingers. 'After a while, we started going out together.'

'And?' McKenna took another scone.

'He fancied me, and I fancied him, even though he was quite fat.' She laughed. 'I was on the bonny side myself, because I've never been like Solange. I call her one of those X-Ray people. You can almost see the bones.'

'And when did you marry?'

'When Iolo realized I wouldn't go to bed with him otherwise, and of course, as soon as he got me where he wanted me, he didn't want me any longer, and that was when the rot set in. He said I'd trapped him, and I wasn't the sort of wife he needed.' She sipped her tea. 'Fool that I was, I kept hoping things would get better, especially after we first came to Bangor. My mother said you have to work at marriage, so I slaved away, and he despised me all the more.'

'How long were you together?'

'Depends on what you mean by together. He's getting on for fifty-six now, and he'd had his thirtieth birthday a week or so before our wedding. I was a year younger, and still a virgin.' The smile returned, teasingly and fleetingly. 'The divorce came through on my thirty-eighth birthday, and it was the best present I'd ever had.'

'I thought you were married for much longer,' McKenna said, picking up his own teacup.

'Well, thank God we weren't, else I'd have thrown myself under a train! Up to then, I'd never understood what people meant by depths of despair, but those days were like a night without end.'

'What was he doing when you married?'

'Lecturing and promoting himself, like now. He's still everyone's golden boy because of those papers he found, isn't he?' Pouring more tea, she added: 'That happened long before we met, though. My family moved to Aberystwyth less than a year before I got married. My dad's great aunt left him a small boarding house, so he chucked his job at the mine, and we left the Valleys for something better.'

'And was it better?'

'Well, Iolo said you'd be hard-pressed to find anything *worse* than where we'd come from, but he was always a terrible snob. His sort usually are.'

'What's his sort?'

'The sort that thinks they're a cut above the working classes, when they aren't. His dad was a steelworks clerk, and his mother came from Swansea, then his father was sent to South Africa for a few years, and they were like nobs come back from the colonies afterwards. His mother's still alive, and I swear she's got more side to her than a double-decker bus. Iolo gets all his big ideas from her, I'm sure.'

'Then he could be a victim of parental ambition.'

'Are you trying to be funny?' she demanded. 'The only thing pushing him around is his own weakness. He lets some people push *him*, because he's scared of them, then he has to push somebody else, to make himself feel better. I was his stooge, and now he's Solange's whipping boy, so I expect he's taking it all out on some other poor fool. People who despise other people really despise themselves, and they can be quite dangerous.' She pushed the plate of scones towards him, saying: 'Have another. You look like a good meal wouldn't hurt.'

'I was always thin. My mother used to be afraid the welfare people would think she was starving me.'

'You're lucky, really. Harry says I've only to look at a cake and he can see it on my hips. Not that he minds, you understand.' The eyes twinkled, and her mouth curved in a smile. 'I've often thought being fat was really all I had in common with Iolo. Solange must half starve him, you know, because he's lost ever so much weight since they got together.'

'How long ago was that?'

'You ask some questions! I think about twelve years since. He met her in France.'

'Did you always know him as Iolo?' McKenna asked, swallowing the last of his scone.

She frowned. 'What d'you mean?'

'He used to use his first name, Edward.'

'Did he? Well, when I met him, everybody called him Iolo, or Iowerth. Or even "sir", at times, which he liked best.'

McKenna put his lighter and cigarettes by his saucer. 'Did he use sleeping tablets? And you say he drinks a lot now. Was he a heavy drinker then?'

'There's an ashtray on the dresser behind you,' she said.

'Harry smokes, but I don't, and Iolo wouldn't have cigarettes in the house, let alone drink or tablets. Shows what a bad influence Solange is, doesn't it?' She sighed, and frowned again. 'I was the one needing help to get me through in those days. I was more in the doctor's surgery than out. I had anti-depressants during the day, and sleeping tablets every night. I was like a zombie, but I didn't care, because it stopped me feeling, and there was so much pain to be felt. People say a marriage gone bad hurts like the ends of a broken bone rubbing together.'

'D'you still take drugs?'

'Good heavens, no! I didn't need them after I left him, did I?'

Turning round in his seat to get the ashtray, McKenna said: 'How well did you know Ned Jones?'

'I didn't.'

Ashtray in hand, McKenna found himself gaping again.

'I'd heard of him of course, but I'd never met him,' Maggie went on. 'There was no reason why I should.'

'How did you hear of him?' McKenna asked, lighting his cigarette. 'Through Iolo?'

'Why d'you keep asking me about Iolo? I thought you wanted to talk about Edith. I knew about Ned because he lived with her.'

'Why should I want to discuss Edith?'

'Because of what happened between her and Iolo,' Maggie said. 'I divorced him because of it, too. I felt gutted at the time, but she did me the biggest favour anyone's ever done.' Watching the expression on his face, she added: 'Don't you know? Oh, dear!'

'Did Edith have an affair with him?'

'If you want to make it sound like something worth having, I suppose you could call it that. He said he was in love with her, and I think she believed he was, too.' Memory extinguished the sparkle in her eyes, and she flushed. 'We had a *terrible* row, and I told her she was the sort who'll let the whole world rub up against her thighs, and never mind if a man was married.' She sighed again. 'To be fair, my marriage was over long before Edith came on the scene, and hers must've been, else she wouldn't have needed to look elsewhere. She thought Iolo'd look after her, the way Harry looks after me. Poor woman! She wasn't so lucky, was she? He left her in the lurch with a vengeance, and I'm not surprised she's been on pills ever since. He seems to do that to women.'

'How did he leave her in the lurch?' McKenna asked. 'Had he promised to marry her?'

'I don't know what he promised, but it made her fall for his wiles. Mind you, he had charm, and a way with words to pull your heart to pieces, but words with nothing behind them aren't worth the breath they take.' She began stacking used crockery on the tray. 'As soon as the chickens came home to roost, Iolo scarpered, and Edith couldn't see him for the dust. He came whining back to me, but I told him I never wanted to set eyes on him again.' One plump hand resting on the handle of the tray, the other on her leg, she stared at McKenna. 'You still don't understand what I'm talking about, do you? Edith had a baby. The middle girl with the silly name is Iolo's daughter. She was all the proof I needed to get a divorce.'

6

He left Margaret to her peace, taking with him the secret which had broken through the weight of time as the weeds with which Harry engaged in battle ruptured the hard, parched garden soil.

The soft sea breeze had made its way further inland, ruffling the trees in Edith's garden, and whispering like voices from the past. He drew to a halt by the kerb, listening to a relay of other voices on the car radio passing urgent requests for personnel and dog handlers to attend the demonstration, then unclipped the seat belt, and found Phoebe crouched on the pavement, staring at him.

'You were wrong about cats having the sense to steer clear of traffic,' she said, holding open the car door. 'That stupid animal was sunbathing on the white lines in the middle of the road, so I've given him a rocket and shut him in the back garden. He'll get the message, if he really *can* think.'

Side by side, they walked up the drive, she with her hands in her trouser pockets, pulling fabric into triangular protuberances. She seemed edgy, a little ill at ease with herself.

'Is your mother in?' McKenna asked.

'She's gone shopping.'

'Will she be long?'

'Probably not. The professor's invited himself over for dinner, and Mama likes to cook him something nice. Solange doesn't feed him properly, you know. She thinks we can all survive on alcohol and lettuce leaves.'

'Isn't she coming, too?'

'She's gone to London. She offered to take Minnie with her, but dear sister couldn't get the day off work, so I expect we'll suffer another sulkfest as soon as she gets home.'

'And where's Annie?' he asked, puzzled by the little knot in his innards.

'She's taken Bethan to Colwyn Bay Zoo. They wanted me to go with them, but I see enough of that sort of thing here.'

'That's rather a pretentious remark.'

'I'm given to those at times.' She led him towards the kitchen through the pooled light in the hall. 'Did you read my essay?'

'Yes, and I think it's wonderful.'

'Do you really?' She frowned. 'You're not just being nice, are you?' Then she smiled. 'No, I can tell you're not, by your eyes. Uncle Ned said the eyes are always a give away.'

'Flattery would be wrong, because your writing's too important for dishonesty.'

She took a jug of lemonade from the refrigerator, filled two tumblers, then took a new blue glass ashtray from the cupboard. 'Mama's stocked up on ashtrays, and she bought two hundred cigarettes from Safeway this morning.'

'How is she?'

'Weird!' Phoebe wrapped her hands around the tumbler. 'Like something in a horror film, metamorphosing into something else. She's as high as a kite, jittery as hell, falling over her own feet, dropping things, laughing like a hyena one minute and weeping buckets the next, and saying she feels better than she's done for years.'

'I think Dr Ansoni should at least know she's stopped the tablets.'

'So do we, but Mama said she'd be wasting her time and his, because she can't avoid the withdrawal.' She took a gulp of lemonade. 'Annie and I had a chat while she was out earlier, and we've decided to monitor the situation, because Annie agrees with me that Mama's been more real in the last few days than we've ever known.'

'Real?' McKenna asked, drinking the ice-cold liquid.

' "Real" as in "here", a real live person instead of a half-dead one. You can't know what I mean because you've never seen her at her worst, when she was so spaced out she couldn't even focus her eyes, let alone concentrate. She did a lot of weeping then, too, only she didn't seem to realize. In fact, she wasn't aware of anything much. She'd wander round the house, muttering to herself, and moving so slowly you'd swear she was wading through sludge. She said her body felt heavy and droopy and stiff at the same time, and her back and all her joints ached, so she could sympathize with Uncle Ned over that much, at least.'

'They were using drugs from the same chemical family, albeit for a different purpose,' McKenna said. 'They cause stiffness in the joints because of the way they act on the central nervous system.'

'I told her that, you know, and I told Uncle Ned his sleeping tablets were making him ache even more.' She ran her finger around the edge of the glass, scowling. 'And I absolutely hate being proved right *all* the time! It seems like I know more than I should.'

'So how did you know?'

'Asking questions, as usual,' she replied, the scowl falling victim to humour. 'Annie had a general anaesthetic last year to have an impacted wisdom tooth pulled, and afterwards, she ached so much she could hardly move because of the drugs she'd had to relax her muscles. So I borrowed Uncle Ned's university library card to mug up on the drugs swilling through my family's veins, as it were, and I could've saved myself the trouble, for all the notice either of them took.'

'Don't judge their weaknesses too harshly,' McKenna said. 'You'll despise yourself if you discover some of your own.'

'With our track record, it's a case of when, not if.' She chuckled. 'We're a real genetic mess.'

'It could skip your generation. Gladys said Bethan has the same colouring as her mother, even though Annie's dark like you.'

'Bethan looks like her father. He's tall and thin and fair. She'll be quite tall, I imagine. Her legs and arms are long already.'

'I didn't realize you knew him,' he said, the knot retying itself in his innards.

'Of course we know him! He's a teacher in Llandudno.

He was engaged to Annie for yonks, and she broke it off when she found she was having Bethan.'

'Why?'

Phoebe shrugged. 'I suppose it made her wonder if she wanted to spend the rest of her life with him. People say a crisis concentrates the mind, don't they?'

'Are they still in touch?'

She nodded. 'It's all very civilized. He's gone to the zoo with them today, and he'd marry Annie tomorrow if he got the chance, but as far as she's concerned, he's history.'

'I see.'

'When George came on the scene last year, I told Annie I'd quite like *him* for a brother-in-law, but she said he's a non-starter, and I don't think it's because he's black, 'cos she's not given to that sort of prejudice. I know they like each other as friends, but there's none of that gut-wrenching stuff they'd need for marriage.'

'Then perhaps you could save him for yourself,' McKenna suggested. 'If you start his training now, he could be well to heel by the time you're old enough to marry.'

'I don't fancy him either, even though he's so gorgeous-looking. We'd never have more than a cerebral relationship.'

'Aren't you rather too young for that kind of decision-making?'

'Not really,' she said airily. 'I know what I like in a man. You must be quite fanciable, especially for someone of Annie's age.' Smiling broadly, she added: 'Did you know you hair's going a bit grey at the sides?'

'You're very observant.'

'I'm very cheeky, too. I'm sorry, I didn't mean to annoy you. It's because you remind me of Uncle Ned in so many ways it seems OK to say whatever comes into my head. You make my imagination work like he did, too.' She paused, reviewing her words. 'That doesn't sound quite right, does it? Why won't words ever say what you mean?'

'You managed very well in your essay.'

'That's different.' She drained her glass, and began making patterns in a ring of condensation on the table top. 'Some days, I feel so miserable and scared I want to die, then on others, I feel wonderfully strong and powerful, especially when I'm writing, even though it's such hard work.' She looked up, eyes dark with concentration. 'And I think everyone feels the same inside, but either they don't understand, or being more than one person gets too frightening, so they take to drink, or drugs, or sex, or anything that'll stop them being alone with themselves. I sometimes wonder if Mama simply let the sad Mama take over.'

'Whatever gifts you have came in part from her, you know.' Lighting his first cigarette, he went on: 'And perhaps she blotted out the reality of the world she lived in because she saw something nearer to her heart's desire, and knew it was just out of reach, whereas you can move between the two as and when you like. For all you know, she might have similar perceptions and impulses, but not the ability to make use of them.'

'Uncle Ned would've said she couldn't perfect the art of escape or achieve the art of revelation.'

'And insight can be excruciatingly painful, which is perhaps why people are so reluctant to admit to it. Drink and drugs and sex at least blur the outlines of harsh reality.'

'I suppose that's what's wrong with the professor.' She dried the table with the cuff of her shirt, and watched McKenna despoil the pristine ashtray with a tube of grey ash. 'I think your inner life is the one that really matters, and it's a terrible waste not to live it, but I suppose you can't if you're afraid of yourself.' She picked up his lighter, tracing her fingers over the engraved initials. 'I watch little Bethan, wondering what she knows and what she'll remember of now, because even though I'm nowhere near grown up, I can hardly remember being her age, and I don't know how I learned all the things in my head. Uncle Ned thought we start learning by looking outwards, referring everything back to our body, and he said most people stop when they know enough to get by, because after that, you have to look inwards, and that's the hard part. But it's the best part, isn't it?'

'It's your inner space,' McKenna said. 'As infinite as outer space, but even more exciting and mysterious because you have your own sun and moon and stars.'

Her eyes gleamed. 'But it can get scary, especially if you're not sure you aren't batty to start with! I wish I had an "off" switch in my head, sometimes, so I won't drive myself completely into the ground. I got really psyched up when I realized I could sort of see sounds, or hear colours, but George said it's not unusual if you're trying to develop your faculties.' She put the lighter back on the table, and sat back, folding her arms. 'We had a really interesting discussion about whether a person's height, or size, or whatever determines their assessment of the world. Do long-sighted people see more than short-sighted ones, for instance, but miss the small details, or do big people feel more than small ones?' She grinned at him. 'Your eyes are glazing over.'

'I've had a busy day, and at my age, you begin to feel it.'

'Annie said I can talk the hind legs off a herd of donkeys. You should tell me to shut up, you know, 'cos I'll go on for ever if you let me.' Unfolding her arms, she rose, and switched on the kettle. 'I'll make a pot of tea. Mama should be back any minute.'

'What time is the professor due?'

'About half seven.' She pulled a face.

'Will Annie be back by then?'

'Dunno.' She counted four tea-bags into the pot, and felt the side of the kettle. 'They might have a meal out. Bethan likes going to a burger bar, even though I keep telling Annie she's running the risk of Bethan ending up like Auntie Gertrude.'

He felt what people always describe as someone walking over their grave, and shivered despite himself.

Phoebe watched him. 'You shy away from some thoughts, don't you?'

'The picture you paint isn't very pleasant.'

'It's a possibility. We never now what *might* happen.'

'That isn't always exciting.'

'I suppose not.' Steam began to force its way from the kettle, and brewing the tea, she added: 'But it's better to look on the really black side so you can recognize the other when you see it. If you're never miserable, for instance, you'll never know when you're happy, and, more to the point, you won't value the happiness when it's there.'

Edith suddenly appeared at the back door, a dress-shop bag over one arm, the cat struggling under the other. Jumping to his feet, McKenna almost upset the lemonade glass.

She smiled vaguely at him, then dropped the fretful animal to the floor. 'What have you done to the poor lamb?' she demanded of her daughter. 'He was trying to climb on to the roof.'

'I shut him out the back because he was lying in the road earlier.'

'Was he? Oh, dear!' Sinking into a chair, she rummaged in her pocket for cigarettes, and as McKenna offered his own, said: 'I do hope he's not getting silly with age.'

'Maybe he's got the feline version of BSE,' Phoebe offered, pouring tea into three mugs.

'Don't be so ridiculous!' Edith snapped. 'You and Annie are obsessed with this BSE thing!'

'With Auntie Gertrude around, it's hard not to be.'

Drawing hard on her cigarette, hands trembling, Edith said: 'Did Ned say Gertrude had human BSE?'

'No.' Phoebe put the mugs on the table. 'He said she was always a bit more odd than the rest of them.'

'Quite.' She knocked ash from her cigarette, and turned to McKenna. 'Did Gladys tell you what happened to her sister?'

'Not really. Annie told me about the little girl who died.'

'She was called Louisa,' Phoebe stated. 'I've seen her grave. She died from consumption.'

'TB,' Edith said, irritation in her voice. 'And it's not in the least romantic, the way novels pretend. That child had a savage, lingering death, and it turned poor Gertrude's mind. She's the way she is because of grief and guilt and family weakness, and not because of anything else.'

Phoebe sat down, wafting away the cigarette smoke. The cat jumped on her lap, nuzzled her bare arm and made her smile, while Edith talked on. 'I do wonder if we weave stories around the realities simply to make them less horrific and more palatable. Gertrude's had a dreadful life, very little of it her own doing.'

'Uncle Ned said once somebody had bad luck, they can expect more,' Phoebe offered, 'because they're being pursued by the world of the dead.'

' "Uncle Ned said" is like a mantra for you, isn't it?' Edith commented. 'And it rhymes with dead. And I'm not being nasty,' she added, as Phoebe's face threatened to crumple into misery. 'I was making an observation.' Drawing on her cigarette, she turned again to McKenna. 'Gertrude was a real beauty in her youth, you know.' As he thought of the human wreck he had kept company with the day before, she went on: 'And she was bright too, even though she was given to flights of fancy at times. With that, and the family's money, she could have taken her pick of the local gentry.' She paused to drink. 'Everyone expected her life to go from one good thing to something better.' Glancing at her daughter, she added: 'And you can stop rolling your eyes like that. All most parents want for their children is peace and happiness, in that order, as you might discover one day.' Then she asked McKenna: 'Was your father in the war? Gertrude's father was exempt from call-up because of the farm, and I've always had the impression they felt the walls of Llys Ifor would protect them from the destruction that touched other families, even in that neck of the woods. Some of the village men never came back from the war, and of course, several people were maimed by the stuff they handled at the explosives factory.' Rather abruptly, she stopped speaking, and looked at him, a hectic quality in her eyes. 'D'you want to hear all this? I don't know how long you've been waiting, but Phoebe's probably exhausted you already.'

'Please, go on,' McKenna said, smiling.

'You can't stop now,' Phoebe insisted. 'You've never told me about Auntie Gertrude before.'

'Because it's not really our business,' Edith said. 'I'm telling you now to stop this BSE nonsense.' She paused again. 'During the war, there was an internment camp near Bala, like the one on the Isle of Man. Enemy aliens and conscientious objectors were sent there, and later, a few prisoners of war. Gladys says the government stockpiled poison gas in the mountains, too.'

'It's probably still there,' commented Phoebe, 'leaking. That's why so many people have cancer.'

Edith stared at her. 'You could be right, actually, but no-one will ever admit to it.' She sighed. 'The internees had to work for their keep, and in 1942, a young Italian prisoner of war was sent to the farm. Ned said he was like a latter-day slave.'

When she paused again, to draw breath and tobacco smoke into her lungs, Phoebe touched her arm. 'Go on, Mama. What happened?'

'Gladys remembers him well, even though they couldn't

say much to each other. In those days, she could hardly speak English, and he obviously couldn't speak Welsh.'

'How old was he?' Phoebe demanded, hugging the cat. 'Was he handsome?'

'I don't know how old he was, and I don't know if he was handsome, but Gladys says she found him sweet and very kind.'

'What was he called?'

'Luigi. Luigi Gianniazzi. He and Gertrude fell head over heels in love with each other, and when her father found out, he told the authorities.' She ground out her cigarette. 'So Luigi disappeared, and Gertrude never saw him again. She tried to find him after the war, but nobody would tell her anything.'

'Oh, what a wicked thing to do!' Phoebe said. 'She must have really *hated* her father.'

'He was trying to protect her from her own wilfulness. She had no future with someone from an enemy country, as Luigi was then, and no-one could possibly know at the time how the war would end.'

'It's still awful.' Phoebe snivelled, her tears making the cat flinch as they dripped on to his back.

'There was worse to come,' Edith added. 'Gertrude was pregnant, and when the people in the village found out, they called her a wanton. She became a virtual prisoner in Llys Ifor.'

'They were wicked, too!' Phoebe said through her tears.

'Were they?' Edith wondered. 'I don't know. They felt cheated and deceived. Gertrude's hopes and prospects didn't only belong to her, you know, and with a baby on the way, she had neither.'

'Is that why you went ballistic when Annie was pregnant?' asked Phoebe. 'Were you scared of history repeating itself?'

'Something like that, yes.' Edith nodded, her eyes darting

from her daughter to her visitor. 'And I wish you'd extend your vocabulary a little. Ballistic is one of your "words of the month", isn't it? Still, I suppose it's an improvement on the other one, although I've yet to decipher what apeshit actually means.'

Phoebe blushed, and while McKenna stifled a laugh, Edith rattled on. 'I don't think the past will lose the power to hurt as long as Gertrude draws breath, but Gladys probably won't mind if you talk about it occasionally.' She reached for another cigarette. 'She'd probably show you the wooden chest Luigi made for Gertrude. He must have been very clever with his hands because it's almost a work of art, carved all over with the kind of shapes and patterns you find in old Italian churches.'

'What's in it?' Phoebe asked.

'Keepsakes, I suppose. Perhaps even love tokens and letters, and I think that's where Gladys put Louisa's little clothes after she died.' She smiled at her own daughter, and ruffled her hair. 'You know those two caskets of Uncle Ned's? Luigi made those from a big branch which came off one of the oak trees in the field during a storm.' She fell silent, chewing her bottom lip. 'We really must see about sorting out Ned's things, and I'm sure he made a will, even though nobody knows where it is. We'll have to ask Gladys about the books, because George wants to carry on with Ned's work if possible.'

'How d'you know?' McKenna enquired.

'I saw him when I walked up from town,' Edith said. 'I noticed him from quite a long way off. He does rather stand out from the crowd, doesn't he? And not because he's black, although we don't see many black people around here for some strange reason. Anyway, we had quite a pleasant chat, which is why I was so long. I'm so glad you had the sense to let him go.'

'You didn't tell me!' Phoebe wailed. 'Why didn't you?'

'I'm sorry,' McKenna said. 'It slipped my mind.'

'Don't speak to Mr McKenna like that. I expect you've been talking so much he couldn't get a word in.' Smiling gently to take the sting from her words, Edith added: 'I think he wants to talk to me, so perhaps you could find something to do for a while.'

'Like what?' Phoebe asked, her mouth drawn down at the corners. 'There's nothing to do. I'm bored.'

'Thank goodness you'll be old enough to have a summer job next year,' Edith commented. 'These long school holidays are a trial for everyone.'

'I wasn't bored when Uncle Ned was alive,' Phoebe stated.

'I know, child. And I know you miss him. Why don't you go over to George's? I'm sure he'd be glad to see you.'

'This is weird!' Phoebe announced. 'One day you hate him, the next you're falling over yourself to be nice about him.'

'I'm allowed to revise my opinions. I've probably been very unfair to him in the past.'

'Maybe you've realized he's not after Minnie.'

'And perhaps my head isn't so full of funny feelings,' Edith countered. 'Just go and find yourself something to do, and don't be late back for tea. And don't lock that poor animal out of the house again,' she called, as Phoebe trudged into the hall, the cat at her heels. 'Shut the front door if you don't trust him not to wander into the road.'

Stubbing out her half-smoked cigarette, she glanced at McKenna. 'Do you ever worry about getting cancer? I'm scared already, and I've never touched cigarettes before. I don't like the taste or the smell, and they make my throat terribly raw.'

He shrugged. 'I'm addicted, I suppose, like millions of other self-medicating depressives, including Professor Williams.' He watched her hands, trembling and jerking of their own volition. 'Phoebe told me he's coming to dinner, but I wondered if you'd cancel the visit.'

'Why?'

He rose to shut the kitchen door, in case their voices carried up the stairs as Edith said sounds travelled through the house. 'I want to discuss some things with him later.'

'What things?'

'Things arising in the course of our inquiries. I spoke to Margaret Williams earlier.'

'How nice for you! I'm sure she made you *most* welcome!'

'She told me she regrets her differences with you.'

'Wasn't that kind of her!' Edith's eyes were alight. 'And I'm sure that wasn't all she told you, was it?'

'You must have known I'd find out, sooner or later.' McKenna's voice was gentle.

'Of course I knew! It's been eating me up with worry, like rats in my belly! Why d'you think I asked you to respect our privacy?'

'I'll do everything I can to protect your privacy, but I don't know what might be relevant to Ned's death.'

'All I ask of you,' she said, her voice straining with grief, 'is that you don't let Phoebe and Annie find out about Mina. They don't need to, and they'd judge her. She'd become an outcast like Gertrude, and they find her wanting enough already, as if they know she's a changeling without being told.'

'Aren't you afraid they'd judge you, too?'

'I'm beyond that sort of care, Mr McKenna.' She snatched a cigarette from the pack. 'Too many others came to push it aside, and I've spent too many years being weak and miserable, savouring the unhappiness I made for myself. If my daughters don't already despise me for what that took from them, they won't despise me for the cause of it all.' Lighting the cigarette, she said: 'I've felt very strange since Ned died, you know, as if the shackles around my personality are corroding and falling apart. I think I'm beginning to mean something to myself again.'

'Phoebe says you've become more real.'

'She's told me all about you, or at least, what she could find out from that young policeman,' she said, wedging her cigarette in the dip in the ashtray. 'I know you've no children of your own, but I'm sure you can understand the bereavements parents suffer as children grow up and go out into the world. I love each of my daughters equally and differently, and each relationship is different. I'm very close to Annie, and more perhaps since she had Bethan, because there's no-one else with a claim to them, but it's rather two grown women together than mother and daughter.' She clasped her hands together, jailing the twitching fingers. 'As I said, I love them all, but I know the greatest bereavement will come when Phoebe leaves.'

'Because she'll leave you with an empty nest?'

'Because she's never belonged to anyone but herself, and because of whatever it is that Ned saw in her and nurtured, when I was too wrapped up in myself to notice. You and George recognize the same thing, and it's what made her teacher so spiteful, and what so frightens Mina.'

'Does Mina know Professor Williams is her father?'

Edith nodded, watching the smoke curl from her cigarette, the ash drop from its end.

'And Gladys?'

'And Ned knew.' She grimaced. 'And, of course, my husband knew.'

'And is that what wrecked your marriage?'

'Adultery's usually a symptom, not a cause. I could never work out what spoilt my marriage, so I came to the conclusion we simply made the wrong choice in each other.' She unclasped her hands to retrieve the cigarette, and held it to her lips, sucking in smoke. Pressure points discoloured the thin skin of her fingers, patches of angry red bleeding into blotches of whiter flesh. 'There were a lot of problems when we first married. My husband hadn't long graduated, he wasn't happy in his job, it didn't pay well, and his prospects were poor. Then I fell pregnant with Annie, which neither of us was ready for, and things overwhelmed us for a while, but we carried on, because you do, don't you? And people say problems bring you together, so you soldier on, even when common sense says you're flogging a very dead horse.'

'And?' he prompted, when she fell silent, gazing blankly at the wall.

'Things got better: new job, more money, lots of chances for promotion, and I went on the new contraceptive pill, which did its job even though it made me feel dreadfully sort of flat and depressed. But while the surface looked rosier, the inside grew bleaker than ever, so perhaps the marriage needed its problems for survival. When they went, it died, because we had nothing else to share.' She replaced the cigarette in the ashtray, and folded her arms, tucking the fractious hands into fists. 'Annie was wise beyond her years when the crunch came, you know. She wouldn't marry Bethan's father because she said there was too much she could call into question about their relationship, and as she wouldn't be able to stop herself doing it, the rot had already set in, so to speak.' She paused, watching him assessingly, as Phoebe watched the world. 'D'you know why your marriage went astray?'

'I suppose the kindest judgement is that we realized we wanted different things from life, and grew apart.'

'Really?' She smiled. 'And do you know what you want?'

'I haven't a clue.' He smiled in return. 'Someone keeps moving the goalposts when I'm looking elsewhere.'

'Or turning the signposts.' Sniffing the smoke from the discarded cigarette, she said: 'I think Annie's on the right track, provided her hormones don't send her off course, but it's strange how she can still take her part in adding to the generational tragedy, like any child who isn't orphaned.' She smiled fleetingly. 'That's my fancy name for the way children dismiss the knowledge their parents learned the hard way, and can't understand parental feelings until they're in the same position, when it's usually too late to make any amends. Even now, Annie can revert to being a child in the blink of an eye when it suits her.' She stopped again, to draw breath, and he wondered if she had ever before expressed the thoughts and feelings tumbling from her mind. 'Anyway,' she added, 'if I've learned nothing else, I've learned from my children what a relationship needs if it's to work.'

'And what's that?'

'Aren't you absolutely weary of hearing our voices?'

He shook his head, wondering as he did so when he had come to need these women more than they could ever need him, and if that need were rooted in the power he wielded in their lives, but as she began to speak again, he realized the ground which shook so humiliatingly beneath him in office was not the same ground trodden here.

'A good relationship,' Edith said, 'must be like a full cycle of the seasons of the year, because if it's trapped in winter frosts, or stifled by the heat of summer, it will perish.' She unfolded her arms, and let her hands rest on the table, watching their tremors as if they were owned by another. 'And that's my profound thought for the week, and the month, and perhaps for ever, and I don't know where Phoebe gets the strength to cope with having her head awash with much deeper thoughts nearly all the time.'

'She puts them on paper and sorts them out,' McKenna said. 'Transfers their power to impress.'

'I hope so, because I'm sure this thinking turned Ned's brain, and for all we know, Gertrude might be another victim of ideas running amok like a herd of rogue elephants in her head.'

As footsteps thundered on the stairs, vibrating through

the kitchen ceiling, she flinched, then Phoebe pushed open the door, said the cat was asleep on her bed, and disappeared, slamming the front door.

Edith cocked her head to one side, listening. 'Sometimes, she makes a huge racket to fool you into thinking she's gone out, and isn't tiptoeing back to listen at the door. She's an incredibly nosy child.'

'I'd noticed.'

'If you hadn't, your faculties would be sadly lacking, wouldn't they? But that's how she grows, feeding on information as the rest of us feed on food, gobbling it up before it escapes or goes off.' She frowned. 'Must I really stop Iolo coming tonight? Solange won't be back until tomorrow, and he's relying on me for a decent meal. The cook walked out because of some row.' Watching his eyes, she added: 'You're going to say "no", aren't you? Why must you prise out every last secret, every morsel of shame?'

'So that I can decide what to discard, or ignore.' He lit a cigarette. 'When did you first meet Professor Williams?'

'Almost a year to the day before Mina was born, although he'd already been at the university a while on a visiting lectureship.'

'And who introduced you? Your husband?'

'No, not my husband.' Something akin to amusement glinted in her eyes for a moment. 'I see Margaret didn't quite tell you everything. She was my part-time domestic. Iolo came to pick her up one day, and it was then the deceit and subterfuge and excitement began. I'd been on my own for some time, so I wasn't taking the pill, and I truly believed Iolo's kisses had the same heat in them that burned all the caution from my own heart, but I was wrong. They were empty of everything except his urgent greed, and when I told him I was pregnant, he fled.'

'Annie told me your husband was here when Mina was born.'

'I asked him to come back because there was no-one else to turn to, but he refused to take Mina as his own. There's just a blank space on her birth certificate where her father's name should be, even though I was still married.' She drummed her fingers slowly on the table, beating out a disjointed, stuttering rhythm. 'He left again, carrying his shame like a trunk full of keepsakes. People say counselling can sort out emotional baggage, but what do you do when that baggage lives and breathes, as Mina did?'

'But your husband must have returned. He's Phoebe's father, isn't he?'

'Yes, he came back, and he brought all his luggage, including the festering resentments of his shame. He couldn't bring himself even to look at Mina, let alone touch her, so I asked him to go, for everyone's sake.' She fell silent, watching her hands. 'I not only gave birth to Mina, you know. It was then I created the ghosts which came to haunt our future, and I suppose that's why we've seemed a divided family. You must have noticed that.'

'I felt you and Mina were orbiting one path, Phoebe and Annie another,' McKenna said, smiling faintly. 'Professor Willliams was your sun, as it were, and Ned theirs, but as his light faded, I began to see other contingencies and intersections.'

'In the near dark?' Edith asked. 'Iolo has hardly any light, and it's very wintry in his shadow.'

'Then why on earth d'you still see him?'

'For Mina's sake.'

'Does Solange know, too? Is that why Mina spends so much time with her?'

'Probably, but neither of them will ever say. Mina stopped talking to me after she found out, and Solange gives little away because she prefers you to think she's as blank and faceless inside as out.' She smiled fleetingly. 'I think she goes travelling so often to escape the suffocating futility of being married to Iolo, recharging her batteries for the next phase in the survival course. We women do that, don't we? Thank God Annie had the sense to see it coming.'

'Perhaps Mina simply finds her glamorous,' McKenna suggested. 'Especially as she has free run of a very extensive wardrobe. Or perhaps Mina's a doll for Solange to dress up and play with.'

'You judge her too harshly,' Edith commented. 'I imagine Mina feels safer with her, because she's no threat to her, and she won't spring any nasty surprises, or dredge up rotting secrets. Solange has no part in the false memories of the past, so perhaps Mina senses she can guide her towards something new and hopeful.'

He rose to empty the overflowing ashtray, then stood by the back door, looking out into the garden, where birds twittered among the quietly rustling branches of the tall old trees. The ginger cat he had seen from Ned's room darted out from the shrubbery, stopped in its tracks when it saw him, then shot back under cover when he moved.

'You've got a trespasser,' he told Edith. 'A big ginger cat.'

'He lives next door but one. Phoebe doesn't mind him in the garden because he's not a fighter, so Tom's quite safe.'

'Among Ned's papers, we found some horoscopes he and George must have pulled off the computer, and Tom's was included.'

'What about Mina?'

'There were predictions for everyone, but not a vestige of truth in any.'

She rose to fill the kettle. 'It's for the best, isn't it? Who'd have the courage to go on living if they knew what was in store? Would you like tea or coffee?'

'Coffee, please,' he said. 'Black, no sugar.'

'You've still got what was left of the sugar.' She tinkered with a cafetiere, spilling a few grounds on the counter, then pulled on rubber gloves, rinsed out a cloth, and cleaned up the small mess. Staring at her back, he thought how shapely and youthful she looked, yet how in every gesture and expression her age was unmistakable. Below the hem of her pretty dress, her legs had a slight stringiness, like the length of forearm showing beneath her sleeves.

'I'd better call Iolo, hadn't I? Tell him he'll have to fend for himself.'

'I'm sure he's capable,' McKenna said.

'I don't know whether he is or he isn't. I don't know much about him at all, except that he's weak.' She rinsed the cloth again, then ran hot water into a bowl, squirting washing-up liquid under the tap. A great froth of scented bubbles rose in the water, spilled over the edge of the sink and took to the air, drifting about the room and out through the door. One landed in front of him, a glistening sphere that rolled and tumbled for a moment, then exploded into a spatter of moisture on the table. Edith dropped the used mugs and glasses into the bowl, wiped the table, removed the soiled ashtray, and took another from the cupboard. 'When Iolo comes here,' she went on, 'we don't have conversations. He talks *at* people, but never listens to them, and I suppose that's how he manages not to hear what he doesn't want to know.' Pulling off the gloves, she put clean mugs on the table, and leaned against the counter, as her daughter so often did. 'When I look at him now, I can't imagine how we came together. He almost makes my flesh crawl.'

'You've worn a great many faces over the years,' McKenna commented, 'and all apparently for the benefit of others.'

'Perhaps I was trying to find one that suited me. I'm not a blank canvas like Solange. She can paint on any face she wants.'

'I find her two-dimensional. She reminds me of the Queen of Spades in a pack of cards.'

'Does she really?' Edith smiled. 'That's not very kind of you, is it? You're supposed to be impartial. Bureaucracy must be, if it's to work properly.' Turning away, she poured boiling water on to the coffee grounds, put the cafetiere on the table, and sat again. 'If bureaucracy had a heart, Mina wouldn't know her father, and everyone might be so much more at peace. Ned might even be alive. Who can know?'

'Is there a connection between Mina's parentage and Ned's death?'

'I know we can only make sense of the past in retrospect, but one thing always leads to another, despite what the horoscopes tell us. Hitler invaded Poland, Gertrude had a baby, and now she dwells out her last years in some terrible twilight, her thoughts the colour of a mountain storm, and just as chaotic.' Pushing the plunger to the bottom of the cafetiere, she added: 'You think I'm being evasive, don't you?'

'Are you?'

'I'm trying to hang on to the last of our privacy for a little longer.' She poured the coffee, smiling wryly. 'Talking with you is like a fencing bout I know I'll lose, but I'm still obliged to put up a fight.'

'Why will you lose?'

'You're part of the imperious officialdom ruling our lives.'

'It rules mine, too.'

'Yes, it does, doesn't it? So why do we credit our adversaries with greater power and freedom?'

'Because it excuses our capitulation. Saves a little bit of face, few remnants of pride.'

'Until now, I thought my pride was a thing of the past,' Edith said. 'I've loathed myself for years, in a lethargic sort of way.'

'Have you ever tried to kill yourself?'

'I thought about it almost every day, but I couldn't get up enough steam to make the effort.' She paused, staring at him. 'Or perhaps something stopped me from abandoning the girls, because there was only me, especially for Mina. She came into the world alone, and she's stayed that way. It's coloured and shaped her whole life, and she never understood why.' A ferocious expression distorted her mouth, and she banged her hands on the table, startling McKenna and setting the crockery jumping and swaying. 'I've been so stupid! I should have faced it out at the time, instead of wallowing in misery and secrets. Secrets fester like bad wounds, and you end up needing major surgery.' She leaned forward, hands clenched. 'And not only did I turn Mina's world upside down, but I dragged her into the nasty secret as well.'

'How did she come to find out?'

'She needed her birth certificate to get into college. Such a little thing, and such a cataclysm afterwards! I knew it would be, and I tried and tried to put off the evil day, but the college wouldn't let her start the course without the certificate, and now she doesn't know what to do with herself. She's no idea who she is any longer, so she can't move forward, and she can't go back. I'm so afraid for her!'

'And are you afraid *of* her?' he asked.

'You asked me that before,' Edith said, her voice weary, 'and I can't put my hand on my heart and give you an answer.' She gulped coffee, then reached for a cigarette, her hands trembling wildly. 'We can't know the truth about our ancestry because we don't have personal memories to retrieve, so we rely on what people tell us. We *trust* what we're told, and make up ourselves and our identity from it, and God alone can say what it does to a person to find out the whole self is a fiction.'

'Some people are more than happy to create their own fiction,' McKenna pointed out.

'Yes, but they know the difference, don't they?' she said irritably. 'Even if they get to the stage of believing their own lies. I created the lies and made Mina live them.'

'Was it your idea? What did Professor Williams think? And your husband? And Ned?'

'Iolo only cared about his own reputation, and my husband said I must lie in the dirty bed I'd made for myself.' She drained the coffee. 'No, he wasn't heartless. I think he was too hurt to realize what he was doing.'

'And Ned?'

She smiled. 'But for Iolo and my foolishness, Ned and I might have been friends. He was an honest man, but his sort of decency can be rather merciless. He called me all kinds of a fool for covering up, and said I must tell the truth. "Tell the truth and shame the devil," he said, and because I wouldn't, or couldn't, it created a rift. He said my world was impinging on his, and alienating us when we should be brought together.'

'Perhaps he had Gertrude in mind.'

'But she had no opportunity to create another reality, did she? And Gladys didn't share Ned's view. She said telling the truth would upset the balances and traditions and received wisdoms, because in the end, Mina would be judged on her own merits and by her own actions, as we all are.'

'And that's what you fear, isn't it?'

She put her cigarette in the ashtray, and wrapped her arms around her body, watching the curling smoke. 'I'll never be free of drugs, you know. They'll control me to the day I die, and be in my thoughts day and night, threatening me with what they might have done that I've yet to see, like a time bomb in my head.' Shifting in her seat, she retrieved the cigarette. 'Annie's been so scared by what a so-called "good" drug did to me that she won't even take an aspirin. Now she's seen Ned killed by another "good" drug, while I'm turning back into myself with the help of a "bad" one. Or, at least, I'm turning into what I can remember about being myself.'

'You won't be as you were,' he said. 'You'll have grown and changed despite yourself.'

'I sincerely hope so, but how will I have changed? Will the drugs eventually make me a monster? And what have they done to my children?' She knocked ash from the cigarette. 'That's why I fear for Mina, and for Phoebe too, if I'm honest, because those good little pills which let women fornicate to their heart's content might have poisoned the cells from which they grew.'

'How? What could they have done?'

'They could have done anything or nothing, but no-one will put our minds to rest. Nobody conceded that tranquillizers can damage unborn children, or told us about the stockpiled poison gas in the mountains, or admitted the power stations were leaking until so much more poison drifted over from Chernobyl that it couldn't be hidden.'

'But millions of women take oral contraceptives.'

'And does that prove they're safe?' She brushed a speck of ash from the table, a frown creasing her forehead. 'Sometimes, I look at youngsters like Mina, and all I see are empty eyes and strange empty minds, as if they're not quite human. Jason's one of them, and you must have seen plenty. They all resemble each other, and I imagine the prisons and children's homes are full of them. It's quite terrifying.'

'The rotten fruit of a poisoned womb?'

'If you like. Mina's not normal, however much it hurts me to say so, and she never was. She was like a wild animal when she was little. She didn't seem to learn, or understand cause and effect, or have any feelings for others, and she got worse as she grew older. I can't find any moral sense in her at all.'

'That's a terrible judgement on her.' McKenna was shocked to the core.

'It's an honest one.' She smiled grimly. 'Tell the truth and shame the devil, eh?' Drumming her fingers on the table, she added: 'And she doesn't look quite right. She looks as if something went amiss in the making, and it's not just her ears, as Phoebe would have you believe, it's everything about her. She suffers all kinds of strange allergies, and rashes, and stomach upsets, and red eyes, but we can never pin point this or that food or drink or whatever. Her whole system goes haywire every so often, and Solange doesn't help. She's made her utterly neurotic with her so-called "diet advice".' Viciously, she ground out the cigarette. 'I hope to God she's not gone on the Pill for that Jason. He's the last person worth that kind of risk.'

'You can't have the same fears about Phoebe.'

'Can't I? She's even less normal than Mina.'

'She hardly lacks moral sense.'

'She has so much of everything it almost overflows, while Mina hasn't enough.' She rose, dropping dirty crockery in the sink and sending more bubbles adrift. 'I suppose they balance each other in a way, but even Phoebe isn't complete.' She pulled on the rubber gloves, staring out of the window. 'Her back view is the most pathetic sight on earth, and it's not because of the puppy fat.' She began to wash the crockery. 'I must sense the heartache she'll know sooner or later.'

'Why should she?'

'Why shouldn't she? Isn't your life a litter of lost dreams and broken promises? What we can have depends on how the world sees us, but what we long for and dream about depends on how we see ourselves.' She picked up a tea-towel printed with one black Scottie dog, and one white. 'Phoebe will never be loved because she's too complex and too knowing, and she lives in a self-created world. She'll frighten people, especially when she tries to drag them into her world, and she won't understand why they can't make the leap of faith she wants of them.'

'And Mina?'

'I destroyed what little self she had by telling her about Iolo. She's got nothing now, so she'll take whatever comes her way and do whatever takes her fancy, and not know until later whether it might be good for her.'

'Are you going to call Professor Williams? It's getting rather late.'

She stacked the clean mugs in the cupboard, rinsed the cafetiere, put the spoons in a drawer, and faced him, the tea-towel over her arm. 'Have we discussed what you came for, or is there something else? I feel almost eviscerated.'

He flinched as the impact of her words reached him.

'I'm not blaming you,' she added. 'I've been so quiet for so long it's rather like a dam burst now I've started talking.'

'Why did you neglect to admit you knew of Ned's long time friendship with Professor Williams?'

'What?' About to wipe the table with the dishcloth, she stopped. 'What friendship?'

'They were at university together. Professor Williams is the "Eddie" I spoke about earlier.'

'Don't be silly!' Edith said, vigorously wiping the table. 'You must be mistaken. They hardly knew each other, and what they did know, neither of them seemed to like over much.'

'I'm not mistaken, Mrs Harris. Ned and Iolo were close friends, for a while at least.'

'Who says so?' she asked, rinsing the dishcloth. 'Is that what Margaret told you?'

'He's been identified by someone else.'

'Who?'

'A prominent scholar who was at university with him, and who knew both of them,' McKenna replied. 'And that might explain why Ned collected so much paper about the professor.'

'Ned collected paper, full stop,' Edith commented,

bending down to examine the contents of her refrigerator. 'I honestly think you must be wrong. I've seen them together countless times, and there was never a hint they had more than a passing acquaintance, and that through me.' She straightened up, rubbing the small of her back. 'You *must* be wrong. One of us would have noticed *something*!'

'Not if Ned and Iolo made a pact never to disclose their friendship.'

'And why should they do that?'

'I hope Professor Williams will be able to tell me.'

Phoebe sat astride the garden wall, scuffing dust with her sandals. 'Have you finished grilling Mama?' she called, as McKenna emerged through the front door. 'Can I come back in?' She swung off the wall and walked to the gate, barring his way. 'What on earth took you so long? It's almost dusk.'

'Don't exaggerate,' he chided. 'The sun hasn't even set. Anyway, I thought you'd gone to see George.'

'He wasn't in. Your car radio's been squawking fit to bust. Will you get into trouble for not answering?'

'They'd telephone if I was needed.'

'The helicopter's been sent to the demo at Welsh Water.' Standing in his shadow as he unlocked the car, she added: 'I couldn't help listening. You don't mind, do you? I saw it fly over about half an hour ago, and it hasn't come back yet.'

'It might go another way.' Clipping on the seat belt, he put the keys in the ignition. 'I must go, Phoebe.'

'Will you be coming again?'

'I expect so.'

'Is Mama OK? She's not upset, is she?'

'She's fine.'

'That's good, isn't it?' She turned, and walked away, closing the gate behind her. He watched as she trudged up the drive and into the house, Edith's words in his mind, then drove to the crest of the hill to turn the car, wondering if the humped and twisted shadow pursuing the girl was the shape of her future.

7

Slumped in an office chair, his uniform shirt in filthy tatters, Dewi clutched an ice pack to his head.

'What happened?' McKenna demanded, looming over him. 'What's wrong with your head?'

'He got into a fight at the demo,' Rowlands offered. 'We've arrested enough for a special night court.'

'Yeah, and I'll have to hang around to give evidence,' Dewi said. 'And most of them only went to make a noise and get their silly faces on telly. This bunch of bloody hippies was squatting in front of the building, and when the helicopter came over, they stood up, waving spliffs in the air, and yelling: "You think *you're* high?", and giggling, like they do.'

'So who hit you?' McKenna asked.

'I didn't see properly, sir. It was a bit of a bear garden.'

'That's not what you told me, is it?' Rowlands countered. 'You said somebody chucked a stone at one of the police dogs, so you chucked a stone back, and somebody else lobbed a missile at you in return.'

'I still didn't see who it was!' Dewi snapped.

'Lucky for you they weren't close enough to get your number,' Rowlands said. 'Let's hope you don't turn up on someone's video, demonstrating police brutality.'

'Was the dog hurt?'

'It dodged, sir.'

'Have you been to the hospital for a check-up?'

'No, sir. I don't need to.'

'So what's under the ice pack?'

'A bit of a lump, and a graze.'

McKenna sighed. 'Get to Casualty now, and don't come back without something on paper to say you were injured. And don't argue,' he added, as Dewi's mouth opened. 'Far better for you to be at the hospital instead of the night court. And don't bother changing.'

When Dewi was out of earshot, Rowlands said: 'Does he often compromise us?'

'Animals are higher than most people on his scale of values. I'd have been hard pressed not to do the same myself, regardless of the fact that police dogs and police horses are well-armoured, and often better trained than a lot of their human counterparts.' Hanging his jacket on the back of the chair, McKenna added: 'Any news about Janet?'

'She's stopped bleeding, but she's still critical, and her father's apparently blaming us, because we didn't insist on her seeing a doctor.'

'She might have been less inclined towards evasion and denial if his portentous sermonising hadn't blighted her common sense. And if Mrs Evans didn't walk in fear of her husband, she might have noticed when Janet most needed her.'

'On the subject of mothers and daughters, we'd better see Annie. The Shrewsbury car is the genuine article, so she could be driving round in another cut and shut, or a re-vamped write-off from an accident.'

'She wasn't in when I left. Neither was Mina.'

'Doesn't she go clubbing with loverboy every night?'

'No-one's quite sure what she does or what she might do, which is why Edith's frightened.'

'The worst she's likely to do is take the same road as Janet,' Rowlands said.

'Edith wouldn't agree with you.' He began to pace the

office, weaving around the heaps of detritus bestrewing the floor.

'Why not? What do you and she know that I don't?'

'Edith lost her heart and her sense to Iolo, many moons ago, and she's looked on the consequences every day since. And even if the worst Mina does is turn out like her father, that'll be worry enough for everyone.'

8

As the sun set, the little breeze off the sea had taken a chill upon itself from the dark water. Whispering through the trees surrounding Iolo Williams's house, it set the leaves chattering, and as McKenna climbed from the car, a single leaf drifted to the ground, then, lifted again by the breeze, began to rattle against the wall.

'Another few weeks and we'll see ground frost of a night,' Rowlands commented. 'I hope I get time to sort out my garden before the weather turns.'

'My little patch almost looks after itself.'

'Iolo's got a nice garden, hasn't he?' Elbows on the wall, Rowlands surveyed the lawns and shrubbery and fine old trees. 'Those holly bushes are a century old if they're a day. He must have a gardener, because I can't see him keeping this much land in order, and even less can I see Solange risking her nails with a bit of toil.'

'Did you check their cars?' McKenna asked, pushing open the gate.

'Iolo's is kosher, as you'd expect. It's too conspicuous for a double-up. Solange doesn't drive, so she hasn't got a car.'

'Does she not? I'm surprised. Has she lost her licence?'

'There's no record of her ever having one.' Scuffing along the wide path towards the front door, Rowlands kicked another tiny brown leaf, and McKenna wondered if in essence there were any difference between the rearrangements wrought by the breeze and the man. 'Not as Solange Williams, that is, although she could be registered under her maiden name. I didn't think to check.'

'We'll ask Iolo,' McKenna decided, ringing the doorbell. Dull light behind dirty glass touched the crowns of the bushes under the window, then a shadow obliterated the light as Williams peered out, a scowl distorting his face.

'Did you make Edith cancel my dinner?' he demanded, pulling open the door. The foul air of his house despoiled the summer night. 'You did, didn't you? No wonder she sounded strange on the phone! You've no right to interfere in people's lives like this!' The hectoring tone made his voice shrill.

'I told Mrs Harris I intended to visit,' McKenna said. 'May we come in?'

'Why?'

'To talk, Professor Williams. I think it's about time, don't you?'

'I've got nothing to say to you!' he snapped. 'And I'm quite sure you won't say anything I want to hear!' He edged the door closed.

McKenna put out his hand. 'Let me add that you don't have a choice in the matter.'

'He told you, didn't he?' he said, his voice rasping. 'That bloody jungle bunny told you! Oh, I'll bet he enjoyed that! Getting his own back with the help of that crazy old man!' He let go of the door, and lunged forward, teeth almost bared, and a froth of spittle at the sides of his mouth. 'Well, I won't have it! D'you hear me? I won't have that bloody nigger ruining my life! And I want my solicitor!' he shouted. 'I want him now!' Without warning, he leapt back into the hall, and slammed the door.

McKenna leaned on the doorbell, hearing it shriek

through the house in counterpoint to Williams's voice screaming down a telephone. Then there was a clatter, and the voice fell silent, leaving the bell to shriek alone. He thumped on the door, and shouted to the man inside.

'You're wasting your breath,' Rowlands said. 'And your energy. Let him stew. I'll make sure he doesn't do a runner round the back.'

McKenna sat on the doorstep, shivering when the breeze touched his flesh, then another large, luxurious car swished to a halt in the road, heavy wheels crunching tarmac, and the city's most expensive solicitor made his way up the path. 'What in God's name are you up to?' he demanded. 'Professor Williams is terrified.'

'We came to interview him.'

'Without benefit of counsel? Really, Chief Inspector, you should know better! I'm not surprised your promotion was shelved.'

While Rowlands sat patiently on an overblown chair, picking at its dirty velvet cover, McKenna leaned against the dark panelling in the hall, half-listening to the solicitor's querulous demands, and watching Williams stamp back and forth, and when he stopped in mid-stride to glare at his observer, mouth working grotesquely inside the crust of spittle, McKenna felt as if suddenly blessed, or cursed, with a smidgen of Phoebe's insight, and looked right through the man to the void at his heart. 'Do you pay any maintenance?' he asked. 'For either of them? Have you ever paid?'

'What?' The solicitor turned to his client. 'What's he talking about?'

'I asked if Professor Williams pays maintenance,' McKenna repeated. 'Or, in your professional parlance, provides ancillary relief.'

'For what?' The solicitor frowned.

'For—' McKenna began, and was cut short by a high-pitched yell from Iolo.

'Get out!' He lunged forward, and pushed the solicitor violently in the chest. 'Get out! Leave me alone!' Snapping like a mad dog, he harried him towards the front door, and out into the night. 'I don't need you. It was all a mistake!' The door slammed so violently a spatter of plaster fell from the ceiling, sprinkling more dust on the furniture and adding to the little heaps of dirt piling up in corners.

'Was that wise?' asked McKenna, as Williams leaned against the front door, panting for breath. 'He won't come running so fast next time you need him, and you surely will.'

'Then I'll get another solicitor! They're like tarts, anyway. There's always another one on the next street corner.' He walked shakily along the hall. 'And why should he know my business? It's bad enough your knowing!'

'The whole world may come to know eventually,' McKenna pointed out.

Williams smiled, a ghastly image. 'I'm sure we could come to some arrangement.'

'No, that won't be possible,' McKenna said. 'We'll do our best to protect your daughter, but that's all.'

'My daughter.' Williams savoured the words. 'People don't call her that, you know. Not to my face, anyway.'

'Quite. You've spent almost two decades pretending she's something else, and much good it's done. By the way, do you pay Edith maintenance?'

'Her husband made sure they never went short, but I give her money for Mina's clothes and holidays, and I pay the college fees.'

'That's another well-kept secret, is it?' McKenna said. 'Like your long standing relationship with Ned Jones.'

'I'm hungry,' the professor announced, making a rush for the kitchen. 'You ruined what would have been a nice dinner.'

'Tough!' Rowlands stood up to follow.

'There's no need for nastiness!' Williams snapped, opening the refrigerator.

The fly-blown light in the kitchen ceiling showed up patches of blackened grease on the tiled floor, and more grease and dirt besmirching counters and cooker hob and table top. Crumbs and bits of food crunched underfoot and littered the chairs, and the huge double sink overflowed with unwashed crockery and glassware.

Pushing aside the debris of other meals, he put bread and cheese on the table, seated himself, and began randomly tearing apart the food and stuffing it into his mouth. While he chewed and swallowed, his scrawny throat describing the passage of his meal, McKenna opened the back door to release the sickening smell from every corner of the squalid room.

Breathing in the fresh night air, Rowlands whispered: 'We should ask environmental health to fumigate the place. He must be breeding roaches by the colony.'

'Don't talk about me behind my back!' Williams gabbled. 'Say it to my face or shut up!' Snatching a plate, some cheese, an apple, and a knife, he pushed back his chair. 'I'm going to the study. Shut the back door.'

'*Do* you pay maintenance to Margaret?' McKenna asked.

'I did until she shacked up with somebody else.'

'She seems remarkably content.'

'Bully for her!'

'You have a new partner, so why begrudge her happiness?'

'Why not?' he demanded, tipping gin into a grimy tumbler. 'She got off lightly.'

'I wouldn't agree,' McKenna said. 'May we sit down?'

'You may as well, as you won't bugger off. You can have a drink if you want.'

'No, thank you.' McKenna shifted a heap of papers from a chair.

Williams grunted, then hacked the cheese and apple into ugly chunks which he stuffed into his mouth and washed down with gulps of gin.

'When we asked you about Ned's papers, you feigned ignorance,' McKenna began. 'In fact, you feigned ignorance about everything.'

'What else could I do?' the other man demanded. 'Come out with my hands in the air?' Chewing apple, he added: 'I didn't kill him, and I had nothing to do with his death. Why should I tell you things you don't need to know?'

'It's not your place to decide what we need to know,' McKenna said.

'Did you need to know about Mina? Did you need to turn Edith inside out?'

'Having to pry is one of the unfortunate consequences of a murder,' replied McKenna. 'So that we can discover what's relevant.'

'Edith isn't, Mina isn't, I'm not, and nor are the other girls.' He paused, mouth working. 'Nor is that bloody nigger, much as I'd like him to be!'

'In our view, Ned's death has its roots in his past.'

'You can't be sure.'

'Give us some credit, Professor. No-one walked in off the street and spiked his food, and, sadly for you, no-one else appears to have a motive for wanting him out of the way.'

'Who *did* tell you?' he asked, his eyes glinting.

'Not George, as you assumed.' McKenna smiled bleakly. 'Bits and pieces of information came together. Gladys Jones showed me a photo, taken on one of your long ago visits to Llys Ifor. Others also remembered "Eddie", and one of your ilk filled in the blanks.'

'If I'd wanted to kill him, I'd have done it years ago, but

there was no need. We made a bargain, and he stuck to his part as if it were written in stone.' Williams smiled, too. 'Anyway, he was as much in it as I was.'

'In what?'

'The manuscript business. It was a game.' He emptied the gin bottle into his glass. 'Then it got out of hand. We were going to own up, but everything snowballed.'

'A game?' McKenna asked.

'It caused Ned's first real breakdown, you know. He was so terrified we'd be rumbled, he got himself locked up in Denbigh Hospital, out of harm's reach.' Lighting a cigarette, he added thoughtfully: 'Or perhaps he did it to get the feel of being behind bars.'

'What exactly did you do?' McKenna asked. 'What did this "manuscript business" entail?'

'Giving people what they wanted! We were both reading Welsh literature and language, and the lecturers were obsessed with the idea of a treasure trove of old manuscripts, if only someone could find them.'

'So you decided to "find" a few,' McKenna said. 'Did you copy them from an obscure book?'

'No, they weren't copies. That's the tragedy we had to live with.' He drained the glass, then rummaged in a cupboard for more liquor.

'Shouldn't Professor Williams have a solicitor before we go further, sir?' Rowlands asked. 'He seems to be admitting to an offence.'

'I don't want a solicitor!' Unopened gin bottle in hand, Williams turned.

'You might feel differently when you've had time to reflect,' McKenna pointed out.

'And when I've sobered up?' he asked. 'It takes more than a few glasses of gin to affect me, more's the pity.'

'None the less—'

'Hear me out, will you?' A whine crept into his voice. 'Let me talk. I know what I'm doing.' The bottle clinked against the rim of the glass as the liquor tumbled out.

'And what are you doing?' McKenna asked.

'Shedding my skin? Copying Edith, perhaps. She says she feels so much better.'

'Does she know? Does your wife?'

'No-one in the whole wide world knew except Ned and me, and now there's only me, and my God, I wish I were dead as well!' He threw the cigarette stub into the hearth, and watched the smoke dragged up the chimney. Slumped in his chair, hands between his knees, liquor slopping from the glass, he said: 'Ned collected paper even then, bits out of newspapers and magazines, old pamphlets, anything he thought might be interesting or useful, and I was looking through his stuff one Sunday afternoon because I was bored, and neither of us had money to go out.' He shuddered gently. 'Ned was lying on his bed, saying he felt hot and sleepy, and I remember chaffing him because he wouldn't take off his tie and unbutton his shirt. I asked him if he went to bed with his coat and tie and boots on, and he said it wasn't decent to show your flesh, and nothing good could come of it. I suppose he was thinking of his sister, the one who's gone completely mad.' Reminiscence softening his features, he half-smiled. 'I've been telling him for years that bottling up all his natural instincts would just make him ill, but the daft old prude still probably died as chaste as the day he was born.' He stared blankly at the dirty hearth, then reached for another cigarette and put the tumbler on the floor. 'Anyway, in among his litter, I found a newspaper article about the messes left over from the war which desperately needed sorting, especially in Germany and Austria, and I figured a job abroad for the long vac would probably pay much better than the usual run of bloody awful student jobs.'

'They weren't much fun, were they?' McKenna asked,

stifling a yawn. 'I sorted other people's dirty linen in a laundry, folded millions of Christmas cards in a printing works, worked from dusk to dawn filling shelves in Woolworths, pulled pints and broke up murderous fights every term-time weekend in one of the worst pubs in Liverpool, and tramped miles around Anglesey delivering Christmas mail.'

'I thought your family was comfortably off,' Rowlands said to Williams. 'Couldn't they shield you from the rigours of student life?'

'I wanted my independence.' He turned to McKenna. 'Tell him to get off my back, or he can get out!'

'Tell me about the manuscripts,' McKenna persuaded. 'Tell me how you forged them.'

'It was a joke,' insisted the professor. 'A game.' He took a swallow of gin, and licked his lips. 'I don't know whose idea it was, or where it came from. It just happened, the way things do, one thing leading to another. We were sick of hearing about these bloody relics, we were bored, I was reading about left-over wartime chaos, Ned's lying on his bed yawning like a hippo because he hadn't slept off last night's sleeping tablet, and then he wondered if the authors of these precious relics would have taken drugs, or chewed leaves, or stewed magic mushrooms.' Shifting in his chair, he went on: 'When I asked him why they should, he said if he deliberately stayed awake after he'd taken a sleeping tablet, he'd feel like a lark in the eye of the sun, and it was worth the terrible depression he had next day.' He ceased speaking for a long moment, staring at the floor. 'He showed me some of the verse he'd written when he was fighting the drugs, and it was so wonderful I felt sick with envy. I looked at him lying on that narrow bed with hands folded across his chest and his old-fashioned clothes, and he still looked like a pathetic runt from the backwoods, even if there was this magic inside.'

'What was he taking?' McKenna asked.

'Mandrax. It was banned.'

'Because it was lethally addictive,' McKenna commented.

'It was marvellous!' Memory glittered in his eyes. 'What the doctor gave me instead was like the difference between a miracle and a sleight of hand.'

'Ned shared his prescriptions with you?'

'Very, very occasionally. The tablets were too precious, you see. He kept the bottle tucked inside his waistcoat pocket, and every so often, he'd get it out, and we'd count the dreams.' He sighed, his bony fingers trembling. 'I told Ned that God had opened the door for us to write about what we saw, and sometimes, the words flowed so fast we couldn't catch them all. I thought it was like clinging to a raft of twigs in a mountain cataract, but when we survived the journey, you can't imagine the exhilaration.'

'And the power, too, I suspect,' McKenna suggested.

'No!' He shook his head. 'Not the power, simply the knowledge, of what lay beyond the edge of the world. You've written yourself,' he added, glancing at McKenna. 'You've hunched over the paper well into the small hours, pen in hand, mind on the run with angels and devils, and the words coming from somewhere you never knew existed. You write, and read, and write, and when you're too exhausted to make another scratch, you read it again, and almost stop breathing for the wonder of what you created.' He paused, smiling with a ghastly weariness. 'Then you sleep on it, and wake up with that excitement still making your heart thump nineteen to the dozen, and get the paper out from where you hid it, because if anyone else reads it while it's so new the magic might vanish, and you read it again, and find the magic's gone anyway, and you're looking at a load of crap.'

'It happens,' McKenna said. 'Nothing worth having comes easy.'

'People say Mozart plucked his notes from the air as if

God were handing them down to him, crotchet by quaver, and if that's true, I know how he felt. In the cold light of day, what we wrote with the help of Ned's tablets was even more marvellous than we thought.' The remnants of the smile soured to a sneer. 'Ned said that monstrous child of Edith's has the gift, and she can get hold of it whenever she wants, without the help of God or medicine.'

'I think he was right,' McKenna agreed, offering his cigarettes. 'Is that why you resent her so much?'

'I don't resent her!' He fumbled in the packet. 'I simply loathe her attitude, her impudence, her mouthiness, and, worst of all, her appalling nosiness. Never in my life have I come across anyone so blatantly and bluntly inquisitive.'

'That's how she gets the knowledge she needs to stoke the flames.' As McKenna leaned froward to light Iolo's cigarette, the other man's odour drifted in his nostrils. 'I don't think she has any control over it.'

'Well, she'll be sorry when she finds herself like us, lashed to a wheel of fire!' commented Williams, blowing smoke towards the dingy ceiling.

Rowlands flicked his own lighter. 'We're still waiting to hear about the manuscripts.'

'We didn't do anything wrong!'

'You've admitted to misuse of prescribed drugs.'

'Don't be so petty! Artists have to reach their visions, by any means, because it's our destiny and our duty to show them to the rest of the world. You can't expect us to be bound by common laws.' Sulkily, he watched his interrogator. 'Anyway, I had my own prescriptions. My doctor didn't believe unsettled nights should interfere with my studies, and he talked as if taking tablets for this and that was the way ahead for everyone. Edith's doctor probably convinced her of a pain- and misery free utopia at the bottom of a bottle of tranquillizers.'

'Did you become addicted?' McKenna asked.

'That bloody dago at the surgery thinks I was! He said my anxieties and insomnia were caused by the drugs, and stopped my scripts.' He picked up the tumbler of gin, and drank again. 'So I took my custom elsewhere.'

'To the off-licence?' Rowlands asked.

'To another bloody doctor!' he snarled. 'One who knows better than to bite the hand that feeds!'

'Edith's beginning to realize how much she lost through drug dependency,' McKenna said quietly. 'Perhaps it's worth thinking about for yourself? Psychotropic drugs release negativity, inhibition, and memory, as you and Ned discovered, but there's an equally powerful downside, as Edith's learned to her cost.'

'You're one to talk!' Williams said. 'You must get through forty or fifty cigarettes a day.'

'And I expect you do, too,' McKenna replied. 'But I rarely drink, and when I had to start upping the sleeping pills to make them work, I stopped taking them.'

'Bully for you!' he commented, reaching for the gin bottle. 'Give yourself a pat on the back for all that self-control.'

'The manuscripts,' Rowlands said, his voice sharp. 'Can we please get to the point of this visit? It's very late, and forgive my deploying the kind of bluntness you so deplore in Phoebe, but to my mind, Professor, there's no difference between your descent into drug-related crime and the teenage deadleg robbing to feed his habit. Except, of course, you can afford to support your habit, and even private prescriptions must come a lot cheaper than anything the local pusher dispenses.'

'I won't tell you again! I did not commit a crime!'

'You engaged in a deliberate deceit, and however much you obfuscate the issue, you gained considerable social, academic, and material benefit.' Rowlands paused. 'In fact, your whole career rests on that fraudulent foundation, and

I'm still not convinced you didn't have a hand in silencing the only person in the world who could expose you for what you are.'

'You can't understand, can you?' he asked, gazing at Rowlands with a strange light in his bloodshot eyes. He nodded towards McKenna. 'He can, though, which is why he'll listen to the bitter end. I *couldn't* hurt Ned, because he was the only person on earth who knew me for what I am, so he was the only person on earth with whom there was no need to perform or pretend. We were in it together, both of us beyond the pale, and when the deceit and pretending stuck in my craw and started to choke me, I could go to him and find myself again. And before you start on the psychological bullshit bandwagon,' he added, looking again at Rowlands, his voice harshening, 'imagine how *you'd* feel in my shoes, if your imagination can stretch far enough. I'm worse off than any slave. For the last God knows how many years I've struggled through shifting sands, fettered with chains I put there myself, producing papers for academics the world over to scrutinize, lecturing to huge audiences, and pretending to a scholarship I don't own and never had.'

'No-one made you,' Rowlands commented. 'And, as I said, you profited considerably, if this house and your car are any indication. And your professorship, of course. By the way, does your wife drive?'

'My wife?'

'Mrs Solange Williams. Your wife.'

'No, she doesn't! And what's she got to do with this?'

'Then how does she get around if you're not on hand to drive her?'

'Taxis! Trains, when there's First Class! Why?'

'And she knows nothing of your deception?'

'No!'

'So, Professor,' Rowlands encouraged, leaning forward

with his elbows on his knees, 'what exactly did you do, all those "God knows how many years" ago?'

'Slipped over the edge into the other world,' he said, almost happily. 'And wrote about it in verse which put the old bards to shame.'

'I know,' McKenna said. 'I've read it.'

'It was out of this world!' he added, gazing up at McKenna as if he had found a saviour. 'We saw further, we heard more, we smelt the earth as never before, we felt everything! We thought we might die from the wonder of it, and even that didn't frighten us.'

'People under the influence are prone to flights of fancy,' Rowlands said acidly. 'And some of them think they can really take wing. We've all done our share of scraping up hopheads from the pavements.'

'You'll spend your life with your head and heart alongside your feet in the dirt,' snarled Williams, 'because you've no imagination. You'll never know how it feels to half-divine the magic. You're pitiful!'

'You sound like an old hippie, Professor,' Rowlands said.

'Sneer if you like. I don't care for your opinion, because I've seen something you don't even know exists.'

'And is that enough to outweigh the consequences?' McKenna asked. 'Because you and Ned squandered your gifts on a dishonest prank you could never claim what you owned. How do you reconcile that? Did Ned's pain come from his guilt and fear, like your confusion and degeneration? And why have you suddenly decided to tell us? What prompted this confession?'

'There's no-one else to talk to now.'

'Is there not?' McKenna enquired. 'People say conscience is the voice of the dead wanting their due, so if you turn around, perhaps you'll see Ned looking over your shoulder, as I can.'

9

'What was all that about, sir? You were making less sense than him in the end.' Rowlands quietly closed the gate to Williams's garden. 'And aren't we bringing him in to make a statement? Suppose he decides to swallow a bottle of pills on top of the gin?'

McKenna stood by the car, keys drooping from his fingers. 'He won't overdose more than he does most nights, and he's in no condition to make a statement. Wait until tomorrow, when he's sober.' Unlocking the car, he climbed into the driver's seat.

'Is he ever sober, as we understand the term?' Rowlands asked. 'And what was that about Ned looking over his shoulder?'

'Provocation.' McKenna gunned the engine, and drew away from the kerb. 'I'm not convinced Ned was party to the fraud, I'm not convinced Iolo wrote the verse, and I'm extremely disinclined to share the view that he's a victim of forces beyond his control.'

'So you think he might've killed Ned after all?'

Driving fast through the web of narrow hilly streets between Williams's house and the main road, McKenna said: 'Not really. He'd have done it years ago if he was going to. What would be the point now?'

'He's got more to lose.'

'According to him, the strain of pretence is near unbearable. Loss of prestige might be a release.'

'I was thinking more about the posh house, however filthy it is, and his fancy car, not to mention his trophy wife.' Rowlands sniffed at his sleeve. 'The stink off that dump's got on my clothes.'

'Living in squalor probably reflects the way he sees himself,' McKenna said, jumping traffic lights on College Road.

'You can delve deeper into his psyche tomorrow, which won't be very taxing, because he's a shallow man, for all his talk of wondrous visions.' The car rocked around the tiny roundabout by Safeway supermarket. 'If he saw anything at all, that is. I suspect Ned's death is hastening the collapse of whatever ethical structure Iolo has, and I think the words he used and the sight he claims were Ned's alone. And,' he went on, roaring down Deiniol Road towards the police station, 'if I'm wrong, it's a tragedy, with Iolo forever condemned as a charlatan for admitting to one lapse.'

'Once a con, always a con,' Rowlands retorted, stifling a yawn. 'His childhood mates would probably tell us he cheated his way through school, and played dirty the rest of the time.' As McKenna turned into the police station yard and parked, he added: 'If he had this wonderful creative spirit, where is it now?'

'Stifled by the contentments of the material world, perhaps,' McKenna said. 'Or sealed up, like the clouds and dreams in Ned's boxes, because it chafed.' He paused, then said: 'Which makes no sense. Phoebe would tell you she can't help herself putting pen to paper, because creative energy rages like Iolo's mountain cataract. Ned dissipated his in arcane research and nurturing Phoebe, but it had to find an outlet.'

'You're still disinclined to look for lumps of clay on the end of his legs, aren't you?' Rowlands asked.

'I've heard nothing to persuade me I should, least of all Iolo's pretentious and pedestrian description of a drug-induced flight of fancy. As you said, people under the influence only *think* they can fly.'

'Well, with Ned out of the way, he can lay claim to whatever he wants.' He yawned again, and stretched. 'Feasibly, drugs *can* let loose greater potential, and people of an artistic bent go in for excesses of alcohol and drugs in any case, but the potential has to be there in the first place. All the

Mandrax in the world couldn't make a silk purse from a sow's ear.'

'I think Iolo's still trying to find this magic in his bottles of gin and pills,' McKenna said. 'But we'll never know, any more than we'll know if Ned only *pretended* to find inspiration in his own bottle of pills because he was afraid of what was in his head; or of going the same way as Gertrude, who had her own distinctions from the herd.'

'Or maybe he got sick of snide remarks about being different, and pretended to join in with the flower power drug culture.'

'Whatever else, joining forces with Iolo ruined him. Even if the manuscript fraud began as a game, once Ned realized the measure of Iolo's corruption, he was effectively muzzled. He couldn't let the cat out of the bag because no-one would believe he wasn't party to the deception.'

'Wouldn't it be more in character for him not to break the bonds of friendship?' Rowlands asked. 'What other friends has he had, apart from an old tramp, an unbelievably odd child, and a black man?"

'Iolo really hates George, doesn't he?' McKenna commented.

'He's a dyed-in-the-wool racist. According to him, Dr Ansoni's a "dago".'

'Only because he stopped his scripts for pills,' McKenna said, finally opening the car door. 'He thwarted him and threatened his ego, which Iolo can't abide, any more than he could bear the prospect of George eventually seeing through the fog of years to the truth.' Walking slowly up the back steps, he added: 'In the morning, you can unravel the roots of his racism, if you want, when you've found out the specifics of making pieces of paper look as if they're hundreds of years old. You can also ask him when and where he met up with Ned, when the strain of his chicanery got the better of him.'

• • •

Diana Bradshaw was waiting for him, lolling in a chair in his office, her smart shoes kicked off and askew on the carpet.

'I didn't expect to see you again this evening,' McKenna said.

'It's more like night than evening, isn't it?' She reached for the discarded footwear. 'What a horrible day! I stayed at the hospital as long as possible, but Janet's still unconscious, so I couldn't talk to her.' Gingerly easing the shoes on to her slightly swollen feet, she continued: 'The doctors say she's as well as can be expected, which really means very little. I tried to get more detail from her parents, and got a mouthful of near abuse from her father, instead.'

'It's easier for him to blame us than look into his own conscience.'

'Well, whatever you might say about Janet's wilfulness, I blame myself for not noticing something was badly wrong.'

'Perhaps it's not a matter of blame,' McKenna suggested, 'but more of a young woman's fear.'

'Fear of what?' she asked. 'Single pregnancies don't attract stigma in this day and age, you know.'

'Maybe not in England, or in other levels of Welsh society, but Janet's circle is very different. It's not a year since her father refused an unwed mother the traditional blessing, humiliating the girl before the whole congregation.'

'How cruel people can be!'

'Men of God are often the least charitable about human failings,' McKenna added. 'By the way, did you see Dewi at the hospital?'

'They wanted him in for observation, but he insisted on going home.' She retrieved her handbag from beneath the chair. 'I told him to take tomorrow off. I hope you don't mind.' She smiled. 'I'm rostered off duty this weekend, but call me if you need anything. Are there any problems I should know about? Any progress?'

'I'll keep you posted.'

'But only during the hours of daylight, if that's possible!' She smiled again. 'I've forgotten the feel of a good night's sleep.'

Feet on the desk and a cigarette glowing between his fingers, Rowlands said, as the firedoor sighed at the top of the stairs: 'Does she know how lucky she is to be getting *any* sleep?'

'Are you going home?' McKenna asked.

'Is it worth it? I won't get there before midnight, and I usually leave before seven. I'd kip here but for the stink of paint.'

'Then call your wife, and tell her you're borrowing my spare room.'

10

The cats were behind the front door, faces pressed to the reeded glass. When a stranger followed their master over the threshold, they disappeared at high speed down the staircase.

Following them, McKenna found empty food and water bowls strewn about the kitchen, the sill beneath the open parlour window streaked with dusty paw-prints, parallel trails of dirt on the wall below, and playing cards littering the carpet, the Knave of Diamonds jammed behind a skirting board. The Queen of Spades had vanished, like her human counterpart.

'Looks as if there's been quite a party,' Rowlands said,

eyeing the cats, now by the kitchen door, and the wreckage all around him. 'Why did you leave the window open so far?'

'So they could get in and out, of course!' McKenna said tetchily, on his way to feed his pets.

'Along with half the local cats, by the look of things.' As practical as Dewi, he re-ordered the parlour, wrung out a clean cloth in hot, soapy water, washed window, wall and table, then made tea and sandwiches while the cats ate supper.

McKenna slumped at the kitchen table, and twitched, like the animals, when the opening bars of Friday's late concert sounded from the garden.

1

Rowlands snored. The deep, rhythmic sound throbbed through the walls of the house and roused McKenna in the small hours. While his brain waded sluggishly through memory for the source of the alien noise, he lay stiff and still, then drifted back to sleep until a brilliant summer's dawn invaded the room.

Sunbeams angled sharply across the pale flowery wallpaper, moving as the sun climbed behind Bangor Mountain, and he sneezed quietly as the scents of early morning weaved through the open window. The sleeping cats were a dead weight at the foot of the bed, deaf to the screeching and mewling of gulls. Turning over to check the alarm clock, he saw a dark shadow flicker on the sun-striped walls, and felt the draught of wings as a huge bird eddied past the window before landing with a thud on the roof. When its jabbering began to reverberate down the disused chimney shaft behind the bedhead, he buried his head under the pillows.

He slept through the rising tide of noise from the waking city, through the wailing of his hungry cats, and came to life only when the shrill note of the alarm began to sputter with exhaustion. He staggered down to the bathroom, Blackie at his heels, Fluff tittuping ahead, then retrieved a litter of envelopes and postcards from the mat by the front door. As he looked through the post, the smells of toast and bacon and coffee finally touched his senses, and he descended the second flight of stairs to find his breakfast cooked, the table laid, and Rowlands, fully dressed, scooping meat into cat dishes.

'They've already been down,' he said, nodding towards the animals. 'They legged it back upstairs when they saw me.'

McKenna grinned. 'They're more discerning than tarts and lawyers, even if they do hang around on every street corner.' Seating himself, he added: 'This is very civil of you.'

'It's the least I could do. I slept like a log.'

'I know. I heard you.'

Rowlands flushed. 'If my wife ever murders me, you won't have far to look for a motive.'

'Separate rooms might solve the problem,' McKenna said, 'as well as giving your conjugal relations a clandestine edge. The upper classes never share the marital bed.' He flipped through the envelopes. 'At least, not with each other, except to procreate.' He grinned again, for no letter from Manchester hid in the welter of paper, and his food tasted even better.

Stock-still in the ivy lavishing the garden wall, a pine marten garbed in golden summer livery watched the cats sail out through the back door. As it leapt from view, the dark glossy leaves quivered, and only then did the cats briefly abandon their territorial circuit.

'What a wonderful sight!' Rowlands said.

'You sound like Iolo.' McKenna smiled.

'That was a real animal, and you saw it, too.'

'And I've seen it before, as well as the jays nesting in that big tree below the fence, the barn owl which holes up in one of the derelict outbuildings behind the High Street shops, and the colony of bats from Burton's attic.' Pouring fresh coffee, he went on: 'A vixen and two cubs came down from the mountain in March, and last week, one of the neighbours found an adder asleep in her back yard.'

Rowlands heaped sugar crystals in his coffee. 'We've got a view of more houses and the tops of a few artificial-looking trees. It's a nice area, but it's too much the work of man, like Iolo's garden.' He lit a cigarette. 'Shall I caution him before he makes his statement?'

'And don't forget to offer him a brief,' McKenna added, surveying the post once again.

'Aren't you going to open your letters?'

'I can resist the temptation.' He picked out a large, lurid postcard stuck about with numerous stamps and five postmarks. 'Eifion Roberts, the pathologist, is touring Germany and Switzerland with his wife,' he said, reading the scrawl on the back. 'But he's not a happy man, because if he hadn't sold his boat last year, he could be tacking down Menai Strait instead of traipsing around crowded foreign places which mean absolutely nothing to either of them. He says his wife's enjoying herself, but only because she's buzzing in and out of shops like a wasp going from one jam pot to another.' Glancing at the collage of mountain peaks and meadows, of narrow streets hung about with timbered houses, and a bell tower in the utilitarian style of architecture, he put the card aside and picked up the other colourful missive which had graced his morning. 'And this is from Jack Tuttle,' he said, examining a sharply focused photograph of the Pont du Gard at Nîmes. 'The weather's dodgy, along with his stomach, because of the ghastly *cuisine*, and his wife is also buzzing in and out of shops, so he'll need the payrise due with his expected promotion to settle the credit card bills.' He picked up his coffee. 'And as there's no promotion in sight for anyone now, he's in for a shock, isn't he?'

2

A lump had grown on Dewi's forehead during the night, pulsing as if he were harbouring alien life. He was reading through a pile of paper, placing each sheet neatly aside as he finished it. As McKenna and Rowlands entered the office, he said: 'I'd like to bring in Jason for questioning about Annie's car. He arranged the deal.'

'We know that,' Rowlands told him. 'But there's nothing to suggest he knew it was dodgy.'

'He insisted on a cash transaction, sir. Edith lent Annie the money, and she's paying it back every month.'

'So as Annie should've known cash equals something amiss, we could do her for knowingly buying a dodgy car,' Rowlands suggested.

'We're interested in the people behind the fraud,' said McKenna. 'Not the victims.'

'She could be involved,' Rowlands went on. 'The family's hardly white as the driven snow. Edith's morals leave a lot to be desired, Mina's a headcase, and the saintly Uncle Ned well and truly mislaid his halo a long time ago.'

'More to the point,' asked McKenna, 'has the pathologist reported back on prescriptions for the Lloyds and Polgreens?'

'No, sir,' Dewi said. 'I've left another message for him.' He paused. 'And I called the hospital. Janet's no better.'

'Is she any worse?'

'They didn't say.'

3

Janet's mother must have retreated to the manse, McKenna thought, facing Pastor Evans in the narrow corridor outside the intensive care unit. Ashen-faced, quivering with the rage which so often precedes grief, Evans hissed words of censure and disgust, then brushed past, leaving behind him the smell of the chapel, a medley of dust and prayer books and polish and maleness which pervaded his daughter's car and person, overwhelming the costly French perfumes she wore in disguise.

Watching the fine grey cloth of the pastor's summer coat swirling about his legs, McKenna made his way to the nursing duty station, a narrow counter overhung by a bank of monitors, where lights pulsed and machines bleeped in harmony and discord.

'Is she conscious?' he asked a tall black woman, whose ornately plaited hair enhanced her height and presence. 'Can I see her?'

The consciousness which had mercifully deserted Janet the day before remained out of reach, and her body seemed shrunken, absent of kinship with the vibrant, temperamental girl who resided in his memory. Watching the regular rise and fall of her chest, he thought of Phoebe's musings on perception, and wondered if life depended for its existence on the memory and participation of an observer.

4

'Jason's out on patrol,' Dewi said. 'He's not due at the depot before lunch-time.'

'When does his shift finish?' McKenna asked.

'Four o'clock.'

'Try to collar him at lunch-time, then, but don't be too pushy. And did you let Annie know about her car?'

Dewi nodded. 'She's furious.'

'Hardly surprising,' McKenna said. 'She can keep it over the weekend, but you'd better tell her we want it first thing Monday morning for the vehicle examiner.'

'You can tell her yourself, sir. She's in your office.'

• • •

She wore a finely-seamed dress, in the style her mother favoured, and looked, he thought, as Edith must have done before she faded, and age rather than youth came to define every curve of her body. 'This week's been like the doldrums,' she said. 'Little winds blowing you this way and that, then a calm period, then a sudden storm, brewing up from nowhere, leaving you breathless and baffled.' She brushed a bead of sweat from her hairline. 'There was a breeze yesterday, but it seems to have died. Did you know this is the second hottest August since records began in 1727? I read it in the paper this morning.'

'I can't imagine people harnessing such information so long ago,' he commented. 'I can't believe they knew enough.'

'Why not?' They weren't inherently less developed.' She grinned at him. 'I expect you think your parents had only just raised their heads above the primeval sludge, don't you?'

'Not quite, although it's hard to tell at times with the Irish.' He smiled in return. 'But they seemed content with less.'

'All we need is food, shelter and warmth. The rest is decoration, diversions from the real business of death and sex, like my car. What's the problem with it?'

'You've fallen foul of the car-ringers.' He lit a cigarette. 'More than a quarter of all recorded crime involves the half million vehicles which get stolen every year. Like a lot of popular mid-price range cars, yours was probably stolen to order, then fitted with number plates derived from a same year model we've already traced. Number plates also come from accident write-offs, which the insurance companies sell to wreckers.'

'But I've got registration documents,' she protested.

'Which only prove that computers can't think for themselves. There's no automatic cross-check when documents go in for change of ownership.'

'So now what happens?'

'If the vehicle identification plate hasn't been drilled out, it will show chassis, engine, marque and year details, and provided the chassis and engine numbers weren't removed and reblocked, we can find out where your car came from.'

'And I'll be minus my car and still in debt to my mother for several thousand pounds.'

'I'm afraid so.'

'Damn and blast that bloody Jason and his "bargain of the year"! What a fool I was.'

'D'you know where he got the car?'

'One of his mates in the trade, he said. According to him, he's got mates in all sorts of trades. I hope you're going to ask him.'

'We'll ask,' McKenna promised, 'but please don't alert him.'

'He probably knows already. Mina was in when Dewi Prys phoned earlier.' She scowled fiercely. 'Oh, damn and bloody hell!'

For no discernible reason, her agitated gestures reminded him of Denise, and he recoiled involuntarily, resentful and even fearful. Later, he realized the similarity depended on a glimpse of some quality common to all women, but only after he had begun to appreciate that real harm had been rendered by the miserable attrition of his marriage.

Sweating profusely, Dewi sat in McKenna's office, legs crossed, hands in pockets. 'What happened at the hospital, sir?'

'Pastor Evans gave me the benefit of his opinion, which, as expected, amounts to Janet's condition being our fault.'

'He can go hang!' Dewi snapped. 'Is she any better?'

'I don't think she's any worse.'

'But she's very ill all the same, isn't she? God! The way the blood poured out of her was horrible!' He rubbed the swelling on his head, and winced. 'Who'd imagine it can go so dreadfully wrong? Mam said even an ordinary miscarriage can be fatal.'

'It can happen. Why not go to see her? She might have come round by now.'

'I'll wait. Her father'll be there, won't he?' He picked at a worn patch of veneer on the desk. 'Has anyone said anything about the demo?'

'Not yet.'

'Should I make a report about it?'

'Only what you remember, bearing in mind that a whack on the head can affect the powers of recall.'

'I was well out of order, sir.'

'And not for the first time. I sometimes think you harbour a death wish.'

'I don't do it on purpose.'

'Yes, you do. We all act on purpose, unless we're mad, and even lunatics can come up with reasons which satisfy their own logic.'

'I lost my temper.'

'You do that too often, as well,' McKenna commented. 'You're prone to acting like a naughty child, especially when you're bored, and you pick fights with Janet, expecting Jack Tuttle or myself to sort you out as if we're your parents. Well, we're not, and it's high time you started acting like an adult at work, as well as at home. You passed your sergeant's exams with flying colours, but I'm not prepared to recommend your promotion at present.'

'Point taken, sir.'

'Then do something about it,' McKenna said tetchily.

'This is the last time I'll help you off the hook. If you must kick against authority structures because they're there, then accept that a couple of broken feet is all you'll get. You've got the potential to be a very good officer, and a similar potential to be a real liability. It's your choice.'

'Iolo declined the services of a solicitor,' Rowlands reported, dropping his files on McKenna's desk. 'He's still hoping to keep his affairs out of the public eye, and he's back to his usual obnoxious self, so he's probably got an almighty hangover.'

'He must have a hangover every day,' said McKenna. 'He probably can't remember being without one.'

'Like you can't remember being without kids once they're born,' Rowlands commented, offering cigarettes. 'He was also very maudlin and self-pitying, but I'm afraid my sympathy wouldn't rise to the occasion. He's a sly piece of work, always on the look-out for himself, and making up his own rules as he goes along.'

'He may be aware of the extent of his dislocation from normality, and that's why he hits the bottle,' McKenna said, taking a cigarette. 'Maybe his brain was glitched in the womb, not enough to cause full-blown mental illness, but enough to condemn him to a no man's land between sanity and insanity. That could explain why he functions as he does, when he's had plenty of time and opportunity to learn what's acceptable and legal.'

'He's adamant he did nothing wrong with the manuscripts because he never made any claims about them. He simply offered them for an opinion, and other people decided what they were. If the experts judged them to be genuine, then genuine they must be. When I pointed out that simply offering them for an opinion was tantamount to fraud, he threatened to have the screaming ab-dabs. And he's paranoid about Polgreen: called him a lot worse than jungle bunny.'

'Guilt-speak,' McKenna decided. 'How did they age the documents?'

'That was also Ned's fault, because if he hadn't cut an article out of some obscure paper, they wouldn't have known where to start.' Rowlands took a sheet covered with notes from one of the files. 'Iolo reckons the world's full of gullible people desperate to jump on the back of some "discovery" and ride to fame, so they could have got away with taking far less trouble, but with the help of this article, they did a superb job.' He scanned the notes. 'Ned allegedly sneaked around the National Library tearing endpapers and the odd blank page out of rare old books, then they copied out their own offerings, with Indian ink and quills cut from seagull feathers.'

'I don't believe it! Ned wouldn't vandalize books.'

'You can't know that, and I think it fits rather neatly. Ever after, he's beset by the enormous awe-inspiring knowledge that in his eyes, he'd done terrible wrong, and would have to pay accordingly, and he caused his own pain in case God thought about letting him off the hook.' He returned to his notes. 'They aged the ink by pouring boiling tea over the paper, then splattered candlewax and butter and oil at random. Iolo also mentioned rubbing in breadcrumbs and dirt, and chewing the edges to mimic vermin damage. His face quite lit up when he was talking, and he wittered at some length about the very long, and very respectable history of faking, but I had to tell him I'd never heard of Keating, de Hory, van Meegeren, or Hebborn.'

'I hope he included his namesake,' McKenna added. 'Edward Williams, AKA Iolo Morgannwg, was faking bardic verse two hundred years ago, as well as rewriting Welsh history, and, like any student of Welsh literature, Iolo would know all about him. That's probably where he got the idea.'

'Ned would've known, too, and knowing the source of the poetry rather puts paid to your romantic notions about the survival of documents.' Slipping the paper back with its fellows, Rowlands smiled. 'You still believe the verses are Ned's own work, don't you?'

'What I believe doesn't matter, but I doubt if Iolo will amaze the world with a bounty of wonderful poetry now he's thrown off the shackles of deception.'

'He's done no such thing,' Rowlands told him. 'He's no intention of admitting to anything except a student prank, which wasn't his idea, and not even that unless he's out of options.'

'We can't justify the cost of having the manuscripts examined unless there's a direct and demonstrable connection with Ned's murder, so Iolo's face will probably be saved, which will be a huge relief to the Welsh academic establishment. You'd better send him home. *La belle femme* should be back soon from her London expedition.'

'I still want to know where the money comes from.'

'Why didn't you ask when you had the chance?'

'I did, and he told me to mind my own sodding business.'

'And where did he meet with Ned when he felt himself in need of honest comfort?'

'They had a weekly date at a pub in Menai Bridge.'

'Did they?' McKenna frowned. 'How come, when Phoebe was usually with Ned?'

'They met while she was in school, and during the holidays, Iolo suffered, which is another reason for him to hate her.' Rowlands picked up the files, and tucked them under his arm. 'And you were wrong about his name change. It wasn't a symbolic separation from Ned and their joint past. People were always confusing the two of them, and he got sick of it.'

5

On his way to Merlin Security, Dewi made a detour to the hospital, and spent an age gazing at Janet's silent shadowy form, a cold sick feeling wrenching at his heart. The image and its misery stayed with him when he emerged into the searing outside light, to make his way to the mortuary. Sunparched bits of leaf and litter crackled underfoot on the narrow flagged path, and he waited respectfully while a tenanted hearse pulled away, followed by a pie and sausage van which had come around the corner from the kitchen area. As the door of the pathology building closed behind him, images from the world beyond began to dance in his sundazzled eyes, like magenta-tinted photographic negatives.

The ground floor offices were deserted. Rounding a corner, he passed a small coffin propped against a 'Staff Only' sign, and went into the autopsy room, where one of the technicians was swabbing the floor and whistling to himself, his tune competing with the hissing of air extractors under the shining tables empty of all but their worn black head-rests.

'I'm looking for the pathologist,' Dewi said. 'He should have some papers for us.'

'Who's "us"?' the other man asked, eying the visitor as if assessing the outcome of his trade.

Dewi fumbled in his pocket for identification. 'Police.'

'Right. I'll go see.'

Gazing around him, buttocks pressed against a huge steel draining board, Dewi decided the place resembled a catering kitchen, provided it was unoccupied, provided he could ignore the strand of lank grey hair stuck to one of the head-rests, and provided he refrained from looking too closely at the tiers of pickled parts on a shelf attached to the wall, but boredom prevailed, and he wandered over. The specimens had an intricate beauty all their own, he thought, surveying the wonderful length of a man's dissected penis, the flower of an excised carcinoma, and a prune skin like a splinter of wood, caught in a sac grown out of a bowel wall. At the end of the shelf, he found a tiny human foetus, no bigger than a baby mouse, cradled in a nest of tissue dark with haemorrhage, and was reading the label pasted to the front when the technician returned, a long piece of paper pinched in his gloved fingers.

Once more out in the sunshine, eyes beguiled by different images, Dewi leaned against the hot metal of his sparkling car, learning from the length of paper that Jason Lloyd's mother, assailed by ills of depressing proportion, depended on the medical profession for both mental and physical equilibrium. Fluctuating blood pressure exacerbated her varicose veins, dermatitis provoked other itches, and infections raged hard on each other's heels through her throat, lungs, and other soft tissues. Scanning the list of prescriptions for tranquillizers and soporifics and antibiotics, he saw that her worn out uterus had fallen to the surgeon's scalpel four years previously, and climbed into his swanky car with his mind's eye overwhelmed with an awful image of Janet, open on a mortuary table with her dead baby nesting in her bloodied innards.

6

'Will Mrs Lloyd remember what she does with her all her pills?' McKenna asked, putting the paper on his desk. 'She's had six scripts for antibiotics in less than eighteen months, so it's a fair bet she didn't even finish each bottle, but I wouldn't lay odds on her being able to lay hands on the left-overs.'

'She only had one script for tetracycline,' Dewi pointed out.

'Is she one of your many acquaintances on the estate?'

'I don't know her to speak to.'

McKenna glanced at his watch. 'You've time to pay her a

visit, and get to the depot before Jason finishes his lunch break.'

'What shall I say if she asks how we know about her tablets?'

'Use your initiative!'

7

The cathedral clock chimed the half-noon as McKenna unlocked his front door. One cat was curled around the cool porcelain pedestal of the washbasin, the other stretched out in the bath, and neither took any notice of him until he splashed a droplet of water on Fluff, and she twitched from head to tail with disapproval.

After he had eaten, he sat in the garden for a while, looking among the glossy ivy for the pine marten's glory, and found his eyes beginning to close of their own volition. He blinked fiercely, and, glimpsing a movement from the corner of his eye, saw one of the feline choristers about to slink into the house. He let it go, too lethargic to bother, and tuned his ears for the outbreak of more territorial conflict.

8

'Jason's mam was out,' Dewi reported, 'and Jason's still on a job, and won't be finished before two. I didn't bother waiting because he's in the Pwllheli area. It'll take him at least forty minutes to get back.'

McKenna yawned.

'His dad was out, as well, so I had a word with the sister who won that wet-T-shirt competition at the Octagon. She said her mam keeps all her left-over pills, in case.'

'In case of what?'

Dewi shrugged. 'In case she can't get to the doctor, or he won't give her more pills when she does get there, or she can't afford a new prescription. I don't know, do I?'

'Did you see the left-overs?'

'They're all over the house. A couple of pills in one bottle, five or six capsules in another. Kitchen cupboards, parlour mantelpiece, bedside table, and more in her handbag, according to the daughter.' He pulled a notebook from his shirt pocket. 'I made a list, but there wasn't any tetracycline.'

'Double check on the trade names,' McKenna said. 'There's a drugs directory somewhere among the junk you shifted into the main office. If you can't find it, ring Dr Ansoni. When will Mrs Lloyd be home?'

'Late. She's gone to Llandudno, shopping.'

McKenna was assessing the need to do some shopping of his own when Phoebe telephoned, edgy with anxiety. 'Annie's taken Mama and Bethan for a drive,' she said. 'She's taking advantage of the car while she's got it, and I can't imagine how she'll manage when you take it away. How will she get to school, and here? And how on earth will she be able to keep an eye on Auntie Gladys?' Before he could respond, she rushed on. 'She can't afford another, because she still owes Mama for this one, and her mortgage eats a huge chunk out of her salary. I don't think Mama's got any more wads of cash to lend, either.'

'If we catch the perpetrator, she'll probably get criminal injuries compensation,' he said. 'But tell her not to hold her breath.'

'She *could* make do with an old banger, I suppose. It needn't cost more than a few hundred pounds, and it wouldn't necessarily be less reliable, would it?'

'My first car was fifteen years old, and I never had a day's worry with it.'

'Mama's worried sick, you know. Could Annie get done for having a dodgy car?'

'Only if she knowingly bought a stolen vehicle.'

'Why don't you say "car"? And what about driving it now she knows it's nicked? What if your traffic cops chase her?'

'Stop fretting!' McKenna said, smiling to himself. 'I'm not surprised she calls you Cassandra.'

'It's nothing to what she's calling Clyde. I hope he's gone before they get back.'

'He's there?' He glanced at the clock. 'I thought he was at work.'

'Oh, he turned up about ten minutes ago, on his way to the depot, and he's in a hell of a mood about something, so don't be surprised if I ring back to say there's been a shoot-out, like in the Bonnie and Clyde film. I just hope they don't make too much noise about it, or leave too much of a mess. That film's a real bloodfest, isn't it?'

'You should be out yourself, instead of waiting around the house for second hand experiences.'

'I don't want to go out. I'm writing.' He heard her draw a deep breath. 'Did you honestly like my story as much as you said? Only what you said made me feel so much better, because my teacher sort of put the mockers on things, and with Uncle Ned not around any more . . .'

'I really liked it, Phoebe. What's your new project?'

'I'm sorting out some ideas about Auntie Gertrude, and her dead lover and her dead baby. And about Llys Ifor, of course. I can't see very far beyond it yet.'

'Perhaps there's no need to.'

'It's in my head day and night,' she said, 'always different and always the same, whatever time of day or night or season of the year I imagine, and whether or not Meirion and Auntie Gladys might have rearranged the animals, or the farm machinery, or the furniture, or themselves, or even

Auntie Gertrude. How can one place positively *invade* your imagination, when there's so much else in the world?'

'Perhaps because it's there, and so are you.'

'Isn't that a bit Celtically metaphysical?' He heard a pen scratching on paper, the faint sounds of voices in the background. 'I'm going to write to my father for a word processor, then I could sort my ideas properly. Modern technology's wonderful, isn't it? George says people often get totally besotted with their computers.'

'Have you seen him?'

'He popped round last night to say he's going home for the weekend. He's still pretty upset, about Uncle Ned, and getting chucked in your cells, and I don't think he feels safe in his flat any more, but I suppose people like him never feel safe, because they know too much about the past. It's not a hundred years since the French were locking up naked black people in cages and showing them off like animals.' He heard a tap of pen against teeth. 'I could ask Mama to let him move into Uncle Ned's rooms, couldn't I? She's had quite a change of heart about him, probably because he's stopped making out like some real cool dude. He could give her a run for her money when it comes to being tense and neurotic, especially about the police.'

'Black people often suffer the sharp edge of policing.'

'Yes, he's told me, and usually because they're there and so are the police. I did think better of you, though I suppose you had no choice in the circumstances.'

'Quite.'

'Never mind. It's water under the bridge, as Uncle Ned would've said.' She paused again, and once more he heard the scratching pen, although the voices were silent. 'When can we have his funeral?'

'Soon, I hope. We should have a date for the inquest next week.'

'George asked again about finishing his work. Mama's

got no objection, though it's not really her decision, but nobody can finish it if you don't find all his papers.'

'We're still looking.'

'Where? Aren't you out of possibilities?'

'Your mother said we could search the house, but we got a little side-tracked.'

'I've been in the attics, and I even turned over Minnie's room when she was at work, but it's clean.'

'Why did you do that?'

'She could've taken them,' Phoebe asserted. 'She's pinched things before, and she could easily have sneaked in when he was asleep, especially if he'd taken one of his tablets. They made him dead to the world.'

'But why should she?'

He could almost see the shrug. 'Because.'

The voices rose again, then a door slammed.

'It's a good job we haven't any guns in the house,' she commented acidly.

'What are they rowing about?'

'Don't know and don't care. They're always rowing, because there's nothing between them but sex and stupidity, and the nastiness that goes with all that. They don't have anything to talk about. Anyway, I must go, I want to finish my writing.' She chuckled. 'It's bizarre the way it takes over, as if it's the most urgent thing in the world, bullying me into doing something every day, no matter how small.'

'Why?'

'Dunno, really, unless it's because I might be dead tomorrow. I wouldn't mean anything then, would I?'

9

In search of novelty, McKenna pushed his way through the crowed aisles of the new supermarket, then walked home,

the ritualistic excitement of Saturday afternoon at the shops
at its height, and the dead weight of cans and bottles in plastic carriers threatening to amputate the fingers of each hand.

Seeing no cans or packets prettified with the winsome
face of one of their own among the shopping, the cats
stalked off to sit on the parlour window-ledge. He stroked
their firm heads and springy ears, and thought if anyone saw
him, as he often chanced a glimpse into the secret lives of
others, he would seem like the lonely, ageing man he was,
with only his pets left to treasure.

The telephone shrilled suddenly, and he was told that
Phoebe had called the police station, upset and almost inco-
herent. When he tried to ring her, the line was engaged, and
he drove away from his house with dry dirt and dust spray-
ing from the tyres, and the knowledge that George's in-
nocence depended on the existence of another with death
in mind.

The front door of the elegant house in Glamorgan Place
stood wide open, a swath of colour draped over the threshold as the westering sun dragged the light of the landing
window in its wake. The hall was empty, each ground floor
room bereft of life, and rounding the dog-leg of the staircase, he almost fell over Phoebe's cat, hunched in a great
mound of fur on the half landing. From one of the bed-
rooms he heard a child's voice, sobbing quietly, and coming
to a room summery with pinks and blues and pale watery
green, he found Phoebe kneeling at her sister's feet, and
Mina slumped in a blue velvet chair. Her pale blue jeans and
white blouse were splattered with deep, gaudy red, huge
glistening beads of coloured glass rolled around her bare
feet, and, trampled into a dark puddle on the green carpet,
he saw a few long strands of gold. Her face was almost hidden by the swing of beautiful hair, and below wads of cloth
binding her wrists, blood oozed, dripping slowly from the
ends of her fingers.

'I called an ambulance,' Phoebe said through her tears. 'I rang, but you weren't there.'

'How bad is it?' Shamefully relieved the blood sacrifice was not hers, he crouched down, and lifted the limp hands in his own. Mina stirred, wincing with pain.

'There's so much blood!' Phoebe's voice was awe struck. 'The bathroom looks like a slaughterhouse.'

He pushed Mina's hair over her shoulders and away from her face, looking into her half-closed eyes. Her skin was marble white, a bluishness seeping into the shadows beneath her eyes. She cried like a stricken animal when he lifted her arms above her head to staunch the flow of blood, and he saw himself in the abattoir, draining a carcase. 'When did she do it?'

'I don't know!' More tears coursed down Phoebe's cheeks, in the tracks of others. 'I was writing. Clyde went soon after I spoke to you, and I thought I heard her go to the bathroom, but I'm not sure when, then Tom started wailing. He was on the stairs, and wouldn't come down, so I went up. She'd locked herself in, and she wouldn't answer. It took me ages to break the door open.' She wiped a hand across her face, smearing her skin with her sister's blood. 'And I had to use her beads for a tourniquet. I couldn't find anything else.'

'Why?' McKenna asked helplessly, feeling Mina's blood on his own hands. 'Why did she do it?'

As the ambulance siren wailed outside, Phoebe scrambled to her feet, ungainly and noisy, and ran downstairs, leaving him alone with Mina. Shallow breaths rattled in her throat, and her flesh was beginning to chill.

He stood aside for the paramedics, his arm around Phoebe's shoulders, then followed the stretchered body downstairs, Phoebe at his heels. Now on the landing window-ledge, the cat was stippled with colour.

'What shall I do?' Phoebe asked, her own breath rasping.

'I'll take you to the hospital. How can we let your mother know? Has she got a mobile phone?'

'She can't remember how to use it, so it's never switched on.'

10

Diana Bradshaw came instead of Edith, and, stripped of her garb of office, had no more distinction, McKenna thought, than any woman of indeterminate years he might pass in the street, and was no less inept in the face of near disaster. In a side room in the casualty department, she and Phoebe huddled together, while he paced the floor.

'She's done it before,' Phoebe offered. 'She took an overdose, but I'm not supposed to know.'

'Why on earth should she do that?' Diana asked. 'She's got everything to look forward to.'

'Because she's not normal!' Phoebe snapped. 'So even if she has got everything to look forward to, she won't see it that way.' She jumped up and smoothed her clothes, then her face blanched as she saw the bloodstains on her own garments, and she fell back into her seat. 'Mama won't know what to do,' she said dully. 'She'll go back on her pills.' Then she swore, as her mother and sister had done. 'Minnie's a selfish, stupid bitch! She doesn't care who she hurts!'

'Perhaps she cares too much,' McKenna said, something falling into place of its own accord amid the chaos left over from Ned's death. 'Perhaps she's running away from the harm she's done, or even trying to make sure she does no more.'

He went outside into the stultifying heat of an August afternoon turned rancid and enervating. Leaning against the nobbled brick wall, he lit a cigarette, and ordered the arrest of Jason Lloyd, then smoked the cigarette to its tip, thinking of the two lovely young women shut inside the building behind him, both beguiled by some guilt or arcane need into a letting of their own life blood.

He lit another cigarette and took out his mobile telephone to dial Iolo Williams's number, waiting an age for an answer.

'Yes? Who is this?' The voice was slurred and despondent.

'Michael McKenna, and I'm at the hospital, where the doctors are trying to save your daughter's life. She cut her wrists.'

'What?'

'I said—'

'Why should she want to do that?' A whine crept into his voice. 'Why cause such a fuss?'

'I don't know,' McKenna said. 'Are you going to come?'

'Me? Why? What good would that do? Edith'll cope.'

'Like she's always done? She certainly backed a loser with you, didn't she?'

'Talk's cheap,' Williams commented, and McKenna heard the chink of glass against tooth.

'Drinking again, Professor?'

'Bullying people again, Chief Inspector? Why don't you mind your own sodding business? You'd drive a bloody saint to drink!' There was a pause, a deep intake of breath, then he said, the whine back in his voice: 'I'll wait for my wife to come home. She'll decide what's to be done. She knows Mina best.'

'Isn't she back from her shopping spree yet?' McKenna asked. 'She spends an awful lot of your money, doesn't she?' He, too, paused. 'One of my officers keeps asking me how you support your life-style, and I must confess I'm at a loss for an answer.'

'Yes, and he had the sodding cheek to ask me!' Williams snarled. 'Bastards! What the hell's it got to do with you?'

'Maybe nothing, but on the other hand, maybe a lot. It

all depends.'

'On what? Who's next in line for persecution.?' He laughed bitterly. 'Don't waste your time! I'm up to my bloody neck in debt, and sinking fast! I've got problems you've never even dreamed of.'

'You'll survive, as long as the currency of your reputation doesn't suffer the devaluation it warrants,' McKenna commented. 'But you don't disappoint, do you?'

'What d'you mean?'

'I rang out of courtesy, to tell you about your daughter, even though I didn't expect you to break the habit of a lifetime by showing compassion. As I said, you don't disappoint.' He disconnected before the other man could answer, then threw his cigarette to the ground and stamped its fire to oblivion.

Phoebe and Diana seemed suspended in the same time in which he had left them.

'There's no news yet,' Diana said quietly.

'There won't be, will there?' Phoebe added. 'He was only gone fifteen minutes.' She turned her hands this way and that, scrutinizing their shape and colours, then held them palms up, and bent forward, peering at the matrix of veins on her wrists.

'What is it, dear?' Diana asked. 'Is something the matter?'

'I'm trying to imagine the pain,' Phoebe told her, and drew her nails viciously across the thin skin on her wrist.

Diana lurched away towards the toilets.

'I can't do it,' Phoebe added, as if there had been no interruption. 'I can't imagine it.'

Sitting beside her, McKenna took the clawing fingers in his own.

'I should pity her, shouldn't I?' Phoebe asked. 'She was probably trying to write what she feels, the way I can, but she had to do it with a razor. She used Uncle Ned's cut throat, the one his father left him. She must have pinched it from his room, and she's made such a mess of the handle. It's mother of pearl, and the blood soaked right in. Will it clean off, d'you think?'

'I expect so,' McKenna said.

She began to fidget. 'Will you take me home? I've got to clean the bathroom before Mama gets back. I couldn't bear her to see it like that, especially if Tom's in there, wallowing. He used to lick off the blood when I fell and cut my knees.'

'Is there no way of contacting her? Has Annie got a mobile?'

Phoebe shook her head, wisps of hair sticking to her cheeks.

'What time will they be back?'

She shrugged wearily. 'Sixish? What time is it now?'

'Ten past four.' McKenna glanced at the wall clock, and rose. 'Wait here while I find Mrs Bradshaw.'

He roamed the unit, peering into curtained bays, and was about to ask a nurse to check the women's toilets when he found her in a small office, beside a desk stacked with X-ray films and cartons of syringes.

'I've seen her,' she said. 'They've almost finished stitching her up.' Her eyes were bemused. 'It's her, you know. I said I'd know her if I ever saw her again.'

'I beg your pardon?'

'Mina Harris.'

'What about her?'

'She's the girl who sprayed my car with brake fluid.'

Sutured and bandaged, Mina was moved to a small ward overlooking the expressway which swept though a man-made ravine behind the city. Phoebe at his side, McKenna looked at the tangled disarray of Mina's wondrous hair, and the ugly little ear on show to the world, then Phoebe rearranged the hair, covering the ear and creating new shadows on the grey skin. Under the closed lids, Mina's eyes moved sluggishly.

'Has she been put to sleep?' Phoebe asked the young nurse fiddling with clips and bags and tubes.

'She had a local anaesthetic,' the girl said. 'While they stitched her wrists.'

'Doesn't she need pain-killers?' Phoebe nagged. 'Won't she be hurting dreadfully?'

The nurse nodded. 'I expect so.' Giving the apparatus one final tweak, she moved away. 'So maybe she'll think twice next time.' Torn between mother and sister, Phoebe decided Edith's need was greater and went home with Diana, leaving McKenna to watch over the would-be suicide, who slept fitfully, mouth slightly open. Through the window beyond her bed, he watched an endless stream of cars, trucks and vans on the road below, and a dirty mist of exhaust fumes creeping slowly up the hillside to join the shadow falling behind the building as the sun dropped towards the horizon. He went outside several times to smoke hurried cigarettes and make short telephone calls, but returned anxiously to his post, only once pausing at the WRVS canteen for a cup of strong tea.

Drowsing in his chair, he was dragged awake by a whimpering, as Mina struggled wildly to free herself from the sheet over her chest and the drip fastened into the back of her hand.

'Don't!' He held her flailing arms, and felt the heat and chill and tremors in her flesh. 'You'll hurt yourself even more.'

As she gasped for breath, he loosened the sheet and helped her to sit up. She flopped against him, then fell backwards on to the pillows, and stared at him without blinking, her eyes bloodshot.

'Phoebe's gone home, to be there when your mother gets

back.' He poured a little water into the plastic beaker on the bedside cabinet, and held it to her mouth. Her lips were desiccated, like an old woman's, and she gulped the water, matted hair tumbling over his hands, then pushed him away. Faint streaks of dried blood, brown against the grey flesh, smeared her hairline and bare arms, and on her scalp, little red pinpricks defined a small bald patch of swollen skin.

'What happened to your head?' he asked.

She lifted her right arm as if it were made of lead, and touched the wound. 'Jason pulled my hair.' Her voice was uncertain.

'Why?'

Her arm dropped, inert on the sheet. 'He was angry.' She screwed up her eyes. 'He said he'd cut it all off.' Then, fearful of betrayal, she turned her head away.

He watched the rise and fall of her chest as breath hissed in and out of her lungs, and thought of the harrowing shock awaiting Edith when she saw the reality of what her daughter had become. Without the camouflage of make-up and underpinnings, Mina had the look of a child who cried too often and too heart-breakingly, her little breasts cleaved by a spur of breastbone, her young flesh sagging like hag's skin.

'Why was Jason angry with you?' McKenna persisted.

'His sister rang his mobile because someone'd been to his house.' She turned her head to look at him again, eyes muddy with distress and incomprehension. 'He said I must've told, but I haven't. I haven't said a word, but he won't believe me.' She wept quietly. 'He says I've ruined everything, and his friends'll slash my face when they find out, then everyone'll know what I did to Uncle Ned, and I'll be put away.' Her left hand clawed its way across the bed, and clutched his arm. 'I didn't hurt Uncle Ned! I swear I didn't!' She tore at the bindings about her wrists. 'Oh God! I can't bear it! I can't!'

Another nurse materialized, in a flurry of pale uniform and crackling plastic apron. 'Stop that this minute!' Holding Mina's arms, she favoured McKenna with a look of absolute disgust. 'What have you said to her? Can't you see what state she's in?'

'She needs a doctor,' he said. 'Or better still, a psychiatrist.'

'She needs to be left in peace! You've no right pestering her.'

The smile which had so entranced Dewi broke suddenly and grotesquely over Mina's face, and her voice wheedled: 'He isn't pestering me. He's just talking. He's a policeman. They've got to talk.'

Snapping her teeth in irritation, the nurse walked away, soft-soled shoes whispering on the lino.

'Stupid cow!' Mina muttered.

He watched as her face was transfigured and refigured by a tide of expressions, until it settled again into pinched misery. 'Do you want some pain-killers?' he asked.

'What for?'

'Your wrists. They must hurt.'

She regarded the bandages, frowning. 'They ache, a little bit.'

And old saying gabbled in his head, reminding him that where feeling was absent, sense was also missing.

'I didn't do anything bad,' Mina added. 'I don't understand why he's so angry. It was just a joke.'

'What was?'

'Jason gave me some powder. It's named for a racecourse, and he said it'd make everybody go to the bog.'

'A racecourse?'

'One of those famous ones, where the Queen goes.'

'Epsom,' McKenna said.

'That's right.' She smiled again, pleased with him. 'Epsom. White stuff in a little plastic bag.' She giggled. 'He said the police'd think it was drugs if they found it in his car.' Another memory re-formed her expression into peevishness. 'And he said Uncle Ned had to be paid back for being so nasty.'

'Why? What had he done?'

'He shouted at me!' She shivered. 'He was horrible to me! And he called Jason an evil little crook, and even though Jason laughed when I told him, I could tell he was really furious.'

'When did Uncle Ned shout at you?'

'When I dropped my files.' Biting her lower lip, she watched her hands, flexing the thin fingers beneath their ugly bracelets. 'I had to write a sort of holiday diary for college, so I took my files to work, and when I came home, I went upstairs, and Phoebe's cat ran across the landing and right under my feet, and I tripped up. Everything fell all over the place, and Uncle Ned came to help me pick them up.' A scowl disfigured her face, and her fingers clenched. 'He was so nosy! He looked at every piece of paper, wanting to know what I was doing with forms for cars in my files, and I said they weren't mine, I was just keeping them for somebody, so he said the only person I'd put myself out for was Jason, and I had to finish with him, because he'd get me into awful trouble.' She fell silent, then added: 'Then he said he'd made a vow never to cover up for anyone ever again, because it led to so much grief, and I still don't understand what he was talking about. And,' she went on, scowling again, 'if Phoebe kept that animal under control, like Mama's always telling her, none of this would've happened. She's lucky I didn't kick its teeth in, and Jason said if it wasn't so fat, he'd stick it in the microwave.'

'What did you do with the Epsom Salts?' McKenna asked.

'Eh?' Her eyes turned slowly to meet his. 'Oh, they didn't work. Nobody even had the bellyache. I mixed them in the butter, because it was nice and soft. Mama's always forgetting to put it back in the fridge, like she forgot about the milk you were asking about. That's why it tasted sour.' She smiled again, almost innocently. 'I don't eat butter, you see. Solange says that kind of fat can kill you.'

11

Leaving Mina guarded by a policewoman, McKenna returned to the station, where, in one of the interview rooms, Jason challenged his interrogators, harsh overhead lights flattening out the contours of his face and making dark holes of his eyes. 'He's fucking stupid, a fucking liar, and a fat fucking sweaty arsehole generally,' Jason commented.

'Whether he is or isn't, your workmate saw you seal up that carton with yards of parcel tape,' Dewi said. 'Then you locked it in one of those big steel cages inside the depot, and put the key on your bunch.'

'I'm always sealing cartons and putting them in cages.' Jason smirked. 'It's part of the job, so things don't get nicked.'

'So how come this one is crammed to the gills with Ned Jones's letters and papers and address book and photos?' Dewi asked.

'Search me!' Jason shrugged. 'Mina Harris gave it me. Why don't you ask her?'

As McKenna listened to questions and denials, tossed back and forth like balls over a net, the ruined card game came to mind, and he thought, fancifully, that the Queen of Spades overlooking the Knave of Diamonds had been symbolic, of death looking over the shoulder of greed.

Diana Bradshaw was in his office again, staring blankly at the wall, her arms wrapped around her body as if she were cold. 'Has that bastard told you what he did with my car?'

she asked. Her skirt was ruckled, her shirt listless, and he noticed the pale trail of an embryonic varicose vein meandering down her left leg.

'The substance of his comment was confined to saying we'd be fools to set any store by the vicious, untruthful allegations being made against him, especially by Mina,' he said. 'According to Jason, she's good for just one thing, and only that until somebody better comes his way. As for your car,' he added, 'you could always ask him yourself.'

'Don't be funny! I'd wring his bloody neck!' She smiled, then sighed, unsure what to do with herself. 'That poor girl! How could she be so stupid? Does she realize what she's done?'

'I don't know. I'm not qualified to form an opinion. I've asked for a full psychiatric evaluation as soon as she's fit to be examined.'

'Phoebe thinks she's completely mad, and utterly stupid,' Diana said. 'But she's a strange creature herself, isn't she? She said Mina carved herself up to make Jason sorry for being horrible, but she doesn't think she intended to kill herself because she cut across the veins. Apparently, you cut down to make a proper job of it.'

'How does she know why Mina did it?'

'She told her, before you arrived. She wanted Phoebe to call Jason on his mobile, so he could see the fruits of his labour.' She crossed her legs, massaging the discoloured flesh. 'I suppose the psychiatrist will diagnose classic dysfunctional inadequacy resulting in sociopathic tendencies and the inability to relate cause to effect, and when we've charged her with manslaughter, some other psychiatrist will decide she was the innocent dupe of a real sociopath who preyed on an overriding need for love and approval stemming from her classically dysfunctional background and deprived family circumstances, so we'll go around in circles for quite a long time, and unless we can attach Jason to the drug and prove the powder he gave Mina was the tetracycline which killed Ned Jones, we're on a hiding to nothing from the start, aren't we?'

'Not necessarily,' McKenna said. 'We've yet to hear what Jason's mother has to say, and she's in a very bad mood, because she was looking forward to an evening in front of the telly after the rigours of trawling Llandudno shops, and is not best pleased to find herself and all seven of her offspring currently occupying our interview facilities. We thought it best to bring in all of them, although Jason and his younger sister are the only ones who haven't yet flown the coop.'

'Isn't she the one who won a wet-T-shirt competition at the local night club?' Diana grimaced. 'Prys was talking about it.' She thought for a moment, then said: 'Where's Mr Lloyd?'

'Long gone, like a lot of these fathers.'

'They remind me of tom cats, sowing the seeds of more irresponsibility and viciousness. I'm not very optimistic about nailing Jason.'

'Forensics should be finished with the carton soon. We only need to find his prints on some of the contents, and we're home and dry.'

'As he's already said he's been everywhere in the house, that wouldn't constitute more than circumstantial evidence.' She glanced at her watch. 'I'm going home. I told my husband I wouldn't be long, and that was hours ago.'

'He must be used to your unsocial hours by now,' McKenna said mildly. 'What does he do for a living?'

She looked sharply at him. 'Don't you know?'

'I know virtually nothing about you.'

'I am surprised! Rowlands seems to think he knows everything, and I can't believe he hasn't told you.'

'Bits and pieces of biased information aren't the best

foundation for conclusions, especially when they might have been embellished in the telling. Truth is often the first casualty in human transactions.'

'What did our masters tell you about me?'

'Nothing. It was all about me.' He related Monday's conversation with the deputy chief constable, then added: 'And what did *you* hear?'

'Another cynical and expedient invention. They said you weren't particularly ambitious, so delayed promotion wouldn't be a problem.'

'Looks like we've both been fitted up, doesn't it?'

'*You* were,' Diana said. 'I deserved dismissal for what I did.'

'Then why did you do it?'

She flushed. 'Wouldn't it be more to the point to ask why I wasn't sacked?'

'Insider trading isn't the worse offence.'

'Is that what you call it?'

'You took advantage of some knowledge for your own benefit. It happens.'

She rubbed her forehead. 'Can I tell you why?' Before he could respond, she went on: 'I'm not trying to make myself feel better, but we women seemed obliged to confess. Men are much better at living with lies.'

'Not always. Ned wasn't.'

'In my view, he's the exception which proves the rule. Professor Williams hasn't let untruth get in his way, whereas I can't function properly because the falseness keeps tripping me up. In the long run, it'll do the same to others.' She smiled faintly. 'I've a fairly good idea why you disappeared all day on Thursday, and I don't blame you.'

'I still had to come back. We don't have many choices.'

'Not if we want to eat and have a roof over our heads.' She took a deep breath. 'A couple of years ago, my husband began having black-outs, dropping things and tripping over nothing. The doctors suspected a brain tumour, but it turned out to be multiple sclerosis. He used to be a dental surgeon, and now he's in a wheelchair, dying slowly instead of quickly.' She sighed. 'Thank God we don't have children to worry about.'

'I'm sorry. I really am.'

Picking at the chipped veneer on the desk, she said: 'There's a theory about this kind of thing, you know. A butterfly stretches its wings in Indonesia or somewhere, and a little while later, there's a disaster on the other side of the world. When I bought that house, I'd no idea you even existed, but you've suffered because of it. You see, with only one salary, we couldn't afford to adapt our old house for my husband as well as pay the mortgage, so when this place came on the market, so cheap, I snapped it up without a second thought.' She paused, and sighed again. 'And I realized later how easily everything can fall apart. First it was our plans, then our prospects and security, then my morality. I was terrified, not because I might be unable to keep the wolves from the door, but of not having a door between us and them in the first place. His private pension isn't very high because of his age, and his state benefit's taxed to almost nothing because of my income, and I know poverty is always relative, but I'm still afraid of the future, especially as I only escaped dismissal by the skin of my teeth. I've no illusions about prospects, here or anywhere else. I'll be shunted from place to place until I cave in and resign. I've seen it happen to others.'

'It must have been a dreadful shock for your husband when you were disciplined.'

'He doesn't know. He thinks the house was pure luck, and I'm on career development, so he's very pleased, and that's how I want things to stay.' She dragged her fingers through her hair. 'I know it's tempting to sanctify the terminally ill, but he's a wonderful person, and a marvellous husband, and I don't want anything to spoil what little time he's got left.'

Checking on the interviews, McKenna found Jason's cock-sure insolence still in full flaunt, then went to hear what Mrs Lloyd was minded to disclose to her interrogators, announcing his presence to the blinking red eye of the tape recorder.

Face mottled, mouth opening and shutting like a fish gasping for air, she turned her bleary eyes on him, and choked back a sob. 'I've told on him! I said I would, and I have. He's been doing it for years.' She twisted in the chair, as if her body pained her for betraying her child. 'Ask Dr Ansoni if you don't believe me. He knows I don't take all the tablets he gives me.'

The contents of her big patchwork shoulder bag were strewn over the table, three brown glass bottles standing upright amid a litter of purse, keys, tissues, lipsticks, used bus tickets, useless lottery tickets, and other jumble.

'Did you tell Dr Ansoni why you needed so many prescriptions?' McKenna asked.

'He knows!'

'But did you *tell* him?'

She dabbed her eyes with a balled-up tissue. 'I couldn't, could I? He'd've stopped my tablets.'

'For the tape, Mrs Lloyd, please say exactly what you mean.'

'Jason's been taking my tablets.'

'And what's he done with them?'

'I don't know!'

'What d'you think he's done with them?'

She looked helplessly from McKenna to the uniformed sergeant at his side, then to the solicitor beside her. He smiled, murmuring words of encouragement in Welsh, and she signed so deeply her body seemed to deflate. 'Dr Ansoni gives me tablets to help me sleep, and for when I'm depressed.' She paused, working her mouth to make it speak. 'I didn't realise at first, and then I was worried to death, thinking I was taking more than I thought, so I told my eldest girl. She said to count them every time I took one, and write on the bottle, and even then I wasn't sure because it's easy to forget something like that, isn't it?'

McKenna smiled his own encouragement.

'My girls must've been talking about it, because my eldest said the youngest'd seen Jason with his fingers in the bottles, and hadn't liked to say because she didn't know if I knew, and she was scared Jason'd thump her.' She patted her eyes again. 'He was always hitting her when they were little. He pulled her hair out by the roots sometimes, when he was really angry.'

'Has he threatened you?' McKenna asked.

She shook her head, rather tentatively. 'I got hold of him, and said it'd got to stop, else I'd tell Dr Ansoni, and he'd tell the police.' She frowned, hindsight perhaps revealing her inadequacy. 'Only Jason said Dr Ansoni wouldn't dare, because he's his doctor, too.'

'Did Jason say what he'd done with the tablets?'

She chewed her mouth. 'My eldest reckons he's been selling them round the estate, but I told her he wouldn't, because he knows it's wrong. There's too many kids taking things these days, and they look so pale and lost and frantic it makes you want to weep.'

'We're interested in some capsules,' McKenna said, 'like little bullets which come apart in the middle.'

'I've been told,' she said. 'I had some red and yellow ones for my chest, after the flu bug in the spring, and there should be most of them left, only I can't find the bottle.'

'Mrs Lloyd had twenty-eight capsules of tetracycline in

early April,' the sergeant reported. 'A week's supply, but she only took them for a couple of days because the drug made her ill.'

'I had the most awful upset stomach, so I rang Dr Ansoni and he said to stop them. He gave me some little white tablets instead.'

'So at least half the capsules are missing?' McKenna asked her.

'I suppose.'

'We've requested fourteen tetracycline capsules from the pharmacy. Once these have been emptied into a plastic bag, the girl can be asked to make a comparison with what she was given.' The sergeant looked through his notes. 'Nothing else we took from the house contains tetracycline, and the tablets in Mrs Lloyd's bag are anti-depressants, paracetamol, and hypertensives.'

Mrs Lloyd frowned. 'Which girl? Mina Harris? She wouldn't need *my* tablets! Her mothers's got enough to sink a ship.'

The big carton was on his desk, bulging sides and straining flaps silvery with the residues of fingerprinting powder. He moved it to the floor, leaving the desk top bare of all but an ashtray, and began to extract the densely packed contents, knowing from experience that the whorls and loops of his own fingertips would be ingrained with the powder for days to come.

Through the open windows, deep luminous twilight beguiled his eyes, and night air, sharp with the scent of smouldering wood, drifted into the room. Elbows on the desk amid the litter of paper, trapped in the slipstream of others' lives, he felt a sudden sense of near desolation.

• • • •

Grabbing the chance for vengeance in both pudgy, sweaty hands, Jason's workmate at the Merlin yard had taken the police first to the carton locked like a Chinese puzzle inside the steel cage in the bowels of the building, then to the well-equipped vehicle maintenance bay behind the building, where Jason and his shadowy assistants stripped stolen cars of their identity before respray and revamp, and onward sale. However else Jason might be described, he was undoubtedly also enterprising and opportunistic, McKenna realized, leafing through pads of blank MOT certificates and a folder crammed with duplicate registration documents. Inside another folder he found boarding cards for the Irish ferries, enough for any number of trips to the duty-free outlets, and tucked behind, seventeen plastic National Insurance identity cards, each with the potential to mine the gold of the benefits system. Wondering at the extent of Jason's hidden empire, he cast around amid the litter for the relics of the man who had seen the other paper and understood its implications, and, in refusing to enter another conspiracy of silence, brought about his own extinction.

The forensic team had neatly tabulated the contents of the carton, packing sheaves of letters and dog-eared, brown-edged clippings from old newspapers and journals into clear plastic wallets. As Phoebe and George had said, Ned's address book was filled with foreign names and streams of numbers, written out in black ink, blue ink, ballpoint and fountain pen, amendments overwritten in soft lead pencil, and in another large, cloth-bound book, Ned had sketched ideas on the common roots of Welsh and Anglo-Saxon, marking the pulse of strong alliteration which threaded both languages, and the oral traditions of ancient cultures. Folded inside the back cover was an article, torn from a scientific journal, about the exhumation of a story-teller's mummified body, recovered with its wonderful grave-trappings from the ice of three millennia.

Leaving aside the evidence of Jason's enterprises, he began to repack the carton. Ned's birth certificate, faded and striated with thin brown lines where it had been folded and refolded, was returned to its envelope, and placed carefully on top of a tiny pocket-book bound in slaty-blue buckram and darkened with fingering, from which McKenna learned that slate was split into Queens, Princesses, Duchesses, Countesses and Ladies, each a specified measure smaller than the other. Bemused, he admired the wit, or the malice, which devolved an English hierarchy of caste upon the native riches of a country transformed by a sixteenth century Act of Union into England's first colony.

More letters were parcelled up with brown paper and thick string, some of their envelopes embellished with colourful foreign stamps, others showing the head of George VI, longer dead than his feckless elder brother, whose faded image adorned a few. Loosely retying the parcels, he put them with the other treasures to read at leisure, thrilled by the prospect, and even a little chilled, as the grave-robbing scientist might feel.

Pages held together by fraying pink tape, Ned's will was folded inside a long manila envelope. He bequeathed his scholarship to George, his personal possessions to Phoebe, his love and gratitude to Edith and her daughters and grandchild, and recorded his hope that Mina might find peace. In a handwritten note at the bottom of the last page, he reported vainly searching his heart for forgiveness for Eddie, for all he knew he warranted pity.

The last parcel spilled its contents willy-nilly over the dusty desk, threatening a cataract of crackled old photographs, postcards cut from soft thick cartridge, and crudely executed engravings on thin, crisp paper with deckled edges. Sifting and sorting, McKenna snapped a rubber band around the postcards, then picked up the first engraving which came to hand, staring at a dark, thick-lipped and flat-nosed face made darker still by its anonymity and lack of expression. A number which looked vaguely familiar was inscribed in the bottom right hand corner. He looked at another dark face, another number, on paper still buckled in places where the ink had soaked in randomly. So much black ink, he thought, counting faces and noting almost unconsciously the near-perfect sequence of numbers which the slave-owners would use in lieu of printed money as the title of their wealth for transactions and collateral.

Marvelling at their differences and not their blackness, struck by the proud cast of a skull or the beauty of an expression, he separated the men, women and children, then remembered where he had seen the numbers before, and was sorely tempted to upend the carton in search of Ned's prize-winning essay. Reluctantly, he put the engravings in a large new envelope, and thought those faces might now have a different kind of value in the marketplace, which Phoebe could realize, perhaps returning Llys Ifor to its one-time glory.

Before reinventing himself in the wake of ethical confusion and degeneration, Eddie Williams occupied the lens of Ned's camera on many occasions, often with the unmistakable turrets of Aberystwyth in the background, but only rarely had he or someone else caught the colour of Ned's melancholy in the camera's eye. Not for the first time, McKenna wondered if there had been love between those two young men, and whether lust, or guilt, or time, or understanding withered it to death.

Trying to recall the chemical process which transformed black and white to sepia, he sorted through other photographs, where other white men displayed their own ethical degeneration, grouping themselves before wounded mountains and the crude machinery of blasting and quarrying, surrounding themselves with white women and white children, and the trappings bought with stolen lives, without a black face in sight, not even peering from under the caps and hats of coachmen, grooms and chauffeurs. Llys Ifor in its heyday was barely recognizable, formal gardens beyond the front door where he had trampled rough grass and crumbling steps, and a man and woman, who must surely be Ned's parents, posed on the lawn with their four children, in tranquillity and sunshine, where he had found only the dark aftermath of tragedy and disintegration.

Expectation lightened faces in the next swatch of photographs, for whereas their ancestors were known only by number, some of these people were named in faded script on the verso. Out of chains and bondage, they were free to go, but from where to what, he thought? A Rachel and a Dogood stood outside the gate of Llys Ifor, a carpet bag of monstrous proportions at their feet, roses which no longer graced the masonry brushing Rachel's shoulder. They smiled with gleaming teeth, like others lined up on a station platform beneath a fret-edged wooden canopy, which reminded him of the tatted borders his grandmother tacked to her kitchen shelves. Amid this dark tide were the sepia faces of intermarriage, and he found them again in another setting, no longer smiling so brightly, and almost bereft of human proportion against a backdrop of smoke-gorging steelworks and massive verticality, straight lines radiating from colliery winding wheels, and conical mountains manufactured from waste, where, on a cynical promise of something better, the remnants of bondage had been exchanged for the blight of another.

Closing the carton lid, McKenna put the engravings and Ned's will in his briefcase, and humped both downstairs to his car. Opening the boot, he turned as he heard creaking door hinges and soft footfalls.

'Are you off, sir?' Dewi asked, his face a pale blur, light rimming his body.

'Soon.' He locked the boot, and made his way back, Dewi behind him. 'Surely you haven't finished with Jason?'

'Refreshment break. Prisoner's rights, and all that garbage.'

'And?' he asked, going into the ground floor office where photocopiers and fax machines were housed.

Dewi shrugged. 'He's still claiming to know nothing about nothing, so we're waiting to hear what's been going on at Merlin yard.' Hands in pockets, he leaned against the wall, watching McKenna feed Ned's will through the copier. 'We told him what his mam and his little sister and his big sister had to say, and got a load of very foul language and precise details of what he'll do to them as soon as he gets the chance. So hopefully, sir, you won't order his release.'

'Indeed not,' McKenna said, putting the original will back in its envelope, 'although I'm not sure what we can charge him with.'

'He assaulted Mina.'

'So she says.'

'He used to tear out his sister's hair.'

'So his mother says.'

'And his fat mate at the yard grassed him up.'

'Not enough, I think.'

'OK,' Dewi said. 'What about Mrs Lloyd's pills, then? Where did they go, if not in Jason's pocket, then down Ned's throat?'

'Who knows? She's got hundreds of pills, she's careless, she's even stupid, and she's his mother, so a pound to a penny, when she works out why we're interested in the tetracycline capsules, she'll be back here saying she's just remembered throwing them down the bog.'

'Great!'

'But then,' McKenna added, stapling the pages of the copy will, 'we haven't taken a statement from Mina yet, and as Jason wouldn't see himself getting caught, he was probably as careless with the bits and bobs of his stolen car enterprise as his mother is with the manna of the NHS.'

'While he's on his mandatory rest, I could ask Geraint

and Dervyn to reconsider previous comment, in the light of
our new knowledge,' Dewi offered. 'Put it to them how any
information could be very helpful to us and them alike.'

'You could. I'm going to see if Mina's fit to be
interviewed.'

'Will you ask about Janet while you're there?'

'I phoned about an hour ago.'

12

A near metamorphosis had overtaken Mina in the few
hours since he had left her bedside. She had been bathed,
her hair was washed and dried and brushed into a glinting
cascade, and the structured form of a lacy brassiere made
a pattern beneath her pale blue satin night-shirt. Almost
bright-eyed, she chatted to the black-garbed shape who
held her bandage-cuffed hands, and under the hard glare of
the ward lights, McKenna could see snarled grey strands
frizzing out of the black helmet of Solange's hair.

She turned, the sinews in her neck pulled tight, then
whispered to Mina, and rose. Almost pushing, she shunted
him into the corridor, out of earshot of the girl and her police guardian. '*Mon dieu!* I come back, and what do I find?'
The huge chunks of silver around her neck glowed. 'Mina
here, *comme ça*!' She threw her hands in the air. 'And my
husband!'

'What about your husband?' McKenna asked.

'He is so drunk it is frightening, and when I ask him why,
he says I must look behind him. So I look, and there is nothing. *Rien!* I say there is nothing, and he says Ned grins over
his shoulder!' She walked away from him. 'I must have a
cigarette.' Her voice despairing, she added: 'I tell him I will
make his doctor come, and he says he wants to see nobody,
not even me, and then he cries, like a silly big baby!'

He followed her along corridors and down staircases to an open fire door at the rear of the building.

Finely shod feet amid the leavings of a hundred other smokers, she rooted in her shiny black bag for a pack of Gauloise and a pebble-shaped lighter covered in brown crocodile skin. 'So,' she went on, blowing smoke into the night, 'I try to pull sense from him, and he says you try to make him see Mina, but he is afraid.'

'I told him she'd tried to kill herself.' Away from the bright lights she seemed even more two dimensional, and he looked in vain for her shadow on the ground or the walls behind them, but as he lit his own cigarette, the flame cast human warmth on her face. 'And I suggested he might want to be with her, given the circumstances.'

'Ah, the circumstances. *Those* circumstances!' She inhaled more smoke, and let it dribble from her nostrils. 'He thinks I do not know, but I tell him different.' Wisps of smoke drifted from her mouth. 'Mina, when she finds out, she tells me, and I ask myself why people are so cruel. Why must she know? Does it make the world better?'

'Edith said something about "imperious authority".'

'Edith is here when I come. And Annie. They bring clean clothes, and Edith helps the child to wash herself.'

'When did they leave?'

She glanced at her watch. 'Not long. Annie, she says Edith is *très désolée*, and she takes her home, and I stay with Mina.'

'Has Mina said anything to you about Jason?'

'She says very much,' Solange answered, dropping ash among the trampled cigarette butts. 'She tells me about the stuff she puts in the butter, and she thinks it is amusing, and she tells me how they play *la malice* on that beautiful black man, and she believes that is *very* amusing, because she says he insulted her.'

'*La malice?*' McKenna asked. 'D'you mean a trick?'

She nodded. 'They enter his *appartement* when he is away, and Jason, he hides something there.'

'How did they get in?'

'The black man gives a key to Ned, so Mina, she says she takes the key when Ned is not looking.' She dropped more ash on the ground. 'I tell Mina, you know. A thousand times I tell her this Jason is bad, I say he is *dangereux*, *un bâtard*, but she says she loves him.'

'I must talk to her.'

'My husband says I am to call his solicitor if you come here.' She smiled, with irony. 'But I call him already, and he says my husband is very rude to him, and he owes him much money. So I tell this man he is *merdeux*, and say my husband owes *tout le monde* very much money!'

Despite himself, McKenna smiled. 'If you have so many debts, why don't you stop spending?'

She folded her arms across her body, cigarette glowing in her right hand, and looked up at him, face expressionless. 'You waste your time to ask *me*. My husband, he spends money like people say it would grow on the spiky bushes in the garden. Me, I keep my clothes and my jewels from when I model.'

'I see.'

'Also, I tell him I do not like to live in a big house, and I think he has no need to have a new car every year.' She dropped the butt, and ground it to nothing, then shrugged. 'But he does not listen to me. He does not listen to *anyone*.'

'Perhaps Edith's solicitor could come,' McKenna said, holding open the door. As she passed, her rich scent and the pungent smell of French tobacco assaulted his senses.

'Perhaps,' she agreed, clicking along the corridor. 'But why make more cost for Edith?'

'He'd be paid by the state, Mrs Williams. People still have the right to free legal representation if we need to question them.'

She shrugged again, the universal Gallic solution, and waited patiently while he made the call, then added: 'You understand she is a stupid girl? A very stupid girl.'

'Because of Jason?'

'*Non!* She is born stupid. She does not understand what she does, what other people do. She does not see that they have reasons.' She trailed after him up the staircase, age telling. 'She talks, she makes one word go after another word, but she has no comprehension.'

'Do you like her?'

'Like?' She smiled again, with more irony. 'I love her, like I love a young animal which is sick and can do nothing to help itself.' She paused at the head of the stairs, panting slightly. 'Edith, she loves her, but she is helpless. She sees there is this great empty place in Mina's heart.' She walked on again, like a shadow without validating form. 'But Edith has Annie, who is good, and she has the other child, who is frightening because she has too much in her head, and, I also think, in her heart, like Ned.' At the entrance to the ward, she stopped again. 'My husband, Mina is all he has. Perhaps she is the punishment of God, for his sins.'

Screens had been drawn around Mina's bed, and through the open window by her side, draughts of hot night air riddled with the stink of exhaust fumes eddied up from the road. She started to yawn almost as soon as McKenna began his questioning, but more, he suspected, from boredom than fatigue. 'But I've already told Solange,' she said, looking fretfully from McKenna to the solicitor. 'Ask her.'

'I must ask you.'

'What?'

'Tell me again about the powder Jason gave you.'

Almost by rote, with the same inflexions in her voice and expressions on her face, she repeated what she had said earlier in the day, only elaborating, with a little giggle, on Jason's proposals for Phoebe's cat. 'He said he felt like tying the thing up, pouring petrol on it, and dropping a match. People in Australia do it all the time.'

'*C'est terrible!*' Solange gasped.

'What happened to the papers Jason gave you?' McKenna asked, appalled by her vacuous acceptance of barbarity.

'Uncle Ned took them, and he wouldn't give them back to me, even when I told him Jason'd be mad with rage.'

'What did Uncle Ned say?'

'He said Jason could go to Hell.' She stopped speaking, biting her lower lip. 'And I'd never heard him swear before, not even when something awful happened.'

'So how did Jason get his things back?'

'I got them, of course! He asked me to.'

'When?'

'At night.'

'Which night?'

'I can't remember. One night last week, I suppose.'

'What did you do?'

'I went into Uncle Ned's room when he was asleep, but I couldn't find Jason's things, so I had to take all these boxes and packets, 'cos I didn't know where he'd put them.'

'And when did you give them to Jason?'

'He was waiting outside.'

'Outside where?'

'The back gate, with his van. He was doing nights nearly all last week, so we couldn't go out anywhere nice.'

'Tell me about the keys to George's flat,' McKenna said.

Her mouth twisted. 'It served him right! He didn't need to be so horrible to me!' Then her mouth resolved itself into a smirk. 'And it's a good thing he was away, because Jason would've beaten him up for what he said.'

'When did you take the key?'

'I don't know.'

'Day? Night?'

'Daytime. Mama sent me upstairs to tell Uncle Ned his tea was ready, but he was in his bathroom, and the key was on his desk, so I took it.'

'Why?'

'Jason wanted it.'

'What for?'

'I don't know.'

'Did Uncle Ned say anything to you about the papers and the key?' McKenna asked, glancing at his notes. Across the bed, the solicitor's secretary held her hands over the keys of her state of the art computerized stenographic machine.

Mina nodded, and yawned again.

'What did he say?'

She sighed, rather peevishly. 'He said he knew I'd taken them for Jason, and if I didn't make Jason give them back in twenty-four hours, he was going to the police.'

'Did you believe him?'

'I don't know. I just told Jason.'

'And did you take Uncle Ned's SOS bracelet?' McKenna asked, almost as wearied as the girl appeared.

She nodded.

'When?'

'The night before he died.'

'How?'

'When he was asleep. He'd taken a tablet. Mama said he took it before supper.' She smiled vaguely. 'Did you know taking tablets on an empty stomach makes them work faster? Mama said so, but she wasn't sure if hot drinks stopped them working altogether.'

'Weren't you out late that night?' said McKenna, racking his memory.

'Yes.'

'So how could you know what your mother said?'

'I heard her when I came in. She was on the phone to Annie.'

'So when did you take the bracelet?'

'Late.'

'Was everyone else in bed?'

'Yes.' She yawned again, and rubbed her eyes with the grubby bandaged wrists, like a tired child.

'Did you wait until everyone was asleep then go into Uncle Ned's room? Did you go up to his bedroom?'

She nodded again.

'Was he wearing the bracelet?'

'Yes.'

'Even if he'd taken a sleeping pill, wasn't it risky to take off the bracelet?'

'I don't know.' She looked shiftily at him, then down at her hands, spread limply on the coverlet.

Jason's knowing smirk and insolent words came to McKenna's mind. 'Were you on your own?'

'Uncle Ned was there.'

'I know that, Mina. Was anyone else with you?'

'Like who?'

'Like Jason?'

Bright spots of colour mottled her cheeks.

'Was Jason with you?' he persisted.

She nodded again.

'Say "yes" or "no", please,' he instructed.

'Yes.' The word was almost inaudible.

'Who removed the bracelet?'

'He did.'

'Then what? Did he go, or did he stay?'

She stared at him, then clutched Solange's bare arm, squeezing so hard the Frenchwoman winced. 'Don't tell Mama! *Please* don't tell Mama!'

Gently, Solange pulled herself free, then held Mina's

trembling hands, while McKenna talked on, relentlessly. 'Tell me about the car.'

'What car?'

'The car you and Jason followed along the expressway. You sprayed it with brake fluid, and nearly caused a serious accident.'

'Well, we didn't! It just stopped.'

'Why did you follow it?'

'Jason wanted to.'

'Why?'

'Because I told him about it.' She smiled at Solange. 'It was outside your house on Wednesday morning, so I wrote down the number and what colour it was.'

'Why do that, *chérie*?' Solange asked.

'I often do it. Jason says it's like train spotting, only more grown up. He gives me a list of cars to look out for, and when I see what he wants, I write down the number, then where it's parked.' She giggled. 'And when we see it again, I spray it with a water pistol, and cross it off the list. Trainspotters do that in their little books when they see a train.'

'Did you tell Jason the car belonged to a police officer?' McKenna asked.

'Of course I did! He wouldn't have been able to find it again if I hadn't, would he?' She frowned at him, working her mouth. 'And I wish you'd stop going on! Jason's got to know about the cars for his job.'

'Why?'

'Because he does. It's his job!'

'How is it his job, Mina?' Solange asked.

'He listens for cars getting abandoned,' she said wearily. 'When they've broken down or the driver's been arrested for being drunk or something. He's got a big scanner in the van, and he picks up police radios and people calling for help on their mobiles.'

'Have you ever been with him when that's happened?'
McKenna demanded.

'I'm not telling you!'

'Why can you not tell Mr McKenna?' Solange asked.

'Jason said he'd get into trouble if his boss found out I
was with him.'

'Let's talk about Uncle Ned,' McKenna suggested.
'When did you put the powder in the butter?'

'I'm tired. I can't remember!'

'I think you can.'

'In the morning!'

'Which morning?'

'*That* morning,' she responded, sullenness pinching
her lips.

'The day Uncle Ned died?'

'Yes.'

'When in the morning?'

'After breakfast.' She scowled, almost viciously. 'Mama
made me wash the dishes before I went to work, so I did it
then. I was going to put it in the milk, only I remembered
what she'd said.'

'What your mother said?'

'About tablets and stuff. Hot drinks stop things working, so it would've been stupid to put anything in the milk,
because nobody drinks milk except me. Phoebe says it gives
her spots, and Uncle Ned said it gave him the stomach ache,
like everything else.' She bit her lip again. 'And I wish you'd
stop going on about it! I've already told you, it didn't *work*!'

The solicitor's secretary, her machinery in a neat grey case,
promised the transcript of Mina's interview within the hour,
assuring McKenna it was a matter of seconds to transfer the
data from one machine to another, and of minutes to make
the hard copy.

'What did we do before computers were born?' Dewi asked idly.

'We managed.'

'Any joy with Mina?'

'She's told us how she poisoned Ned, but there's no joy involved, except for a sadistic bloody psychopath like Jason Lloyd.'

'Well, he's banged to rights on the vehicles, so that's some comfort,' Dewi said, following McKenna away from the ward where Solange had elected to remain. 'Geraint doesn't know owt from nowt, because he's thick, like most of these backwoods types, but Dervyn got verbal diarrhoea once he knew Jason was behind bars and couldn't come after him with a baseball bat, as is apparently his wont if people upset him.'

'If he can't get hold of some poison.'

'That was a one-off, sir, and sheer opportunism, and if Ned hadn't made such a very noisy song and dance about all his ills, he might be alive today.'

'No, he wouldn't, because he'd crossed Jason,' McKenna said. 'And one day, Edith, or Phoebe, or the cleaner, or even Mina, would have found him with his brains splattered around the room, instead of less bloodily, and, I hope, less painfully, dead in his favourite chair.' As Dewi yawned, fist against his lips, he added: 'Why are you here, anyway?'

'To let you know you were right about Jason. Your mobile's been switched off for ages.'

'They interfere with hospital equipment.'

'Do they? I thought that was a bit of fiction to beef up TV drama. Anyway, where Jason's concerned, it's like mother like son with a vengeance, 'cos he was *extremely* careless with things at Merlin yard. There's been a huge amount of respraying, none of it in Merlin's own colours, or like the boss's personal vehicles, and forensics turned up a load of windows, most with the original numbers etched in, which happily for us, match up perfectly with a lot of stolen vehicles.' Following McKenna across the car park, he continued talking in lists: 'Equipment and die stamps, all well used, for grinding and reblocking engines and chassis, nearly two dozen VIN plates out of missing vehicles, and odds and ends like ashtrays and whatnot, which sometimes have the vehicle marque and date embossed in the making. Oh, and there's an enormous bunch of keys, so hopefully one of them belongs to George's flat.'

About to carp at him for the repetitious use of vehicle, McKenna bit his tongue. Dark shadows smudged Dewi's eyes and cheekbones, and the bruise from yesterday's injury seeped down his face like watery ink.

'Interviewing Jason's kin was like having a conveyor belt on the go,' Dewi added, 'which is probably why I've got a storming headache. And his boss was ringing every half hour, wanting to know when we'd be done with the fat man, and how much longer forensics would be turning his office and yard upside down.'

'D'you think Mr Merlin's involved with the car thefts?' McKenna asked. 'Jason couldn't have run the business on his own, and it's hard to believe his boss noticed nothing.'

'Why?' Dewi unlocked his car and reset alarm and immobilizer. 'Edith let an awful lot pass her by, didn't she? It's dead easy to con people when they trust you, even when gut instinct tells them something's amiss.'

'Point taken,' McKenna said, envy niggling as Dewi sat behind the wheel. Hood folded down, the dark vehicle's long, raked shape was almost sinister. 'Are you off home?'

'I'll finish taking Dervyn's statement first, as he knows so much about Jason and his mates in the used car business.'

'What's the *quid pro quo*?'

'He hasn't asked for anything. Maybe he's glad to get things off his chest.' He turned the ignition key, letting the engine tick over. 'Phoebe rang a couple of times, and Superintendent Bradshaw called to say we've done a very good job.' He gunned the motor. 'I said we should be able to locate her car, because we found the papers for its scrap twin, so we know the new number.'

'Have you put out a bulletin on it?'

'It's in the computer, sir, along with all the others. The vehicle examiner wants everything ready for Monday morning, including Annie's car.'

'She knows.'

'Phoebe said it doesn't matter if you're late ringing back.'

'I'll probably visit the house.'

'This must be dreadful for them, and none of it would've happened if Mina hadn't taken up with that villain.'

'Unfortunately, she's the sort of girl who'll always end up with some villain or other,' McKenna said. 'She needs cheap, quick thrills to make her feel alive, because she can't bear life's usual tedium, and where we see Jason's wickedness for what it is, she sees it as a source of constant excitement.'

'Does she actually understand what she's done? Does she *know* she killed Ned?'

'I honestly can't say, and in her present frame of mind, it wouldn't be wise to tell her that what she thought were Epsom Salts was the drug which killed him,' McKenna replied. 'Common sense tells me she must understand, but she seems not to, so perhaps Solange is right to call her stupid, in the true sense of the word.'

'Did she really come good, like you said? I didn't think she had it in her to be good for anything but spending hubby's cash.'

'Hubby hasn't any cash to speak of. He's drowning in debt, robbing Peter to pay Paul, and Paul to pay back Peter.'

'Serves him right for conning people about that poetry,' Dewi commented. 'What goes round comes round.' He paused, flicking the indicator switch. 'I saw Janet again, while I was waiting for you. Her father's gone, but her mother was there. She looks terrible.'

'Who does? Janet, or her mother?'

'Her mother. Janet's still out of it completely, but she isn't any worse. If she can hold her own while her body starts to get over the trauma, she should be OK.'

'Then we should pray she can,' McKenna said.

'I am doing,' Dewi answered, roaring off into the night.

13

The front of Edith's house was in total darkness, only a faint nimbus of light defining the gable wall and the trees overhanging the garden. Debating with himself on the wisdom of retreat, McKenna crunched up the drive and around the side, pushed open a heavy wooden gate smelling of sun-scorched wood and, faintly, of creosote, and into the back garden.

A cloud of midges danced under the trees, and there was a shiver of autumn in the air. A clothes-line, slung between a concrete post against one boundary wall, and the branches of a huge old beech tree, sagged under the weight of laundry pegged along its length. In the wedge of fuzzy light spilling through the back door, and the elongated rectangles from the kitchen windows, he saw the pillowcases and quilt cover and sheet from Mina's bed, the clothes she had worn when she was stretchered into the ambulance, Phoebe's much larger shirt and trousers, and what must be, he thought, the carpet from the bloody bathroom, a large square of pale pink, indented with curves and slits, dripping on to the grass at the end by the tree, and stippled with leaf shadows. Or perhaps, he mused, the darker patches were splatters of blood, as indelible as Rizzio's on the floor of Holyrood House.

They must have heard the closing of the gate, for Phoebe appeared in the doorway, throwing an enormous amorphous shadow across the garden and the clothes-line. The cat materialized by her feet, creating another black hole in the light.

'I'm sorry I couldn't come earlier,' he said. 'I know you've been trying to call.'

'Solange telephoned,' she said, drawing him into the house. 'And that bloody excuse for a man she married called, as well. He wanted to come round, but Mama told him not to.'

His eyes adapted to the soft darkness, the lights in the kitchen were dazzling, making masks of the faces of Edith and her daughters. She sat on the far side of the table, a mug of coffee steaming in front of her, a cigarette in her hand, and the ashes of many more in the blue glass tray. Annie rose, to pour coffee for their visitor.

'I actually said if he wasn't too drunk to stand upright, he should be at the hospital,' Edith added. 'And I also said all the drink and drugs in the world can't stop things happening, and can't shield you from the consequences, either, but Iolo's a fool, because he still seems to think they can.' She stubbed out the cigarette, and reached for another, summoning a smile. 'I told Phoebe it was too late to expect you to come, but she would insist on calling.'

'You wanted to see him, Mama, only you wouldn't ask,' Phoebe said.

'I did, and I didn't,' Edith countered. 'Have you anything to tell us we don't already know?'

He sat down between Annie and Phoebe, close enough to feel the heat of their bodies and smell the scents of fresh air and scouring powders. Coloured plastic buckets, wrung-out cleaning cloths, and rubber gloves, littered the counter beside the sink, and he could hear the whine of a washing machine on fast spin behind a closed door.

'I've told them about Mina,' Edith added, pushing the ashtray towards him. 'I should have done it years ago. Secrets do nothing but fester.'

'I've wondered if Professor Williams prevailed upon you to keep quiet,' McKenna asked.

'Not so I noticed,' Edith said, 'but perhaps he did. We're both responsible for her, and we've both failed her, because we started whatever it was that finished with Ned's death.' She gazed somewhere over his shoulder, into the night. 'I think we broke her heart, and she couldn't put it back together again. Or perhaps it was so wounded and scarred it just stopped working.'

'Or perhaps she never had one in the first place,' Phoebe added waspishly.

'Don't!' Annie snapped at her. 'You're too young to know.'

'Know what?'

'How it makes sense of all the things I never understood.'

'Like what?' Phoebe enquired.

'Like Mama being afraid and sad, when I couldn't see why, and why Mina was always unhappy even though she seemed to be Mama's favourite.' She paused, searching for words. 'I was jealous of her, and nasty to her, because she was my sister, but so different.'

'If you'd seen her as my child, too, your life might have been easier,' Edith said.

Once again, McKenna thought, he was caught in crosscurrents, as their dynamics adapted to crisis and aftermath, closing the wound in the family body opened by the bereavement of Mina, and in their distress, he wanted less to leave them than before.

'And,' Phoebe said, 'I suppose that's why Mama didn't drop on you like a ton of bricks over Bethan, because most mothers would've gone ape. She could've put you in some awful place for fallen women, and they'd have punished you every single day for sinning, and never let you out, in case you had some fun, or worse still, more sex.'

'I think your mother was too busy punishing herself,' suggested McKenna.

'Probably,' Phoebe agreed. 'And you'll go on doing it even more now, won't you, Mama?'

'I don't know what I'll do.' Edith fumbled with her lighter.

'World in freefall again.' Phoebe sighed.

'Well,' Edith said, her cigarette glowing, 'I won't go back on the pills, so you can stop worrying.'

Phoebe clasped her mother's free hand, stroking the fine skin on the back of it with her thumb. 'I know you won't, Mama.'

Smiling, Edith squeezed Phoebe's fingers, holding tight. 'But there's such a very thin line between things being tolerable, and even good, and things being absolutely and unimaginably bloody terrible, you see. All it needs is one small step, one little omission or neglect, one tiny, *tiny* shift.' She looked across at McKenna. 'And I seem to be going willy-nilly backwards and forwards over that line all the time.'

'The winds of circumstance,' Phoebe said. 'Uncle Ned talked about them a lot. A breeze one day and not a leaf moving the next.'

'And a vicious storm blowing up from nowhere the day after.' This from Edith.

'It makes life exciting,' Phoebe added, 'and the storms don't really come out of the blue. You can always see the clouds on the horizon.'

'Only if you care to look,' Annie said. She turned to McKenna. 'Solange says she's failed Mina, too. She told us what Mina did to Uncle Ned, not that we didn't already know in our hearts.'

'Mina did exactly what Jason told her to do,' stated

McKenna. 'No less, and no more, and perhaps in her mind, only to prevent something worse.'

'I didn't know criminal stupidity was a defence,' Phoebe commented. 'It wasn't when Derek Bentley was topped, was it?'

'Oh, for God's sake!' Annie exploded. 'Are you a couple of valves short of an engine, or is there just a swinging brick where your heart should be?'

'Too much emotion interferes with creative thinking,' Phoebe said mildly.

'And not enough kills it stone dead,' Edith countered. 'Ask your Uncle Iolo if you don't believe me.'

'If that's the case, he wouldn't know, would he?' Phoebe prattled on. 'Will Minnie go to prison? That's what's screwing up Mama at the moment, and not so much because Minnie wouldn't survive there, but because Mama couldn't survive it for her.'

'Don't presume too much.' Tears glinted in Edith's eyes. 'You're not the only one to know Ned's death for the tragedy it is.' She looked across at McKenna again, and he wondered where she found her strength. 'Have you found the rest of his papers yet?'

'Jason had them hidden at the Merlin yard.' He pulled the long envelope from his briefcase. 'And I found Ned's will.'

'So I was right! I *thought* he'd made one.' Fingers shaking, Edith reached into the envelope, her daughters clustered at her side and reading with her, and as the last page was turned, Phoebe choked, blundered from the room and crashed upstairs. Alarmed, the cat streaked after her.

'Oh, dear,' Edith said, left hand flattening the folded papers. 'Oh, dear.'

'She'll wake Bethan.' Annie sighed, making for the door to quell the thuds and bumps coming from above.

Again, Edith read the last few paragraphs, scrabbling blindly for her cigarette, then put the document in its envelope. Behind the veil of smoke, she asked: 'What does he mean about Iolo? Why can't he forgive him?'

From somewhere at the top of the stairs, McKenna heard Annie's voice, urging quietness on the cadences of Phoebe's distress.

'The recovered mediaeval manuscripts on which Professor Williams built his career are no such thing,' McKenna told her. 'He faked them when he was a student.'

'I see.' She nodded, as if to herself. 'Why aren't I surprised?'

'He claims Ned was involved in the chicanery, and that both of them wrote the poetry under the influence of Ned's sleeping tablets, but I don't believe him.'

'Nor do I,' decided Edith. 'Isn't it amazing how one little thing makes everything else fall into place? All this secrecy! And for so long!' Dousing the cigarette, she added: 'And for what? I know I said otherwise when you asked, but I always felt there was an atmosphere between Ned and Iolo, even though I couldn't think of a logical reason for it. If my common sense hadn't been so befuddled by drugs, I might have challenged them outright, and perhaps none of this would have happened.'

Rising, he put the will away, leaving her with the copy. 'I'll let you have the original for probate as soon as possible.'

She smiled wryly. 'Are you sure you'll know which is which?' She too stood up, holding the edge of the table for support, and, like him, listened to the voices from upstairs. 'Phoebe hasn't even *begun* to feel the loss of Ned yet, you know. She's still in that wonderful limbo which opens up after a terrible shock, then closes around you, so you just function, but scarcely feel. I only pray she'll be able to grow through the sorrow instead of letting it wither her humanity.'

'And you?'

'Oh, I'm in limbo, too.' Her voice was tinged with irony. 'And perhaps if I pray very, *very* hard, God will let us both stay there, but I doubt it. Sooner or later, the feelings batter their way through, and when that happens, Phoebe will think she's been hit by a ten ton truck.' Still leaning on the table, she added: 'And then I'll have another damaged child, won't I?'

'Life marks all of us in one way or another. Phoebe has the means to make something good from the bad.'

'Like Ned.'

'Like Ned.' He nodded. 'You don't have a copy of his Eisteddfod essay, do you?'

'Phoebe has one.' She made for the stairs, McKenna behind her, and called softly to her daughters, who sat in a huddle beneath the landing window, its colours now leeched by the moon. 'Mr McKenna wants to borrow Uncle Ned's essay, dear. Will you get it for him?'

'Why?' Phoebe whispered, rubbing her eyes.

'To read again,' McKenna said. 'I'll make a copy and let you have it back tomorrow.'

As Phoebe scrambled to her feet and padded away around the dog-leg, Annie dragged herself upright by the banister rail, came downstairs, and stood on the bottom step hugging the ornately decorated newel post, her face almost as aged as her mother's, her eyes almost as dark. 'You haven't told us what's happening with Mina. Have you arrested her?'

'I questioned her, but I didn't tell her she was responsible for Ned's death.' He paused. 'We can't proceed further without a proper psychiatric evaluation, and not just because of the wrist-slashing.'

'But she can't come home, can she?' Annie persisted.

'She'll stay in hospital until we're in a position to make a decision, and she'll be transferred to the psychiatric unit when she's medically fit.'

Edith took a deep breath, which rattled in her chest. 'Tell me what *you* think will happen. Please!' She touched his arm. 'We won't say a word, and we won't hold you to it.'

He found it hard to think straight, to be guided only by professionalism. 'Jason will be charged with Ned's murder, and the car thefts. He'll also be charged with assaulting Mina.' He paused again. 'Her evidence ties him to the murder, but of course, it implicates her, too. If she's found unfit to plead, for whatever reason, we could have a problem.'

'And if she isn't?' Annie demanded.

'There would still be much to consider in the way of mitigating circumstances, and, given the situation, I don't think the Crown would press too hard.'

'For what?' Edith asked, frowning. 'Press for what?'

'Imprisonment, Mama,' Annie said.

'Some cases are better resolved with probation and an order for psychiatric treatment,' McKenna said.

'All the treatment in the world won't make her understand the devastation she caused,' Edith said. 'She's like her father!' Then she shook herself angrily. 'Oh, God! I'm passing the buck, just like him.'

'Come on.' Annie let go of the newel post to take her mother's arm. 'You're going for a bath, and I'll make some cocoa.' She began to tow Edith up the stairs. 'D'you mind if Phoebe shows you out? I expect we'll see you again soon, in any case.'

'I expect so,' he agreed, his heart lurching on its moorings. Phoebe waited on the half-landing, papers drooping from her fingers, until Annie and Edith disappeared, then came down and handed the essay to him. 'Thank you,' he said. 'I won't break my promise.'

She opened the front door, and crunched beside him down the drive, their shadows falling over the gate and into the road, the night-scented stock sweet and nostalgic in the cool air. 'Why d'you want it?'

'I have a need to read it again.'

She scuffed the toe of her sandal on the pavement. 'You must have found the pictures of the slaves, then. The old ones with the bond numbers.'

'We found everything you and George told us about, and you should take great care of those engravings. They could be valuable.'

'Anything connected with Uncle Ned is priceless.' It was a statement of certainty. 'And George'll be over the moon. I'll ask Mama to let me ring him tomorrow.'

Unlocking his car, he said quietly: 'Try not to hate Mina too much.'

'I can't hate her, can I?' She folded her arms, and leaned against the wall. 'She's my sister, well, my half-sister, and I've always known she's stupid, but now I know why.' Above her head, a breeze began to snatch at the leaves. 'And I feel sorry for her, like I would if I'd heard about something awful happening to someone I don't know and can't help, but I don't really want to go down that road, even though it might be easier than admitting at least half of me is blood kin to a psychopath.'

'Which road, Phoebe?'

'Pitying her. Uncle Ned said pity amounts to arrogance. He also said it lets the other person off the hook, and it lets you off the hook of having to feel kinship for them.'

'I see.'

'And I agree with him,' she added, pushing her body away from the wall. 'So I'll no doubt have a few nightmares about her before I come to terms, or whatever the saying is, and I'm absolutely sure I'll find it very hard to stop myself giving her a dose of her own medicine.'

'As long as that remains a dream.'

'And I really hope Jason rots in hell,' she added, her voice hard with intent. 'But there's a problem with that ending, too, because Minnie's so besotted she'd happily go to hell with him.'

14

McKenna's street was overhung with an acrid pall of smoke, as Bangor Mountain burned once again, flames crackling and leaping through the trees, sparks bouncing down roof tiles all along the terrace. He put his briefcase and Ned's relics on the parlour table, closed the windows on the shouts of fire-fighters and the sizzle of water on flame, then went to the kitchen to feed the cats, who appeared to have spent the after-noon and evening without the company of friends. A large brown moth fizzed round and round inside the parlour lamp-shade, and another had flattened itself against the outside of the window, eyes red, underbelly caterpillar-furred.

He made a pot of tea, opened his last pack of duty-free cigarettes, and sat in the kitchen reading the paper. The name discs on the cats' collars pinged against their dishes, reminding him of the tolling bell-buoy in Dun Laoghaire harbour, where only last week, waiting for the ferry home, he had watched the huge catamaran come in to dock, its wash setting the old South Rock lightship heaving against its mooring. The lightship occupied a well-thumbed place in the internal library of his childhood memories, and he still half believed the rusting hull was where the Irish ma-rooned the pox-ridden and mad, like the smallpox boats which once bobbed on the Thames, or the Ships of Fools cast out on the oceans of history.

Scanning newspaper storylines, he was struck by coinci-dence to find an article about the late Iris Bentley's lifelong fight to clear her brother's name, and realized his own in-ternal narratives had been dominated all week by women, and looked set to continue that way. The letter from Denise's solicitor demanded a response, and, noting how the stain in front of the cooker was creeping back, he knew there could be no freedom from the haunting, threatening misery of her and their marriage unless she released himself from bondage.

He cooked two slices of Welsh rarebit, eating at the kitchen table and looking forward to a day without mail, then stacked dishes in a bowl of hot sudsy water, the sights and sounds and scents of Edith's kitchen potent in his mind. A fresh pot of tea to hand, he slumped on the worn chesterfield in the parlour, cats by his feet, and finished reading the paper. Struggling as usual with the crossword, he found himself writing 'FE' and 'EF' in the margins, Mina Harris in mind, any compassion he might find for her blighted by the thoughtless destruction she had brought about. He scribbled over the rough letters, the clue resolved, sure that in the last cataclysmic moments of life, Ned betrayed her, scoring his nails across blistering skin to write the first letters of the Welsh words for 'Eddie's daughter'.

Filling another space in the half-completed grid, he wrote 'cataclysm', thinking that Mina, like Ned, had already experienced her own, while for Edith and Annie and Phoebe, and perhaps even for Solange, the nightmares were yet to come. Edith's would be the most devastating, he decided, when she learned that her carelessness had provided Mina with the God-given opportunity to poison Ned. When Phoebe's pain grew less excoriating, she would write about her sister, transforming chaos into something lucid and explicable, but until then, he would willingly foster her nightmare, but not to access her wonderful dreams. Iolo Williams would find no peace or redemption because he stole another man's dreams, counterfeiting the whole currency of their world, and writing 'degenerate' on the empty line in the middle of the grid, McKenna wondered if the professor's whole persona were a fabrication from which he was unable to extricate himself. Take away the unbelievably unremitting nastiness, and what was left but a brittle shell?

Newspaper slipping off his knee, he dozed, thoughts disintegrating into sleep as a personality might scatter into confusion, without certainty of awakening, either literal or metaphorical.

15

For Solange, true pity for Mina came to outweigh futile pity for her husband, and she lingered at the hospital until the girl fell into a deep, untroubled sleep, then clipped along quiet corridors, down staircases to the softly lit reception area and its empty banks of strawberry pink seats, and out through the ever-revolving door. Standing amid more discarded cigarette ends, she looked across the car park for a taxi, then, sighing, returned through the swishing door to ask the night clerk for change for the payphone.

Call made, she went back outside, and feet amid the litter, smoked another pungent cigarette, shivering occasionally from fatigue, and the dreadful nagging disquiet which grew as relentlessly as the earth turned under the glare of the moon. She started as a figure spilled through the revolving door; another woman, older than herself, and graceless in anxiety.

Panting slightly, the woman nodded, and Solange wondered why the women of this country so despised their bodies, and hid them inside ugly garments as if they were the source of deepest shame.

'Are you waiting to be picked up?' the woman asked.

'I wait for a taxi,' Solange said.

'My husband's coming for me,' the other woman replied. 'He should be here soon.'

'You are visiting at the hospital?' Solange asked, blowing a plume of smoke into the night.

'My daughter.' The woman coughed, scrabbling in her handbag for tissues.

'What is wrong with her?'

'She was expecting a baby,' the woman said, staunching tears, 'but she lost it. She nearly died.' She gulped. 'Still, they say she's over the worst. My husband wept when I told him.'

'Ah, quel dommage!' Solange patted her arm. 'But there will be other babies.'

'She isn't married.'

'So?' Solange shrugged. 'It happens all the time. It is nature.' She dropped her cigarette and ground it to shreds as a taxi came into view, light winking on its roof.

Only a few yards behind, indicator blinking, Edwin Evans's car rounded the corner.

Author's Note

This novel was inspired by the story of Edward Jones (1752–1824), born in Llandderfel, Meirionydd. Henblas, his family home, still stands as a working farm.

A gifted harpist, Edward was in the service of the Prince of Wales (later George IV) from 1775, and is generally known by the title *Bardd y Brenin* (King's Bard). Apart from music, his abiding passion was the collection and preservation of the relics of Welsh culture, and he became an important antiquarian scholar. His first significant publication was *The Musical and Poetical Relicks of the Welsh Bards* (1784).

He died, unmarried, on Easter Sunday 1824, and was buried in the churchyard of St Mary-le-Bone, London.

ABOUT THE AUTHOR

Born into an Anglo-Welsh family, and brought up in rural Cheshire and Derbyshire, Alison Taylor studied architecture before commencing a career in social work and probation. She has been instrumental in exposing the abuse of children in care, and has written a number of papers on child-care and ethics. She has a son and daughter, and has been resident in North Wales for many years. Her interests include classical and Baroque music, art and horse-riding. She is currently working on a mystery entitled UNSAFE CONVICTIONS.